Praise for Traci Hall and her Scottish mysteries!

MURDER IN A SCOTTISH GARDEN

"In her second Scottish Shire mystery, Hall capably juggles multiple story lines and vividly evokes the Scottish backdrop."

—Booklist

MURDER AT A SCOTTISH SOCIAL

"Witty characters match the well-crafted plot. . . . Cozy fans will want to see a lot more of the compassionate Paislee."

—Publishers Weekly

MURDER AT A SCOTTISH WEDDING

"Down-to-earth characters and two mysteries to solve add up to a solid read."

—Kirkus Reviews

"Intriguing. . . . Fans of all things Scottish will have fun."

—Publishers Weekly

MURDER AT A SCOTTISH CHRISTMAS

"This latest adventure of a charming Scottish family is perfect for readers who like thorny mysteries and puppies."

—Kirkus Reviews

Books by Traci Hall

MURDER IN A SCOTTISH SHIRE
MURDER IN A SCOTTISH GARDEN
MURDER AT A SCOTTISH SOCIAL
MURDER AT A SCOTTISH WEDDING
MURDER AT A SCOTTISH CASTLE
MURDER AT A SCOTTISH CHRISTMAS
MURDER AT THE SCOTTISH GAMES
MURDER AT A SCOTTISH HALLOWEEN

And writing as Traci Wilton

MRS. MORRIS AND THE GHOST
MRS. MORRIS AND THE WITCH
MRS. MORRIS AND THE GHOST OF CHRISTMAS PAST
MRS. MORRIS AND THE SORCERESS
MRS. MORRIS AND THE VAMPIRE
MRS. MORRIS AND THE POT OF GOLD
MRS. MORRIS AND THE WOLFMAN
MRS. MORRIS AND THE MERMAID
MRS. MORRIS AND THE VENOMOUS VALENTINE
MRS. MORRIS AND THE DAY OF THE DEAD

Published by Kensington Publishing Corp.

Murder at a Scottish Halloween

TRACI HALL

Kensington Publishing Corp.
kensingtonbooks.com

KENSINGTON BOOKS are published by

Kensington Publishing Corp.
900 Third Avenue
New York, NY 10022

ISBN: 978-1-4967-5783-8 (ebook)

ISBN: 978-1-4967-5782-1

First Kensington Trade Edition: July 2026

10 9 8 7 6 5 4 3 2 1

Printed in the United States of America

The authorized representative in the EU for product safety and compliance
is eucomply OU, Parnu mnt 139b-14, Apt 123
Tallinn, Berlin 11317, hello@eucompliancepartner.com

I would like to dedicate *Murder at a Scottish Halloween* to the amazing cozy mystery readers who have shared their time with me.

Getting to know some of you in person, off of social media, has been a true pleasure.

Adaiah, Jenny, Katherine, Katie, Heather and Shawn, thank you!

Chapter 1

All Hallows' Eve

Thursday morning at the Shaw household was unusually loud as Paislee's grandfather, Angus Shaw, and her son, Brody Shaw, debated right versus wrong. The reason for the exuberant back-and-forth was that vandals had graffitied the entrance of Lady Shannon Leery's mansion with *Down with Tories* and the word *SAORSA*, which meant freedom.

"Just the porch, though?" Brody asked. The three sat around the wooden table for breakfast. He waved his piece of toast, sending crumbs flying that an alert Wallace, Brody's black Scottish terrier, quickly licked up from the hardwood floor.

"It's not right tae destroy anyone's home," Grandpa stated firmly. "Lady Leery's family has always been a boon tae Nairn." Her grandfather was in his late seventies, and his silver-gray hair had become more silvery-white. He was very fit, as he fished and had an active lifestyle. He wore black-framed glasses, and his full beard was the color of snow.

Paislee agreed but was swallowing tea so couldn't say so.

A snapshot of the Leery Estate had made the front page of the newspaper with pictures of Lady Shannon Leery, her son Shawn Marcus, and her daughter, Aila Webster. They were the last of the

Leery bloodline despite valiant efforts by Shannon's children. The tall bronze nymph in the koi pond had been knocked over and painted blue.

"I've got brilliant memories of the Leery gardens," Brody replied. "I hope it's only paint, which will wash off. That stag statue used tae be bigger than me, remember, Mum?"

"I do," she said.

"The article states the Leerys are Conservative, and that isnae always popular." Brody drank his orange juice, on his second bowl of Weetabix. Paislee didn't begrudge a pence of what it took to feed him. He was now taller than her. He had auburn hair and brown eyes, like her da.

"So, vote," Paislee said. "Don't deface property." When her bestie Lydia Barron-Smythe had returned from a trip to Greece with her husband, Corbin, she'd been shocked that many of the Grecian ruins were covered in graffiti with no respect for the ancient monuments. In Scotland it was illegal to wield spray cans and kids under sixteen couldn't even buy aerosol.

"I'll vote when I'm able," Brody said in a very serious tone at odds with his changing voice and freckles.

"And which party will ye join?" Grandpa tapped the photo, then returned to his oatmeal and toast.

Brody would rather starve than eat oatmeal, no matter what they did to spruce it up, though Paislee and Grandpa both liked it—especially with cream and fresh berries.

Grandpa was a member of the Labour Party, and Paislee was in the middle, a Liberal Democrat who just wanted everyone to get along.

Brody, in his second year, offered intelligent observations thanks to the Citizenship class he was taking in the Key 3 courses required for his certificate of completion. Paislee's mother said she might come for the commencement ceremony. Brody hoped to nab a football scholarship and get his Bachelor of Science degree in sport, fitness, and coaching, like Calum Waters, Brody's latest hero. "Not sure. A unionist."

There were six main political parties in Scotland. The Scottish National Party wanted independence from the UK. The group's rise in popularity had been affected by a scandal involving missing funds, and their leader, Nicola Sturgeon, had cried innocent of embezzlement although her husband, now ex, had been charged. Some members of the SNP had defected and created Alba in 2021. The other four were: Conservative (Tories), the Labour Party, the Liberal Democrats (Lib Dems) and the Scottish Greens—all unionists. They didn't want to leave Great Britain. There were pros and cons to each position.

"Guid lad." Grandpa circled the word SAORSA in the article with his finger. "It's a shame aboot all the bloody wars over 'freedom' where people died for an ideal."

"War is romanticized in the movies," Paislee said, "though I like *Outlander* as well as the next person." Fit Highlanders in kilts? Jamie and Claire's love story? She sighed and sipped her tea.

"You think Jamie is verra fine," Grandpa joked.

Paislee hid her smile by ducking her head.

"Would you fight tae the death"—Brody stabbed his spoon toward his grandfather—"over something?"

"Cannae say there's been an issue in me lifetime I would've fallen on me dirk for besides protecting me family. I earned enough to provide food and shelter." Grandpa nodded at Paislee. "Stories of the Highlanders are told with pride but in truth, the sides were muddied. Our ancestors fought for freedom and in the end, we had tae learn tae compromise. Not much has changed. I believe Great Britain and Scotland can help each other."

Paislee shifted, impressed by his insight. "We are blessed tae live in a time where we have plenty tae eat and means tae provide, even the poorest of us in this community. It wasn't always so."

"Money, food, and shelter are worth fighting for?" Brody asked.

"And love!" Paislee said.

Grandpa waggled his brows. "I'm too old for that. Your future has more at stake. Mibbe you can go intae politics after your football career."

Brody burst out laughing, sounding like the child that he was. How she wanted to protect him, but he was a young man now. He knew about his father and had forgiven her for her transgressions, accepting that her choices had been made from love.

"No, thanks. I want tae coach when I retire, at like, forty. That's older than Mum."

"Funny lad." Paislee chuckled at the poke. She was about to be thirty-one next week and it stung.

Grandpa passed Paislee the part of the paper with the sales—Halloween costumes at Tesco were half off for the very late shopper.

Brody and his mate Edwyn, both thirteen, weren't dressing up this year and Paislee was more than a little misty eyed about it. They'd attend a boy-girl Halloween party at the ice rink, which ended at ten, as there was school tomorrow.

Emma would be at the ice rink. Would she wear a costume? Brody had a mad crush, but they weren't official.

Edwyn didn't have a girlfriend by choice. He had blond ringlets and green eyes like his da, Bennett Maclean. He was into gaming and no longer played football. The split had left Brody at odds, and Paislee hoped her son didn't get hurt by Edwyn's wilder choices.

In America, her half-siblings, Natalie and Josh, were dressing up to go guising, or trick-or-treating, as they called it. Her mother promised to send pictures later. Nairn was seven hours ahead of the States. Natalie would go as Barbie, and Josh, a Ninja Turtle.

Paislee's nod to Samhain was a white T-shirt she'd embellished with a knitted black cat wearing a witch's hat. She had a matching hat for when she and Grandpa would hand out candy, and she'd knitted bat wings for Wallace. Grandpa had fake vampire teeth and a black cape for his role as Dracula. The wee bairns in costume always made her smile.

"Are you sure you won't want tae dress up tonight?" Paislee showed Brody a Batman costume, on sale.

"Naw." Brody scratched his nape, about due for another trim. He kept his hair in a short style, similar to Calum. Paislee encouraged the fandom as it meant university aspirations and regular haircuts. "I'm no wean. What's the plan then?"

"I'll drop you off at six at the rink, for pizza," Paislee said. "Four hours seems like a long time tae hang out with your friends. If you want tae come home early, just call me."

"I willnae," Brody assured her.

Paislee bit her tongue.

"You doin' anything fun?" Brody asked.

"We're giving candy oot," Grandpa said. "Wallace will be a bat."

"Brilliant!" Brody brought his empty dishes to the sink, rinsing them and putting them into the dishwasher that none of the Shaw family were tired of using. He let Wallace outside, then raced upstairs to prep for school. He took extra time with his appearance these days.

"Brody might end up a Lib Dem like you." Grandpa sighed. "Wanting everybody tae get along."

"So?" Paislee said. "It's better than being so wound up that you graffiti somebody's house. We can all agree it wasn't right."

"Not just somebody," Grandpa said. "But Lady Leery. Nobility, aye, but the guid kind. The Leery family would share their food—deer, fish, whatever—withoot a qualm, tae anybody in need."

"I wonder if she was the only one tagged?" Paislee traded the adverts page for the article and skimmed it. Darcey McClintock was a controversial journalist who often had her pieces featured.

"We would've heard aboot it, I think," Grandpa said. "Mibbe not though. The election is over. The SNPs lost ground. I've always been a Labour man meself."

"They gained seats due tae the SNP scandal. So did my party, but not enough tae take over the Conservatives," Paislee said.

Wallace barked at the back door, and she let the pup in. Brody skipped down the stairs, sliding around the corner post of the railing to the foyer.

"Can Emma give me a ride tae the ice rink tonight?" Brody balanced on one leg, phone in his hand, then hopped to the other. The boy was always in motion.

"Emma doesn't drive."

"Emma's mum." Brody rolled his eyes.

Paislee realized she had no reason to say no other than it meant not being in charge. "Okay."

Emma's mother was a hardworking lady with three part-time jobs trying to make ends meet after her divorce. Janet . . . no, not Janet. Crystal? Paislee couldn't remember, though they'd met twice now at school. She'd had an opinion about Paislee's lack of dating, thinking it strange.

Paislee and Brody were all right after she'd told him about his dad, and that was all that mattered. She and Mack, well. She averted her face as it heated with the memory of the detective inspector's kisses. Back in August he'd promised to kiss her often and he hadn't stopped.

Brody looked up from his mobile. "Emma and her mum will pick me up at five thirty. Emma wants me tae dress up but I'm not wearing a costume. No way. I'd be laughed oot of the ice rink."

"That's up tae you, honey."

If there was one thing that could make a boy change his mind about what was cool, it was a girl.

"Not gonna do it," Brody repeated. "It's not like she's my girlfriend."

Paislee laughed. "Do you want her tae be?"

"Not enough tae dress up." Brody's lip jutted and Paislee silently wished Emma luck in getting him to change his mind.

"We have tae hustle." Paislee and Brody called goodbyes to Grandpa, who murmured a reply from his chair at the kitchen table. Today was his day off and he planned on relaxing by reading or working on a puzzle.

Cashmere Crush, Paislee's yarn and bespoke sweater shop, kept not only Grandpa employed part-time, but also Elspeth Booth. Elspeth and Grandpa worked alternate days from noon to six. Rhona

Smythe was her only full-timer, clocking hours Monday through Friday, starting at ten. The end of October meant business quieted down until December, when things picked up for Christmas.

Gran had taught her that business had an ebb and flow. She dearly missed her grandmother. Seven years had passed since her death and so much had changed, yet the values she'd instilled remained important. Her granny believed that one should never discuss politics or religion outside the home, unless you were with close friends. She wouldn't have approved of the graffiti on Lady Leery's porch, believing it a right-or-wrong issue.

After dropping Brody off, Paislee drove to Cashmere Crush. Rhona's red sportscar was parked in the back by the cement stairs.

The nineteen-year-old brunette hopped out with her customary enthusiasm. She and her boyfriend, Artie, were moving to Inverness in the spring, and until then were saving every pound. Aibreann, her best friend, was going with them and the young women planned to open a dance studio.

Lydia, an excellent estate agent as well as Rhona's family by marriage, was locating a property with a business and living space to buy. Artie's mother had sold their house and given her son half as a nest egg while using the other to buy herself a condo overlooking the Moray Firth. Artie, close to his mum, lived there with her for now and shared the expenses.

"Morning!" Rhona's tiara sparkled despite the clouds. Her pink princess costume reached the pavement.

"You look adorable," Paislee said.

"Thanks. Artie is going tae be my Prince Charming for the parties tonight." Rhona flashed a dimple. "There's a costume contest at the Grotto with a cash prize."

"I want tae see pictures." In a few years, would Brody be willing to dress up to make his girlfriend happy? Paislee hoped so.

They went up the stairs and inside, Paislee flicking on the lights as they prepped for the day. She was going to miss Rhona terribly when the lass went on to greener pastures.

"I'll bore you with them tomorrow," Rhona promised.

"Not possible." Paislee located the witch's hat she'd knitted to go with her shirt, and put it on.

"Cute!" Rhona said. "And they all sold oot, too."

"Good thing." Paislee cringed at the clutter. "My back storage room is so full I don't have space for merchandise that isn't selling."

Rhona jerked her thumb behind her to the storage area. "What if you had new shelves fitted exactly tae the walls so it was organized tae make the most of it?"

Paislee considered the slew of cardboard boxes, yarn, patterns, and junk. "Not a bad idea."

"Mum just got it done for her closet and it created double the space," Rhona said.

The Smythes had buckets of money, so Paislee winced at what that might cost.

"I know that expression, Ms. Thrifty." Rhona powered on the store laptop. "There's a program we can use tae get plans. For free. And I bet Lachlan Felling, Gemma's boyfriend, would give us a guid deal on hardware."

Gemma was Artie's mother. She'd quit her prior job to be a manager at Lachlan Construction. Within an hour, Rhona had put in the backroom dimensions and created a shelving design that appeared very promising, all without spending a thing.

"That's incredible." Paislee eyed the current situation of overstuffed, lopsided metal shelves. "And, overwhelming."

"I'll help," Rhona promised.

"When?" Paislee arched her brow at the hardworking teen. "Between here and teaching dance tae the kids, there is no spare time."

"I like tae be busy. Besides, I can work on it when things are slow. Or on a Sunday, when we arenae open tae the public."

That had merit. Knock it out in one fell swoop.

The front door opened, and Paislee turned to greet the first customer of the day at—she gulped—eleven. There was slow, and then there was slllowwwwww.

Her welcoming smile widened as Lady Shannon Leery came in, with Dowager Countess Sorcha Grant at her side. Though Sorcha was younger by twelve years, the ladies appeared practically the same age until you looked closely.

The dowager countess was an actual noble, able to trace her ancestry to the first king of Scotland, while Lady Leery held an honorary title given hundreds of years back to those with money and estates, like Lydia's father-in-law, Laird Garrison Smythe.

Shannon Leery was now Shannon Leery Thornton as she'd married Gavin Thornton, a longtime admirer who'd stayed in the background of her affairs and loved her always.

"Good morning!" Paislee left the mess of the backroom and walked toward them.

The dowager countess wore her gray hair with pride. Sorcha's clothes were subdued but quality. Tweed and fine wool, while Shannon had the latest fashions. Neither wore a Halloween costume.

Paislee's happiness faded as she could think of only one reason for the pair to be here together, and it had to do with the article in the paper about the vandalism of Lady Leery's porch.

The astute older woman broke into a grin as she elbowed Sorcha. "Paislee is ontae us. I told you, Sorcha, she's no fool."

The last time they'd arrived at Cashmere Crush they'd wanted her help to solve a crime. What could she do about someone with a spray can and a grudge?

"Dinnae be frightened," Sorcha admonished good-naturedly. "I'm also here tae discuss gifts for Robert's wedding party over Christmas. He and his bride will tie the knot on December twenty-sixth, and I'll host the event at Ramsey Castle."

Rhona, though related to Laird Smythe, wasn't nobility herself and dipped her head respectfully. "Guid morning."

"Lady Leery, and Dowager Countess Grant, meet Rhona Smythe."

"Related tae Laird Garrison Smythe? A grand family," Lady Leery said. "If large. Call me Shannon."

"I'm Sorcha."

"Oh, I couldnae do that. Mum would have my hide," Rhona said. "Will Ms. Shannon, and Ms. Sorcha be all right?"

"And who is your mother?" Sorcha asked with a twitch of her lips. "She taught you wonderful manners."

"Petra Fuller. My da is McDermot Smythe."

"Petra Fuller?" Shannon tapped her chin. "She was a bonnie lass and didnae last long on the marriage mart."

Rich as well as beautiful, Petra would not have been interested in Sorcha's philandering son Robert, or Shannon's partying offspring, Shawn, though the ladies would be aware of her as a possible mate.

"Why don't you do inventory of the skeins?" Paislee suggested. "Start with the cashmere."

"Sure." Rhona grabbed a clipboard and pen, leaving to give them privacy. Soft music played.

"She's a pretty thing," Sorcha said. "Polite and wealthy too."

"Way too young and sweet for either of ours," Shannon said.

"Robert had tae go oot of the country tae find his bride, but he managed it." Sorcha leaned her elbow on the counter by the register. "I was a wee bit worrit, I can admit now."

"The bride tae be, Princess Dona de Chevron, is from a small European country I cannae recall the name of but she is quite beautiful." Shannon smiled at her friend in understanding. "Robert did well, in the end."

Sorcha sighed. "He just has tae not muck it up and aye, Ramsey Castle will be saved for the next generation."

"What are you thinking?" Knitting items for a noble wedding would up Paislee's credentials, which was good for business.

"I suggested the vests and ascots in cashmere," Shannon said. "Scarves in the Grant tartan."

"Which was an excellent idea. I'll need four for the men. Robert, Patrick. The bride's brother and her father. Matching sashes for the ladies—the bride, me, her mother. Cinda. Patrick insisted she be included." Sorcha tilted her head, her cunning eyes narrowed. "I know it's October thirty-first, but can you complete this by December twentieth? We'll need photos. The sooner the better, actually."

"Absolutely." Paislee would work around the clock to deliver. This would be a feather in her knitted witch hat.

"Splendid." Shannon smiled and changed the subject, as Paislee had known she would. "Did you read the paper this morning?"

"Yes. It was awful, what happened tae your property." Paislee glanced toward Rhona at the front of the yarn shop as she counted the skeins of cashmere, about to move to the next shelf of merino wool.

"It was unacceptable." Sorcha's gaze burned with anger equal to her friend's.

"Did they catch the vandals?" Paislee asked. "Not only graffiti on the porch, but the statue in your koi pond was painted blue."

"No," Shannon said. "It just happened this morning."

"Like they even tried!" Sorcha scoffed.

"I'm assuming you called the constables," Paislee said. She couldn't think of a reason not to do so. "What did the police say?"

"I had tae fill oot reports." Shannon's mouth pursed. "I miss the old days when I could simply give the information and someone else would file it. My handwriting is not what it used tae be."

"It was a sacrilege." Sorcha's regal brow rose.

"I'm really sorry," Paislee said again. "What can I do tae help?"

"Well, what can you do, darling lass?" Sorcha asked.

Her thoughts precisely.

"What we mean tae say, is that you are not local nobility, so you cannae understand what it's like tae be targeted in such a vicious way." Shannon shivered.

Paislee realized that the lady was sincerely bothered and responded with her heart rather than a smart comment. "What happened, exactly?"

"Well, I'm living at me and Gavin's home, so I wasnae at the estate. Shawn and Aila are both staying there as they will inherit and need tae figure it oot. Shawn called me at five a.m.—not the call you want from your grown son in a panic, having heard the vandals. I think Malcolm chased the intruders off with the hunting rifle, truth be told."

Malcolm was the butler at the Leery Estate and not one to back down from an intruder. Paislee would trust Malcolm with an emergency far more than Shawn.

Shannon paused to take a breath. Sorcha patted her shoulder and took over for her friend. "Aila had been ill, so she'd taken cold medicine and was zonked. Didnae hear a thing. Shawn had his girlfriend Margot with him . . ."

"They called the police," Shannon continued, "and then me. I went right over. The stag in the maze had been knocked over as well as the nymph, and graffiti sprayed everywhere. Doon with Tories? How unoriginal."

"Was anything taken?" Paislee asked.

"No. Just ruined," Shannon said.

"Are you able tae clean it up?"

"The police just finished photographing the damage, so aye." Shannon tilted her chin. "Shawn will handle it."

Shawn Marcus was the landlord for the businesses on their street, and he was dating Margot, who managed a wellness clinic a few doors down. He'd had many health scares...was it a liver transplant? Maybe a kidney. Her memory wasn't what it used to be. No matter—the operation had been a success, and he was healthy.

Everyone seemed to be in a *steadier* frame of mind. Paislee had learned that just because your children were grown didn't mean that you stopped worrying over their sometimes idiotic choices.

"That he will." Sorcha stepped back from the counter. "*SAORSA* was painted everywhere. Freedom. Freedom from what? Following the law? I want these people caught and punished. What right do they have tae destroy private property?"

"We're going tae the paper and have a talk with Darcey

McClintock. Where did she get that photo? The paint was still fresh. Makes me wonder if she could be behind it," Shannon said.

"Why would she do that?" Paislee asked. It was risky if one wanted to keep their job.

"Why not?" Sorcha shrugged. "The Scottish National Party is prevalent around here. Could be she's a member and protesting against us."

"Us?" Paislee queried.

"Tell her," Shannon said. She looked at Sorcha with an expectant expression.

Paislee braced herself for what was to come. One never knew with these two.

"Well." Sorcha sighed. "The Leery Estate was not the only one under this SAORSA's spray can, that's all."

"What do you mean?"

"They were at Ramsey Castle the day before yesterday." Sorcha folded her hands before her. "Spray-painting. Knocking things doon."

"Did they do damage?" Paislee asked, incredulous. She hadn't heard of the disturbance, and they read the paper every day.

"Aye," Shannon said when her friend didn't respond. "They trampled her entire corn field. Cowards."

"What did the police say?"

"We didnae call them," Sorcha said. "Robert, Patrick, and I cleaned it up ourselves. Radicals want one thing—publicity. We cannae have word of this reaching the de Chevron family. It's challenging enough tae hide my daughter's mental illness." She exhaled. "From the way Dona's mother, Queen de Chevron, spoke on the phone, they think Scotland is still full of raging Highlanders ready tae plunder, and they're worrit aboot their daughter's safety."

Shannon flipped her sleek blond bob. "I think when Sorcha didnae report the incident, well, the vandals made sure tae take photos and send them tae the paper. I will find oot who is responsible. It's our next stop after this."

Paislee believed the culprits deserved the wrath of the ladies in Nairn. "Have you talked tae the other local nobles?"

"I've left a message for the dowager countess at Cawdor Castle. The family is in residence in October through the spring, so they keep it closed tae the public. I dinnae ken the thane as well," Sorcha said.

Thane of Cawdor was a title in Scottish nobility, and the current thane was the 7th Earl Cawdor, and the 25th Thane of Cawdor, Colin Campbell. He was the Vice Lord Lieutenant of Nairnshire, married, and had four children. He cared very much for their community.

"I'm friends with his wife, Isabella. They're hosting a fundraiser tonight, which has caused a rift in the already tense family dynamic. She said that so far, they havenae been tagged with graffiti or property destruction," Shannon said. "They have a lot of extra security in place. She blames the recent elections for making people mental."

"We protect a way of life." Sorcha's expression turned grim. "Our castle works verra hard tae employ locals as well as donate tae charities. We've had tae tighten our belts as it is, and there are days I want tae walk away from the bleeding pile of stone. But what then? If I dinnae make the effort, what will happen tae the history of our land and people?"

"Folks dinnae feel the same responsibility toward the land as they used tae," Shannon said wearily.

"Too busy trying tae make it through their own day, I suppose," Sorcha conceded. "It's a heavy burden. Can you imagine trying tae marry off a princess? Dona de Chevron is almost thirty, which is cutting it close for those childbearing years."

"You both are incredible examples of how tae live with integrity, while saving what you've inherited," Paislee said softly.

"I fear Robert and Patrick will give it up once I'm gone," Sorcha said. "I've threatened to haunt them if they do."

Shannon gave a hoarse laugh. "I hadnae thought tae come back from the dead. Today is the best day for it, All Hallows' Eve."

"I could join Muriel at Cawdor Castle," Sorcha continued, her lips twitching. "Or the Wraith at Rait Ruins."

Paislee shivered. While Muriel was often spotted throughout the year, the Wraith only came out on All Hallows' Eve. The poor lass had been trying to escape her father's rage, and he'd chopped off her hands while she'd been hanging from a window in the tower.

"Muriel is less spooky," Paislee said. "You wouldn't want tae be a scary ghost, would you?"

"If my children sold Ramsey Castle, aye, I would," Sorcha promised. "I pray Robert and Dona have a dozen babies, and Patrick and Cinda too." Her only daughter had been institutionalized and would not have children.

"Muriel is a lonely ghostie," Shannon said. "She haunts the tower and guards the holly tree. I've seen her and felt her sad presence."

"You have?" Paislee asked in surprise. "Not once for me, no matter how many times I've taken the tour."

"I have too," Sorcha said. "Just a hint of blue from the corner of my eye. Puir Muriel Calder, kidnapped as a baby by the Campbells, wanted tae bring peace by marrying Sir John Campbell of her own free will, tae ensure the Calder, or Cawdor, line. One of the legends states that she guards the holly tree still because she died tae protect it from bloodthirsty vandals." She curled her fist. "Vandals, even then."

"I've never heard that version. I thought she was an old lady." Made Paislee regard the petrified branch with a little more respect. No more tree, no more Thanes of Campbell.

"It's been over five hundred years," Shannon said. "Stories get jumbled. You've heard how the original Thane of Cawdor had a dream aboot a donkey carrying around baskets of gold?"

"Aye." Paislee had been taught this at Gran's knee. "Wherever the donkey lay down was where the thane would build his castle. He built the tower around the holly tree, tae protect it."

"Now you ken why—he made a deal . . . angel, or demon, no one remembers, but for so long as the tree is safe, the Thanes of

Cawdor can claim the land." Shannon's eyes glittered. "I learned this as a wee one, 'So long as the branch is safe in the tower, the Thanes of Cawdor will remain in power.'"

"Easy tae remember!" Paislee said.

"If Muriel Campbell was willing tae die for the holly, why shouldnae I be prepared tae do all in my power?" Sorcha placed her hand over her heart. "I would die for Ramsey Castle."

"Nobody is going tae die," Shannon said perkily. "Unless it's that journalist at the paper. If she's behind this slanderous photo, I might kill her myself."

Chapter 2

"Probably not something you should announce if you're planning a murder," said a male voice.

Paislee's stomach tightened with . . . longing. She whirled to find Detective Inspector Mack Zeffer standing behind her. Seafoam-green eyes, russet hair. Clean-shaven.

He'd entered through the back door of her shop as quiet as a cat. Blue suit jacket stretched across broad shoulders, buttoned against the autumn chill.

Shannon's mouth made an O. "A jest, DI, obviously. What are ye doing sneaking aboot?"

Paislee chuckled with nerves and happiness, and well, she liked that Mack held his own beneath the lady's glare.

"Quite sneaky!" Sorcha seconded with a huff. "Let's go. Paislee, I'll be in touch aboot Robert's wedding. I expect that what we discuss is in confidence?" Her brow arched.

"Of course." Paislee's mirth fled. She would tread cautiously as she wanted to snag that custom order.

Rhona opened the door for the regal figures as they exited Cashmere Crush, wishing them a wonderful day.

"Do I dare ask what secrets you need tae keep already this morning?" Mack asked her. His eyes warmed and she could stare into them for hours.

Somehow, Paislee had fallen head over heels in love with Mack Zeffer. Since August, she'd been on the wildest ride of her life. The feelings were dangerous, thrilling, and exciting. The out-of-control emotions made her understand why people behaved so uncharacteristically while under the effects of romance.

Love was as intoxicating as top-shelf whisky.

Mack had been a rock for her when she hadn't realized she'd needed one. He loved her too, which evened the playing field a wee bit. He cared for Brody, and even though he hadn't wanted children he said that because Brody belonged to her, that his feelings encompassed her son.

"I can't tell you details because I don't have them, but it seems Robert Grant is getting married at last tae a princess named Dona de Chevron, in December. I'm sure Sorcha wants grandchildren tae carry on at Ramsey Castle. She asked me tae supply some cashmere vests and sashes for the wedding party."

Paislee didn't share about the vandals at Ramsey Castle. It didn't pertain, and just because she was in love with Mack Zeffer, he was still a detective. If it was important, she would find a way to share that didn't break bonds of trust.

"That'll be a gold star for Cashmere Crush." Mack tugged her knitted witch hat. "Cute." He turned to Rhona as the young woman joined them with an elaborate curtsy. "And I like your costume too."

"Thanks! I am, alas, just pretending tae be a princess. I'm gonna look up the country the de Chevrons rule. Mibbe they have a son?" Rhona's smile showed she was teasing. "Me and Artie have three different parties tae go tae tonight with Aibreann and Foster, and the costume contest at the Grotto. Now that they're officially a couple, Aibreann is dressing as Little Red Riding Hood, and Foster will be the wolf. It'll be a pure blast."

"Well, be careful," Mack said. "The police have extra patrol cars oot tonight tae crack doon on drinking and driving."

"I am the DD," Rhona said. "I'll be extra cautious."

Mack's nod shifted his thick hair, kept even shorter than Brody's. He guided the subject back to the Lady Leery situation. "Should I have Constable Jays check on the journalist's safety?"

"They were joking," Paislee assured him. "Writing the article about the vandals is Darcey McClintock's job. Whether or not she has a grudge against the nobles in Nairn, I couldn't say. I've never noticed Darcey McClintock's political leanings."

"Did you find the vandals?" Rhona asked. "Mum and Da think it's wrong tae deface property."

"Not yet." Mack's eyes shuttered. He knew something about the case but wasn't going to share.

Fine.

Made her feel better about not repeating what Sorcha had told her about her castle also being vandalized. Still, she said, "Could the Cawdor family be next?"

"I dinnae ken," Mack said. "Why would you think so?"

"Oh . . . no reason."

"Isnae the castle closed for the season?" Rhona asked.

"I heard an unsubstantiated rumor that there might be a fundraiser tonight."

Mack seemed on the verge of a smirk but stepped closer to her instead, so that there was a mere handsbreadth between them. "What are you doing this All Hallows' Eve, Paislee?"

Her pulse sped. "Brody has a party at the ice rink, so Grandpa, Wallace, and I will hand out candy tae the weans at home." Paislee studied him, trying to imagine Mack relaxing enough to don a costume. "Would you like tae join us?"

He exhaled, the scent of spearmint reaching her cheek. "Mibbe? It all depends on how late I stay at my sister's place in Stonehaven. She feels sorry for me and invites me for burgers with the kids on Halloween. I want tae tell her in person that I've found someone special."

Paislee's heart went to gooey sentimental mush in an instant. He'd been very private about his family. "That's sweet, Mack."

"Prepare tae be bombarded by questions and social media requests," Mack said.

Her stomach twirled with nerves. Would his sister like Paislee?

The front door opened, and Paislee, who'd inched closer to Mack, leapt back. He chuckled. "The day I cannae make you blush is the day I need tae worry that you dinnae care."

"You will never have tae worry about that." Paislee cursed her redhead blush that inflamed not just her face but her entire body.

Rhona was helping a customer, so Mack pressed a firm kiss to her lips, which immediately tingled.

Kissing was all they'd done. They were going slow, and Paislee appreciated that he was in no rush.

He loved her and that was enough.

They didn't talk more about the next steps, agreeing to be in the moment. It was terrific that he wanted to share their relationship with his sister, his closest relative.

Would she have the same eyes as Mack, and hair? Paislee knew that her name was Michele with one *L.* She was on her second marriage and had two kids younger than Brody—a boy and a girl.

That after their father's death, Michele had been the closest to Mack and helped him when he was depressed. The money he'd earned as a child model had kept his family afloat. His mother had wisely managed the finances until her death. At eighteen, he'd been determined to right the wrongs of his childhood by being a detective.

"I look forward tae meeting her," Paislee said.

She was afraid to meet her. Would Mack break things off if his sister didn't care for Paislee?

"She will love you," Mack said.

The door opened again. Another customer? Paislee peered around Mack and smiled at Mary Beth Mulholland. The woman was very pretty, plump, and married to a solicitor. She knitted and was part of Paislee's weekly Thursday night Knit and Sip.

"I've gotta run," Mack said.

"Don't rush your visit with Michele on my account for tonight," Paislee said. "I'll pick Brody up at ten and be home right after, if you find yourself in the neighborhood for a cup of tea. Or, we can get lunch tomorrow at the Lion's Mane. They have the fish and chips special on Fridays."

She just wanted to know that she would see him again.

"All right." Mack seemed to feel the same. "Until later." He went out the back and Paislee walked toward the front of the yarn shop.

"I hope I didnae chase the detective off," Mary Beth said.

"No. He was already leaving."

Mary Beth gave Paislee a side hug along with a smile. They didn't have to talk about it. Everyone knew she and Mack were dating and her friends unanimously approved.

Lydia and Corbin were in Germany, but Lydia would be back next week for Paislee's birthday and to check in with her estate business. They had staff to manage their new home while they were away to set up the Smythe Winery. Since the flight from Germany was less time than it took to drive to Edinburgh, it really was not going to be a hassle.

Change happened.

Change didn't have to be bad.

"How did the girls' costumes turn out?" Paislee asked. Twins, Anna and Iona, were ten, while Suz, Blaise and Shep O'Connor's little lass, was now eight. Though their mothers were friends, the three weren't close, as the twins went to Fordythe Primary and Suz attended a private school.

Halloween had been a mainstay topic for the last several weeks at Knit and Sip, with Suz finally deciding to be a unicorn, and the twins, Anna and Elsa from *Frozen*.

"I've got pictures," Mary Beth said.

"I want tae see!" Rhona said. She'd rung up the customer she'd helped and now joined them.

"They were so excited this morning I could hardly get them tae sit still and finish their breakfasts." Mary Beth tapped her phone and chose a photo. Both grinned ear to ear. "Anna is Elsa and Iona is Anna. Anna is always Anna so wanted tae be someone else."

"Makes perfect sense," Rhona said.

"Do they get tae wear the costumes tae school?" Paislee asked.

"No. I'll bring them tae change intae after lunch." Mary Beth pocketed her phone. "I help with the parties and I've made four dozen cupcakes with blue icing."

"How fun!" Rhona said.

"They were verra guid, too, if I do say so myself. I used angel food cake mix and organic blueberries for the color."

"Healthy and yummy," Rhona said. "Now that is impressive."

"I had some boxed to bring here later before I remembered we arenae doing Knit and Sip. I miss our Thursday nights, but the girls are getting older by the second and I just dinnae want tae miss a thing," Mary Beth said. "I could hardly believe it was Brody last week when I saw you two together. He just shot right up!"

"I know it." Paislee sighed and placed her hand on the high-top table.

"You both are wonderful mums," Rhona announced. "I dinnae want kids and neither does Artie. The world is such a dangerous place. Bombs, car accidents, and other stuff beyond your control."

Paislee realized the lass had to be thinking of Artie's family, and the incident concerning his brother Cam several years ago.

"I guess I never thought aboot it like that," Mary Beth said. "I always wanted tae be a mother." She fanned her face. "And when I saw Arran Mulholland? I didnae care aboot anything but being his wife. It was love at first sight."

"Where did you meet?" Rhona asked.

"University." Mary Beth's brow furrowed.

Rhona straightened the stack of shawls while they talked. "What's your degree?"

"Ah, I dropped oot tae support Arran and worked at an office. It was the best deal of my life. He promised that I would never have tae worry aboot money, and he was right. Mibbe once the girls are older, I might go back tae school, but why? I like making our home a haven."

"So long as you are happy," Paislee said. "What's brought this on?"

"Och, one of the other mums at school made a snide comment aboot how it must be nice tae live off my husband. She has no idea how hard I worked tae support us while he went tae law school. Or how much we wanted bairns. I was lucky with two, but she doesnae ken aboot the miscarriages we had." Mary Beth's cornflower-blue eyes welled.

"Let me have a wee chat with her." Paislee immediately sprung to her friend's defense.

"And you'd just show up at Fordythe Primary?" Mary Beth's shoulders shook with quiet laughter.

"Why not?" Paislee shrugged. "It wouldn't be the first time I was in trouble with Hamish McCall." She shuddered. He was the youngest (and handsomest) headmaster in Fordythe Primary history.

"You were in trouble?" Rhona asked with total surprise.

"There was a stretch where puir Paislee couldnae get Brody tae school on time no matter what. Just before Angus arrived tae live with you. And hasnae that been a blessing?"

"It has!" Paislee and Hamish had dated but it hadn't gone anywhere. He'd recently rekindled his romance with his university sweetheart, who had moved to Nairn. Jerry McFadden and his girlfriend Freya went on double dates with them, but Jerry wouldn't have if Paislee'd had a problem with Hamish.

Paislee and Hamish had been friends. And now that Paislee understood the overwhelming, all-consuming love for Mack, well, there was no substitute.

A customer entered the yarn shop and Rhona greeted the older woman. "Welcome tae Cashmere Crush. How can I help you?"

"My daughter-in-law bought a knitted black witch's hat she'd gotten here. Do you have more?"

"No, ma'am, I'm sairy." Rhona placed her hands behind her

back. "They're sold oot until next year. Would you like the pattern? You can make one yourself. They are simple tae do."

"All right." The woman perused the shelves. "Do you think I can complete the hat in a few hours? For tonight before the kids come guising."

"Two hours, maybe three," Paislee said, joining them.

"Let me see the pattern. I'm just above a beginner level." The woman nodded at Paislee, and Paislee's hat. "Aye, that's the one." She tilted her head. "Any chance I can have that? I'll pay extra."

Paislee, Mary Beth, and Rhona burst out laughing as Paislee removed the hat. "Deal."

With wishes for a happy Halloween, and money in the register, Paislee set to work on another knitted witch hat for her own costume.

Mary Beth returned home to prepare lunch for Arran, who joined her a few times per week. Rhona handled the customers until Elspeth arrived at noon and then they each took a lunch break.

By quarter till four, it was starting to get darkish. "I've got tae run but honestly, if we don't have any customers past five, go ahead and lock up. Rhona, have fun tonight. Elspeth, you too. Are you still going tae the church with Susan?"

Susan, Elspeth's blind sister who suffered from macular degeneration, had a trained labradoodle named Rosie for a service dog.

"Aye. This is the second year that Father Dixon has done the haunted maze at the adjoining cemetery. We had over a hundred kids last year and he anticipates it will dooble. Parents want a safe, fun option tae go guising. Rosie's lead is decorated with glowing pumpkins."

Rosie was a sturdy dog that, when standing, reached Susan's thighs. Rosie assisted Susan with balance and guidance so Susan could be more independent in her daily activities. This helped Elspeth and Susan's relationship, which had been strained due to Elspeth being Susan's caretaker. They were finding their footing again as sisters and friends.

The dog was also a companion for Susan, who answered phones part-time at Margot's clinic. Elspeth, retired from office work for Father Dixon, had too much time on her hands so she worked at Paislee's twenty hours a week, as did Grandpa.

Both seniors promised her that if they wanted to cut down further or not work at all, that they would just let her know.

Grandpa claimed it gave him purpose, and he liked flirting with the ladies who were there to buy yarn or bespoke sweaters. Elspeth had a crush on Grandpa, but Grandpa's heart belonged to Paislee's granny.

"I bet you have a big turnout," Paislee said. "Say hi tae Father Dixon, and Susan, for me."

"I will," Elspeth said. "We have a contest for the best costumes—not a cash prize, though, like what's for the older crowd at the Grotto. People are verra creative."

"Lots better than my witch hat." Paislee would try harder next year.

"Father Dixon asked if you'd purchase a hundred trash bags for the All Souls' Day cemetery cleanup, since you and the Shepherd family are next on the donation list."

When Elspeth had worked at the church, she'd devised a system to ask the parishioners to pitch in so that it didn't fall on just one family for supplies, but a list of volunteers that went alphabetically. Shaw, and Shepherd. "Yes, of course. See you later!"

Paislee, wearing her freshly knitted slouchy witch hat, left as the sky turned gray. By eight thirty, it would be very dark.

She picked up Brody at school, who seemed to be arguing with Edwyn. Emma wasn't around, or his good friend Sam. Two boys stood behind Edwyn, sneering. She recognized one of them from the football team. He was older and a pretty good player. Darryl Barclay.

Paislee honked to get their attention. None of the kids acknowledged her. Brody got in the front seat and tossed his backpack behind him.

"What's going on?" Paislee asked.

"Nothing."

"Now, that is an out-and-out falsehood. I saw you and Edwyn fighting just now. And Darryl. Who is that other kid?" He looked familiar and was probably also a footballer. The lads were growing so fast it was hard to keep them straight.

"Mum! It doesnae matter. It's a school thing. Not a big deal." Brody focused out the window and ignored her.

"All right." Paislee silently counted to ten. "You know you can talk tae me?"

"Yeah." He read the digital clock with an exaggerated groan. "I barely have time tae change before Emma picks me up. Can I have extra money for the ice rink?"

"Besides pizza money?" Paislee realized they wouldn't have dinner together but what else would the kids do in that four hours besides eat? And skate. And eat. "I have cash in my bag I'll give you—remind me."

"Thanks."

Ten minutes later, they'd reached the house, where it had gone from a little dark, to twilight.

Her grandfather had turned on the solar-powered candles in the pumpkins on the porch, so lights flickered merrily. Grandpa had carved a fish, Paislee a ghost, and Brody had done a stencil of a Scottish terrier.

"Cool!" Brody said, seeing them lit up as she reached the house and parked beneath the carport.

"They turned out great." Paislee turned off the engine.

Brody dashed out and up the steps into the house. He'd forgotten his backpack, so Paislee grabbed it and brought it in. Wallace waited for her in the foyer, snuffling and wagging his body hello.

The pup left the foyer for the top step outside to sniff the pumpkins. The best thing about the solar-charged fake candles was not having to worry about fire.

Paislee put Brody's backpack on the hook and called for Wallace to come in, then closed the door.

"Heya, lass. Was that a ghostie whooshing up the stairs?" Grandpa had gelled his thick hair back, styled like Dracula. He wore black pants and a white shirt that he'd top with a black cape later to complete the costume. Pointy plastic teeth poked from his shirt pocket.

"Just your great-grandson behaving like a dervish." Paislee hung up her jacket and handbag, dropping her keys into the ceramic dish by the front door before she turned to join her grandfather in the hall.

"Probably been eating candy all day," Grandpa said.

"That would explain it. I feel bad for the teachers at school tomorrow."

"Mibbe they'll skate all that energy off at the rink." Grandpa stepped toward the kitchen. "Can I get you a cup of tea?"

"Sure. That'd be great." She grinned as she saw the treats he'd made for them arranged on a wooden charcuterie board Brody had made in one of his electives.

Sliced meat and cheese, crackers, veggies, and a variety of dips tempted her. "I thought we could snack until the fish chowder is ready. I baked a loaf of bread tae go with it."

"Thank you, Grandpa. Brody will eat at the ice rink, so a light meal for us is perfect."

He handed her a mug of Brodies with fresh sliced lemon. "Here ye are."

She inhaled the citrus and smiled. "I could use some afternoon pep. I'm dragging a little today."

"And, it might be a long night," Grandpa conceded. He nibbled on an olive.

"Yum!" Paislee piled snacks on a napkin and sat down. "What did you do today?"

"Finished the book, and started a new puzzle," Grandpa said.

"That's nice. I literally sold the hat off my head for a profit." Paislee patted the one she currently wore. "This is not as tight of a weave, but it was fast, so I'd have it for tonight." Wallace wagged his tail, and she scratched under his collar.

"Looks fine tae me," Grandpa said.

Her phone dinged. It was a message from her mother, with pictures of Josh and Natalie. Her half sister was dressed as Barbie, and her half brother a Ninja Turtle, as they'd planned. Sometimes costumes were changed last-minute if something happened.

"So cute!" She showed Grandpa, and then sent heart emojis as Brody came downstairs, his hair styled. He'd changed into new jeans and a T-shirt with his favorite band. Black, of course. Like his sneakers.

"Hungry?" Grandpa asked. He went to the stove where the fish chowder bubbled on low.

"Always." Brody pocketed his mobile. "Emma will be here in a few minutes. Can you come oot and say hi tae her mum?"

"Happy tae." Paislee stood and got money as well, handing her son more than she normally would in case he wanted to treat Emma to an ice cream or something. Was that why he'd asked for extra cash?

"You're the best." Brody filled a small bowl of chowder and blew on it, quickly swallowing a bite. "Grandpa, this is so guid. Will you save me some for when I get back?"

"I can always make it again, but, me lad, I doot your mum and I will eat all of it. I made a large pot."

Paislee attached Wallace's batwings with a special harness. "Come on. Let me get a picture of you guys."

Brody rolled his eyes but did as she asked. He held Wallace and Grandpa added his teeth before he grinned. It was so precious that she sent it straight to her mum and Lydia. Both immediately hearted it.

A knock sounded on the front door and Wallace zoomed around the kitchen. There was no danger of the wings taking flight, but they were fancy. Grandpa swooped the pup up in his arms, his cape flaring dramatically.

Paislee answered the door, hoping it would be the first of the wee bairns to come guising, but it was adorable Emma dressed in black with long black braids. Wednesday Addams.

"Boo!"

"Would you like a treat?" Paislee reached into an orange plastic pumpkin she'd had since Brody was a babe and pulled out a chocolate skeleton.

Emma held out her palm. "Yes, please. Mum didnae even buy any for the house because she's always on a diet. Thank you, Paislee. Angus!" She fluttered her fingers at Grandpa in the hall, pocketing the candy.

Brody shrugged on his jacket.

"Phone?" Paislee asked. "Money?"

"Aye, and aye." Brody slid past her down the stairs to the lawn.

It wouldn't be cool to grab him for a hug, so she didn't, and crossed the yard to say hello to Emma's mum.

The brunette woman in her mid-thirties rolled down the driver's-side window of her sedan.

"Hi, Crystal," Brody said as he got in the back. Emma went around the other side to sit next to him.

"Hi, Brody. Thanks, Em. Now I feel like a taxi driver."

Emma stayed in the back with Brody.

Teens.

Crystal. That was right. "I can drive Emma home, since you're dropping off," Paislee said.

"No, thanks. Emma is actually staying with her friend from school. I have the night shift at the hospital, answering phones. I'll be checking in and I'd better get an answer. No messing around." Crystal glanced over her shoulder at her daughter.

"Mum!" Emma groaned, mortified.

Was there a probability of messing around? Before Paislee could ask more questions, she was handed a card with Crystal's name and phone number.

"Just so that we are in contact. Aye, I am one of *those* mums."

"I don't mind. Uh, Brody, make sure that Crystal has my number, too, would you?"

"I already do." Crystal patted the steering wheel. "Home and mobile. All right. Have a nice night and I'll probably see you when I drop Emma off tae watch Brody play football on Saturday."

With that, Crystal drove away. Well!

Her mind was kept occupied by the groups of kids coming by for the next three hours. At nine, they were officially out of candy, even Grandpa's private stash, so they turned off the porch light and pumpkins.

Wallace had been a hit, and in many pictures with his batwings. Grandpa had played it up as Dracula. Considering this was the first Halloween that she and Brody hadn't spent together, it hadn't gone too terribly bad.

Paislee had a bowl of fish chowder and a slice of bread. Her grandfather could certainly cook. She was grateful for the gift of Angus Shaw in her life, which reminded her of how he'd come to be in it, thanks to Mack investigating her uncle Craigh and discovering her homeless Grandpa on a park bench. "I bet Craigh misses your cooking."

"Not me, eh, but me fish chowder?" Grandpa snickered.

When Paislee and Brody eventually traveled to America to visit her mum and siblings in Arizona, Grandpa wanted to join them as her uncle lived, under a different name, in the Florida Keys.

"He didn't appreciate you like we do." Paislee didn't feel the least bit bad about saying so, as it was the unvarnished truth.

After putting the snacks away and doing the dishes while Grandpa showered to get the gel from his hair, Paislee checked her phone for messages. Say, from Brody. Or Mack.

Nothing from either of them.

She saved the picture of Grandpa, Brody, and Wallace as her new screen saver.

Grandpa got out of the shower. "I'm off tae get Brody," Paislee said. "I'll be right back."

"Let him know that there's plenty of chowder left, silly lad."

Wallace jumped at her heels.

"You want tae come too?"

The pup raced to the front door.

"I'm taking Wallace!"

"Okay," Grandpa said from behind his closed bedroom door.

She got the lead from the basket under the foyer table and attached it to her dog's collar. It was black but had reflective strips that glimmered in the dark.

The unlit pumpkins looked sad on the porch.

"Want tae get your boy?" Paislee asked, lifting Wallace into the Juke. It was a short ride to the ice rink.

The pup put his nose to the window and chuffed, wagging his stubby tail.

Wallace was seven and in optimum health. Their veterinarian, Dr. Kathleen, always gave the pup kudos during his routine visits. It hadn't always been that way but after Wallace had scared them to death by eating socks and getting sick, Paislee had invested in a dog trainer.

Best money ever.

She reached the ice rink, and the queue of cars to pick up the kids was long. Eventually it was her turn. Brody hopped in. He didn't look good. Pale, with clammy skin.

"Hey!"

"Hey."

"Did you eat too much junk food? You're a wee bit green around the gills," Paislee teased.

"It's not funny."

"Oh."

She pulled onto the street and glanced at Brody. His hands were shaking as he cuddled Wallace to him. "Brody?"

He bowed his head.

Her mum senses were screaming that something was wrong. She studied him closer. He had all of his appendages. Wasn't bleeding. That she could see, anyway.

Did this have to do with Emma? She recalled the scene earlier at school. Edwyn, and Darryl Barclay.

She pulled over to the side of the road and put the car in park. "Brody, love. Tell me what is going on."

"I cannae."

"You will."

"Mum!" He brought his gaze to hers and his face was pale as the moonlight on the firth.

"I am not leaving here until you tell me what happened."

"I cannae. I'll get razzed at school tomorrow."

"So?"

"Mum. I cannae tell you." His lips tightened as he squeezed his eyes shut.

"I'll call Edwyn if you don't."

"He's an eejit."

"Yeah? Why?" It felt like they were getting somewhere.

"Darryl wants him tae rejoin the football team."

"I don't understand. Edwyn doesn't want tae, so it's not Darryl's decision."

"They were shoving Edwyn around a little. Shoulda stayed oot of it, but Edwyn is, was, my friend." He blew out a breath. "Not anymore."

Paislee bit her lip to keep from responding. She had to listen, but this was very hard.

At thirteen, Brody didn't need her to swoop in with a bandage to fix a scraped knee. His problems were different as he learned how to navigate through life.

"Edwyn has been hanging oot with the gamers, ye ken? Smoking." Brody shook his head and patted Wallace. "He doesnae care aboot university. He's got his da's store."

Paislee knew that Bennett was aware of his son's feelings about football and college. Not sure about the smoking.

Bennett wasn't a dumb man and was a caring, involved parent.

"Can we go home now?" Brody asked, still not looking at her. Until he did, she knew he wasn't being completely honest.

"Grandpa saved you some chowder."

"I'm not hungry. I just want tae go tae bed."

Paislee didn't move the car. Her son not hungry? That was a first. There was more to the story. How to get at it?

"What did you eat? I gave you extra money . . . did you fill up on chips and burgers? Popcorn? Ice cream?"

Brody's skin turned legitimately olive green as he reached into his front denim pocket and gave her most of the money back. "No. Now can we go?"

She recalled Crystal's warning for her daughter to stay in contact and at the ice rink.

"You got your phone?"

Brody fisted his hand on his knee. "Why cannae you leave it alone?"

"Brody. Son. Talk tae me."

Tilting his head back, Brody finally faced her with large, scared eyes.

"Fine. You're gonna be mad. So, you might as well know."

Paislee's belly shot straight up to the back of her throat. Panicked, she swallowed it back down. "Start talking."

His teeth chattered.

She felt bad, but she could only help once she knew what had gone wrong.

"Darryl dared me tae get video of the Wraith at Rait Ruins. A full minute long."

"What? When?"

"Tonight."

"Tonight?" Paislee's thoughts shuffled over one another like the tumble dry in her combo washer and dryer.

"Yeah. Mum, I saw the Wraith. I saw her, and she came for me." Her son gulped. "I dropped me mobile and ran as she screeched behind me."

First of all, Paislee believed in ghosts as much as the next Scotsman, and second, there was no mistaking the fear in her son's eyes.

"Worst?"

What could be worse?

"The guys are gonna tell everyone at school tomorrow that I'm a wee babe, just like Edwyn told them."

Chapter 3

"What are you talking about?" Paislee demanded. She'd heard what her son had said but couldn't fathom it.

"Edwyn put Darryl up tae daring me tae go by myself, in front of Emma. How could I say no?"

Och, Paislee wanted to give Edwyn a good lecture on being a decent friend but knew that wouldn't help the current situation. As a kid in school, Paislee had been teased for being a redhead with such light skin. Lydia had been cruelly mocked for being tall. They'd hidden out in the library, their bond deepening for being targeted over things that were out of their control. Looks.

She empathized, and yet her son had left the ice rink. It hadn't occurred to her to tell him not to leave. Crystal had gone over those instructions with Emma. It was something Paislee would go over moving forward.

If her son was ever ungrounded from his room.

"Do you have an idea where your phone might be?"

"At the ruins, by the base of the tower."

Paislee Shaw was very aware of the time nearing midnight on All Hallows' Eve, when the veil between the worlds was thinnest.

When the Wraith of Rait Ruins was free to wander the grounds where she'd died, to gain vengeance for her own death seven hundred years ago. This was the single night when the ghost had been repeatedly spotted for years and years, but only on All Hallows' Eve.

Paislee one hundred percent did not want to go to Rait Tower, once a tall stone monument but now partially crumbled into rubble and next to one of the oldest, creepiest, most haunted cemeteries in Scotland.

She absolutely did not want to go to the ruins by herself, with only her thirteen-year-old son, and their dog.

It was a night when anything could happen.

Her phone dinged.

Mack.

Oh. Mack was strong, protective.

He had a gun.

Not that a gun would hurt a ghostie; even one with no hands would be more powerful tonight of all nights.

"We have tae get your mobile," Paislee said, proud of herself that her voice didn't shake to give away her trepidation.

"Mum! It's *dark*."

"That's true. I bet Mack might have a . . ." Gun. "Large torch. Should we ask him tae help us? He just texted tae check in."

Brody chewed his thumbnail. He was probably also thinking it might be nice to have the DI with them.

He shrugged, not committing.

"Should we have him meet us there?"

Her phone rumbled with a text message.

"Hm, he's at the station. We can swing by and pick him up."

Another rumble and then her shoulders drooped.

"There's been an accident by the farmer's market." Paislee exhaled. "That's okay. We can do this, Brody."

Knowing the DI was at least close by, rather than hours away, boosted her courage.

"Awright." Her son opened the glove box and withdrew a very small torch that had been in there for years.

"Does it work?" Paislee asked, doubtful.

Brody flicked it on. A stream of light beamed but then flickered to nothing. He shook it, but the battery was dead.

"I can use my mobile and the Juke's headlights. Do you have a general idea at least of where you dropped it?"

He nodded. "The Wraith was huge, Mum, and so scary. She called me name. She knew me!"

"What?" That was strange. She'd never heard of a ghost calling someone by name—but Paislee also believed her son had seen something. He wasn't the kind to be spooked unless there was a reason.

"I am never going tae sleep again. I call dibs on the couch."

"Brody," Paislee said. "Let me answer this text from Mack and let him know where we are. Then, we can get your phone and go home."

"In case the ghouls get us?"

Paislee wanted to agree but played it cool. She hoped that her son had an explainable and understandable case of sugar overload and nothing more. "Brody, take a deep breath. Relax."

"This ghost is real for absolute sure—she didnae have hands, Mum. No. Hands. I was videoing her and she reached toward me, and I freaked oot and just bolted like a numpty bairn. I didnae realize I'd lost me mobile until I was halfway back tae the ice rink."

It was just over three miles. As a family, they sometimes tromped along the river and hiked in the woods around Cawdor. But never during the darkest night. Halloween.

Paislee hefted her chin. She'd drive the Juke as close to the ruins as possible, perhaps closer than the car park allowed, and then put the brights on, targeting the tower.

Mack didn't answer her text message.

You are a grown woman, Paislee Ann Shaw. She took the SUV out of park and drove away from the luminous recreation center, seeing the ice rink in her rearview mirror.

After ten minutes or so, Paislee veered off the main street with its decent lighting and followed a darker side road on the right toward Rait and Cawdor, and Rait Ruins. Eerie fog drifted over the hills. Another few miles beyond the cemetery and they'd reach Cawdor to the left.

Her son was fast and ran often, thanks to football. On Sundays when Paislee, Grandpa, Brody, and Wallace traipsed around the forest and river to hike it was more leisurely; though they catalogued distance without a problem. Brody's best time was a five-minute mile.

Clouds scuttered across the ominous sky, covering the moon and stars. The streetlamps were more sporadic this far from the town center, leaving the road dark and forbidding. She put her headlights on the brightest setting, but it barely cut through the fog.

"Let's turn around, Mum." Brody adjusted Wallace on his lap and peered at her over the console. "I dinnae need a phone. I can buy a new one when I'm sixteen or something."

Brody, like every other person she knew, was attached to his mobile. Her son was different in that he wasn't allowed to take it to bed, and he was very active during the week and weekends with football. Still, it was his social lifeline.

They passed the historic cemetery with barren branches and mossy-green, aged headstones. An empty pickup was on the side of the road. It was fine to visit during the day but at night, on All Hallows' Eve, this was very scary.

There. She'd said it. This was *scary*.

"And you came up here by yourself?" Paislee asked. "That's very brave."

"Edwyn wouldnae come with me." Brody's teeth chattered with fear. "Go past this section toward the tower."

"Here?" Paislee slowly inched the vehicle over the dirt. She flipped the high beams on and illuminated the crumbling stone tower.

"Aye. You know the story of the Wraith, Mum?"

"Yes." She cleared her throat, going for calm and matter-of-fact. "The de Rait family wanted control of the tower and were going tae trick the other clan by inviting them inside for a meal of peace, to end the fighting, which meant no weapons inside for either party during the feast. The chief's daughter betrayed him and alerted someone on the other side, so when the de Raits attacked, the opposing clan was ready. There was an awful battle with few survivors."

"Why would she do that?" Brody asked.

"One of the legends is that she'd fallen in love with the other chief's son." Paislee glanced at Brody as she put the Juke in park, the engine on. No other vehicles were around.

"She shouldnae have done that." Brody stared at the base of the tower. "Her own da chased her and cut off her hands when she dangled from the window to escape."

That was the gory version, and probably what appealed to teen boys.

"People parent a little differently these days," Paislee said in a light tone.

"Mum!" Brody wrapped his arms around Wallace. "The Wraith came around the tower there, and Darryl told me tae get her on video tae prove I wasnae scared. For a minute or more. I was terrified already, but she was, well, she was scarier than I ever imagined. She didnae have hands, and her body glowed all white."

"Where was that?" Paislee located the flashlight app on her mobile.

Her palms began to sweat, and her pulse fluttered.

Through the windshield, she squinted into the night. Skeletal trees, naked of leaves, protruded from rocks and the occasional headstone to the left of the tower.

Was that white fluttering behind a stone? Like the Wraith's gown?

Paislee swallowed a gulp and glanced toward her son, who was focused on the base of the tower, gripping Wallace like a furry life preserver.

"Do you see that?" Paislee pointed toward the white behind the headstone.

If they were envisioning things, maybe it would be best to do it together. She'd never witnessed a ghost full-on like this before.

She felt things, sure, and believed with her whole soul that there was something more after death that remained a mystery, but it would be her first tangible proof of a ghoul. Of course, on Samhain, All Hallows' Eve.

Brody looked toward where Paislee pointed and shook his head. "Nah. The beams from the headlights are making too many shadows."

"Stay here." Paislee gripped her phone. "I'll go check it out."

"I'm pretty sure I dropped me mobile closer tae the tower, but I dinnae remember exactly. Should I come with you?"

"No. Don't let Wallace out either." Paislee opened the car door, which squeaked in the night. "I don't want to chase him if he gets loose, got it?"

"Yeah."

Paislee climbed down to the mix of dirt, stone, and dry grass. Her stomach had flipped around so many times she was seasick.

She slowly, dreadfully, walked toward the fluttering white mystery behind the stone, not sure how to address what was there. Could be a ghost, or her imagination.

"Hello?"

Paislee heard a sound she couldn't place and stopped in her tracks. Human, or inhuman, from the cemetery to her far left. The white object in front of her remained low to the ground—the noise hadn't come from it.

"Who's there?" she called in a tremulous voice. She peered from the rock to the barren mossy trees and shadowed tombstones. The cemetery was hundreds of years old. Who knew how many ghosts resided here?

Her skin was pebbled with goose bumps; the primal fight-or-flight response urged her to flee. A chilly breeze barreled by her to the stone, lifting what might be a lock of hair, or a straggly piece of moss.

The practical part of her mind reminded her that most ghost

stories turned out to be false. What if the white object was someone who needed help?

She inched forward until she reached the four-foot boulder as a white gown gusted upward before settling down. The material was shiny like polyester.

Did they have polyester eight hundred years ago? She had a bad feeling this wouldn't be a ghost after all. The boulder had shielded a three-foot tombstone covered in moss.

She heard the creak of the Juke door opening and Brody racing toward the tower. He dipped down and retrieved something with a victory yell. "Mum! I found me phone!"

A curse, yes, a human curse, groused to her left amid the tall, thick trees and tombstones.

An icy chill spiraled to her bones. "Get into the car, now!" Paislee's shout was filled with fear that somehow, she wasn't supposed to be here. She was not wanted. Danger hummed like electricity before a lightning storm.

Brody started toward her instead of following her directive, but she pointed to the vehicle. Her son had to be in the car, safe. "*Now.*"

She peered around the stone with trepidation and full-blown alarm, to the decrepit headstone.

The forlorn figure of a pretty young lass, with both her hands, lay on her back, her half-lidded gaze toward the sky.

A shadow moved behind an oak tree, the moss appearing to be like hair. She squinted into the night. Was someone really there? Was this her imagination? She'd admittedly had her share of chocolate pumpkins.

"I've called the police," Paislee said. Her voice warbled with fright. She hadn't yet, but would. She gripped her mobile tight and sent the weak flashlight toward the trees.

What might have been footsteps bolted into the night, toward the River Nairn. Soon after she heard a splash. Deer. Rounding the tombstone, Paislee knelt and pressed her fingers to the woman's wrist for her pulse.

Her skin had been painted an opalescent white. Her eyes, half-mast, her cheeks made up to look ghoulish. A trickle of red at her temple dripped into her brunette hair. The voluminous gown surrounded her like a shroud. Was the red part of the costume?

Not likely. The angel was dead, having joined the Wraith of Rait on this All Hallows' Eve.

A floral fabric backpack had been tossed behind the rock, with a collection of keychains dangling and a university ID. Ailis Barclay.

Any relation to Darryl?

With shaking hands, Paislee managed to call Mack on his cell phone.

He answered, "What's up?"

"We're at Rait Ruins. There's a . . . a young lady named Ailis Barclay, is dead, Mack. Her brother plays football on Brody's team." Poor Darryl. Their parents, Doug and Julie Barclay. Her stomach rolled with grief.

"Where are you?" Mack's tone was calm.

"By her body." Paislee sat back on her heels, shuddering. She didn't want to let her gaze settle on poor Ailis but couldn't help it. Long brown hair, lace along the collar and sleeves of her costume. Something green sparkled from the confines of the lace around her neck. A necklace? She couldn't tell for sure.

"Where's Brody?"

She'd leaned closer but Mack's impatient question had her gazing back toward the Juke. The lights blinded her.

"In the car." Her teeth chattered.

"Join him. Lock the doors and wait for me. There's been a series of protests tonight, including a break-in at Cawdor Castle nearby."

Paislee hated to leave the young woman alone in her death. Had she fallen over the stones and hit her head? Why was she dressed like the Wraith of Rait? Could be the handless Wraith wanted revenge, and this had been the one night a year she'd been strong enough to take it.

"Paislee?"

"Sorry, Mack. Going tae the car right now."

Paislee stared into the shadows of the cemetery to the left and quivered, sensing that she was not alone. Whether her company was alive or dead she couldn't tell. The area around poor Ailis seemed as if it had been trampled. Sneakers—not paw prints or hooves. The footprints could have been hers. Pink trainers peeked beneath the white gown.

She got up, stumbled over her own feet—boots—and raced back to the Juke.

Once inside, Brody instantly locked the doors. "What took so long?"

After a deep breath, Paislee said, "Honey, a young woman has had an accident."

"The Wraith got her!" Brody showed her his phone in his hand. "Let's go home. Now. Before we're next."

"We have tae wait for the DI."

"I dinnae want tae." Brody dug his fingers into Wallace's wiry fur. "She's dead for real?"

"Yes. I'm sorry." Would Brody know Ailis, without the makeup?

"How?"

"I'm not sure. She had a mark on her forehead. She might have tripped on the stones and accidentally . . . died."

"On Samhain?" Brody arched both brows at her like she was bonkers. "No way. Accidents like that dinnae just happen. Ever. The Wraith got her. Coulda got me." He trembled in fear. "Like Darryl wanted, and Jimmy. Edwyn."

Sirens blared as the police and ambulance showed up in force. Paislee recognized the Scots-pale features of Constable Monroe, who parked next to her.

After exiting the police vehicle, Constable Monroe shook her head at Paislee, as if she couldn't believe her terrible luck. Paislee rolled the window down.

She was about to share what she knew but rolled the window

back up and exited the car instead so that Brody wouldn't overhear the gruesome details.

Mack's blue SUV crunched over the gravel and pulled to a stop behind the patrol car. He hopped out and looked for Paislee, then Brody, who remained with Wallace in the Juke.

"Why didnae you stay in the car, like I told you?" Mack asked Paislee.

"I didn't want Brody tae overhear me, that's why," Paislee said.

Constable Monroe's mouth twitched.

"Fine." Mack, in DI mode, nodded. "Why were you oot here at the cemetery?"

"Brody was dared tae face the Wraith of Rait Ruins while at the ice rink earlier. I think Ailis and her brother Darryl were playing a trick on him. Ailis Barclay is the one behind the rock. She might have tripped on a tombstone." Tears spilled down her cheeks, which Paislee quickly wiped away.

"For sure that's Ailis?" Monroe nudged the brim of her police cap upward.

"Yes."

"She was a smart lass. Going tae university for business. Must be home for the holiday—her parents will be gutted." Monroe's compassionate gaze hardened.

"That's all I can think about," Paislee admitted, folding her arms to her stomach.

"Why was Brody here again, with you now?" Monroe asked.

"I sent Mack a text explaining how Brody had dropped his mobile, so we were at the ruins looking for it," Paislee said.

"I never got that message," Mack said.

Paislee read her messages. Sure enough, it hadn't sent. She showed him and Monroe. "Sorry."

"Why not wait until morning?" Monroe asked. "This is full-on creepy at night. You'd have a better chance of finding the phone. Any luck?"

"Brody thought he knew where it was, by the base of the

tower." Paislee lowered her arms to her sides. "Aye, he found it. He was supposed tae video the Wraith and come back with proof or else be made fun of at school tomorrow."

"Kids," Monroe said. "Zeffer, you want tae handle interviewing Brody, or should I?"

"I'll do it," Mack said.

Monroe gestured toward the ambulance, and paramedics, who let her know with a headshake that there was nothing to be done for Ailis. "I'll call the ME."

"Puir bloke is having a busy night," Mack said. "The accident near the farmer's market had two fatalities. Drinking was involved."

Paislee sent a quick prayer that those she loved would be safe and followed Mack around to the passenger side of the Juke. Wallace waited on Brody's lap, tongue lolling as he observed Paislee and Mack. Brody stared down at his mobile.

"Hey, Brody." Mack tapped on the window. "Will ye come oot for a moment?"

Brody exited, leaving Wallace in the car as he shut the door, so the pup didn't get loose.

"I have a few questions and then you can get on home." Mack placed his hand on Brody's shoulder and squeezed with empathy. "What happened?"

Paislee stayed by Brody. Not hovering, but watchful.

"Lost me mobile." Brody glanced at Paislee, then showed his phone to the Detective Inspector. "Got it now."

"I'd like details of what you were doing here in the first place," Mack said.

"Darryl and Jimmy are brilliant footballers on my football team. They run circles around me at practice and I wanna be just like them. Anyway, Edwyn said I was too much of a wee baby tae come here alone. They wanted us both tae get video of the Wraith, but Edwyn's not playing football anymore, so . . . he didnae care."

"They didnae have any leverage over him," Mack said concisely.

Brody scowled. "Edwyn deliberately put the heat on me alone. In front of Emma. Had tae do it or look like a wean."

Mack tapped his pen against his notebook. "How did you get here? Three miles or more from the rink. Bike?"

"Ran." Brody's cheeks flushed. "I'm pretty fast. Followed the river shortcut but that was even more scary, so I took the road back even though it added distance."

"Dinnae blame you there," Mack said. "Why did they want you tae get video instead of a picture?"

"Dunno. I didnae ask a lot of questions." Brody shuffled his feet. "Darryl is cool. He's the best player on our team next tae our captain, Pedro. He's for sure going pro."

Mack knew of Brody's footballer-star dreams and had played with Brody in the back garden. "Got it. You didnae want tae make him think you werenae tough."

"Failed epically." Brody scuffed his trainer to the dirt. "Cannae go tae school tomorrow."

"I realize this feels big but let's just take it slow. Did you record the Wraith?" Mack asked.

"Yeah."

"And you found your phone." Mack's tone lifted. "Can I see what you've got there?"

Brody blushed so hard that she could see it as the moon cleared before being covered by another cloud. "It's embarrassing. I squealed like a girl."

Mack briefly thinned his lips, a flash of anger on Brody's behalf in his gaze. "Dinnae blame you. The fact you made it up here on your own withoot anybody? That's verra brave. I wouldnae at your age. Not for a hundred pounds."

Brody shrugged in misery and kept his mobile gripped in his palm.

"What happened next?" Mack asked.

"I was breathing hard when I got here because I'd jogged at a fast clip from the river tae the cemetery. I waited for a minute or so at the tower." The vein at Brody's neck pulsed. "I heard noises and thought I'd pass oot. I planned on getting the fastest video ever once the Wraith showed. But, it had tae be at least sixty seconds."

Mack, who didn't believe in ghosts, still listened with compassion.

Brody's shoulders bowed. "Everybody knows the Wraith comes through the veil on Halloween. I had my eyes partially closed. I heard her and opened them all the way. She was glowing *white*. For real." He sucked in a breath. "I hit record. It was a blur, and I dinnae remember exactly what happened, but when she called my name I screamed."

Brody shook from head to toe.

Mack's eyes narrowed. "Your name?"

"Yep. Broooody." Brody gulped, his mobile still tight in his hand. "I must've dropped me phone right then."

"May I see the video?" Mack asked.

Brody reluctantly put in the password and opened the photo app, then gave it to him. Paislee looked over Brody's arm when Mack pressed play. Brody's heavy breaths combined with his muttering, "I'm here at Rait Ruins. Looking for the Wraith. It's Samhain and the perfect night tae see the ghost with no hands." Brody waved the phone from the rocks, to the tower, to the top of the tower down to the crumbling pebbles. It looked like large rabbits had been at work along the base.

Suddenly the shimmering opalescent figure, which absolutely resembled a ghoul, came into Brody's line of vision. He actually stepped toward her. The ghost, Ailis, called out, "Come closer, me lad, and I will drink your soul."

The video shook because Brody's hand must have shaken. He sucked in a breath. "Just need a minute of video then I'll leave."

"Brooodddyyyyyy."

Her son screamed like anyone would have. Only, instead of dropping the device immediately to run like hell to safety, Brody waved the mobile toward her, and the cemetery trees. "She knows me name," he said in a high-pitched voice.

A loud *thunk* sounded from when the phone hit the dirt, and then the video showed the trees and the night sky. After a minute, Ailis's chuckle was recorded.

"Puir lamb," she said. Her voice grew nearer. "You owe me one, Darryl. Where did he drop his mobile?" Her voice and footsteps could be heard as if she was searching the dirt for Brody's phone. She said, "I will turn it in at the ice rink." Shuffled steps. An exhale. The whirl of satin as she turned. "Blake? That you?"

More shuffled steps.

Ailis asking, "What are you doing here? Get oot of here." She sounded angry as she hurried toward . . . wherever she'd gone.

Then, a squeal . . . from Ailis? Blake?

There was a murmuring of low voices, but it was too hard to make out words. Ailis was out of the range of the audio as well.

Mack turned it off.

"I never heard that before." Brody, eyes wide, put his fingers to his throat and gulped as if he might be sick. "That wasnae the Wraith of Rait Ruins."

"No, son," Mack said in a gentle voice. "That was Darryl's sister, Ailis Barclay. My guess is this prank, meant in jest, took a dark turn."

Chapter 4

That night, Brody slept on the couch with Wallace. Word spread quickly that Ailis Barclay, who'd gone to Nairn Academy, was dead. There would be no school on Friday as the shire held a day of mourning.

In the middle of the night, Paislee woke with a start, recalling how Ailis had shouted out for Blake. Who was that? A friend? Boyfriend?

If they'd had plans to meet and he'd been late, well, what a disaster. He'd feel terrible about not being there for Ailis. The recording from Brody's mobile hadn't been clear.

Paislee, restless, switched on her nightstand lamp and reached for her tablet. She logged onto social media and typed in Ailis Barclay's name.

Brown hair, pretty face, green eyes. So young and sweet. Odes to Ailis were everywhere. *Gone too soon.* There were a lot of posts with a guy named Blake Harrington. Charming, blond, about her same age. Ailis had shared a picture of herself in full Wraith costume at Rait Ruins at eight Halloween night. Her post read that she and Blake would be at the Grotto Bar by ten—the trophy for best costume was in the bag.

In the posts, Blake hadn't dressed up.

Paislee heard a shout from downstairs and practically leapt from her bed, bolting from her room and sailing down the steps as Grandpa, wild-haired and minus his glasses, came out of his bedroom.

She made it to the lounge where Brody sprawled, asleep on his back, hand over his forehead. Wallace licked his cheek. Grandpa caught his breath.

"Hey," Paislee murmured softly as she kneeled by the sofa.

Wallace acknowledged her with a tail wag but didn't budge from Brody's side.

She smoothed his hair off his forehead, and he calmed but didn't wake.

"Puir laddie," Grandpa said softly. "It was a rough night."

"This might be the first time someone has died from Brody's friend group—not that he and Ailis were friends, but him and Darryl," Paislee whispered.

"Should I stay home from work tomorrow?" Grandpa asked.

The shop was slow. Rhona could probably handle things by herself. Paislee nodded. "Good idea."

"I'll keep Brody preoccupied," Grandpa said. "A trip tae the giant movie theater in Inverness?"

"Let me know when you need the Juke, and I'll bring it to you." The digital clock on the telly blinked four. "Is this the first he's stirred?"

"He's been restless all night, but I've had my door open." Grandpa gestured toward the staircase. "Sleep, lass. Between us, Brody is well guarded."

Paislee hugged her grandfather and went upstairs. She dozed very lightly but didn't hear any more shouts of terror in the night.

The next day, Paislee arrived at Cashmere Crush at quarter till ten. She'd made it out the door without waking the guys, who were both sleeping. She and Mack texted good mornings. He'd requested a rain check for fish and chips today at lunch as he was swamped because of the break-in. Rhona waited for her, eyes red, on the back stoop.

They went in.

"Did you know Ailis?" Paislee asked. She tossed her bag beneath the counter and prepped the register.

"Friends from school. Her and Aibreann had shared literature classes and a love for poetry. Do you know what happened tae Ailis?" Rhona asked.

"Brody and I found her, but no, I don't know. I haven't had a chance tae read the paper."

"There was nothing really aboot it," Rhona said. "Just that a young woman home from uni was discovered deceased at the ruins in a Wraith costume. Your names werenae listed but I figured it oot from the description of local yarn shop owner. You are the only one in Nairn."

Paislee took her mobile from the back pocket of her denims and placed it on the counter. "It happened so late. They are probably still investigating." She wanted to be available for Grandpa, Brody, or Mack.

"Thanks tae social media, it was not a hard guess tae put it together with Ailis. She'd posted a picture of herself." Rhona's eyes were sad. "What an incredible costume. I bet she would have won."

"It was." It had been authentic enough to frighten Brody and Paislee.

"Why were you up there?" Rhona got the broom from the back room and started to sweep. Her outfit today was black pants, and a charcoal jumper. Her hair was in a clip.

"Brody was pranked by Darryl, Edwyn, and Ailis, and lost his mobile."

"Pranked?" Rhona's brows rose.

"Yes. It's all I can do tae keep from calling Bennett about Edwyn. Brody had nightmares all night." She couldn't say anything to Julie because her daughter was dead. What an awful way for Darryl to learn a lesson.

Was that really even fair? Jokes should be fun.

They couldn't really discuss what happened further because they had a steady run for yarn. Mary Beth was in with the twins, who'd had a marvelous time guising the night before. Each girl had loaded up a cloth pumpkin with candy.

Mary Beth had discreetly asked about the tidbit in the paper, also surmising Paislee to be the local yarn shop owner.

"I don't know anything more," Paislee said. "Trust me, I will share when I do."

Mary Beth was teaching Anna and Iona each to knit, so they bought a fun pattern for a coin purse to make. Anna chose pink yarn, and Iona blue.

Around noon, three people in costume entered the store. One wore a Guy Fawkes mask from the movie *V for Vendetta*, the other was Robin Hood, and the third was Maid Marian.

Rhona tried to chat with them, but after doing an intense loop of the interior, they departed without a word. "Weirdos. There are more Halloween parties tonight because of the weekend; however, I have retired my princess costume. Artie stepped on the hem."

"Oh no!"

"I have pictures before it happened." Rhona went to her social media page and showed her photos to Paislee. Artie made a very handsome Prince Charming. "We were thinking of going tae other parties this weekend, but I'm not in the mood, and I know Aibreann willnae be either."

"How did Aibreann's Little Red Riding Hood turn out, and Foster's Big Bad Wolf?"

"They placed in fourth at the Grotto. I'll show you." Rhona skimmed her thumb to Aibreann's page. The current post was a picture of Aibreann and Ailis, in secondary class, with a broken heart emoji.

Crying softly, Rhona tucked the phone away and went into the restroom to wash her face. When she came back out, dry-eyed, it was well past noon, and they left the subject of costumes alone.

"If you're all right, I'll run home and check on Brody. We might have an early day today." Paislee was feeling the lack of sleep.

"Give him a hug from me," Rhona said.

"I will." Paislee drove home for lunch, thinking to leave the Juke for Grandpa and Brody if they wanted an adventure out. The movies were a terrific distraction.

When she arrived, the house was relatively quiet except for Brody's music upstairs. Grandpa worked on a puzzle at a special table made for just that purpose, which Lydia and Corbin had bought for him.

"Hey," Paislee said.

"Hiya!"

"What are you working on?"

The wheeled table had an adjustable height so you could be comfortable on a stool, or chair, or even standing.

Grandpa wore fleece-lined house slippers, jeans, and a gray flannel shirt. His glasses were in his perfectly combed hair.

"This beauty is the German countryside," Grandpa said, his focus keen. The harder the pieces to match the happier he was to tackle the puzzle. He framed his favorites and hung them in his room.

Paislee wandered toward the puzzle. It was inevitable that she looked for a piece to fit—Grandpa said he didn't mind.

The German countryside was lovely and the property inviting. She knew Lydia and Corbin's new winery project would soar.

Her gaze went to the side table where the landline was plugged in. With extreme weather it was good to have a backup in case the power went out, including cell towers.

Brody's phone was plugged in downstairs, following the rule in their house. A notification went off.

"I had tae turn it on silent," Grandpa said. "It's been nonstop, but Brody doesnae want tae talk tae anyone, not even Emma. She called the home phone, she was that concerned. Sweet lass."

Crystal had Paislee's phone numbers, all of them. Had Emma been in trouble before, so she knew to make specific rules?

"That's strange. They've been attached at the earbud."

Grandpa gave a sage nod. "Last night spooked him."

Paislee stepped toward the stairs. "Should I go talk tae him?"

Grandpa waved an edge piece. "I dinnae think so. Give him time—he will come around."

The home phone rang, and Paislee answered it, as yet another text message popped up on Brody's mobile.

Besides Ailis in costume, what else had he seen or heard while recording? She picked up the mobile and typed in the password as she lifted the receiver to the landline. She had zero compunction about looking at the messages. This was her mobile, there were rules, or he could lose the privilege of it.

"Hello?" She propped the handset between her shoulder and ear as she scanned the text messages. Emma, Sam, Coach Harris.

"Paislee? This is Coach. Wanted tae check in on Brody. He's supposed tae be at practice today, even though school is oot."

"He's not doing well." Paislee clicked on the photo app.

"I understand. It's your decision, of course, but if he misses practice today, he should absolutely be there tomorrow."

"I disagree," Paislee said.

"I've talked tae the Barclays and Darryl willnae be there, but they understand why I think it's important. We've got tae give these boys an outlet for their emotions. Hard drills will do that."

"Hard drills?" Paislee repeated. She put Brody's mobile on the table.

"Running, exercise."

"I'll ask Brody, but I don't think he'll want tae come. Today especially! It's too soon."

"I knew Ailis. The hazings at the tower happen all the time. It's a rite of passage tae face the Wraith—not sure how it came tae be that Ailis agreed tae act the part, but damn, this has really crushed the community." Coach Harris's low voice was filled with sorrow.

And my son, Paislee added to herself. He'd been hurt. "I'll ask him, Coach, but I don't want him penalized for not showing up either day."

"He willnae be," the coach promised. "It'll be better for him tae think aboot something other than what happened. The grapevine says you both found Ailis at the ruins. Is that true?"

"Grapevine is correct. I'd driven him tae the tower tae find his phone because he'd dropped it. Out of being scared. Brody doesn't frighten easy, but this was intense."

Coach Harris murmured consolation. "No pressure then, but I highly recommend physical activity of some kind."

"I hear you. It will be up tae Brody." They ended the call, and she replaced the handset rather firmly.

"Coach Harris is holding practice?" Grandpa deduced.

"Today, and tomorrow. Not sure how I feel about it. I can see his point for directing the boys' energy, but what if Brody isn't ready tae be with his friends? He's not even answering his phone."

Paislee retrieved the mobile, scanning messages without reading them. It was a hard position to be in regarding privacy. Brody had agreed to the rules that it was her phone and there were to be no secrets kept on it.

"I need tae look at what he saw last night." She clicked on the photos icon.

"Didnae you when Brody showed the DI?"

"Over their arms . . . it was spooky, no lie." Paislee clicked on the video her son had taken. "Ailis made a great Wraith."

Grandpa joined her, observing over her shoulder as they stood in front of the kitchen window. "Is that fog? Pure creepy."

"Yes." Paislee's stomach clenched as she recalled the fog and mossy trees. "I was giving Brody kudos for braving the cemetery and ruins. I wouldn't have done it. Darn Edwyn. I have half a mind tae let Bennett know how his son was behaving. Tae set Brody up like that?" She fumed, which felt better than fear.

Grandpa gave a low whistle. "Cryin' shame. It's an awful way tae learn that sometimes your friends dinnae always stay your friends."

On the video, Brody's hand shook as he said, "I'm here at Rait Ruins. Looking for the Wraith. It's Samhain and the perfect night tae see the ghost with no hands."

He scanned the eerily dark and foggy tower, then the cemetery, and the crop of boulders where they'd later find Ailis's body near a headstone.

Perspiration dotted Paislee's brow. Even though she knew what was coming, she tensed when Ailis appeared suddenly at the base of the tower and Brody screamed. Dirt piles made it difficult for him to walk.

She'd have bolted, but Brody, wanting to prove his bravery, crept toward the apparition.

"That's terrifying," Grandpa stated. "What is on her skin? She's tucked her hands oot of the way. Or else the sleeves are extralong. I would have been fooled in a heartbeat, thinking it was a ghostie."

"Right?" Paislee's pulse skipped even though she knew it was a fake. A trick. A prank gone too far. "She was hoping tae win the costume contest at the Grotto."

Ailis, in a low, husky voice, said, "Come closer, me lad, and I will drink your soul!"

Brody stopped, the mobile quivering.

"She must've been a theater major." Grandpa held out his trembling hand. "I'm proud of Brody for sticking it oot like this, but no wonder he was beset by nightmares."

Brody had stopped and sucked in a breath. "Just need a minute of video and then I'll leave," he promised. He skimmed the phone around the tower and cemetery once more as if to prove to the viewer he was there. Alone.

"Brodyyyyyyyy."

Brody shouted in terror. "She knows me name!"

At that, her son dropped his phone on the ground, a mix of grass and gravel.

Again, the sound of Ailis's laugh was eerie and brought goose bumps on Paislee's skin. She neared where the phone had fallen. "Puir lamb. You owe me one, Darryl. Where did he drop his mobile?"

Steps could be heard as she neared the device.

"I will turn it in at the ice rink."

After a big exhale, the sound of the satin fabric could be heard as she whirled.

"Blake? Is that you?"

Chills erupted down Paislee's spine.

Blake never replied. Thanks to social media she knew what he looked like, how cute a couple they made.

"What are you doing here?" Ailis asked, her tone remaining belligerent, but this time Paislee detected a hint of fear. "Get oot of here."

Ailis's footsteps headed toward the rock and tombstone where Paislee had found her. "She must have tripped at this point here," Paislee said.

Ailis, or Blake, or something, made a squealing noise or squeak followed by a thunking sound.

"And whoever was there didnae help her?" Grandpa asked in disbelief.

"What if they were scared that they'd be blamed somehow. Not good at all . . . what other reason could there be for their silence?"

Grandpa tilted his head and put his glasses on to peer at Paislee in disbelief. "I can think of several. None of them guid."

She was about to turn off the video, thinking that it was over, when she heard voices arguing.

"Wait. Who is that?" Paislee put her finger to her lips. They hadn't gotten this far last night.

"What are they saying? Can you turn it up louder?" Grandpa asked.

Paislee adjusted the volume on the side, but it didn't get any clearer. It seemed like possible footsteps back and forth but no more words. The cemetery was full of deer and wildlife. Possible ghosts.

After five more minutes the video clicked off.

"Ran oot of media storage," Grandpa said. "I'm impressed that the battery lasted so long."

"I'm going tae call Mack." Paislee shifted toward Grandpa. "It feels important."

"Didnae he already watch it?"

"Yes, but he hasn't gone as far in the video. I bet he assumed, like I did, that it was over." Paislee went to the beginning of the video, looking for clues as to who else might be there with Ailis.

The first time that Brody scanned the cemetery and tower to prove to Darryl that he was there, Paislee slowed the video to each frame. Dirt had been mounded unevenly along the tower's base. "Could this be caused by rabbits?"

"Badgers, mibbe," Grandpa said. "What's left of the tower is aboot tae topple over. It's a hazard. We used tae climb all over it when we were lads, but no more."

Impatient, Paislee tried to find any clue as to who'd been with Ailis last night and not waste Mack's time during an investigation. He was focused on the break-in at Cawdor. She studied the video closely, slowing down each frame. At this speed she could see when Ailis's hands had briefly come untucked from her voluminous sleeves. She zoomed in on the girl's makeup. It was really well-done. The lace at the sleeves and collar. No necklace. She'd probably been mistaken. "Did you see her hands?"

"Aye, just barely," Grandpa said.

Paislee slowed the video for the section where Ailis had warned Brody not to come closer. "If he'd gotten nearer tae her, he might have noticed that she was a real person and not the Wraith of Rait Ruins."

He'd bravely scanned the area before she called his name. He'd dropped his mobile and bolted.

Paislee scrolled the footage, back to the cemetery to the left of the boulders where Ailis had tripped and fallen.

Her stomach roiled. She recalled the alarm she'd felt when staring into the trees. She'd talked herself into thinking it was a deer. This was the wrong height for a deer's eye. The moss could be hair, or the hair could be moss. "Grandpa! Is that a person?"

"Mibbe, or it could be a ghost," Grandpa said. "It's the cemetery, lass, and way too unfocused."

Paislee zoomed in on the screen and blew out a breath. "No. That's a person in a mask." She squinted. "Maybe two people even."

Paislee, shivering in her warm cozy kitchen, dialed Mack. She kept the phone on speaker so Grandpa could hear too.

"Afternoon," Mack said, answering on the first ring. "How's Brody holding up?"

"He had nightmares all night. Mack, I think we might have caught a very blurred image of someone in the cemetery with Ailis on the video Brody took last night. Remember when she yelled out for Blake? That was her boyfriend."

"Aye. How do you know that?"

Paislee blushed, feeling called out for being nosy. "It's all over social media."

"We're trying tae find Blake Harrington, tae ask some questions." Mack paused, then said, "What did you see? Could it have been Blake?"

"I don't know. It's way too blurry. I think someone was there when Ailis tripped and fell but they didn't help her or call for help either."

"Is this what we watched together last night? I'm familiar."

Grandpa's silver brow arched over the black frames of his glasses. He rounded the table to get out some crackers from the pantry. The candy was all gone and this required snacks.

"It's past that section. I have it zoomed in very close, but I can't identify the figure. The smooth features suggest a mask. We heard some voices, but again, have no idea what they said."

"Why were you watching the video again?" Mack asked.

"Brody isn't talking tae his friends and he's holed up in his room. He was scared, and I need tae know all the details so that I can help him." Paislee accepted a cracker and nibbled the corner. "I came home at lunch tae check on him."

"Can you stay there for a few minutes? I'd like tae pick up the phone for evidence."

"Evidence? But Ailis tripped."

"I'll explain when I get there." Mack used the tone of voice that assured her she'd learn no more until he arrived.

Paislee had been gone almost an hour. "All right, but hurry. I should get back tae Cashmere Crush." She ended the call with Mack.

"I can lock up for you," Grandpa offered.

"I wonder why Mack wants Brody's mobile?" Paislee put the phone on the side table to charge. Something had shifted regarding the events last night and she decided to stay home. "Let me call Rhona . . . she knows how tae close."

Grandpa nodded. "Still, I'll get shoes on just in case. Cannae have the DI thinking I'm a lounge aboot."

"You're partially retired, Grandpa. You don't need tae change!" Paislee called the shop on the landline.

"Cashmere Crush," Rhona answered.

"Hi, love. It's Paislee. How are things going?"

"We've only had one customer. It's a dreich day and nobody wants tae brave the weather. The skies are pouring. Tears for Ailis?"

"Don't make me cry," Paislee warned. "Why don't you close up and head home? I want tae stay here with Brody. He's not feeling well."

"It's only one in the afternoon—are you sure?" Rhona asked.

"Yes. Full pay."

"I will then. I've sorted some of the odds and ends on the back shelves, but Aibreann is having a rough time, and it might be an ice cream emergency," Rhona said.

"Scoops has a new flavor, triple chocolate fudge."

"I'll pick up a carton and head tae Aibreann's house."

"You're a wonderful friend," Paislee said.

"She is like a sister tae me. Like you and Aunt Lydia."

Not that Lydia was an aunt, but the title was meant with love and affection as there were an abundance of Smythe cousins in the area.

"We are blessed in our friendships," Paislee said.

"What will the schedule be for tomorrow? I realize there's no school on Saturday, but do you need me tae cover?"

"No, thank you. Meri and I are both working, but if Brody goes tae practice, I want tae be there. Could be another half day."

Grandpa mouthed, "Yer the boss."

"All right," Rhona said. "If you need anything, let me know. Otherwise I'll be in on Monday."

"Bye now."

Paislee was tempted to run out and buy some triple chocolate fudge for the house but would wait until Mack arrived.

"It's the benefit of owning your own business, tae take a day or two if you need it," Grandpa declared.

"You're right." Paislee went to the kitchen window and looked out at the chestnut tree in fall foliage, clicking on the electric kettle. "Feels strange tae be home rather than at work, but Brody is my priority."

She made herself a cup of tea and brought her knitting project, an infinity scarf in soft blue, to the table where she sat and waited for Mack.

"Rhona said that there wasn't really a mention of Ailis in the morning paper. Just descriptions of a dead university lass discovered by a yarn shop owner."

Grandpa lined an edge piece to his puzzle. "I saved it if you wanted tae read it later."

A knock sounded at the front entrance. Paislee set aside her knitting and tea to walk down the hall. Wallace, upstairs with

Brody, barked. Her son's bedroom door opened, and Wallace came out, but Brody stayed in his room. Wallace darted down the stairs to meet Paislee in the foyer.

She smoothed her hair before opening the door and her tension eased as she smiled in welcome at her handsome detective inspector.

Mack had on a navy-blue raincoat over his clothes and an umbrella that he closed and left on the porch beneath the small overhang. The rain was a steady drizzle.

"Come on in," Paislee said.

Mack removed the raincoat, and Paislee hung it on a hook by the front door. His customary blue suit was styled to woolen perfection, skimming over his lean yet muscled physique. He smelled like the outdoors.

"Thanks," Mack said.

Grandpa exited his bedroom and waved at Mack. "DI. Cup of tea?"

"Aye, that sounds wonderful. Make it strong, eh?"

Mack ushered Paislee before him, Wallace scampering down the hall ahead of them. He curled up in his dog bed by the back door and Grandpa tossed the pup a chewy bone after putting on the kettle.

Paislee looked at Brody's mobile plugged into the wall socket. "It's almost back tae a hundred percent charge. Why do you want it? Don't tell me that my description of a blurry masked man cracked the case."

Mack exhaled and sat down at the kitchen table. Grandpa handed out steaming mugs of hot water and a selection of tea bags before he pulled up a chair. Paislee's tea was still warm.

"It's not that." There was a somber mood around Mack she'd never seen in him before. "What a wretched day."

"Death is terrible." Paislee went to the pantry for her emergency stash of chocolate-covered almonds, bringing the glass container to the table. She hadn't had lunch, her stomach queasy. "Especially of someone so very young."

"Ailis went tae university," Grandpa said. "Was she an actress? Her performance was superb."

"I dinnae ken," Mack said. "Monroe has handled the interviews with the Barclays, and I havenae read the full report yet."

Paislee untwisted the top and poured some almonds on a napkin. She passed the container to Grandpa, who helped himself, and then to Mack.

"No, thanks." Mack shook his head at the container.

"Long night?" Grandpa asked.

"It was, it was. Can you show me the figure that you believe you saw on the phone?"

"Sure!" Paislee brought it to the table before sitting down again. "Emma just sent another message tae Brody. Poor thing is worried about him." She opened the video.

Mack blew on his tea, black and straight, before sipping.

She replayed the video again, suppressing her nerves as best as she could, knowing what was going to happen next.

Placing the mobile in the center of the table, Paislee paused it when they reached the part where Ailis had warned Brody not to come closer.

"Here." Paislee picked up the phone and zoomed in on the masked figure, giving it to Mack.

He frowned, adjusting the image.

"Do you see it?" Grandpa propped his elbow on the table as he leaned toward Mack and the phone.

"I do. It's so blurry," Mack said. "Mibbe our tech department will be able tae make sense of it."

"The tech department?" Paislee asked.

"Aye." Mack hit play again. "You say you heard voices?"

"I think so. But after several minutes pass."

It was hard to listen, waiting. Paislee chewed a chocolate-covered almond and swallowed it down, about to reach for another when she stopped the video. "Here!"

Mack's face was creased with tension.

Paislee adjusted the sound.

"Mibbe you have audio people?" Grandpa suggested.

"We do." Mack sighed. "We just dinnae ken what we're looking for."

Grandpa asked, "You think this could be Blake?"

"He's wanted for questioning. I cannae give you much information." Mack hunched his shoulders as he shared, "We need tae know if Ailis was part of the heist at Cawdor Castle last night. Why was she really home from university?"

"I don't understand." The chocolate in Paislee's mouth tasted like bitter coffee.

"What heist?" Grandpa asked.

"There were a series of vandalized estates in Scotland last night. The homes were tagged with *SAORSA*, like what had happened at Lady Leery's estate. A pamphlet showing a unicorn trampling a lion was nailed tae several doors."

"A unicorn and lion?" Paislee asked. "Lady Leery didn't mention it and it wasn't in the paper. Grandpa?"

"Not in this morning's news," Grandpa said.

"It wasnae brought up during the interview with Shannon Leery, Shawn Marcus, and Aila Webster regarding the graffiti." Mack drummed his fingers against the mug. "Were they hiding it? I'll be conducting a second interview. Is this what Sorcha Grant reminded you of, tae keep her confidence?"

"No." Not a unicorn or a lion, just that Sorcha had been victimized as well. The ladies hadn't been forthcoming with how their visit with Darcey McClintock had gone. She'd give them a ring later. "What does it mean?"

"I believe it's in response tae a petition going around regarding laws for fireworks." Mack sipped his tea and winced when he burned his tongue.

"Was anything stolen from the other houses?" Grandpa asked. "Shannon's was simply vandalized with nothing taken."

"What happened at Cawdor last night was different than the other places that were covered in graffiti," Mack said. "We arenae sure why."

"The castle was open when it normally wasn't because of the fundraiser." Cawdor was just a few miles from Rait Tower. Paislee calculated that a fast walker would be there in less than an hour. Ailis had worn pink trainers. Was she a runner, like Brody? "Was the theft a planned operation, or rather a crime of opportunity?"

"I'll know more after my interview with the Dowager Countess of Cawdor. I cannae imagine it will go over well, but her head of security found a broken gate latch on the property that could be an access point. Several valuable items were stolen."

Paislee recalled Shannon and Sorcha's concern for Cawdor being next to be targeted and that they had brought up the fundraiser being a possible weakness.

Their fears had played out. Would they be in touch with the DC of Cawdor to offer condolences? Did they even know about the theft?

"Paislee," Mack said in a solemn tone. "I'd like tae clarify something you said, aboot Ailis tripping. We dinnae believe that what you heard was Ailis hitting her head on a rock. We found an emerald in her clothes. Her parents say she doesnae like emeralds."

"A necklace?" Paislee touched the divot in her throat. "I saw something sparkling in her collar but didn't get a good look. She was wearing trainers beneath her costume. I thought for comfort." What was the *thunk* she'd heard, then?

"All the better tae run to Cawdor Castle in?" Grandpa suggested.

"A loose stone that we dinnae ken the origin of as of yet. It muddies things. We are taking sole prints from the scene. You wore boots last night?"

"I did."

"Brody had trainers?"

"Yes, but he wasn't over by Ailis. Mack. How did Ailis die?"

Mack put the phone into a plastic evidence bag. "This footage could lead tae answers. Now, I need tae talk tae Brody before I go."

Chapter 5

Paislee shook her head at Mack, in mama-bear mode. "Talk tae him? You already did!"

"That was before we found the emerald. Her family says she doesnae like emeralds, or own any emerald jewelry, so why does she have it?" Mack asked. "Did Ailis steal it? And then what . . . Did she meet up with Blake at the ruins? And argue? It seems like that on the audio."

"Ailis had posted a picture of herself in costume at eight at the cemetery, saying she wanted tae be at the Grotto at ten," Paislee said. "There was no announcing the prank or a segue that she was heading tae Cawdor for some thievery or vandalism." She couldn't fathom it. "How, Mack?"

"They're conducting an autopsy on Ailis Barclay tae determine cause of death. The evidence at the scene didn't match with a fall. Was her car in the photo?" Mack asked. "I've been focused on Cawdor but will make reading her social media posts a priority."

"No vehicle of any kind." Paislee tilted her head. "I have an emerald bracelet, and we're talking chips that aren't valuable. What size is this emerald?"

"I cannae tell you that. I'd like tae chat with Brody before I interview the Dowager Countess of Cawdor." Mack tapped the table. "I've got tae hurry."

"You can't tell Brody that Ailis's death is under investigation," Paislee stated. "He had nightmares all night, thinking she'd hit her head after tripping on a rock."

"Give me some credit for being tactful," Mack said indignantly. "But, I cannae lie."

Grandpa removed his glasses.

It took Paislee several minutes to be convinced to get her son and bring him downstairs to be questioned.

"I'll be sitting right here," Paislee said.

"Angus is welcome tae stay too," Mack said. "I just want tae toggle Brody's memory from last night. You both must be verra quiet, or you willnae be included."

"Fine," Paislee said. She wasn't happy . . . but a young woman was dead. Being investigated, which meant they thought there was a chance poor Ailis had been killed.

She climbed the stairs and knocked on Brody's door.

"What?" Brody grumbled.

"The DI is here." Paislee tried the door handle, but it was locked. "Will you please come down for a few minutes?"

"What does he want?"

"He needs tae take the phone," Paislee said.

"Dinnae care. Never want it again."

"Brody, sweetheart, please come down. Mack isn't going anywhere until you do."

The music turned off. Brody opened the door, not looking at her, his shoulders slumped. His hair was a wild mess, and his eyes were red and bloodshot. "I just want tae sleep."

Paislee checked his forehead with her wrist, but it wasn't warm. Stress could make you ill.

"You can go back upstairs after you answer a few questions." She kept her voice soft and reassuring.

Brody nodded and slouched his way down the steps, his body loose.

She'd make a butter and crisp piece for him while they were

downstairs. It was a disgusting sandwich, but he loved it, especially with sour cream crisps.

"I dinnae ken anything more," Brody said over his shoulder. He reached the foyer. Wallace raced from his bed at the back door down the hall toward him. Her son gave his pup an absent-minded pat.

Grandpa had refreshed their tea mugs and poured Brody a glass of orange juice.

"Hi." Mack watched Brody closely as he sat down. "First off, I'm sairy. This is an awful way tae celebrate Samhain. I willnae keep you too long. You may have caught the last footage of Ailis Barclay while she was alive."

Brody's hand trembled as he reached for the juice. "Mum says you want the mobile—take it. I dinnae care."

"Thanks. It will be returned once we get what we need."

"Keep it."

Mack nodded. "I understand. It's been traumatic."

Brody drank his juice. Paislee got out white bread, butter, and sour cream crisps, quickly putting the concoction together as Mack and Brody went over what Brody had seen last night. Keeping the sandwich on the counter for when the interview was over, Paislee returned to the table.

"Brody, did you see a car in the car park? Either time—when you were there first, or later, with your mum?"

Brody scowled. "I think there was a car when I first got there. It was dark though."

"Was it running, or parked? Was someone inside it?"

"I didnae pay close attention. It was in the cemetery. It wasnae there when me and Mum came back tae find me phone."

"Paislee, do you recall a car?"

She thought back to the empty lot. "No. The only vehicle we saw the whole night was an abandoned truck closer to the main street."

Mack turned to Brody. "What aboot when you returned tae the ice rink—did you go by the river, the way you said you came?"

Brody shrugged. "I bolted, scared tae me soul, and ran along the road. Dinnae remember parked cars . . . I wasnae thinking clearly."

Paislee and Grandpa exchanged a look.

Whoever had robbed Cawdor Castle might have been in the cemetery afterward, if the police could somehow tie the emerald to Ailis and the stolen jewels. She had no prior connection to the loose gemstone.

Ailis's death was being investigated.

Had she been killed? Had she been part of the heist? Had she been home to visit her family for Samhain, or were there underlying reasons for the visit that included stealing from the Campbells? Cawdor Castle was connected by various waterways to Rait Tower.

"I heard a splash in the river," Paislee said. "I thought it was deer or some wildlife."

"When?" Mack had his pen poised to jot her answer down on his tablet.

"We were at the ruins around ten thirty," Paislee said. "So, then."

"We're trying tae trace when and how Ailis arrived at the ruins. Her family's property is several miles away. She owns a two-door Fiat. An older model. Silver. Her friends said that she let her boyfriend borrow it sometimes." Mack focused on Brody. "Was the car you saw a Fiat, or two-door?"

Brody ruffled his hair, his expression sheepish. "Dunno. I took off, like the Wraith was after me. I ran with me head doon, a total eejit."

"You are not an idiot," Paislee said firmly.

"No, son, you are not," Grandpa said with assurance.

"Not even a wee bit," Mack agreed.

"I feel verra stupid," Brody said. "If I could turn back the clock, I'd tell Edwyn and Darryl tae stuff the dare. I had this grand plan tae ask Emma tae be my girlfriend when I got back tae the ice rink, but instead I went intae the loo and boked." His nose scrunched. "Dropping me mobile meant not having proof, so none of being terrified had been worth it. And then tae find oot it was Ailis, and they'd played a trick on me?" His lip quivered. "Not going tae school ever again."

Not an option, Paislee wanted to say but didn't.

"What were you going tae do?" Mack asked. "After the ice rink party?"

"Come home and sneak oot tae find me mobile, but Mum just wouldnae let it go, and so we went together." Brody didn't meet her eyes.

"Thank the guid Lord," Grandpa said.

Paislee's hands shook, so she wrapped them around her mug of tea. If he'd snuck out that night, he might have discovered Ailis's body on his own. Worse, he might have disturbed the thieves who'd (possibly) killed the young woman who had been in the wrong place at the wrong time.

Maybe. What if they discovered that Ailis had developed a drug habit or drinking problem while away at uni to explain her behavior?

Her being part of the vandals didn't track. Not when she'd been so sweet about intending to return Brody's phone to the ice rink.

Where was Blake Harrington? Why hadn't her boyfriend been with her?

"You promised—no more sneaking out. Do I need tae install motion cameras?" Paislee's voice was harsh from fear that sounded like anger.

She hated to admit it, but she'd recognized her mother's tone just then. Had there been caring and fear in her upbringing that Paislee hadn't realized until just now?

Brody didn't look at her. Paislee inwardly counted to ten. The calming technique worked to a degree. Maybe if she counted to a hundred, she wouldn't feel like screaming.

"Can I go back upstairs?" Brody stared at the mobile on the table.

"Not yet," Mack said. "Just answer a few more questions, please."

Brody studied the empty glass. Paislee got up to refill it with water and brought the crisp and butter piece with her, setting both before her son.

"Thanks." Brody inched the food away but sipped the water.

Mack asked about the timing of his return to the ice rink. "I see the video was at nine fifteen."

"I left the rink at twenty till nine," Brody said. "I easily run a six-minute mile, but I went along the river so it took a wee bit longer. Got tae the tower. Didnae immediately see the wraith—Ailis. There were these boulders that looked like monsters. Dirt piles freaked me oot. Like, fresh, tae bury someone in. Every horror movie I ever saw screamed danger. I heard a sound." His mouth twisted. "Darryl had plenty of time tae call Ailis and set me up."

Nobody liked being made to feel like a fool. And it had all backfired so horribly. Paislee patted Brody's shoulder.

Wallace lay down by Brody's feet.

"You can help me find oot how she died," Mack said. "You will be the hero of the hour. Nobody will laugh then."

"No thanks." Brody nodded at the text messages. "I read some this morning before I went upstairs. Emma feels sairy for me. Not the best impression. Darryl accused me of not doing anything tae stop what happened."

"Oh, son!" Paislee covered her lips with her fingers.

"Sam, my other friends—not Edwyn, mind ye, but others—all want tae know how I am. I am going mental. Nobody, especially not Darryl or Jimmy, saw me return, because I was in the bathroom tossing my pizza." Brody exuded misery. "I am so sairy that Ailis tripped. I am not responsible for it, am I? If I'd known she'd fallen I would have helped her, even if I am a joke."

Mack's phone rumbled within the confines of his suit pocket.

He removed it and frowned. "Brody, you did nothing wrong. You were verra brave—a heck of a lot braver than I would have been. That cemetery is damned eerie during the day. At night?" He stood. "It was a jest that didnae turn oot as planned. Darryl is looking for someone tae blame, but it's not you, and we are all assured of that."

"Blame for what?"

"Ailis's death is being investigated. It's possible that there is more tae what happened last night than a simple trip and fall in the cemetery."

Brody paled. "Do the Barclays know that?"

"Yes."

Brody finally looked at Paislee, fear and sadness replaced with compassion for the family they knew through football.

"Your true mates will come around." Mack pocketed the plastic bag with Brody's mobile along with his own. "I'll be in touch, Shaw family. No need tae walk me oot."

In other words, the DI was in a hurry to follow the next clue.

She believed that Mack would come through with answers to set everything back to rights, as much as possible. The echo of the door closing traveled down the hall.

Paislee looked at her son. "It scares me tae think how close you were tae being . . . involved."

"What happened?" Brody took another drink of water.

Grandpa nudged his plate toward him along with some chocolate-covered almonds.

"They are investigating, so nothing is certain. You remember how the Leery Estate was covered in graffiti?"

"Yeah." Brody swiped his hair from his forehead.

"Well, last night there were more noble houses or estates tagged with that same word, freedom. *SAORSA*. Down with Tories."

"So?" Brody bit into his sandwich. White bread, butter, and sour cream–flavored crisps. Her son swallowed and took another bite.

"Cawdor Castle was robbed. The police are investigating tae see if Ailis was somehow part of the heist."

His lunch was gone in three more bites.

Grandpa didn't ask but warmed up the fish chowder he'd made yesterday.

"Robbed?" Brody shook his head. "There's lots of stuff, I suppose. Dinnae they have guards? Security?"

"The ladies were in yesterday and talking about the fact that the castle would be open for a fundraiser . . ." Paislee tapped her fingers on the table.

"Normally the castle is closed during the winter." Grandpa poured the hot chowder into a bowl and brought it to the table. "The family resides there. Crackers?"

"No, thanks, Grandpa." Brody stirred the thick soup. "I havenae eaten since . . ." His face turned green as he recalled what had happened again last night.

"I hope that the constables can find something tae help." Paislee quickly changed the subject. "Coach Harris wants tae hold football practice this afternoon and tomorrow. I told him I didn't think you'd be up for it. Whatever you want tae do is fine with me, and with your coach."

"What aboot Darryl?"

"He won't be there, understandably." Paislee imagined his family preparing at the church even now, on All Saints' Day. Gran would have been at mass today, but Paislee wasn't as strict. She'd go on Saturday afternoon for All Souls' Day, and the cemetery cleanup.

"I cannae wrap my head around what happened, or why," Brody said. "Can I think aboot it?"

"Of course."

"Thanks for the grub but I cannae eat anymore." He stood and raced up the stairs, Wallace at his heels.

His bedroom door slammed closed.

"If only I could take on his pain, I would," Grandpa said.

"Me too." Paislee reached for the bowl of chowder, hating to waste food. It tasted like sawdust, but not because of the chef.

Afterward she cleaned up the dishes and read the small article that was barely a blurb in the paper about the yarn shop owner finding the university student.

Darcey McClintock had written about the fundraiser at Cawdor Castle with a number to contact if you wanted to donate to the farmer and the Highland cows. She would be glad to help however she could.

She let Brody sleep through afternoon practice, worried. Knitting kept her mind from falling apart. She finished the infinity scarf and started a blanket.

"It will be better in the morning," Grandpa said.

There was no further word from Mack that night. She sent him a hug emoji that he answered with a heart.

In the morning, things were worse.

The rain had stopped, but the skies were heavy and seemed on the verge of a deluge. Paislee left her room, listening for sounds inside Brody's, but there was nothing.

She hoped that he'd slept all the way through the night without further bad dreams. When she reached the kitchen, she saw Grandpa making pancakes. Brody had come downstairs with Wallace at some point and was now sprawled on the couch.

"He was awake twenty minutes ago and hungry, so I asked if he wanted pancakes. Of course he did, but then, he's oot again."

Paislee peered at her son. What could she do?

"I pray it rains so hard," Paislee whispered to Grandpa by the stove, "that Coach has tae cancel practice." She looked around the kitchen. "I'll get the paper."

"It wasnae there earlier," Grandpa said. "Hope it isnae soaked."

Paislee, barefoot, walked down the hall and ducked her head outside. She glared at the skies.

The delivery man must've been in a hurry, or new, or afraid of getting wet, because the paper—yes, in recycled plastic—was in the fall-brown grass.

She hitched up her pajama bottoms at the knees to clear her ankles, dashed down the steps to the yard, and picked up the wet paper.

"There goes your black bun at Christmas," she said in a warning tone. They'd complained but to no avail.

She shook the excess water from the plastic and returned to the stoop, her toes cold and damp. Removing the paper from the wrapping, she realized that it wouldn't be so bad. She could hang the worst of it over the bathtub downstairs or on the back porch. She tossed the outer plastic into the bin and went inside.

Walking on her tiptoes, paper in hand, she went to the bathroom and grabbed a small towel she sometimes used for Wallace's fur when it got damp, and dried her feet. Unrolling the paper, Paislee gasped to see her son's face on the front page, with Ailis Barclay's Nairn Academy photo and her university school ID.

Grandpa, spatula in hand, joined her in the bathroom, as she'd had the door open and he had heard her sharp inhale. "What is it?"

"Brody!"

Stomach clenched, she brought the paper to the table, not caring whether she was dripping water or not.

His school photo, which she thought was cute, but he hated, and the football team picture, with Brody's face circled.

"Darcey McClintock!" Paislee fumed. "This woman has some nerve. How can she post a picture of a minor?"

"Those are public photos." Grandpa's tone was calming but his eyes flashed with anger. He went to the pan and flipped the pancake before it burned.

Brody was still out like a light.

Wallace had left the sofa to sniff around the mess she'd made on the floor, no doubt interested in the pancakes.

She skimmed the article. "Local Nairn student finds body when school prank goes awry." Well, Darcey had that right anyway.

"What else does it say?" Grandpa asked.

"There is a sweet piece on Ailis Barclay, and a number tae call if anyone has information about that night." Paislee wiped tears from her cheeks.

"Are you okay, lass?"

"Aye, yes. It's alarming when you're not expecting it. I feel so bad for the Barclay family. I'll probably see them at church later, for the All Souls' Day Feast after we do the cemetery cleanup. What can we do tae help them, specifically?" Paislee sat down on the kitchen chair. She had to buy trash bags before they went. She'd make a list.

"Paislee, hinny, sometimes there is nothing tae do but let the time pass."

The smoke alarm went off as a pancake burned.

"And that's what I get for giving advice when I should've been paying attention tae my cooking," Grandpa said. "I'll join you for the cemetery cleanup—I feel closer tae Agnes and Bruce. It boggles the mind how much ivy can grow in a year."

"Gran likes things tidy, but I don't think Da cares one way or the other."

Brody woke, getting up so fast he banged his knee against the coffee table. "What's that smell?"

"Your breakfast," Grandpa teased.

Her son, rumpled hair and all, made it to the kitchen table, where he saw his face in the paper, next to Ailis's. "I dinnae understand. Why are we in the paper together?"

"The article is very sweet. Darcey wrote that you were very brave tae go tae Rait Ruins at all that night."

"I wasnae," Brody said.

Changing the subject, Paislee asked, "What do you think about practice today?"

Brody nodded glumly. "I need tae go and just get it over with. Especially if what happened has made the paper. I didnae ken anything had happened tae her, or I wouldnae have run away. Do you believe me?"

"Of course!" Paislee sent her son a look of love that he didn't see as he was glaring at the paper.

"I was hiding in the ice rink bathroom when she died. That doesnae feel brave at all, so can we not talk aboot it?"

"For now," Paislee said. "You are brave, son." She blinked tears of pride from her eyes and got out the plates for breakfast, and orange marmalade, which her son preferred to syrup.

"What time is practice?"

"One in the afternoon." Paislee had her bag of knitting at the ready to spend the time. "I have work until noon, and I'll pick you up at twelve thirty. Then after practice we have the annual cleaning of the graves. It's our turn tae buy the bulk trash bags."

"Do I have tae go?" Brody groused.

"Yes. Church too."

"It feels weird not tae have my phone," Brody said. "I dinnae want *that* one. Can I save for a different model?"

"Sure," Paislee said. "Let's find out what's on sale for our plan. Same rules as always."

"Fine by me." Brody appeared relieved to not have his old one back. She didn't blame him.

After breakfast, Paislee stopped at the Nairn newspaper office. She entered and waited at the front desk. "Is Darcey McClintock in?"

"Go on back. Third office on the right," the young woman said, not peering up from her computer.

Darcey had short, bleached blond hair that was styled to be messy. Paislee liked the look in theory, but it would never work for her.

She knocked on the partially open door.

"Enter!"

"Hi. I'm Paislee Shaw."

"Brody's mother?" Darcey swiveled in her office chair toward Paislee. A computer took up one corner of her desk, and a printer the other. Reams of paper were piled on the floor next to it. "Cute kid."

"That he is."

"You like the piece? We can get you discounted copies if you want them for a scrapbook. Talk tae Susie up front."

Darcey was missing the point. "I'm here tae tell you that if you ever put him in another article without my express permission as his mother—his guardian—I will sue the paper."

"It was a nice article!" Darcey protested. She was dressed head to toe in black, with red lipstick.

"It was, I agree. I have one job in this world and that is tae protect my son—you should have asked my permission before blasting his face in the paper for any stranger tae see."

"Doesnae he want tae be a famous footballer?" Darcey queried. "You cannae keep his identity a secret."

"I can protect his name until he's older," Paislee said. "This is not up for discussion." Pausing at the door, she tossed Darcey a bone. "It was a lovely article about Ailis. I hope it brings answers."

With that, she left and drove the less than a half mile to Cashmere Crush. The blasted skies had the nerve to clear to a light bluish gray.

She had to focus on the positive, like the smiling Meri McVie, who helped occasionally on Saturday if Amelia Henry, her other part-timer, wasn't available. Amelia was immersed in police training school at Tulliallan and hadn't finished her first year of two yet. Located near Edinburgh, she came home for weekends with her pup, Snowball. She worked one Saturday shift a month just to keep her hand in.

Meri had also read the paper and had nothing but empathy for Brody, and the Barclays. "Cannae imagine losing a child."

"It's a brutal, tragic thing. You know, Darcey McClintock had covered the fundraiser last night at Cawdor Castle, so why didn't she mention the robbery? She was all over the vandalism at Lady Leery's estate."

"What robbery?" Meri peered down her nose at Paislee. She had short hair, silver glasses, and a no-nonsense attitude that made her a brilliant judge in the piping competitions. She'd done a stint on the board of the Nairn Highland Games but went back to her beloved bagpipes, as the games held too much drama.

"Oops—forget I said a thing." Had Mack asked her to keep that under wraps? She didn't think so. "I don't think it is a secret, but just in case."

"All right, I willnae say a word." Meri mimed locking her lips and tossing the key. "What robbery?"

"Halloween night there was a theft at Cawdor Castle. There were also several nobles' homes vandalized."

Meri's voice lowered. "Was Ailis involved?"

Thankfully Meri's question veered in the direction of the conversation. Paislee wasn't sure what Mack would be okay with her sharing; however, Meri could be trusted and had proved that many times.

"I don't know. I think she was expecting her boyfriend, Blake, but he wasn't there. The police have Brody's phone, since he had video of Ailis on it, tae prove tae the other lads he saw the 'Wraith.'"

"The article this morning said that it was a trick gone wrong," Meri said.

The front door of Cashmere Crush opened. Instead of retrieving her from the hot seat, Paislee felt pinned and wished she could duck out the back and hide at the harbor.

Lady Shannon Leery and Dowager Countess Sorcha Grant entered the yarn shop with their chins high.

"We'd hoped tae find you alone," Shannon said. Her blond bob had been sprayed into a shellac that didn't budge.

"I am not. You remember Meri? She's a judge for the piping competition."

"Of course," Sorcha said, not unthawing. "The article in the paper today was not acceptable. I will have Darcey McClintock fired, if you'd like."

Oh—they were angry on Brody's behalf. How sweet.

"It was a shock tae see his school picture staring at me this morning, but the piece she wrote about Ailis was a touching tribute tae a young life. I've already been in this morning tae let her know that I won't forgive a second time regarding Brody's inclusion without permission." Paislee felt she and the reporter had seen eye to eye.

"This world is often cruel. It's why we must celebrate each victory." Shannon cleared her throat and gestured to the back room. "Is there a place we can have a quiet conversation?"

"Let me work up here at the front and handle any customers." Meri knew her own worth and wasn't bothered by the ladies' sometimes haughty attitude.

"Thank you, Meri," Sorcha said. "I know you'll be the soul of discretion."

"That you do," Meri agreed. She grabbed the feather duster and walked to the first high-top table.

Paislee hid a smile as she ushered the ladies to the cramped back space. There'd been an attempt at sorting boxes, which hadn't gone far. "Rhona has suggested an overhaul of this back area, and I think she's right. Until then, one of you can take the armchair and I'll grab some stools."

She returned in an instant with two. Lady Leery was perched on the edge of the old stuffed armchair.

"Here we are."

Sorcha took a stool and sat next to Lady Leery. This put her corduroy-clad knee at the lady's nose.

"If you're sure we cannae get Darcey fired, then let me share the real reason we're here. We know that Cawdor was robbed last night," Sorcha said.

"You do?" Paislee shouldn't have been surprised.

"Of course. My new grounds manager was talking tae the gardener at Cawdor this morning aboot the robbery and he told me while we were potting seeds in the greenhouse that the dowager countess is furious. She'd only agreed tae the fundraiser tae keep the peace with the thane regarding that blasted petition he has going around for regulating fireworks. It has set off hard feelings from the public."

"A guid deed punished," Shannon tsked.

Sorcha lowered her voice. "Randall Fowler runs security there and he showed the furious thane a broken gate by the river. Easy in, and easy oot."

That's what Mack understood as well.

Shannon twirled the large diamond on her left hand. "The castle is full of historical artifacts and unimaginable wealth. I've never blamed her for wanting tae keep it closed tae the public, but one must do what one must tae support the property."

"And the crofters on it. The DC agreed tae host champagne and tapas from seven till nine tae raise money for the family with a small holding on their acreage," Sorcha said. "The man was in an accident and cannae work for a few months until he heals. Simon Sinclair came up with a rather clever idea tae foster their two Highland cows with money as well as manpower."

"It's a brilliant idea. I read about it in Friday's paper though it was on page four," Paislee said. "I thought Darcey did a nice job there too. She knows how to hit the heartstrings."

"The family willnae starve, but it's nice tae have enough tae pay the other bills too," Shannon said. "We've dropped off venison from our estate."

"And we've shared veg we canned from our harvest," Sorcha said. "Now, this is through the gardeners, mind, but I hear they garnered ten thousand pounds in two hours over champagne and appetizers done by that chef they hired for the castle . . . Pat Amblin." She checked behind her and at the front of the shop, not wanting to be overheard. "Depending on the value of the items stolen, well . . . the DC threatened legal action."

"What?" Paislee asked. Her head raced with the ten-thousand-pound figure. "The DC against the thane?"

"It willnae be the first time," Shannon said sagely. "The woman wants what is hers, or she perceives tae be hers. It's tricky."

"I called Shannon right after breakfast when I realized that the news of the theft wasnae in the paper. Mibbe that troublemaker

Darcey heeded our advice? Do you realize that she, well, it's what she told us anyway, but that she just shared the photo of Shannon's estate withoot a photo credit or due diligence of where the information came from?"

Shannon's lips pursed in anger. "Just received it via email and didnae care that it didnae have a source. That's shoddy journalism."

"Mibbe that's why there was no article aboot the theft at the castle," Sorcha said. "In the old days the editor would run things by us before blasting our faults tae the world. It's a different time. Could be the thane has an in, or the DC of Cawdor, to keep the story squashed."

"Darcey was there, getting coverage of the fundraiser." Paislee tapped her finger to her chin. "No word about the theft, just the piece about Ailis, and Brody. I wonder when it happened?" Paislee made a mental note to make a timeline.

"The owner of the paper now is a Conservative and an ally of sorts," Shannon said. "It's why that photo was such a shock. I prefer me privacy. The various editors dinnae always agree. Some journalists will do anything tae sell papers."

"Is Darcey a journalist and an editor?" Paislee asked.

"The paper is so small that perhaps many of the staff wear many hats," Shannon said.

"We feel like this was different than the other vandalizations," Sorcha said. "Nothing was stolen at my property. Or Shannon's. Destroyed, yes, with *SAORSA* painted everywhere."

"That's what Mack said too. I didn't tell him that you'd been tagged, Sorcha, but maybe you should." Paislee glanced toward the front where Meri was folding shawls. "I wonder if Cawdor Castle was also graffitied. The DI mentioned that a symbol of a unicorn trampling a lion was left at the other properties vandalized on Halloween."

"There were?" Shannon asked, looking at Sorcha.

"Out with it!" Paislee said.

"Fine. We each received the same threatening pamphlet." Sorcha hooked the heel of her boot on the rung of her stool. "I still have it at Ramsey Castle."

"Shawn did the right thing and hid it, not letting anyone else know aboot it. I wonder if we were the practice runs before Halloween night?"

"And Cawdor was the big event?" Paislee shook her head. "I don't think so. Nobility all over Scotland was tagged. What did the pamphlet say?"

"It's the unicorn stomping on the lion with a message aboot SAORSA rising in power and for the people not tae take the idea of legislation for fireworks quietly," Shannon summarized.

"And Cawdor was the only theft?" Paislee didn't understand it, and when she thought of Ailis and her part in the evening, things grew cloudier.

"That we know of," Shannon said. "Rich people dinnae like tae be made fools of."

"Hate tae break this tae you, but nobody likes being made a fool." Paislee thought of Brody, hurting because he had been pranked by people he considered mates.

"You're right," Sorcha said. "So, what happened at Cawdor that went different?"

"You know the DC, Sorcha," Shannon said. "You are her equal. Why not invite us all over tae tea?"

"At Ramsey?" Sorcha sounded uncertain.

"Why not?" Shannon persisted. "Paislee is a friend of ours and the dowager duchess wouldnae dare protest if we were at your home."

"Can you imagine if she found oot aboot my lovely cashmere items in the Grant tartan?" Sorcha rubbed her hands together. "Mibbe you could get another client, dear."

Shannon looked properly horrified. "You must be jesting. Inviting her over tae discuss business?"

"What else would we talk aboot?" Sorcha said. "We cannae just ask her if she was robbed, and what was taken."

"Not directly," Shannon mused. "Conversation. Tea. Brandy."

"Well . . . I've never had her over. Perhaps if we share that we received the unicorn and lion pamphlet, she might be intrigued enough tae join us." Sorcha stretched her leg, uncomplaining on the hard stool.

"Do I need tae be there?" Paislee asked.

"Yes," the ladies said in unison.

She had so many apprehensive thoughts, but kept them to herself. The chances of meeting with the Dowager Countess of Cawdor were slim, so she didn't argue and waste her energy.

The truth was that Cawdor Castle was normally closed to the public from October to spring. It had opened for a champagne fundraiser at the last minute to assist a farmer on their property. It would bring in positive feelings, perhaps to balance the contentious petition started by the thane to regulate fireworks. Darcey's article had been good enough but not as vibrant as some of her other messages.

"I think Rhona is right and you could use this space much wiser," Shannon said, rising to her feet, somehow graceful despite her age and the overstuffed chair.

"You are a guid lass." Sorcha easily straightened up, the physical work she did at the castle keeping her strong. "How did you vote in the recent elections?"

"My gran taught me tae never discuss politics," Paislee said. "Or religion. It was considered cheeky even tae ask."

Both ladies chuckled, unabashed.

"Agnes was an incredible woman," Shannon said.

"I never met her," Sorcha said. "But if she believed in guid manners, we would have gotten along just fine."

Paislee knew her Gran might have been a wee bit jealous of Shannon Leery and her effect on the men, but Sorcha's down-to-earth side would have appealed. Her Gran believed in tradition, yes, but as a teacher, she saw where the practicalities of the common man struggled. It was why she had been so active in the church.

"I believe you're right," Paislee said.

"I like tae hear that," Shannon said. "Just as I am right aboot Sorcha inviting us tae tea at the castle tae discuss the pamphlet fiasco. Troublemakers behind the scenes."

With that, the ladies swept out of Cashmere Crush leaving Paislee tongue-tied. She had nobody to blame but herself.

Chapter 6

The gray skies puffed like angry cotton balls but didn't rain—not even a drizzle.

Paislee picked Brody up at half past noon, thinking she'd have to drag him to the car, but he bounded out in his practice clothes and hoodie, and carrying a water bottle. He hopped in the front seat.

Coach Harris had been right. These boys were used to running and needed an outlet.

"Hey," Paislee said.

"Hi."

"Did you already have lunch?"

"Yeah. Grandpa made beef stew." Brody pulled a granola bar from his pocket. "And sent me with snacks. Hungry?"

Paislee had been hoping to run in for a bite but accepted the bar. "Thanks." She put it in the cup holder for later. "You have extra?"

Brody displayed five more granola bars.

Paislee laughed.

"Grandpa said that Ritchie from the flower shop called, and the arrangements are ready when you want tae pick them up for the cemetery."

"Good." Every year she ordered loose bouquets to adorn the graves of her family. She had Ritchie make up a dozen extra carnations for headstones that didn't have anyone to commemorate them.

She put the Juke in reverse and drove to the park where the rec league practiced. Coach Harris was just arriving, and she parked next to him. Born in Scotland but of Haitian descent, he'd been very talented, earning awards and accolades as a footballer before a knee injury took him from the pros.

Brody considered the way to "retire" was to coach.

If you still loved the sport so much, then Paislee approved. She couldn't imagine ever giving up her knitting needles. These days it seemed as if her son often had the ball attached to the toe of his cleat.

"I'll look for Emma and sit with her," Paislee offered.

"Nah. She better not come. I have tae concentrate on my game, like Grandpa said." Brody opened his car door and jumped out.

"Does she know that she's not invited?" Paislee asked the empty car as the door slammed closed.

"Brody!" Coach Harris offered his knuckles to Brody, who bumped them with his. "This is an awful time. I'm not gonna ask how ye are, because I get that you're a jumble of things. Want tae run it oot?"

"Yeah."

Coach tossed him the ball. "Go. Two laps, left tae right foot drill, then come talk tae me."

Brody nodded, the ball like an extension of his foot.

Paislee got out of the car. "You were right," she said.

Like the noble ladies, he preened. "Love tae hear it." His smile faded. "You okay?"

"Aye, and I am not interested in running drills." Paislee patted her bag of knitting. "I've got scarves tae knit."

Always scarves, and hats to match, for the upcoming Christmas season, though it was just fall. Today was All Souls' Day, and Gran was in her heart, as was her Da—and poor Ailis Barclay.

Coach ran to the field and soon had the team warming up.

Paislee got comfortable in her camp chair, sitting outside and bundled up. She enjoyed the seasons. One just had to dress for the weather.

Lydia called and Paislee answered, having time for a chat. "Hey!"

"Hi—is now a guid time?"

"Sure is," Paislee said.

"What are you doing?"

"Watching Brody practice, knitting, and now talking tae you."

"Multitasker!"

"Have tae be, as you know."

"I do. Paislee?"

Her skin dotted with alarm at Lydia's tone. It could be good, or bad, but her bestie was about to tell her something important. Like when she'd decided to marry Laird Corbin Smythe. Like when she'd announced moving to Germany with Corbin to operate a winery.

She put the knitting needles in her lap, over the scarf in aqua blue. "Yes?"

"Did you read the paper today?"

"The one that had my son's face all over it? Yes."

Paislee realized that the Smythes might have been targeted, as Laird Garrison Smythe had a very, very grand estate.

"I was coming home for your birthday, but now Corbin is too. His father was so upset by the damage caused by those cowards that he had a heart attack. He's in hospital in Inverness."

"He's all right? How can I help? How is Mary?" Corbin's stepmother had been terrible to Lydia and Corbin, but Corbin had been willing to throw away his inheritance, and all that went with it, for Lydia's love. His family had come around.

"I'm afraid she's not doing verra well. Mary said that a pamphlet with a unicorn trampling a lion was tacked to the front door."

"What about the word *SAORSA*?"

"Aye, that too. I never thought I'd feel sairy for the Smythes, but this vandalism is terrible. The great Garrison dooned by a heart attack."

"When are you coming? We'll be cleaning Gran and Da's graves later today and then have dinner at the church afterward. I should be done by seven."

"Tonight, but not that early. We're closing up the winery so that Corbin can focus on his father. Mum and Da are driving up with Baxter and will meet us at our house, tae be supportive. I've already called the staff tae prep so we have groceries for us all. Will you come over tomorrow?"

Their house in Nairn was a perfect mix of old and new, to suit both Corbin's and Lydia's tastes. Her best friend sounded forlorn and upset. "Of course. Let me know what time."

"Bring the family. Wallace loves the back garden." Lydia exhaled and when she spoke again, her tone was lighter. "I need tae see you. I never realized that a two-hour plane ride could be a deterrent. Love you!"

"Love you too." Smiling, Paislee got back to her project while watching Brody. Other parents were bundled up on the sidelines or watched from the warmth of their cars. She recognized Sam's mother and waved. She felt as if she was being watched but didn't see anybody she knew. Spectators in coats and hats, with gloves and scarves just to be warm, were everywhere on the field.

At two thirty, the boys were worn out and seemed to be in better spirits.

Sam gave Brody a pat on his shoulder before joining his mother.

So long as Brody had one ally, Paislee would feel better about the kids going back to school on Monday.

"I didn't see Jimmy today."

"Nope. Not sure what tae say tae him anyways." Brody stretched his right arm behind his back, and then the left.

Paislee packed up the camp chair as Brody wiped sweat from his forehead with a sports towel.

"I'm knackered," Brody said.

"You still have tae help," Paislee said. "Besides, I thought you liked checking out the tombstones."

"That was before finding Ailis at the cemetery," Brody said.

Death was a fact of life. Living in Nairn and being part of the church and community meant having a purpose.

"Someday you'll be taking care of my grave," Paislee said. "I'll be thirty-one in a few days, so I am on borrowed time."

What was meant in jest landed flat.

Brody climbed into the back seat and stretched out, putting his forearm over his eyes, clearly not wanting to talk about it.

Paislee didn't push. She didn't know what to do. So, she drove them home—grateful to Gran for leaving her the house. Grateful to Lydia for making it safe for another hundred years.

She parked in the carport and Brody jumped out, running inside before they could talk further.

"I'm not doing great here, Gran," Paislee mumbled as she exited the vehicle and trudged inside, the bag of knitting and her handbag over her arm.

Music blared from upstairs.

"Dare I ask?" Grandpa left his room, dressed for outside in boots, jeans, and a jacket over his arm. A tam sat on his head.

"He's been through so much," Paislee said.

"What happened now?"

"Brody doesn't want tae go tae the cemetery with us today. Ailis's death is hitting hard."

"And if he stays home?" Grandpa asked.

"He will wallow in sadness."

"And if he goes with us?"

"The same? He can wallow with us," Paislee decided. "I don't want him tae be alone."

"I can see both sides, but, as a parent, I think dragging him oot for fresh air and community is the right choice."

"Thanks, Grandpa." Paislee took a deep breath, her nose twitching at sensory deliciousness. "What is that?"

"I made chicken and dumplings for the potluck at the church." Grandpa raised his hand. "I'm not going but figured you could use it. Will Elspeth be there?"

"You know she will," Paislee said.

He finger-combed his snowy white beard. "She'd asked aboot it one day when we were talking last week. I think she was angling for a dinner invitation, but this will have tae do."

"You are something else," Paislee said.

"And will Mack be going tae church tonight?"

"No." Paislee closed her mouth. She hadn't heard from him since a good morning text earlier.

"I made extra chicken and dumplings tae have at the house if he wants tae join me." Grandpa took off the tam and smoothed his hair before replacing it in the exact same position.

"And why on earth would Mack want tae join you for supper?"

"I've got some ideas aboot the vandalism," Grandpa said.

"Do I know them?" Paislee checked her watch, then mumbled, "For Heaven's sake." They were to meet at the cemetery at three and it was a quarter till. "Brody!" she yelled from the bottom of the stairs.

Of course he didn't hear her.

"Hold that thought," she said and then climbed the stairs. She knocked and turned the knob. Locked.

She pounded.

Brody opened the door, still in his practice clothes.

"Turn off the music, now."

Eyes narrowed as if he wanted to argue, Brody followed her directive albeit reluctantly.

"If you lock this door again . . ." Paislee began.

"I was changing!"

"I knock before I enter. You can give me a shout if you are mid change."

"I dinnae want you barging in," Brody stated.

"I knock. I shouldn't have tae knock. And the music is way too loud."

Brody rolled his eyes.

Paislee counted to ten. Fifteen. Twenty. "I want you in jeans and downstairs in ten minutes. No arguments. Or, or . . ." What could she do? He was a teenager now. Taller than her. He'd had some tough blows this year.

"Yes?" Brody asked, his tone wiseass.

Next time, she needed a plan before just blowing off steam.

"If you are not downstairs in ten minutes ready tae help me at the cemetery for our family plot, then you will be grounded. Grounded means no practice. You can go tae school and come home for an entire week. Seven days."

"No practice?"

He sounded like she was taking away his orange marmalade.

"Your choice," Paislee assured him. "And while we are at it, I don't want you tae be disrespectful tae me. I am your mother." She held her son's gaze until he nodded.

She went downstairs, breathing hard.

Paislee missed those days when he was a toddler, and she could scoop him up for a hug. This, this was work. She had never shied away from a challenge.

"It's going tae be a long five years," she told Grandpa.

"You have no idea." Grandpa patted her on the shoulder.

Brody was down at the allotted time. She was glad that he wasn't the kind to pout or sulk, so that when she hugged him, he hugged her back.

The Shaw family left their house and drove to the florist to pick up the flowers, stopping to buy a hundred extra-large trash bags, and then went to the cemetery by the church where Gran and her da were laid to rest—only ten minutes late.

About a hundred people were gathered in the parking lot. Father Dixon's assistant, a young man named Rooney Crowe, took attendance on a clipboard. "I need an accurate number tae buy pastries. Coffee and tea will be available all afternoon."

"Thank you," Paislee said.

"Welcome," Rooney said. "How are you? Father said you and Brody found Ailis's body on Samhain." He had to be in his mid-twenties, with dark brown hair covered by a cap. Blue denims, and a zippered hoodie. Thoughtful, he'd waited to ask while Brody and Grandpa were getting the flowers from the back of the car.

Paislee looked around the lot. "It's been hard. I can't imagine how the Barclays are holding up. I don't see them here." They'd been on the list to bring a hot dish.

"They called oot, understandably so. Father Dixon has been at their home all day." Rooney leaned closer to Paislee, snapping peppermint-scented gum. "Did you know that the police asked if Ailis could be part of the vandals tagging houses on Halloween? They've been asking all kinds of questions aboot her."

The trouble with living in a small shire was that it was very difficult to keep things secret. Paislee shrugged, noncommittal. "I didn't know her that well. I know Darryl more from being on the football team with Brody. The family seems very nice."

"Ailis was a few years behind me in school," Rooney said. "She was a theater kid through and through. I was in the band. We had our separate groups, ye ken?"

"I do."

"I hear her boyfriend is a real jackass." Rooney chomped his gum.

"How so?" When Paislee had been on social media night before last looking Blake up, he'd seemed like your average university guy who was into partying before studying. They'd been a cute couple, which wasn't hard when both people were attractive.

She wondered if Mack had found Blake yet, to question him.

"Heard he was at a party all night on Samhain and totally ditched her at the ruins. If I had a girl as hot as Ailis, I wouldnae be messing around, right?" Rooney chewed his gum, cracking it.

"I suppose." Rooney had a jealous tone that put Paislee on guard. "You went tae the same primary? Secondary?"

"Secondary." He tipped his cap back. "It's ancient history but we had a summer love."

"You did?" She guessed that Rooney had the cute nerdy-guy vibe.

"Summer lovin'. It wasnae a big deal." Rooney tapped his pen to the clipboard. "There's video of Blake and Ailis arguing that's gone viral on social media. They were at the cemetery, and she was in full costume, telling everyone tae meet up at the Grotto."

"I saw the post about meeting at the Grotto, but not the argument."

"Think it happened later." Rooney leaned closer to her. "I'll find it and show it tae you."

"Don't show me," Paislee said. "Show the police."

"Blake was driving her car, and he kicked Ailis oot." Rooney switched the wad of gum to his other cheek.

Paislee's mouth gaped and she quickly closed it. "Nobody deserves tae be treated like that. Did you tell the constables?"

"Nah. I dinnae mess with the cops."

Brody and Grandpa, arms laden with two bouquets and a dozen extra carnations, walked from the car toward Paislee and Rooney.

"We also have a hot dish for later," Paislee said. "It's in a thermal container so fine in the car for now."

"Thanks for volunteering." Rooney snapped his gum. "All Souls' Day is the best day of the year tae care for our ancestors." He eyed Grandpa, then Brody. "You're lucky that the Shaws bought plenty of land. The cemetery is running oot of room, so space is at a premium. Let me know if you ever want tae sell off some of your plots. It could bring in a tidy sum."

"I didnae come here today tae bargain," Grandpa said, offended. "I came tae pay respects tae my deceased wife, and deceased son. Get oot of our way."

Rooney, flustered, melted back. "Sairy, mate."

"That was cool!" Brody nodded at Grandpa.

Paislee seconded the thought. "And rude on Rooney's part." She didn't really know the young man, but she didn't care for Father Dixon's assistant.

"Makes me wonder if he pockets the money," Grandpa said.

"Would he?" Brody asked in alarm.

"Let's mind our own business," Paislee said. Would Rooney convince unknowing parishioners to part with their plots for a steep price, and then put the cash in his bank account?

Shady.

Paislee sent a text to Mack about the young assistant, Rooney Crowe, bringing up the police looking into Ailis, and Blake kicking Ailis out of her own car. Dinner with Grandpa if he was free, and last, she asked if he'd found Blake.

Mack didn't answer.

As this was out of her control, she put it from her mind.

Paislee, Brody, and Grandpa spent the afternoon cleaning the Shaw headstones. A dozen tall markers were in a wrought-iron fence with a gate. Her da, Bruce Shaw, who had died when Paislee was sixteen, and then her gran, Agnes Shaw, seven years ago.

The flowers, hardy white mums, yellow daisies, and soft peach carnations, added a cheerful ambience. She had a dozen individual carnations, with baby's breath and fern, to decorate headstones that had no flowers. It didn't take long to find twelve and tidy them. Each of the members of the church took turns looking after the ones who had no family here to do so. Brody discovered a person buried in 1850 and cleaned it up, adding a carnation.

At five, she received a text from Lydia, with a reminder about lunch the next day, and an update that Garrison was well enough to argue about leaving the hospital.

"We have an invite tae Lydia's tomorrow," Paislee said. The sky was growing dark and the wind from the water brought a chill.

"I thought she was in Germany," Brody said. "Is she coming home for your birthday?"

"That was the original plan, but it seems Corbin's dad had a heart attack. The Smythe property was targeted by the vandals last night. Garrison is okay but Corbin wants tae see him."

"Dinnae blame him," Brody said.

Paislee heard the sorrow that he hadn't met his father, who had died a military hero without ever interacting with Brody, though he'd watched from afar.

She patted her da's tombstone, adjusting a bit of greenery at the base of the loose bouquet. Regret settled over her like a mist.

"I've prepaid for me funeral," Grandpa announced as if discussing the weather, which at the moment was cloudy.

Brody and Paislee turned to him.

Brody was tying a bag full of twigs and leaves. They'd cleaned the ivy off of the stone as well as the moss. The earliest headstone here was from 1820. Daniel Shaw.

"Thanks?" Paislee said, unsettled. Because Gran had been sick, they'd had time to go over what her grandmother had wanted. The prayers to be said, the songs sung.

Brody moved the bag of ivy toward his great-grandfather. "When? Where will you be?"

"I had thought here, in this plot. Next tae Agnes." Grandpa looked at them with concern. Her grandmother hadn't forgiven Grandpa in life for a wild stag night that had resulted in a son he hadn't known about until later.

Paislee and Grandpa both believed now that she had forgiven him, from the afterlife.

"I think you should be here," Brody said. He looked around at the tidied Shaw plots that connected them all.

"I do too," Paislee agreed.

"I talked with Father Dixon when I had that cough last winter." Grandpa seemed embarrassed.

He'd been frightened of dying from lung cancer, like his dad had done. The kind doctor had prescribed medicine for walking pneumonia that had cleared the cough.

"Does he know what you want then?" Paislee straightened, her heart beating extra hard.

"Aye. I want a tombstone in the shape of a River Nairn salmon," Grandpa said, eyes twinkling.

Brody burst into laughter.

"And you paid for that, did you?" Paislee quipped.

"Naw. Just a boring headplate next tae Agnes."

Her grandmother had chosen a marble angel on a pedestal. Both her children had died, and she hadn't forgiven Angus for breaking her heart. Yet, she'd had so much love to give still. Paislee and Brody were the recipients of her guidance and wisdom.

"I dinnae think Gran would've liked a giant salmon next tae her," Brody decided. "Guid choice. But dinnae go dying anytime soon. I need my family."

"Not planning on it, Brody, but preparing." Grandpa placed his hand on the angel's wing where Gran was buried. "It's a relief in a way tae know that I will be here, with Agnes and my son. Your mum, and you. Your children too."

"We are all connected." Brody studied the tombstone where her da had been laid to rest after dying in a boating accident. "There is no guarantee of a long life."

"No. It's why we must make the choice tae be our best each day," Grandpa said.

"It is up tae me." Brody put his hand on his heart. "I've heard that always, but it's the first time I've really understood what it means, tae be responsible for my actions. I cannae care what Edwyn thinks, or Darryl, or even Emma."

"Yep. You're ahead of the game, me lad." Grandpa scratched his beard and cleared his throat. "Took me a wee bit longer."

"Are you glad you came?" Paislee glanced up at Brody as he slung the bag toward the other by the fence.

"Yeah. I am."

"Family," Grandpa said. "Nothing is more important."

Chapter 7

Paislee and Brody sat with Elspeth after a short Saturday mass in the hall for the Feast of All Souls' Day. Grandpa had opted to stretch his legs and walk the two miles home rather than have Paislee drop him off.

They'd piled plates high with delicious selections, including Grandpa's chicken and dumplings. Elspeth had brought a savory sausage and potato casserole.

"It's a shame your grandfather is so stubborn aboot church," Elspeth said. "He's a fine cook though. I've never had better dumplings."

Rich chicken gravy nestled around and over the steamed dough. She used her fork to slice one in half.

"Christmas and Easter," Paislee said. "Tae make Gran happy. His church is the River Nairn." There was a powerful healing force in nature that Paislee couldn't deny.

Elspeth sighed. Paislee would wager that her frustration belonged more to the fact that she couldn't sway Grandpa from loving Gran with all his heart. Plenty of widows and widowers went on to remarry, and while Grandpa appreciated the ladies, he was married to Agnes Shaw for all eternity.

"I cannae wait tae be an adult and have the football field be my church." Brody alternated bites of Elspeth's potatoes and sausage and Grandpa's chicken.

"Brody!" Paislee chided, half-heartedly. She knew to pick her battles and today had been a win with his help at the cemetery, realizing for himself the power he held in forging his own destiny with his choices, and not complaining about the mass.

When she'd been a teenager, attending mass had been the last thing she'd wanted to do as well. However, Paislee knew how to pray and when things were too hard, she bowed her head to let go her troubles.

She couldn't imagine not having faith in something more. It wasn't like she preached her beliefs—they were hers. She tried to be the woman her grandmother had been, with integrity to walk the walk of being a decent human.

Sometimes religion, like politics, colored the view and it was simpler to connect on a heart level.

"Can I get dessert?" Brody asked, his dinner plate demolished.

Paislee still had half of her food left, and Elspeth even more. "Wait for me, and for Elspeth."

"I am a slow eater," Elspeth protested. "I would never stand in the way of a growing boy. Try the mince tart."

"Please, Mum?"

Paislee sighed. "Go ahead. Make sure you only take one."

"Of each? They're small!"

"Two then, and let others have a chance."

Brody stood and hurried to a table manned by a fellow parishioner. It was laden with desserts. There were so many to choose from that he might be a while.

"Brody's a guid boy." Father Dixon brought a dinner plate to the table. "May I join you ladies?"

"Of course," Elspeth said as Paislee nodded. The table was for six, so they had two more spaces.

His expression was sad, but he forced a bite into his mouth. "There are days when I wonder if I am at all effectual in my duties, as a shepherd tae my flock."

Paislee sipped her tea, resonating with his statement on not doing a good job in the parental role.

Elspeth patted his hand. She'd worked with the priest for decades before her retirement, and the two were friends.

"You always question the guid you do, Father. You have been a gift tae our community."

"I look intae Darryl Barclay's accusing gaze, and what can I say? Ailis's parents want comfort that their daughter will be in Heaven."

"She's been baptized," Elspeth said with assurance. "Confirmed."

"Yes, that is verra true. I cannae know her heart. Did she belong tae a ring of thieves? Did she steal an emerald from Cawdor Castle? What if she was using the prank for Brody as a cover, for a reason tae be at the ruins?"

Paislee grew alarmed by Father Dixon's candor. He sounded uncertain.

"I've known Ailis since she was a wee babe," Elspeth said, her tone unwavering. "I taught her Sunday School classes. She always wanted tae make people laugh. The lassie was an entertainer, through and through. Not a bad seed."

"Why was she at the cemetery with the thieves if she wasnae one of them? Rooney showed me a post of Ailis arguing with her boyfriend on Halloween. She was already in her Wraith costume."

Rooney seemed the kind to stir the pot. Paislee jumped in to explain more of what had happened that night. "As you know, Brody was pranked by Darryl Barclay. I'm assuming that they had Ailis plan the hazing as a joke." The priest had spent the day with the family and probably had firsthand knowledge of *why*. "What did Darryl say?"

"That young man is angry, sad, and looking tae blame someone—God, Brody, himself. He knows that Brody isnae responsible. He swears that he'd been pranked at fourteen before joining the football team. He and his mate Jimmy went together."

"They wanted Edwyn tae go, but Edwyn backed out." Paislee's cheeks heated with disappointment.

"Darryl and Jimmy had a positive experience and decided tae take the prank tae the next level," Father Dixon said. "Convincing Ailis tae dress up as the Wraith for the best scare ever. Tae make

Brody get video as proof of his bravery. They were going tae back him moving forward in his football career."

Paislee glanced toward her son, who had selected something at last. Something tall with whipped cream.

Father Dixon forced down another bite of roasted potatoes.

Elspeth gave his hand a firm pat.

"It's a rare day that I cannae enjoy a meal. I'm conflicted over what happened tae Ailis. Darryl is taking this tae heart. I've recommended tae his family that they seek counseling, but his mother is grief stricken and didnae hear. His dad is drinking too much. Lord knows I dinnae blame him, and I'll be pouring a dram as soon as this day is done."

Elspeth made soothing noises toward him, and the priest's shoulders relaxed.

"Is there anything I can do tae help the family?" Paislee asked. "I imagine they will be getting inundated with food. I've been focused on Brody, admittedly."

"I've sent a ham and homemade rolls. Meals are what we send because we dinnae ken what else tae do," Elspeth said.

"Ailis died on Samhain. Julie Barclay is worried that her daughter's soul is in limbo. I dinnae think it is. Was she a criminal?"

"Father, so what if Ailis was part of the robbery ring?" Elspeth posited. "You would still love her. She would still be welcome intae Heaven. That's what we believe because of our faith. That is what you must continue tae believe. Be that strength for the Barclay family as only you can."

"You're right." Father Dixon exhaled.

"But, Father," Elspeth continued, "Ailis wouldnae be involved in such a thing. She could be wild but never cruel. Careless sometimes though not on purpose. You see?"

"I miss your guidance, Elspeth," Father Dixon said. He attended to the rest of his meal with improved appetite.

The Ailis that Paislee had heard on Brody's phone had been fun and kind, had wanted to return the phone to the ice rink. And then what—she randomly went to Cawdor to steal an emerald she didn't like?

Brody arrived with a whoosh of teenage energy. "Hey, Father Dixon."

Father Dixon shook off his melancholy and smiled. "Brody. How are you holding up, son?"

"All right. Better. Mum and Grandpa said time will make the nightmares stop." Brody sat down. His choices for dessert were Dundee fruit cake, famous for its almond topping, and cranachan, a tasty dessert with raspberries and cream.

"Time. There is truth there," Father Dixon said.

"How is Darryl?" Brody asked.

"He's in a difficult way, as you can imagine."

Brody dipped his spoon into the whipped cream and raspberries. "He blamed me for not saving Ailis, but I didnae even see her afterward. I thought she was the Wraith of Rait Ruins."

"It was a joke that went awry. Darryl and Jimmy both think you have the talent tae be as guid as Pedro." Father Dixon stared into Brody's eyes with a reassuring gaze. "They thought you'd have Edwyn with you."

Brody's mouth thinned. He swallowed the bite of cranachan. "I didnae. He made sure I'd look like a wean if I didnae go alone."

"Not nice," Father Dixon said.

"No. I am not sure what Monday will be like, especially if Darryl is still upset with me. I wish I never had tae go tae school again."

"Well, understandable, but not practical. I think Darryl will need a friend," Father Dixon advised.

"He set me up." Brody's auburn brows lifted high.

"He feels badly aboot that, believe me. He is blaming you, but he is really blaming himself," Father Dixon said.

Brody got up, unable to finish his Dundee cake. "Mum, can we go? I dinnae feel guid."

"Of course." Paislee said her goodbyes. Brody was back to being mute, and the drive home was heavy with angst.

He went straight to his room and Paislee winced when he slammed the door, but she didn't yell at him.

She felt a wee bit like slamming doors herself.

"Should I ask how the dinner went?" Grandpa asked. Wallace remained downstairs with her grandfather, who was working on the puzzle.

The pup had a chew toy to keep his attention. The bass from Brody's music shook the ceiling.

"It was fine, until Father Dixon suggested that Brody should forgive Darryl for setting him up and then blaming him for not staying tae help Ailis." Paislee put her handbag and fall jacket over the chair in the dining room.

She clicked on the electric kettle.

"Brody did nothing wrong, and is the victim here," Grandpa said. "Asking him tae get over it is a difficult task. The forgiving part is a tough one, but I think he'll come around. He has a braw understanding of life far beyond his years."

"You're right."

"Rosanna called. I told her what was going on. She sends her love tae you both." Grandpa, glasses on top of his head, looked over the puzzle, a German landscape. The project was about halfway done. "You're welcome tae assist."

"I'll join you here, but I will knit while you search for the right pieces."

Paislee made her cup of tea, gathered her bag that always had a project of some kind in it, and sat at the kitchen table.

She read her messages, but there was still no reply from Mack about whether or not he'd located Blake Harrington, Ailis Barclay's boyfriend. The message had gone unread, including her suggestion to check out Rooney Crowe.

"What ideas did you want tae share with the DI about the vandals?" Paislce asked her grandfather.

He was half perched on a tall stool as he surveyed the puzzle. "As you are well aware, Bonfire Night has been escalating each year."

Bonfire Night, November 5th, also known as Guy Fawkes Day, was a tradition that harkened back to 1605 and the failed Gunpowder Plot.

In the last several years, gangs had taken to protesting on this night, using fireworks as weapons against each other, as well as the police.

Opponents were using this as a platform to try and regulate industrial fireworks. The Scots, being ones for doing their own thing, didn't want the Tories or anybody else telling them that they couldn't have their personal fireworks. Heaven help the Conservative who took away their sparklers!

"The Dowager Countess of Cawdor agrees with the thane regarding the regulation of fireworks, which hasn't gone over well with many people. She's heard the grumbles too. Simon pitched the idea of a fundraiser for the injured farmer on their property tae show everyone that they care. Her caveat was that it had tae be done before November, so she could prepare the castle for the holidays. Otherwise, it would have been closed tae outsiders, per usual."

"Did you know that there used tae be two unicorns on the Scottish coat of arms?" Grandpa glanced over at Paislee from his stool.

"No. It's currently a lion and a unicorn," Paislee said. She felt a flashbulb go off over her head.

"That's right. The vandals are using the symbol of the unicorn trampling the lion." Grandpa gestured with a piece of the puzzle.

"This is political," Paislee said.

"I'm afraid it will turn oot tae be that way. My real fear is that the violence will escalate on Guy Fawkes Day."

The music turned off from upstairs and Brody came down. His cheeks were flushed, his lashes damp.

"Can I interest anyone in a movie?" Brody said.

That night, the Shaw family binged the Marvel movies and ate popcorn, and didn't bring up poor Ailis once.

★ ★ ★

Sunday morning, Paislee went downstairs. Brody had once again slept on the couch with Wallace.

Grandpa's door was closed.

She heated the electric kettle for water and chose a Brodies tea bag.

She looked out the kitchen window Lydia had designed, eager to see her best friend today. It had been a rough few days.

Her phone dinged.

Not Lydia, but Mack. Her smile widened.

Are you awake?

Yes.

Can I bring you breakfast?

Yes. Brody and Grandpa are still sleeping so you have to be quiet. We can visit on the back porch.

She had space heaters and comfy blankets for the chairs.

While waiting for Mack, Paislee quickly brushed her teeth and combed her fine hair but opted to keep her flannel jammies and robe on.

She met Mack at the front door. Wallace understood that it wasn't playtime and greeted him with a tail wag and low woof.

"Morning," Mack murmured into her ear. He carried a bag of breakfast sarnies that had her stomach rumbling.

"Bacon?"

"And egg," Mack confirmed. "I brought extras for the others."

"Thoughtful. Let's take our feast outside." Paislee nodded toward Brody, who stirred restlessly on the couch.

Mack paused, his brow furrowed as he murmured, "Nightmares?"

"Aye."

She opened the back door, and they went out to the covered back porch. Wallace dashed down the steps to sniff around and make sure things hadn't changed since last night before returning to the porch.

Paislee flipped on the tower-style heater and handed Mack a

knitted throw for his lap. She sat next to him on the rocking bench, and he placed the bag of food on the low table, near the mugs of tea.

It was romantic, just them in the early fall morning. The trees retained their colorful leaves, squirrels chittered, and birds chirped. The ugly shed was hidden by Brody's goalie net. The clothesline had been ignored since she'd gotten her dream appliances.

"Maybe I should take the poles for the clothesline out," Paislee said, thinking aloud. "It would give Brody more room tae run."

"I'm happy tae help you," Mack said. "But I'm not especially handy."

"You have other skills." Mack happened to be one of the smartest men she knew. And he was an excellent kisser.

"Do I?" Mack chuckled as he opened the white bag and pulled out two sandwiches, along with napkins.

They were still learning about each other and she treasured every new thing. "Grayson's has the best breakfast sandwiches," she said with approval. "Brown sauce." She looked at Mack in alarm. "You do prefer the HP, yes?"

"Oh, aye," Mack said. "My palate isnae so refined that I've given it up for the ketchup and mustard sauce."

She bit into the delicious toasted white bread. "So good. They always have the perfect amount of bacon."

"Three rashers. Smoked." Mack watched her with an indulgent smile. "I am so besotted with you that I would give you half."

"You would?" Paislee leaned to him and kissed him. "That is true love. And I am so taken with you, Mack Zeffer, that I wouldn't accept it."

They finished their breakfast under a warm glow that had little to do with the heater.

"What's on the agenda for Sunday Funday?" Mack asked.

"We are going tae Lydia and Corbin's."

"I thought they were in Germany?"

"Oh—Corbin's dad had a heart attack."

"What?"

"Garrison is all right, in the hospital, but Lydia and Corbin were very concerned. They flew in last night." They hadn't had a chance to have a regular conversation as Mack had been busy working the Ailis investigation.

"I hope he's okay."

"Laird Smythe is a strong-willed man. His estate was targeted by the vandals on Halloween."

Mack nodded but didn't comment.

Had he known that already? Yet, Laird Smythe's heart attack had been a surprise. "Lydia said that he thinks of himself as a businessman more than a laird and the wanton destruction was shocking."

Mack remained silent.

Now Paislee was very curious as to why.

"The vandals had tacked up the unicorn pamphlet everywhere. Just like Lady Leery's place." Sorcha still hadn't shared. "Grandpa thinks the symbol might mean more coordinated efforts from the criminals." Paislee sipped her tea. "Do you know if there was vandalism like that at the Cawdor estate?"

Mack looked at his watch. He'd kept his phone in his pocket rather than have it out on the table, as Paislee had hers. "I suppose our pleasant idyll had tae end. It's only eight thirty. I have tae be at Cawdor at nine thirty for a coffee with the dowager countess. We are meeting at the new café."

"I've heard that the food is excellent there—Meri told me it had just opened. Some famous chef is running the place. Pat Amblin."

Mack patted his belly. "I'll be full after our breakfast, but I didnae want tae meet with her while hungry. She's . . . cunning. Which is fine—she's had tae be, I suppose. I will need all of my wits aboot me if I am going tae get answers aboot what happened that night other than what she wants tae tell me. This will be our second interview, and I've learned precious little."

"She was robbed, though. Surely she wants your help in getting back whatever was taken."

"That's the only reason she's granted this meeting." Mack readjusted the fluffy blanket so that it fit over both of their laps. Their shoulders touched, as did their thighs.

"Do you know what was taken besides the emerald found near Ailis?"

"The dowager countess hasnae given a precise list. She's barely admitted that there was a crime. She wants my help yet resents needing it."

"Doesn't she have a security crew?" Paislee reached for her tea, holding the cup.

"I've put in a request tae speak with Randall Fowler again," Mack said. "Because she had the fundraiser that night, the guards were spread thin. I felt sairy for them. First robbery in years. Wouldnae be surprised if they were all sacked."

After a fortifying sip, Paislee cleared her throat. "The ladies know about the robbery, though it hasn't been published in the paper anywhere."

Mack's brow rose. He reluctantly pulled his phone out of his inner pocket and opened an app. "How?"

"I heard that the Ramsey Castle grounds manager is friends with the gardener at Cawdor Castle." Paislee stared into her mug, closing the subject. "It's impossible tae keep a secret in Nairn."

"Unfounded rumors withoot a name attached tae the story dinnae help. Sure you cannae cite your sources?" Mack's eyes glittered with annoyance.

Paislee realized that his irritation was directed at the nobles, for keeping secrets, and not at her. Could she give up Sorcha or Shannon just yet? "I will ask, but for now, no."

"I can guess. You have lofty friends." Mack put his phone next to the empty wrapper. "And Lydia now a Lady as well."

"Don't let her hear you say that. It was almost a deal-breaker."

Her best friend hadn't been treated well by the Smythes. Corbin had promised it would never happen again, and it hadn't. Lydia commanded respect, even from Corbin's evil stepmother, who took superstition to another level.

"Lydia has a fair head on her shoulders," Mack said. "She willnae be turned by money or power. My point is that you have three such women in your corner."

"It's not always easy. Sometimes they want favors."

"Favors?"

"For example, Dowager Countess Sorcha wants me tae go tae her castle sometime and have lunch with the Dowager Countess of Cawdor, who sounds terrifying, and Lady Leery."

"Why?"

"Tae discover what happened Halloween night. I don't know why I need tae be included in these schemes."

"Sorcha Grant cannae just ask the DC, one countess tae another?"

"They must be afraid too," Paislee said with a chuckle. "I am not looking forward tae the meal and I hope that it doesn't happen."

"If you go, please, Paislee, be careful," Mack said.

"Of what? I am always cautious."

"Sometimes people in power trample the commoners withoot thinking." Mack's tone was light, but his gaze serious.

"Lady Leery introduced me tae Dowager Countess Grant and my fortunes have changed for the better, being able tae have my cashmere goods in the gift shop at the castle. It's not something I'm likely tae forget."

"It was savvy business on her part, as well as yours—not a favor but an even barter," Mack insisted. He reminded her of Lydia.

Paislee glanced at Mack. "I am grateful."

"But worthy. Dinnae forget that."

Paislee blushed.

Brody came out of the house to the back porch. "Morning," he mumbled groggily. "Why are you oot here?"

"We didn't want tae wake you." Paislee gestured to the enclosed porch and blankets. "Besides, it is cozy."

"It is." Brody shuffled to the armchair closest to the heater and sat down. Wallace left his spot by Paislee's feet to lie by Brody's. He'd put on slippers at least.

"Bacon sarnie?" Mack asked.

Brody grabbed a blanket. "Aye, please."

Mack handed him one from the bag.

"There are two more in here," Mack said. He looked at his watch and sipped his tea. "How are you feeling?"

Brody unwrapped the sandwich but then put it on the table. His eyes were shadowed. "Did you find oot what happened tae Ailis?"

"Not yet."

"Until you do, I am going tae continue tae feel terrible."

"Well, that adds pressure." Mack crumpled the empty sandwich wrapper into a tight ball. "Investigations take time."

Brody exhaled. "School tomorrow is going tae be awful, and Mum willnae let me stay home. I dinnae feel good."

"You have tae go," Paislee said. "It might be like when you went tae practice and things were better than you thought they were. Tae get it over with."

"I dinnae think so." Brody extended his legs and Wallace jumped up on his lap.

The pup rested his head on Brody's chest.

"Your mum is right. Sometimes facing a situation that is uncomfortable is better than dragging it oot."

"That's what Father Dixon said too." Brody leaned forward and picked off a small piece of bread.

"When was this? Was that Rooney person there?" Mack asked. "I ran his name through the system. He's had some speeding tickets."

"We were at dinner last night after the cemetery cleanup at the church hall. Father Dixon spent a lot of time yesterday with the Barclay family. Darryl feels guilty for what happened because him and Jimmy set it up." Brody's eyes flashed. "Set *me* up."

"It was a rough night. Rooney wasn't at dinner." Paislee glanced at Mack. Did he know Rooney Crowe personally?

"Darryl blamed me, though," Brody said. "Him and Jimmy."

"You were not responsible," Mack said firmly.

"What did you see on the video?" Brody asked. "Did it help at all?"

"It's still being examined by the specialist."

"Was it one person? Two? A ghost?" Brody patted Wallace's black fur.

"I dinnae ken," Mack said. "Doubtful a ghost, though."

"We heard several voices." Paislee looked from her son to Mack beside her. "Possibly three."

"It could've been an echo," Mack warned.

"Could it have been Blake Harrington, her boyfriend?" Paislee asked. She wanted to remind him to find the viral social media post of the pair arguing but Mack was answering her question.

"We dinnae ken. Blake is still at large," Mack replied.

"Waiting for answers is so hard," Brody said.

"It is." Mack's expression was filled with empathy. "Doesnae get easier as you get older either."

Brody fed the crumb to Wallace. "Older is supposed tae make you wiser."

Paislee didn't berate her son for feeding their dog, as Brody was miserable. Very miserable if he couldn't eat a bacon sarnie from Grayson's.

"I've heard that before," Mack said.

"Mum's birthday is on Wednesday. She should be verra wise now that she's over thirty." Brody's droll tone had her chuckling.

"Do you have plans for your birthday?" Mack asked.

"Not really. Maybe?" Paislee looked at Brody, who shrugged. "I think Lydia was planning something, but now that her father-in-law is in the hospital, I don't know that we feel like celebrating. Ailis, too."

"Life continues and the hard part is celebrating life because death happens. Makes those special days more important. Trust me on that," Mack said. "In my career I've seen a lot of heartbreak. Each day I choose tae look for something guid."

"Every day?" Brody asked.

"Every day. Sometimes it's harder than others."

Wallace woofed.

"I didn't know you did that," Paislee said. "Brody mentioned just yesterday about realizing that we are all responsible for our choices." Her heart filled with love.

"Scotland is a moody land of highs and lows, but I love it, in my soul. I hike, or go intae nature. Push myself mentally and physically. Being a detective inspector lets me use my mind tae solve puzzles." Mack tapped his temple.

Brody nodded with understanding.

How had she gotten so lucky?

Paislee reached for Brody's hand and squeezed.

Mack tossed the sandwich wrapper into the open white bag.

"Brody, I promise that I will solve the tangled web of what happened tae Ailis. You can count on me."

Chapter 8

Brody perked up at Mack's promise to find answers to what had happened to Ailis. Paislee believed the DI, and so did Brody.

She released Brody's hand and sat back, accidentally jostling Mack's elbow. "Sorry."

"Dinnae be." Mack's expression was one of regret, as if he wished he could stay here on the back porch all morning. "Listen, I've got tae leave, or I might be late for my appointment at Cawdor Castle with the dowager countess." He stood. "She has information for me that will be key."

"Thanks for the sarnies," Brody said. Wallace jumped from his lap to the porch and waited at the door. Her son grabbed the bag of sandwiches.

They all went inside. Paislee walked Mack to the front stoop to get the paper and shared a sweet kiss goodbye. The window curtain across the street twitched. Nosy Mrs. Florence. Had to be one of the worst gossips on the block.

"Good luck today, Mack." Paislee held her fingers to her lips, marveling at the tingle, and the speeding of her heart.

"I am rather determined tae find oot what the DC is hiding, and if it will pertain tae the case." Mack kept his back to Mrs. Florence's window. "We have an audience?"

At Paislee's mute nod of embarrassment, Mack kissed her again.

"She will need tae get used tae it. We are doing nothing wrong." Mack stared into her eyes with promise and love.

Paislee rose on her tiptoes to kiss Mack, enjoying his pleased chuckle as she dashed inside with the paper.

She shuffled to the table in a daze.

Grandpa, freshly showered, joined them and reheated the sandwiches from Mack, for him and Brody. There were two for Brody, of course. Paislee's stomach was jumping with excitement, and she could barely manage to sip her tea.

"Grand of Mack tae drop off breakfast," Grandpa said.

"It was," she agreed, not wanting to talk too much and burst this ridiculous bubble of joy.

They read the paper. No new news about Ailis, but Darcey McClintock had a piece about the vandals on Halloween and how everything had been in sync. The lion being trampled by the unicorn pamphlets had been tacked on doors or fences, and *SAORSA* spray-painted everywhere.

"What do they want?" Grandpa asked. "With this kind of cohesion, there should be a message or a call to action."

The pamphlets had been words of caution. "Maybe you can help them get organized," Paislee teased.

"Grandpa can be a rebel instead of a Labourer."

"Rebel is not a government faction," Grandpa countered, smoothing his beard like a movie villain. "That sounds like anarchy."

"Extremes are rarely good for anybody." Paislee read the last bit of the entertainment section, reminded of the fundraiser for the farmer on Cawdor property. Paislee shared the story with Brody. "He just needs assistance until he heals from an accident."

"Highland cows?" Brody nodded. "What kind of help?"

"I can find out more." Paislee's phone dinged. "Ach, a command lunch with the DC at Ramsey Castle." She didn't protest and sent her RSVP. Yes. Noon. Monday.

"What time are we leaving for Aunt Lydia's?"

"Let me find out. Their flight was late last night." Paislee sent off a message asking about what time and what they could bring.

The answer was immediate.

1:00

Your appetite.

"That's not a problem," Paislee said. All three Shaws enjoyed eating. "We can pick up flowers from Ritchie's on the way. I think they'll be staying in Nairn a while. A bouquet is always nice."

She sent another text about Corbin's dad and got a thumbs-up.

They spent a pleasant half hour on a video call with her mom and her half siblings. Family mattered. Brody didn't bring up the dead Ailis or being pranked, but kept the conversation on Josh and Natalie and trick-or-treating, then All Saints' Day, and the tradition of cleaning the cemetery to honor the dead on All Souls' Day. Her mother had taken part in the ceremony when she'd lived here.

"Will you want tae be buried in America, Grandma Rosanna?" Brody asked. "We have loads of room in the Shaw plot. You can be next tae Grandpa Bruce."

Her mother coughed in surprise. "Sweet of you, Brody, but I will be laid to rest here, with my husband and kids." Her mother then had to explain to her children about the November 2nd All Souls' Day tradition of cleaning the cemetery for your ancestors.

"That sounds creepy," Josh said. "And really great! I'd do it."

"I don't like to be scared," Natalie said.

"Scotland is full of cemeteries," her mother said, as if warning her daughter away from the entire country.

"History," Paislee countered.

They wound up the chat with a promise to call later.

"On Mum's birthday," Brody said.

"Is that coming up?" Rosanna asked, her lips twitching.

Josh started to say something, and Natalie covered his mouth and then ended the call.

Paislee laughed happily at her siblings' antics.

Last year at this time, she'd had no idea of the surprises to come from a relationship with her mother, and half brother, and half sister; from telling Brody about his dad, Calan Maxwell. From a dream kitchen. But most wonderful of all, had been falling in love for the first time in her life with Detective Inspector Mack Zeffer.

"Grandpa, we have tae go shopping. I have money saved for you-know-what." Brody hooked his thumb toward Paislee.

"Nothing big, you guys." Paislee couldn't imagine a single thing that she wanted. She had everything. "Let's find out what Lydia has planned."

Brody gave her a side hug. "Love you, Mum." He dashed up the stairs while Paislee's mouth gaped.

"What was that for?" Paislee wondered aloud.

Grandpa chuckled. "That little boy is still in there. It's nice tae see, eh?"

"You're so right."

Still practically floating from the morning of surprises, Paislee dressed for the day in a fall sweater and a long skirt in brown plaid. She brushed Wallace, who had been invited too, and put an orange and brown collar on him.

They arrived at the Barron-Smythe house with a giant bouquet for Lydia and Corbin. Brody had used the new brown-and-orange lead for Wallace.

"Aunt Lydia lives in a mansion," Brody said once they'd driven down the long, paved driveway toward the giant house.

It was true that Lydia and Corbin's forever-together home was on a luxurious estate with a view of the ocean from the top floor. It wasn't as near to the Moray Firth as Lydia's condo had been. Mack had bought it from her and paid in cash.

Mack's mother had been a whiz with Mack's earnings as a child model after his da had been killed in a suspicious oil rig accident. Her investments had allowed them a good life. He spoke of her, and his favorite sister, with love. His mum's death had sent him into a depression that his sister stood by him through.

Life had been full of tragedies, as he'd said, but also joy.

It was important to celebrate the wins.

She tried to imagine their future together—where would they live? Would Mack be comfortable moving into her place?

Paislee couldn't imagine leaving it as there were many memories with her gran and Brody as a baby, and now Grandpa. It was more than four walls and a roof, but a home.

She loved the condo, with the view of the dolphins and the gray waters of the Atlantic. The wind dancing across the waves. The heated enclosed balcony where she and Mack had snuggled.

They were taking things very slow, and Paislee enjoyed each kiss. The condo wasn't her home.

Maybe Brody would marry someday and want to be in the Shaw house with his wife? His family? She put a halt to those thoughts as they went nowhere.

Paislee parked next to the Barron sedan that had a cute paw print decal on the bumper. Sophie and Alistair, and their dog, Baxter, were already here.

Lydia raced out of the house, which was an older home that had been completely refurbished. The best of old and new. The first of many marital compromises.

"Shaws!" Lydia, tall and thin, her charcoal eyes gleaming, hugged them all separately, and then together, pulling Paislee up the six steps to the porch. It was open and wrapped around the house.

Inside, the interior was bright and airy.

To the left of the marble foyer was a sitting room, open now to show Lydia's parents, Sophie and Alistair; Corbin; and Simon Sinclair, a good friend to Corbin and Lydia as well as the best mate to the Thane of Cawdor. Fifty, trim, and with thick auburn hair, he wore a tailored suit complete with tie.

Baxter, a sassy Maltese mix the Barrons had rescued after their previous pup had passed, hurried toward Wallace. The pair were friends and sniffed around each other. Wallace, though bigger, didn't play rough. Amelia's little Snowball was about the same size as Baxter.

"Welcome," Corbin said, holding out his hand to shake Grandpa's, then Brody's, then offered Paislee a hug.

She hugged him back, looking into his anguished brown eyes. He had ebony hair and was normally clean-shaven. Not today, though. Scruff layered his jaw.

"How's your dad?"

"Fine. Stubborn. Left the hospital withoot being discharged. I needn't tell you that my stepmother is losing what's left of her mind aboot it. She's called her psychic friend, who said that Da needs tae wear some kind of amulet."

"Rose quartz, for the heart chakra," Lydia said.

"It's supposed tae be verra helpful," Sophie said in her positive way. "It certainly cannae hurt. It's terrible tae feel so hopeless."

"Let me put them over here." Lydia brought the artistic bouquet to the tall sofa table. "These are gorgeous. Flowers just lighten the mood!"

Paislee noticed dark shadows beneath her bestie's eyes, proof that she hadn't slept very well either.

It was a lot to coordinate: a winery, a house, and an ill father-in-law along with house guests, even if it was your own parents.

"Paislee, Brody, Angus," Simon said, greeting them with a polite smile that didn't reach his eyes. "What a nightmare this has all been. The thane is torn up."

"About Ailis's death?" Paislee asked.

Simon paled. "Aboot the break-in. The lass's death too," he quickly added.

Brody bristled. "I think a dead person is more important than some stolen . . . whatever it is that was stolen. We still arenae clear. An emerald?"

"You're right!" Simon said. "I didnae really know the Barclays. Sairy tae sound careless. I've been in conversation with the thane, but the Dowager Countess of Cawdor has been giving me the cold shoulder. I dinnae know anything aboot an emerald."

"An emerald was discovered on Ailis's clothes," Paislee explained. "It's why the constables are concerned she might have been part of the thieves."

Brody unclipped Wallace's lead from his collar to free the pup, who stayed at Brody's side.

"It was my fault that the castle was open tae visitors," Simon said.

"How so?" Lydia's father, Alistair, asked. The man stood by his wife, who was seated on an armchair. His hair was dark and his clothes plain, but good quality. He held a tumbler of amber liquid. Baxter lay at Sophie's feet on a tiny blue dog bed made of plush fabric. Sophie had explained that this gave their dog, who traveled with them when possible, his own space. If in doubt, Baxter had his cushion.

"The DC and the thane always keep the castle closed while the DC is in residence from the fall through the spring. Guarding the home and protecting the branch."

"The branch?" Sophie asked in surprise. She and Lydia shared a love of fashion, and her pink pantsuit was custom-made. Her smooth bobbed hair had been dyed brick-red.

"The sacred holly branch," Simon said. He repeated the rhyme Paislee had heard from her noble ladies. "So long as the branch is in the tower, the Thanes of Cawdor will remain in power."

"The Dowager Countess of Ramsey shared that she'd learned that rhyme in primary school," Paislee said. It was inspiring that the Cawdor/Campbell family could trace its origins to one location.

"The Cawdors have been in power for almost a thousand years," Simon continued. "That is documented. Before then probably too."

"That's a long time," Brody said.

"The Campbells kidnapped Muriel Calder, which is now Cawdor, when she was an infant. One of the sons married her and ensured the line," Grandpa said. "And the fortress."

"That's how things were done," Corbin said. "Not a heroic practice in hindsight. But, Muriel went along with the marriage tae John, ensuring the safety of the holly tree, protected in the tower."

"I've seen the artifact." Alistair shook his head. "Sairy tae tell ye this, Corbin, but it's a dead branch."

"Petrified now, yes, and documented to 1367." Corbin nodded at Simon. "Still there. So long as the branch is in the tower, the Thanes of Cawdor will retain their power."

Brody murmured the poem with the men. *So long as the branch is in the tower, the thanes shall remain in power.*

"It was alive and there is magic in it still," Simon said with a straight expression. "I think someone tried tae steal it on All Hallows' Eve."

"Come, sit doon," Lydia said, gesturing to Paislee, Brody, and Grandpa, her tone annoyed with her husband's friend. "Simon, I know you're upset, but they havenae even taken their jackets off yet."

Simon flushed an ugly crimson at being called out by his hostess. He dipped his head. "My apologies."

A man in a subdued brown suit came to take their coats. Paislee removed hers and followed the butler as he said, "They will be here when you are ready tae leave again."

The closet was the size of Paislee's bedroom and perfectly organized for boots, coats, hats, umbrellas, and wellies. What a setup!

"Thanks!"

Returning to the lounge, Paislee sat on the sofa next to Grandpa and Brody. Wallace stayed near Brody's feet.

Corbin handed out whisky to those who wanted it. Lydia, Paislee, and Sophie opted for a crisp white champagne. It was quite delicious, which meant expensive.

Brody had a fizzy water in a crystal glass.

"Next year at this time, we will be drinking our own brand from Smythe Winery," Corbin said. "Slainte!" Everyone had a sip.

"So, you believe that the holly branch is magical?" Brody asked Simon. Her son was undeterred by the paranormal element. When one had a unicorn for the country's mascot, well, the supernatural was part of daily life.

Paislee sipped her champagne.

"Aye, I do," Simon said. "You've heard of the castle being haunted by a woman in a blue medieval gown?"

Brody shivered. "Muriel." He raised his palm. "I've had enough of haunts tae last forever."

Simon swirled the amber liquid in his tumbler as he shared, "On Halloween, Muriel set off the alarm around the branch." He lifted his angst-filled gaze.

"Are you sure someone wasnae playing a trick?" Alistair asked. He and Sophie had an insurance business in Edinburgh where Sophie did the accounting.

"It wasnae a prank," Simon said. "I've seen the footage. The thane warned me that the DC is holding a grudge aboot the break-in."

"Muriel the ghost is on film?" Grandpa asked with suspicion.

It was unusual for a sighting to be documented.

"Not clearly, but there is a blur of blue and suddenly the motion lights went off and activated the alarm." Simon drank his whisky. Corbin topped it off.

"I want tae see it," Alistair said. Sophie made a humming noise which could be taken for anything from approval to doubt.

Lydia surveyed her guests from her seat next to Corbin, calculating the mood. She sat back after evidently deciding things were fine.

"Me too," Brody said. "I bet it's a trick."

Grandpa patted Brody's shoulder in commiseration.

Paislee set her champagne down on the side table. "I'd like tae compare it tae the video that Brody caught on his mobile the other night."

"You have ghosts on film too?" Simon's tone rose.

"We aren't sure what we've got," Paislee said. Could the image in the trees be a spirit? Or a person in a mask? Or...moss.

"Let's absolutely compare notes as well as footage." Simon stepped toward the threshold of the lounge as if ready to do so immediately.

"I'll need to wait. The constables have Brody's mobile as he may have the last footage of Ailis before she died," Paislee said. "She was dressed as the Wraith of Rait Ruins."

"A trick. Did you show yours tae the constables?" Brody asked. "DI Zeffer was at Cawdor earlier tae talk tae the dowager countess."

"The thane and the DC didnae want tae. Since I had already pressured them aboot the fundraiser and opening the house, I am persona non grata and cannae push. 'Tis brutal knowing I let doon one of my best mates." Simon's shoulders bowed.

Brody patted Wallace, dozing by Brody's feet. "I feel like that aboot my friend Darryl."

"Who's that?" Lydia asked. "Have we met him?"

"Mibbe at a football game." Brody shrugged. "Darryl is Ailis's brother. Ailis died at Rait Ruins, setting up a prank on me."

Corbin walked to Brody and kneeled so they were eye to eye. "I heard the older kids do that tae the younger ones they think are cool. I'm sairy aboot Ailis, and the Barclays. It's terrible all around."

"Thanks." Brody held Corbin's gaze. "I'm glad your da is better."

"Me too. We've got tae find the vandals responsible. Everyone was in costume because it was Halloween." Corbin stood to his full height and looked at Simon. "The break-in that night during the fundraiser, on a night where people were dressed up. Intentional?"

"Mibbe. The guests are wealthy members of society and even though the fundraiser was a last-minute invite, most treated it as a pre-party tae other Halloween festivities, as it was done by nine. Over ten thousand pounds was raised tae help the farmer injured on the property two weeks ago." Simon stared into his tumbler. "The DC insisted it had tae be soon, as November and December are for Christmas."

Paislee swirled her champagne. Was two weeks enough to plan a heist?

Corbin realized that their party was short one. "Where is Mack?"

"Working," Paislee said.

"He might still be at Cawdor Castle talking with the DC." Brody kept patting his dog's head. "She's not being open with him."

"The head of security is a man named Randall Fowler. He and I dinnae get along. He hates me, and this fiasco is adding fuel tae the fire." Simon sighed. "If the thane has tae choose between me and the DC? I'm gone."

That matched what Sorcha had told her, and what Mack knew. Investigations went smoother if everyone had the same information.

"Do you know if the castle was vandalized outside as well as the theft inside?" Paislee would gather as much news as possible before the meeting at Sorcha's.

"I dinnae," Simon said. "The thane and I spoke with Pat Amblin at length yesterday at dinner. He didnae mention it. Of course, we were talking aboot a different subject entirely."

"Pat Amblin, the chef?" Corbin asked. He and Lydia were big foodies, so Paislee wasn't surprised that he would know of the man.

"Yes, that was a lucky score for Cawdor, and the food at the fundraiser was amazing. Pat's sauces are divine. His girlfriend, Poppy Drummond, manages the brand-new hotel by the golf course with an incredible rooftop bar. Oasis. She invited us tae drop by anytime this week for a whisky tasting."

"I'm in," Alistair said.

"You werenae invited," Sophie said, appalled.

"You are all invited," Simon said. "Monday afternoon at four. I let her know that Corbin and Lydia would be back, and she wants tae meet you both. She said you could bring friends and family. I like her."

"Like her, like her?" Corbin asked.

"No. I *respect* her," Simon said. "She's young enough tae be my daughter."

Not something that always mattered when wealth and men were entwined.

"Simon did say Poppy was Pat's girlfriend, Uncle Corbin," Brody said.

"My mind must've been on the subject of whisky." Corbin shrugged both shoulders theatrically.

Grandpa raised his empty tumbler. "Can I horn in?"

"All of you are invited," Simon repeated with assurance. "It will be a grand time."

"I'm . . ." Paislee began to say, about to make her excuses.

"Paislee, dinnae even think aboot backing oot," Lydia said. "I want you tae be there too. The hotel is next tae the arcade and Brody will be oot of school by then. Three thirty, right?"

"He likes tae be picked up at four tae give him time tae talk with his mates," Grandpa said. "Right, Brody?"

"Not tomorrow." Brody concentrated on petting the space between Wallace's ears.

"Fine." Paislee realized she wasn't going to get out of it and gave in. "Elspeth is working tomorrow, and she is a pro at helping Rhona close." Business at the shop had been slow. "Meri said that the food at the new Cawdor Café is incredible."

"We should go for lunch, us girls," Lydia said. "This week."

"Mum is already supposed tae have lunch with the ladies, so she's busy tomorrow," Brody said, throwing her under the bus. "Mibbe later this week?"

Paislee blushed. "Honey!"

"And, Aunt Lydia, what are the plans for Mum's birthday?" Brody leaned his arm on the cushioned armrest of the sofa.

And she wished she could melt into the floor. She arched her brow at Brody, but he pointedly was not looking at her.

"I have something up my sleeve, but I'll need tae talk tae you and Angus aboot it in private." Lydia sipped her champagne, waggling her brows. She quickly set it aside.

"No surprises!" Paislee said. "I can't take them now that I'm over thirty."

Everyone chuckled.

"I love being in my thirties," Lydia declared. "It's empowering."

"I liked my forties best," Sophie said.

"And fifty isnae bad." Simon read his phone. "Poppy will give us a private room for twenty tomorrow. She's a brilliant businesswoman, like you, Lydia."

"That's important tae thrive," Lydia said. "I'm sure I will like her too. Any chance she knits? We could use another tae fill my space."

"You don't knit but you bake, Lyd. And nobody could take your place." Paislee smiled at her best friend.

Simon acknowledged Paislee with a slight nod. "We can ask." He surveyed the room with approval. "The Thane of Cawdor has had revitalizing Nairn on his agenda for decades. This new energy is exactly what he wanted. It's not for fame or money that he works so tirelessly but because, like Muriel Campbell, he believes in this community."

"The ghost?" Brody asked.

"Aye. Though kidnapped as a babe, she still married John Campbell and protected the holly tree," Simon said. "Her merging of Calder, or Cawdor, with the Campbells ensured the castle remained strong."

Paislee didn't share Sorcha's theory that Muriel haunted Cawdor because she'd lived and died to keep it safe.

"The thane is a guid man," Corbin said. "What's this aboot a new law he'd like tae suggest?"

"There's a petition going around tae regulate the fireworks," Simon said. "I've been helping him with it, but it hasnae been supported by many who fear they will lose their rights tae have their own fireworks."

The butler in his subdued brown suit entered and announced that lunch was ready.

Paislee followed them to the formal dining room that was inviting rather than imposing. Lydia had a wonderful gift for design.

"You've hardly touched your champagne," Paislee said. "It's so delicious I'm on my second glass."

"I've been so worried aboot Corbin and his dad that I didnae sleep. I cannae really eat. And I havenae been able tae bake, which is my go-tae stress relief." Lydia peered at Paislee with widened eyes filled with worry. "This house is too damn big. There are too many people in it. The responsibility of being a lady . . . it is too much."

"Oh, Lydia."

"We need tae do a girls' lunch, you, me, and Mum. I feel like I'm aboot ready tae snap."

"Tell me when."

"Tomorrow?" Lydia grabbed her wrist.

"I have a lunch at Ramsey Castle."

"That's right. Brody said you were busy. He's adorable and I've missed him." Lydia arched her brow knowingly. "Why are you going?"

"The noble ladies are worried about the vandals. There is more tae it that I can't get intae right now." Paislee was used to telling Lydia everything, but it was harder to share over weekly phone dates and rushed text messages.

"Tuesday then?"

"Maybe. I can't make a firm date until we know more about Ailis."

"That's okay." Lydia hugged Paislee tight. "I've missed you."

"Lyd?" Corbin called.

"Coming!" Lydia's smile was bright and without a care as she joined her husband.

No matter how hard Paislee tried, she was unable to get her bestie alone the rest of the day, as if Lydia was avoiding her.

Chapter 9

Leaving after the delicious champagne and late lunch, Paislee had been in a mellow mood on Sunday evening.

Brody had called it a food coma. It was apt. The Shaw family had relaxed on the couch, watching movies.

At half past eight, Brody lobbied hard to stay home the next day. They'd argued and finally the mellow mood had burst.

Paislee had been very firm with him, though she was tempted to give in and allow him to stay home for a mental health day. She made the parental choice to send him to school and have him face his fears head-on.

Lydia didn't return her calls or texts, and Paislee was worried about her best friend, who was also completely overwhelmed. However, Sophie was an amazing mother, and Paislee was very glad she was there staying with Lydia and Corbin for moral support.

Simon had never answered her question about whether or not the grounds at Cawdor had been vandalized like the others. They hadn't exchanged emails yesterday, but she had his phone number from when they were on the Highland Games committee.

She sent Mack a text at nine, wishing him a good night.

He answered without giving much detail that he'd stop by later. But, later, he texted that he was caught up with something and would see her Monday.

She woke up the next day cross and at odds with herself. She tripped over her own feet, banging her knee on the bedpost.

"Ouch!"

Brody was in the shower and so didn't hear her. Just as well, as the *ouch* had been followed by several inventive curse words that would have disappointed her granny.

Over breakfast, Grandpa offered to loan Brody his mobile for the day, but Brody declined. "I dinnae want it, thanks. I will get a new one when the DI finds oot what happened tae Ailis."

"I see." Grandpa cleared his throat and returned to reading the paper. There was nothing in it pertaining to the death of the young lady, or the vandals who had attacked the nobles' estates with graffiti.

"Maybe Darcey has the day off," Paislee said grumpily.

"I feel safe in wishing you both a guid day," Grandpa said. "It can only get better. Both of you in blue moods!"

After dropping a silent and brooding Brody off at school, she drove to Cashmere Crush. Rhona was there and sitting on the back stoop watching something on her mobile.

"Paislee, you will never believe this." Rhona was dressed in denim coveralls with a flannel shirt and designer trainers, her brunette hair in braids on either side of her oval face.

"What is it?" She thought of the social media post of Blake and Ailis's argument that Rooney said had gone viral.

"You know the guy they've been looking for, Blake Harrington, Ailis's boyfriend?" Rhona tossed a braid over her shoulder.

"Yes." Paislee sat next to Rhona, who hadn't gotten up, to see the video. "Did they find him? Rooney from church told me they'd argued, and he'd kicked her out of her own car."

"No, not that one. I've seen it though. Epically brutal. This is new, from this morning. Blake claims the constables are going tae set him up. He doesnae know what happened tae Ailis. Watch!" Rhona hit the play button on the video.

A handsome, buff, twenty-year-old man who exuded university-boy charisma flashed his white teeth. "The constables are trying tae frame me!"

"Where was this filmed?" Paislee asked.

"It was live this morning. He's around the harbor somewhere, or he was. He had Ailis's car. If he was smart, he ditched it."

"What if he hurt her somehow?" Paislee asked. They still didn't have the cause of death for the young woman.

"Unless he did that." Rhona's eyes widened. "Then he should be caught. He totally left her—taking his girlfriend's car and stranding her at the ruins."

"He's not one of the good guys," Paislee said.

"Nope." Rhona shrugged. "*If* he did that. Not cool. I hate tae judge someone if it turns oot tae not be true."

"I wonder if Mack has seen this, or the other constables?" Paislee stood and wiped dirt from her pants.

"We could show them." Rhona shook her phone. "Want me tae run tae the station?"

"Sure. I'll get us open. That might be crucial information."

"On it!" Rhona stood and raced with all of her youthful dancing athleticism down the steps and alley, past Scoops on the corner, to the station that was to the right a few blocks.

If Paislee had tried that, she would have passed out.

She went in and opened up the store, making sure to water the marigolds in the flower box at the front of the shop on Market Street.

Rhona returned a half hour later with a pretty blonde who had big blue eyes and an upturned nose. The two were chatting like old friends. The woman was maybe thirty to Rhona's nineteen, but they had the same vibrant energy. Paislee's thirty was dodgy in comparison.

"Paislee, this is Marion McGinty."

"Hi," Paislee said. "Nice tae meet you."

Paislee had dressed for the fall weather in a bulky sweater. Marion, slender but strong, had on black running shoes and jogging togs that left little to the imagination. Between Rhona and Marion, Paislee knew she should find time in her packed schedule for a gym.

"I'm here with my husband, visiting from Glasgow, and oot for a morning jog. I'd asked for a local breakfast place Rhona might recommend, and we ended up talking."

"I'm a chatterbox," Rhona said.

"It's cute!" Marion patted Rhona's shoulder.

"What did you decide?" Paislee asked.

Marion balanced on the toes of her running shoes and then rocked back as she scanned the shop with interest. "For?"

"Breakfast."

"Oh, well, Rhona suggested Grayson's but I'm a veggie girl." Marion scrunched her nose. "I'll probably find a juice place for a protein smoothie."

"Give up bacon?" Rhona said in mock horror.

"I couldn't do it." Paislee grinned at Marion. "I know you're going tae be healthier and live longer but I'm willing tae trade a few years tae eat bacon."

Marion burst out laughing. "I've had it. I understand. It's a choice, for sure. What do you do here?" She perused the shelves filled with all colors and styles of yarn.

"I sell bespoke sweaters and knitted goods. We pride ourselves on carrying yarn that has been sourced humanely."

"You are not blind tae the earth's plight," Marion said.

"No. I am doing what I can. Giving up bacon?" Paislee shook her head.

"Long life is not a guarantee," Marion said sadly. "We read in the paper aboot that puir university lass. Have the coppers caught who did it?"

"Not yet," Rhona said.

"They will," Paislee said with assurance. The last thing the Thane of Cawdor would want was a drop in the tourist industry.

"Paislee and Brody were at the ruins that night. They found Ailis," Rhona said.

"You were?" Marion reached out for Paislee with compassion and touched her hand.

"We were. It's really upset Brody. He didn't want tae go tae school or anything today, but I made him, for his own good."

"But then he gets tae go tae the arcade this afternoon," Rhona said. "Paislee is the best mum, balancing rules with fun."

"I love the claw game." Marion curled her fingers.

"I'm no good at it." Paislee hadn't spent her free time at the arcade but reset at the beach, collecting sea glass.

"There's a system and once you crack it, it's easy," Marion said.

Paislee's business phone rang, and she left Marion with Rhona. "Cashmere Crush!"

Rhona showed Marion the rows of sweater vests, jumpers, and cashmere. The young woman was very animated. It made sense that she was a runner.

"I'll be back tomorrow with an idea of what I want tae make," Marion said. "Bye, Rhona and Paislee. I hope your boy feels better. Rhona said he got footage of that night? No wonder he's puirly."

"We'll see if anything comes of it. Until tomorrow, then." Paislee picked up the latest project she'd been working on, a beige scarf in a mermaid pattern, and got to work.

The morning was busy, and Paislee was tempted to cancel the meeting with the noble ladies at Ramsey Castle. Mary Beth was in to visit and bought aqua-blue yarn for her daughter Iona, who had flown through the coin purse project and wanted something else, but didn't stay long.

She received simultaneous texts from Shannon and Sorcha at 11:30.

Sorcha: **New plan—noon, at Cawdor Café.**

Shannon: **Don't be late. Wear a dress!**

She showed the texts to Rhona and Elspeth, slightly in a panic.

"I don't have time tae change clothes. As it is, traffic tae Cawdor takes longer than Ramsey Castle."

"You should leave right away," Rhona said. "You will barely have time."

"You can borrow one of the cashmere shawls from the display!" Elspeth handed a pretty cocoa colored soft shawl to Paislee.

It really did dress up her khakis.

"Are you meeting the DC of Cawdor?" Rhona asked.

"Maybe. I'd better bring her a gift. But I don't have anything for the other ladies."

Her staff came to the rescue with knitted fall pumpkins she'd made for table decorations. Each lady received a trio in a gift bag.

"This is perfect," Elspeth said. "Please, drive safe."

"Thank you," Paislee said.

Rhona walked her out the back door to the Juke. "Have fun! I want the scoop if Pat Amblin is as cute in person as he was on TV."

Paislee put the gifts in the car along with her handbag and drove to Cawdor Café. The memory of Meri's recommendation of the food had her mouth watering.

She was ten minutes late, but they would have to handle it, considering she'd just gotten the change of venue, and she wasn't a lady of leisure.

None of the nobles she'd met were ladies of leisure, which meant they were bossy but hardworking. Who would be in control of the lunch? Sorcha and Shannon both had strong personalities.

Paislee parked in the separate lot for the café after entering the castle grounds. Ramsey Castle was impressive, as was Leery Estate. Cawdor Castle was just that little bit more.

The gardens were lush, and impressive. Sorcha's garden was more for utility, but Shannon had pleasure in mind when she'd designed hers.

She couldn't wait to hear what Sorcha and Shannon would say afterward. Also, what would the Dowager Countess of Cawdor be like?

Mack had been MIA other than a *good morning and have a nice day* text. No information. This meant that he was still involved with things he couldn't share with her.

He wouldn't take the promise made to Brody lightly.

The building resembled a medieval stone cottage, with a

thatched roof and a sign outside that swung from a newel post. It read, CAWDOR CAFÉ. CHEF, PAT AMBLIN.

There was status in his being here for both the chef and the DC. Celebrity chefs were sought after in higher end venues and hotels.

Paislee, juggling the three gifts as well as her handbag, entered the dining room and recognized Pat Amblin, handsome like a young Bobby Flay, holding court over Lady Leery, and the dowager countesses—plural.

All of this ego in one place.

It should have been too much, but it wasn't—no, it was just right. Pat's easy charm made her welcome. He included her as if she wasn't the most common thing in the room besides the cottage stone floor.

"Hello, everyone. Apologies for being late," she said.

"I warned them that timeliness was not your strong suit," Sorcha said with a friendly smile.

"I was worrit that you werenae going tae come at all. Better late than never." Shannon had the nerve to wink.

"We have never met." The DC of Cawdor dipped her white head. "I'm Dowager Countess Cawdor." There was no invitation to call her by her first name, Angelika.

"Paislee Shaw." She sat down at the only available seat at the table for four. She should have brought something for the chef as well, but hadn't realized he'd be part of the experience today. Should she keep the gifts back?

"And I'm Chef Pat Amblin. I'll supervise in the kitchen, coming in and oot tae check on your meals. I've prepared a sampling of dishes from my world-famous tasting menu."

Chef Amblin wasn't cocky, just stating a fact.

Paislee swallowed, her mouth watering at the tease.

The conversation was centered around the café, and the chef, and it wasn't until dessert that the energy calmed a little. Their full bellies had them satiated.

Over tiny cups of espresso, Sorcha said, "You have my admiration, dearest. Trust you tae come oot of this with your head high."

"What does that mean?" The DC of Cawdor glanced at Paislee before returning her steely gaze to Sorcha.

"We can speak freely," Sorcha murmured. "Paislee was the one who discovered that puir dear girl, Ailis Barclay, on Halloween night."

"You did? If she was part of the group tae rob us, we will press charges against the family," the DC said firmly. Though in her eighties there wasn't so much as a wobble in her tone.

"I didn't know Ailis well," Paislee said. "Our families go tae the same church."

"Church of Scotland?"

"St. Bridget's Church."

"Catholic?" Her chin trembled.

"Yes. Born and raised. My son, Brody, too." She sipped the espresso. Normally she found coffee too bitter, but this was perfection after the meal.

"Paislee's grandmother taught her tae never talk aboot religion or politics," Shannon said in a light tone.

"Did I ask her political affiliation?" the DC of Cawdor inquired haughtily.

"You did not," Sorcha said.

"I don't mind answering, even if it isn't popular," Paislee said. Her vote, like her religion, was her choice. She was not ashamed of either.

"Please tell me you are not part of the green movement," the DC of Cawdor said. "You have a hippy air around you."

"Lib Dem," Paislee said, allowing her mouth to lift in a smile.

"Like my nieces," the older woman scoffed. "It could be worse. I have a second cousin who is a proud member of the SNP. He's been jealous of the Cawdor land and title his whole life."

Chef Amblin stopped by their table, taking off his apron to sit next to Paislee. "And how was your meal?"

"Delicious. My friend Meri stopped by here and raved over it. She was spot-on."

"What was your favorite?" He sat close to her, in a flirty way, but she didn't take it personally. It was probably his personality.

"I couldn't pick," Paislee said.

"I preferred the savory sauces tae the sweet," Sorcha said. "But that is my boring palate, not the fault of your craftsmanship. Have you thought of bottling them for sale?"

Shannon sucked in a shocked breath that Sorcha would discuss business at the table.

The DC of Cawdor raised a brow at the chef. "Would you?"

"I could, I suppose. If that was all right with you? Cawdor Café Condiments?" Pat Amblin's mouth twisted. "Not that. My girlfriend, Poppy, was asking aboot something like that as well. Why not make use of this name I've built a career with?" He shrugged, but appeared thoughtful.

"Poppy, who manages the Oasis Hotel?" Paislee asked. It was a lovely if unusual name. "We're meeting her this afternoon."

"You are? Why is that?" Pat Amblin's gaze narrowed.

"A whisky tasting." Paislee kept her tone light. "I'm close with Lydia and Corbin Barron-Smythe and we were all at a lunch yesterday. Simon Sinclair was included, as he and Corbin are also good friends."

"Related tae Laird Garrison Smythe..." The DC studied Paislee closely. "There are more Smythes in this shire than Highland cows, and that's something. Guid stock. Why the hyphen for their surnames?"

"It was important tae Lydia and Corbin that she be considered equal." Paislee rubbed shoulders with nobles but that didn't mean she herself was snobby. If she'd been born to money, she imagined she'd be more like Sorcha. She didn't share the news of Garrison's heart attack, and the reason Lydia and Corbin had returned to Nairn, or how awful Lydia had been treated before their wedding.

"Lydia is a savvy estate agent who donates time and money to various local causes," Shannon announced, as if protecting Lydia from any possible disparagement.

"We will consider the idea of sauces." The DC shifted her attention from Pat to Paislee. "What do you do again?"

"I own Cashmere Crush on Market Street, a bespoke sweater and yarn shop. I've been there for over ten years." She gestured toward the gift bags at her feet. "I brought gifts of table decorations for you but should have brought one for Chef Pat as well. It's really nothing . . ."

Of course, the ladies all wanted to see their pumpkins.

Pat also exclaimed at the quality.

"For fall," Paislee said. "I will bring them tae you, Chef Amblin, if you'd like, for the café. A gift!"

The DC of Cawdor rubbed her thumb over the round curve of the pumpkin. "You might understand that operating a property of this size means being mindful of the bottom line."

"I do," Paislee said. She nodded at Sorcha, who didn't say any more about what she had received at Ramsey Castle—the lion and unicorn pamphlet.

Shannon drummed her fingers on the table. "I think we can all agree that owning land of historic value comes with its challenges. How do you handle security?"

"Randall Fowler is in charge," the DC said. "I can introduce you if you'd like, considering your recent problem at the estate."

The chef cleared his throat. "He's at the . . . away, at the moment."

"Where?" the DC demanded.

"The police station, tae talk tae the constables."

"Why?" The DC's face grew red. "They were just here, pestering me and the staff. Everything is journaled tae the exact minute—who was here, when they left. How much was donated tae the family. We were spread thin with guards, and I blame Simon Sinclair." Her scowl traveled from Pat to Paislee, as if knowing him clouded the DC's opinion of them.

"They had further questions for Randall aboot that night. Is it possible he alerted someone tae where the fence was weakest? They asked us all," the chef said. "As if it might be an inside job."

"That's ridiculous." The DC touched a silver pendant. "I would stake my life on the fact that Randall Fowler is loyal tae Cawdor Castle."

Paislee glanced at the other ladies, who had previously been in such tenuous positions. Sometimes you couldn't even trust your closest allies, and that included family.

"I am sure the situation will be cleared up soon." The chef, crimson-faced, lifted his chin and stalked away to the kitchen.

"Temperamental," the DC of Cawdor said. "But Pat Amblin is worth it. I will give the idea of bottled sauces serious consideration."

Without giving Sorcha credit?

"I shouldnae have allowed Simon tae sway me, but I've a soft spot for the Highland cows, and this particular crofter has a magic touch with the fold." The DC snapped her fingers. "The fundraiser was supposed tae create goodwill and offset the criticism of the thane's petition for regulating those blasted fireworks. Darcey McClintock's article didnae help, as I'd hoped."

Paislee liked the cows too, but preferred goats and sheep. She decided to take the conversational bull by the horns, as neither Mack nor Simon had answered her. "Was your property vandalized?"

"What do you mean?" The DC of Cawdor put the pumpkin back in the Cashmere Crush gift bag.

"What happened tae me was in the papers," Shannon said. "Graffiti. SAORSA. Doon with Tories."

"And at my castle too," Sorcha said. "I received a pamphlet against the petition."

The DC leaned toward Sorcha. "It wasnae in the papers."

"I wanted tae keep it quiet. Protesters want their name and cause in the news. They defiled my property. I'm not giving them airtime." Sorcha's eyes flickered with righteous anger.

"We each received a pamphlet berating the Conservative Party," Shannon continued. "Warning the regular folk tae guard their power against the aristos. Neither of us shared with the police nor the paper. That Darcey McClintock is not tae be trusted."

The DC of Cawdor narrowed her eyes. "I'd invited her here tae write a positive article aboot the fundraiser. She left by eight after interviewing Pat and I. Sampled plenty of the tapas." She glanced around the table. "Randall said he chased off two people who had spray paint cans, a man and a woman, at the gate. I wonder if it was Ailis and her boyfriend, Blake?"

"When?" Paislee asked. She finished her espresso.

"Samhain. At midnight."

Paislee thought back to the time she and Brody had been at Rait Ruins. "Ailis would have been dead by then. It couldn't have been her. Blake maybe."

"I see. Well, someone managed tae infiltrate the tower. If not for Muriel Campbell setting off the activation alarms around the holly tree, we wouldnae have known anyone was there. The tower was closed off—my caveat for opening the place for the benefit."

"Someone besides Muriel was in the tower?" Shannon asked.

"A real person. A man. I gave the description tae the constables in charge. Six feet, and in a Guy Fawkes costume."

"Of course." Paislee exhaled. "That isn't much help."

"I believe they wanted tae steal the holly tree. Doon with the monarchy nonsense." The DC of Cawdor pounded her fist to the table.

"Could it be a clue?" Paislee asked. "The costume? Although it had tae be a popular one this year. I've seen it all over."

"It's in two days," Shannon said. "Bonfire Night."

November 5th.

"It's ridiculous tae celebrate the capture and death of a Catholic radical with fireworks and bonfires," Sorcha said. "But it's been happening for hundreds of years, so who are we tae stop it?"

"Grandpa said it was in 1605. We used tae have two unicorns

on the coat of arms, but now there is the lion and the unicorn, tae show Scotland and Great Britain are allies."

"I dinnae care aboot that," DC of Cawdor said. "One thing the thane and I agree on is that the fireworks need tae be banned or regulated. The gangs of youth last year targeting our police and first responders with petrol bombs and industrial-grade fireworks was shameful. If people cannae control their anarchist impulses, then we need tae help them manage their behavior."

Paislee had watched the news the prior Bonfire Night, otherwise known as Guy Fawkes Night, November fifth, with horror. Edinburgh had been hit particularly hard, as had Glasgow and Dundee.

Angry youth. The Conservatives posited that the towns and villages could manage the bonfires and fireworks safely without harm to their citizens—but the citizens demanded the right to have sparklers, fireworks, and bonfires.

"If people could be trusted tae make good choices," Paislee said.

The DC held up her palm. "It is obvious by the mayhem that is only getting worse, putting our shire in harm, that they are not tae be trusted. We need tae manage things for them."

Paislee bowed her head, agreeing, but still resisting that yoke of authority.

Her phone dinged.

Brody, wondering where she was. How had it gotten to be half past three?

"I have tae go. I'm l—"

"Late," the ladies said in unison.

Chapter 10

Paislee drove to the school, making it in fifteen minutes. Brody stood alone, his hands in his pockets, his backpack at his feet.

"Hi. Sorry about that," Paislee said.

"Busy?" He climbed into the front passenger seat.

"At lunch with the ladies. The new café is incredible."

Brody buckled up, remaining silent.

"I'm going tae run home and pick up Grandpa for the whisky tasting at the Oasis Hotel with Poppy Drummond."

"I dinnae care. Do I have tae go?"

"Don't be rude, son. I think it would be good tae get your mind off of things." Paislee glanced at Brody. "How was school today?"

"Awful. Edwyn ignored me. You know we always go tae Bonfire Night together? This will be the first year we dinnae. Emma kept giving me sad eyes, like I'd hurt her feelings, and I didnae mean tae. She should just leave me alone."

Bonfire Night in Nairn had a carnival feel, with caravans selling toffee apples and hot chocolate. Simple joys of childhood. "She probably just wants tae be your friend, and let you know she's there if you want tae talk about what happened."

"No thanks. I want tae forget what happened."

"I don't think that's the healthiest way tae handle it. Would you like tae talk tae Father Dixon, or a school counselor?"

"Didnae you hear what I said, Mum? Dinnae wanna talk aboot it. That means no talking. Tae nobody." He ran his fingers across his mouth like a zipper being closed.

Gritting her teeth, Paislee asked, "Was Darryl at school today?"

"No. Not Jimmy either. Which sucks because tomorrow it will be like the first day all over again, tae see them after Ailis's death."

Paislee sighed. She and Emma had wanting to help in common. "Did you get homework?"

"None of the teachers gave us any," Brody said. "It was a light day—even the faculty was sad."

"How about we get an ice cream?"

He shook his head.

This was bad if ice cream couldn't fix it.

They arrived at home, and Paislee turned the engine off. Brody hopped out, dragging his backpack like it was filled with rocks.

"Hey!" Paislee called as she entered. She caught Brody and Wallace as they went up the stairs and into his bedroom, so low energy he didn't even slam the door.

"Gran! What should I do?"

She eyed the photos of her family that Lydia had arranged artistically on the wall, pausing at the one of Paislee and her granny when Paislee was pregnant.

Grandpa poked his head from his bedroom and gave a somber smile. "She always had the best advice, eh? But she never had tae deal with finding a dead person. That seems tae be a uniquely *you* problem."

"Thanks, Grandpa." She tilted her head. "And you are uniquely suited tae help me solve these puzzles."

"I've tried my hand at them." His cheeks pinkened with pleasure. "Not letting bad people get away with murder feels grand. I understand why Amelia went intae constable training. I'm too old or I'd be doing it too."

"I normally would say that age is not a factor, but no way do I want you out chasing criminals." Paislee tossed her keys in the ceramic dish by the door and hung up her coat, and her handbag.

"Tea?" Grandpa asked.

"No thanks. I need tae call the shop and make sure they're okay. I haven't heard a peep from Elspeth or Rhona."

"You trained them well, and it's the slow fall season."

She laughed at having her words parroted back to her. "Don't forget we have our outing at the fancy new hotel, with whisky tasting."

"Didnae you notice me nice shirt? Dinnae have tae wear a tie, do I?" Her grandfather shivered. His white oxford was tucked into khaki pants and he'd no doubt wear his tan checked jacket with it.

"You look nice tae me." She frowned down at her khakis. "I should probably go put on a dress or slacks."

"Is Brody coming?"

"Yes, whether he likes it or not."

She hurried up the stairs and knocked on her son's door. She tried the knob—unlocked, good, and said, "Hi! We are leaving here in fifteen."

"Not changing my clothes."

"Fine with me."

Normally getting out of the school uniform was the first thing on the agenda, but Paislee wouldn't argue.

She went into her room and chose a fall dress that Lydia had selected for her. It was soft and probably cost more than what Paislee would spend on a dress, but it fit perfectly and made her feel pretty.

Taking her hair from the clip she routinely kept it up in, as it was fine and had zero body, she flipped it over and ruffled it before straightening again. She gave it a quick spray, knowing by the time they reached the hotel it would be flat. Oh well.

Paislee added a bit of tinted lip gloss and some charcoal liner beneath her ice-blue eyes. "Good enough," she said aloud.

Leaving her room for the hall, she could see that Brody was already downstairs, as was Wallace. She was glad he hadn't fought her further on the outing and would give him extra money to play at the arcade with.

To her mind, the arcade was a waste of coin, but the kids all loved it. Her family was ready to go and waiting in the foyer.

"This is a treat," Paislee said, "not having tae yell."

"Grandpa wants his whisky," Brody said.

"And didnae you change yer mind aboot having a fancy ice cream at the hotel?" Grandpa countered.

Paislee chuckled. It would be all right. Her life with her guys was going to be better than all right.

"Aye. Whipped cream and a cherry too," Brody said.

He'd decided to change into his new jeans and trainers and ditch the school uniform after all.

"You look pretty, Paislee," Grandpa said.

Brody nodded. "You do, Mum. Meeting Mack at the hotel?"

"No. He's busy. I haven't really heard from him today."

She didn't bring up Ailis, and neither did Brody or Grandpa.

They arrived at the new hotel next to the strip of businesses with the arcade, and parked in the car park. Paislee's car was the oldest one in it.

She recognized Corbin's new Mercedes SUV, and Simon's Land Rover.

The Juke had some life in it and Eddie, her mechanic, thought it might be a good car for Brody when her son was ready to drive.

Boggled the mind.

She turned off the engine, and the trio went into the hotel lobby. A fountain was in the center of a marble floor. Lights and fresh plants made it look like they were somewhere tropical. "Isn't this nice?"

"It is." Grandpa reached out to put his finger in the water, then flicked it back at Brody. Brody grinned.

"Don't even think about it," Paislee warned her son.

"Hey, Paislee," Sophie Barron said.

She and her husband, Alistair, were standing with Lydia and Corbin, and Simon.

Simon was talking to a woman with bleached short blond hair, shimmery hazel eyes, and a stunning figure as she rounded the hotel counter and joined them.

"Hi, all! I'm Poppy Drummond." She shook hands with everyone, treating them all equally.

Smart. One never knew who might someday be a future customer. Poppy was in her thirties. Very confident.

Paislee could see that confidence would be an attractive quality to a successful man like Chef Pat Amblin.

"This hotel is lovely," Lydia said. "It feels verra Italian villa."

"That was the aesthetic I was going for." Poppy folded her hands before her, never losing her charming smile.

"Are you from Nairn?" Grandpa asked.

"No, born and raised in Edinburgh—not the nice parts," Poppy said with a self-deprecating laugh. "I wanted more. Went tae every business course I could find. I wanted tae be a model but was told I was too short and curvy. One thing aboot me, is that I will find a way. I unapologetically love beautiful things."

"We are going tae be great friends," Lydia said. "Simon was right aboot that! This is my best friend in the world, Paislee Shaw. Her son, Brody, and her grandfather, Angus."

Brody was tongue-tied.

"Nice tae meet you," Grandpa said. His appreciation of the ladies didn't detract from his love of his Agnes.

"I've hired Chef Amblin tae assist my hotel chef for an *exclusive* celebration from the rooftop tomorrow evening. The views for Bonfire Night will be incredible if you'd like to join us. Unless you have other plans?" Poppy asked.

"We usually watch the fireworks from the bandstand," Paislee said. "I'm up for trying something new." A year from now, Paislee would wager this posh hotel would be fully booked.

The Barrons, the Shaws, and Simon all accepted the invitation as well. Since Brody and Edwyn weren't doing their normal thing, it was a good time to change direction.

"Will you have toffee apples?" Brody asked.

Poppy blinked. "Let me talk tae Chef Amblin and see what I can do. I havenae had those delicious treats in years."

"Sticky, but worth the risk of my teeth," Lydia said.

"I lost a filling once," Alistair said, tapping his jaw. "Not for me, pet."

"Puir Da," Lydia said. "Poppy, this is Alistair and Sophie Barron, my parents. They moved tae Edinburgh and have a business there."

"Nice tae meet you," Poppy said. "I love the city but consider Nairn home. I've been here since I turned twenty, and learned hotel management, starting up at the Muthu Newton, and then the Dolphin, and now here at the Oasis. This new build has two hundred grand suites, all exuding luxury, from the bamboo sheets tae room service. Would you like tae go on a tour, or just get tae the whisky?" She winked. "I've reserved the Barrel, which is a private tasting room."

"Grandpa wants the whisky," Brody said.

"I can wait, lad. Is anybody else interested in a tour?"

Paislee, Corbin, and Lydia nodded.

"I've seen it," Simon said. "I have a call tae make so I'll meet you in the Barrel in aboot twenty minutes."

Poppy smiled, seemingly thrilled to show off the hotel. "Here at the lobby level, we have conference rooms and a business center. A gym. A convenience mart."

Paislee followed around the large fountain with bronze dolphins in the center. From the corner of her eye, she saw Marion McGinty with two men, and waved hello as the elevator doors closed.

She realized that Marion and Poppy had similar bleached blond hairstyles. Lydia used to have different hair colors and styles all the time but lately she wore it in a caramel-colored bob. Paislee wasn't brave enough to chop or color her hair. Her luck, it would fall out.

"We have an outdoor heated pool, as well as an indoor one."

The marble floors were protected by sage carpet runners, and everything was trimmed with a hint of gold.

"This way, for the rooftop," Poppy said. "It's the crown jewel of the hotel."

They all fit in the spacious elevator to the tenth floor. Paislee exited behind Lydia and Corbin, with Brody and Grandpa on either side, the Barrons behind them.

The rooftop had a glass dome, so was protected from the elements. You could see the Moray Firth, and the beach, and the harbor.

Wooden pallets were being piled up to create an epic bonfire tomorrow night. "This will be the best seats around," Poppy said. "Because we just opened a few months ago, we arenae at full capacity, which is why I can offer them this year tae you all. I hope word of mouth will make sure we are booked for next year."

"We will spread the word," Lydia said.

"That we will," Corbin seconded. "This is an incredible space and the hotel is right in the middle of the village, so convenient tae everything."

"That's what I like aboot it too," Poppy said. "It's just a few minutes' walk from the train station or the bus."

"We'd stay here in a heartbeat," Alistair said.

"Except that you are staying with me and Corbin at our home," Lydia reminded them. "No hotels for you guys."

"You might get tired of us," Sophie protested.

"Never!"

Paislee tried to catch Lydia's eye to see if there was a chance for a talk one on one, but again, while loving, Lydia wasn't answering Paislee's questions.

Fine.

Paislee wasn't going anywhere.

They returned to the opulent lobby and Poppy escorted them to the private, dimly lit room. It smelled rich, as if it had history, despite being modern. Dark wood paneling, with ivory chairs.

Simon and Pat Amblin were having a murmured conversation. They stopped talking, the tension around them clear, and stood.

"There you are," Pat said. He left Simon and joined Poppy, kissing her cheek.

Poppy arched a brow at him as if to remind him that she was at work and to respect that fact.

Pat stepped back, his arms behind him as he accepted the silent rebuke.

They were both attractive, but one person usually had more power than the other in a relationship, or it was close enough, like with Corbin and Lydia, that it balanced out. With Pat being famous and talented, it might make Poppy feel like she had to prove herself all the time.

"Let's sit here," Poppy suggested. She waved her arm, and Paislee detected a delicate unicorn head tattooed on her inner forearm. The large chunky bracelet she wore had hidden it earlier. The mahogany oval table easily seated fourteen—six chairs on each side and one at each end.

A tall table on wheels had been set up with several decanters of amber whisky and thick short glasses.

"Brant, our certified whisky specialist, will be here in a few minutes tae explain aboot the different varieties we have here." Poppy sent her confident smile around the table.

"It's like a wine sommelier?" Lydia asked.

"Aye, exactly." Poppy nodded with enthusiasm.

"I was telling you aboot their winery in Germany," Simon told Poppy. "Once up and running their wines might be a nice addition tae your wine list."

"Definitely," Poppy said. "I think the vineyards in Germany are incredibly underrated. It's the perfect time tae bring them tae light."

Paislee smiled at Lydia. If they could get their wines in a fancy hotel, that would be the equivalent of her cashmere goods at Ramsey Castle.

Corbin nodded. "We're just starting oot, but I'm happy tae send you sample bottles as we get up and running."

"The German Riesling is my favorite light wine of all the brands," Poppy said.

"Since Lydia and Corbin started this venture, we have a new appreciation of wine," Sophie said. She smiled with pride at her daughter.

"I like it all!" Alistair said. "Wine, beer, and whisky."

"Brant should be here any second." Poppy tapped her fingernail on the table as she looked at Brody. "Did I hear that you were hoping for ice cream?"

Brody blushed. "Aye, yes, please."

"A delicious choice. How many of you would like something other than whisky?"

Sophie and Paislee raised their hands.

"I can have the kitchen make you sundaes. The ice cream is churned here in house. Whipped cream?"

Lydia pouted her lower lip. "This is a really tough choice. I love ice cream too! We need tae make a Riesling ice cream."

Paislee's bestie had a sweet tooth, as did her grandfather. "I'll share with you, Lyd," she said.

"Perfect!" Lydia smacked her full lips. "I adore a world where I can indeed have it all. Thanks, Paislee."

"A Riesling ice cream?" Simon said to Corbin. "That could be the thing that makes you unique in the sea of wineries. What a combination."

"I like the idea." Corbin winked at Lydia. "We have so many ideas that we need tae be at the implementing stage before coming up with more."

"I hear you, hinny," Lydia said.

"I'll just put it in me notes." Sophie immediately jotted it into her mobile app. "We can circle back around tae it later after things settle doon."

Poppy checked her watch then stood. "Let me step oot for just a minute. Pat, would you mind coming with me?"

Pat, who had been perusing the bottles on the high table, clenched his jaw but nodded and smiled at Simon and the rest, shrugging his shoulders good-naturedly at Paislee.

He was about to get a lecture but probably had it coming.

The pair left the room.

Corbin chuckled. "Busted."

"Why?" Brody asked.

"They are dating but she is at work," Lydia said. "He shouldnae have kissed her in front of us."

"But they like each other?" Brody made sure that he had the facts right. It was an interesting time in history, where the rules were changing.

"They do. It's just being polite."

"But people kiss on the cheek all the time," Brody said, confused.

"Not as much anymore," Simon said. "Times are a changin' and we need tae be aware of protocol. Right, Corbin?"

"Right. Being polite is never a bad thing, Brody. You can almost always rely on guid manners tae get you oot of a bind." Corbin smiled at Brody.

Grandpa gave light applause.

"It was nice of Poppy tae invite us for tomorrow. Was she just being polite? Because I totally want tae see the bonfires and fireworks from here."

"She meant it," Corbin assured Brody.

"It was a nice thing for her tae offer, so we will make sure tae leave guid reviews for the hotel," Lydia said. "Can you imagine if we had our wine sold here? Thanks, Simon, for the introduction. Poppy is a go-getter."

"Not a problem. I feel like I'm in the hot seat with Pat though, and I dinnae really like it."

"How so?" Lydia sipped her water.

"Pat was telling me before you guys arrived that he'd met you, Paislee, earlier today at lunch. And that the ladies were discussing what happened on Halloween. He mentioned Randall Fowler being questioned and the DC of Cawdor later almost sacking him for talking oot of turn. As you just saw, Pat doesnae always know tae be discreet."

Chapter 11

Discretion mattered in business, well, and in life, really, Paislee thought. The famous chef was probably not used to it. He'd grown to fame by his flamboyant behavior.

She wondered if the relationship would last. Poppy and Pat could be a power couple, like Lydia and Corbin, or their egos might clash if they each wanted different things.

Brant, the certified whisky expert, arrived at the same time as the ice cream. Pat and Poppy entered behind them, their expressions smooth and untroubled.

Paislee found the information interesting, but much preferred the ice cream sundae. Homemade vanilla, homemade fudge, warm caramel, fluffy whipped cream, topped by toasted almonds and a cherry.

Lydia mostly ignored the whisky and shared Paislee's sundae.

Brody barely finished his, but he did. Paislee was impressed. Sophie gave the rest of hers to the guys around the table to share.

Poppy sat back with her inner arm revealed, relaxed now that the introductions had been done, and people were chatting easily.

"I like your unicorn tattoo," Paislee said toward the end of the afternoon. "It's patriotic."

"It was a wild moment of my youth," Poppy said. "I'm tempted tae get it removed but it's supposed tae really hurt, so I havenae followed through."

Brant, covered in tats, chuckled. "You should do what I do and cover it up with more ink." He showed the Scottish flag of blue and white. "This used tae read *I Love Mary*."

Everyone at the table laughed.

"Anybody else have tattoos they regret?" Corbin asked.

"I don't have any," Paislee said.

"Me either. Not opposed," Grandpa said. "Just never had something I wanted permanently."

"I have a flower," Lydia said. "On my ankle. Believe me, I gave it a lot of thought of where I might wrinkle."

Poppy laughed. "I saw a cartoon of old people in nursing homes playing 'guess the tattoo' games. It's a factor tae consider."

"Not the visual I want in my mind," Pat said. "I have the chef's knife on my upper arm that can easily be covered by a chef's jacket. I had just graduated from culinary school and was making a statement tae my family, who were not supportive. They've since come around, but sometimes you have tae be your own motivation."

"Something Pat and I have in common," Poppy said warmly.

Paislee assumed he was no longer in the doghouse.

"There is no guarantee of a long life," Simon said. "Take that Ailis, for instance. What dreams did she have that were cut short?"

Poppy rested her forearms on the table. "I feel terrible for the Barclays. Ailis used tae work at the Dolphin Hotel with me. I hired her tae clean rooms, before she moved tae Inverness. I didnae like her boyfriend Blake at all. He was a rat. I told her tae dump him."

Brody stiffened at the reminder of Ailis.

"Have they found Blake yet?" Simon asked.

"Not that I know, but I havenae been tuned in tae the news." Poppy had a cold tone that surprised Paislee.

Had her dislike of Blake transferred to Ailis?

"That seems extreme," Lydia said. "Why would you say that?"

"They were partying in the empty rooms," Poppy said. "Like I wouldnae find oot. And when I confronted her, she denied it. I showed her Blake on video, and she couldnae defend herself. I was never sure if she was in on it or not."

"Oh no!" Sophie said.

"Blake could have taken her keys—either way, I told her tae dump him, or she could find another job. She moved tae Inverness." Poppy shrugged. "I wouldnae be surprised if he had something tae do with what happened tae Ailis."

"Have you told this tae the police?" Paislee asked. "They're searching for Blake tae question him."

"No." Poppy tapped the tattoo on her inner forearm. "I dinnae mingle with the police."

"What do you think of the petition going around aboot governing fireworks?" Simon asked. "The thane really wants tae bring this tae the next level. What happened in Edinburgh last year was criminal. Punks aiming fireworks at the police. Surely you agree that was wrong."

"I wouldnae sign it," Poppy said.

"Why not?" Pat asked in surprise.

"I think people can manage themselves withoot the government getting involved," Poppy said.

"But they didnae," Simon countered. "And rumors abound that this year's Bonfire Night will be even more deadly. There's talk of it being canceled in Edinburgh as a precaution."

"Cancel Bonfire Night?" Brody asked.

"I cannae believe it," Lydia said. "It's an institution. Like taking away Burns Night, awful poetry and all." The tradition was that every January 25th, to celebrate the poet Robert Burns's birthday in 1759, Scots held a supper with much whisky and attempts at poems to rival the bard. It was hilarious.

"Would you sign a petition tae have legislature controlling the fireworks?" Simon asked the others at the table.

"Yes," Lydia said.

"Aye," Corbin seconded.

"We would too," Alistair said. "Our insurance business is close tae the offices for the SNP, which is concerning. Conservatives and the SNP members were having actual fistfights in the street."

"It was surreal. We want people tae be their best selves, but last year I was afraid I'd lose me home and business," Sophie said. "Laws are required for everyone's safety."

"People's freedom tae choose shouldnae negatively impact others," Pat said. He looked at Poppy with a scrutinizing gaze.

Paislee wondered if he was realizing that his girlfriend wasn't aligned with him politically.

"I guess there's still that rebel lass inside me, resisting authority. I'm sairy aboot your house and business, Sophie and Alistair," Poppy said. "You shouldnae be scared tae lose your livelihood."

"The thane thinks that managing the bonfires and fireworks will allow for a bigger, better display funded by the individual towns," Simon said. "At no cost tae the people."

"Free is always nice," Sophie said.

"I love sparklers," Brody said.

"Sparklers are verra cool and one of my favorite childhood memories," Poppy said. "How would they regulate those?"

"I'm not sure. Right now, the only laws are that you must be eighteen tae buy them, even industrial grade fireworks, and the gangs last year were literally firing them at each other." Simon curled his upper lip.

"It's a way for them tae blow off steam," Poppy said.

"Join a gym," Corbin suggested. "Learn golf."

"Fair." Poppy sighed.

"Play football? Run?" Brody shifted on his seat. "We saw the drone footage in class last year of what happened, and it's not okay tae hurt other people."

"We can all agree on that," Paislee said. "It's not okay. Poppy, I think you need tae tell the constables about Blake and Ailis."

"You can, if you want tae," Poppy said. "I'm no snitch."

She sounded like she was twelve just then, her accent deepening, and Paislee imagined her growing up as a young tough lass in a rough neighborhood.

Pat noticed too, his grip on the whisky tumbler tightening.

"I will feel a lot better when we get answers," Lydia said, reaching over Paislee to touch Brody's shoulder. "Aboot Ailis."

"Brody and Paislee found Ailis that night, so they need closure," Corbin said firmly. "Simon is in hot water at Cawdor Castle, as is Pat, but we need tae find oot what happened, and if Ailis was part of the robbery. It seems like she wasnae as innocent as we all thought if she was sneaking parties at the hotel."

"You're right," Poppy said. "Wait—are you thinking Ailis might be involved with the vandalism at the nobles' estates as well?"

"This needs tae stay between us," Simon said, "but it's been confirmed that there were several items stolen—expensive items—from the castle. The police wonder if Ailis and Blake might have been involved."

Paislee wiped whipped cream from her mouth with a cloth napkin. She'd known this already. Who else might be aware of the police's suspicions? Everyone seemed focused on Simon.

Poppy sat back. "Pat told me that the fence was broken on the Cawdor property. That's a short trek along the river near Rait Ruins."

Pat bowed his head and scowled at Poppy. Pillow talk? Gossip? That lack of discretion seemed to be a character flaw.

"Four miles isnae short." Simon poured himself a glass of water rather than more whisky. Paislee appreciated his self-control.

Pat sipped from his tumbler. "People walk in the country all the time. The Barclay family had a nice property with lots of hiking."

"Ailis had a car, though," Paislee said. "That Blake took that night, after they had an argument, leaving her stranded."

"Proves the point that she wouldnae have had trouble walking, and in fact might have been forced tae," Poppy said.

It sounded to Paislee like Poppy believed Ailis could be guilty. Having worked with the young woman, she had reason to be suspicious.

Lydia sighed. "I didnae really know the Barclays that well. Simon, have they found any of what was stolen?"

"Not yet."

"What was it?" Paislee knew about the loose emerald found next to Ailis but hadn't heard of anything else.

"Again, let's keep this here between us." Simon leaned forward, his arms on the table. "A jeweled Fabergé egg, and several diamond necklaces. The size of the stones combined with their historical value make these items priceless. The thieves fit them intae their pockets easily. The thane and I believe that they wanted the holly tree tae make a statement."

"And the thief was stopped by the ghost of Muriel," Brody said.

Poppy's brows rose. "A ghost?"

"We have a blur on the security camera," Simon said.

"I saw it myself," Pat said. "Randall showed me. You cannae make her oot but there is definitely a tinge of blue and a feminine shape."

"The Muthu Newton Hotel was haunted, and the Dolphin too. This hotel is brand-new. No ghosts." Poppy sighed. "It better stay that way at the Oasis."

Brody and Grandpa spun a coin at the end of the table. Since her son didn't have his mobile, he had to find other forms of entertainment than scrolling.

"I wonder if Ailis will join the Wraith and become the next ghost tae haunt Rait Ruins." Poppy looked at Paislee, her tone almost casual as she asked, "Do you think Blake killed her?"

Paislee sucked in a shocked breath. It was the first time someone had put the idea so bluntly. "The constables want tae track Blake down and find answers. It's *possible* that Ailis fell and hit her head against the tombstone or a boulder." Though Mack had told her the evidence didn't support her theory, she could keep a confidence. "There are rocks all over the place. However, I am almost positive that she wasn't alone. Someone out there knows more."

"I'll talk tae the police then. No way should Blake get away with hurting Ailis." Poppy's eyes cleared. "Let's find him—the sooner, the better." She stood. "I have a dinner banquet tae oversee. You all are welcome tae stay and visit. Do you have any further questions for Brant aboot the whisky?"

"No, thank you, Poppy," Corbin said. "We should get going too. We have dinner with my dad and family tonight."

"Please, come tomorrow around five up tae the rooftop. I've talked tae my chef already and he and Pat are collaborating on the menu, which will include toffee apples. Until later," Poppy said.

She and Brant left together.

"Poppy is verra savvy. I ken she'll put the word oot aboot Blake and help find him if she can." Pat stood and shook hands all around. "See you tomorrow."

The chef left. Paislee and the others also decided to call it a night and began gathering coats and saying goodbye.

She had a message from Mack about dinner—she invited him over for pizza and he agreed. Her evening was perking up. He offered to pick the pies up and meet her at the house.

Perfect.

Grabbing her jacket, she slipped the mobile into the side pocket of her handbag.

Simon gave her a quick hug goodbye. His thick hair was showing just a few strands of white at the temples. "I'll poke around at the castle for answers, and let ye know if I find oot anything useful. I'm truly sairy that you and Brody were the ones tae find puir Ailis."

"Thanks, Simon," Paislee said. He was a kind man, dedicated to Nairn.

"I want tae see Muriel." Brody tilted his head and stuffed both hands in the central hoodie pocket. "Can you tell it's a ghost? Ailis wasnae really the Wraith." His jaw firmed.

"Tell you what." Simon settled his leather jacket over his shoulder. "I'll forward the footage I received from Randall, and you can check it oot for yourself. No posting on social media, though, okay? It's on me laptop, not mobile, so it'll be later tonight."

"We willnae share it!" Brody promised. "Thanks, Simon."

"Can't wait," Paislee said. An actual ghost on film! Brody seemed cautious, as if not willing to believe in a spirit. He'd been cruelly pranked. Would this change his mind? Or hers?

Grandpa and Lydia were conversing, heads together.

Simon clapped Brody on the shoulder. "I'll send it tae your mum's email. I've got it from being on the Nairn Highland Games committee."

"We'll be home all night." With Mack on his way, Paislee wasn't leaving. She missed him and it had nothing to do with the case.

"Great." Simon stepped around Paislee and Brody to Lydia and Sophie, hugging them goodbye, and shaking the men's hands.

"He's pure grand for an old guy," Brody said to Paislee in a quiet voice, thank the good Lord for that.

"He's just turned fifty," Paislee replied. "But, I agree. Simon has class."

Simon made his way to Corbin. "Give my regards tae your family, Corbin. Glad Garrison is on the mend."

"Us too," Corbin said. "Hard tae believe anything could take him doon. Vandals have the same mentality as the punks throwing fireworks at the police."

"I'll support the thane's proposition," Alistair said. "I'm happy tae fund whatever you want tae coordinate, Simon."

Sophie, Grandpa, Lydia, and Paislee murmured agreements.

"Turning Conservative?" Corbin asked Paislee, lips twitching. He knew Paislee's heart was about being kind to her fellow man no matter the affiliation.

"I will also sign the petition," Paislee said. "It's not a political line for me but one of safety." As she'd told Darcey earlier, she did not take lightly the responsibility of raising Brody into a wonderful young man.

The Shaws went to the Juke and climbed in. Paislee started the engine. "Hope you're not too full. Mack is coming over with pizza."

"Pizza and ice cream?" Grandpa peered into the back seat at Brody as he buckled up. "Red letter day, me lad."

"I'm sorry we didn't get tae the arcade," Paislee said.

"Ice cream was better, and hearing what everyone else knew aboot Ailis was also important. I stayed quiet and listened," Brody said.

"Smart boy." Paislee grinned at her child as she backed out of the space. "What did you think about what Poppy said regarding Blake and Ailis partying at the Dolphin Hotel? Is that something she might have done?"

"Ailis was always a cool girl, popular, you know. Darryl said she would sneak him beers sometimes."

"Oh." Paislee turned forward and headed toward the main street.

"Edwyn thought she was cute."

Figured.

"Can you believe they might cancel Bonfire Night in Edinburgh?" Brody sounded truly appalled. "I hope that doesnae happen here in Nairn or Inverness."

"If I had tae choose between village-run fireworks or none at all, I would pick the village event," Grandpa said.

"I would too." Paislee imagined that the recovery costs after a night of fireworks, sparklers, and bonfires was actually astronomical from out-of-control fires or personal injury.

"Yeah, I suppose," Brody agreed, reluctantly.

They arrived at the Shaw home just as Mack did. Paislee parked under the carport, and he parked on the street. The nosy neighbor across the street peeked from her window curtain. What did Mrs. Florence think of Mack being at the Shaw house more often? Paislee had learned long ago not to listen to gossip. She lifted her nose and unlocked the door.

Mack held two large pizzas that he brought inside the house. They all walked in together as Wallace raced down the hall to meet them.

"Hi!" Paislee said, ushering him before her into the kitchen.

Wallace barked hello and circled their feet as his tail wagged.

Brody let the dog out. Instead of darting upstairs to his room as he had been doing since the Ailis incident, he remained downstairs.

"How's it going?" Mack asked. "I cannae stay long but I've missed you all."

She felt the same way about him.

"We found oot that Ailis and Blake used tae party in empty hotel rooms, at the Dolphin," Brody said.

"What?" Mack put the boxes in the center of the table. "Please dinnae tell me that you are going tae be as nosy as your mother and your grandfather."

"Hey!" Paislee said.

Grandpa chuckled. "A chip off the old block."

"Not what I want tae hear." Mack tapped the top box. "Can I have pizza first? Pepperoni?"

Paislee, mood lighter than it had been in days, retrieved plates and napkins and brought them to the counter.

"What can I get you tae drink, Mack?" Paislee studied him beneath her lashes, not bothering to hide her happy smile.

"Whisky?" Her grandfather went to the pantry and brought out the Macallan that he'd gotten last Christmas.

Brody laughed. "Grandpa!"

"A strong tea will be fine. I feel like I am missing the punchline of the Shaw family joke. Care tae let me in on it?" Mack crossed his arms and stepped back, but he wasn't really mad.

Paislee put on the electric kettle. "We had a whisky tasting at the new Oasis Hotel."

"All of you?" Mack's russet brows rose.

"Brody and I had ice cream instead." Paislee chose a ceramic mug that matched the other four-piece set. "It was very good."

"Made there at the hotel," Brody said. "Caramel sauce, hot fudge, and whipped cream. A bright red cherry."

"Poppy Drummond is the manager, and she's invited us tae watch the fireworks from the rooftop tomorrow night." Paislee set the selection of tea bags by the kettle.

"That makes me feel better, actually," Mack said. "All of you are going?"

"You can come too," Paislee offered. Had he been hoping to

join them for Bonfire Night? They were newly a couple, so she didn't know the rules.

"Sairy, cannae." Mack crossed the kitchen to Paislee, by the sink. He looked into her eyes and smoothed a piece of flyaway hair over her ear. "We've gotten leads from our informants aboot something going doon tomorrow night tae rival last year's mess in Edinburgh. I was hoping you'd stay home and warm, hanging oot by the fireplace. I could bring you sparklers."

"No way!" Brody said. "We're not staying home. It's the best night of the year for fireworks, next tae Hogmanay."

"Miss Bonfire Night?" Paislee shook her head. "It's always felt like the kickoff tae my birthday festivities. Can't imagine not celebrating it."

Mack gave a single nod and pressed his lips into a thin line. "All right, it was just a thought."

Brody let Wallace inside. "How many sparklers? You could still bring some over if you wanted tae. I like them a lot."

"If I wanted tae," Mack said with a chuckle. "Mibbe next year. This Bonfire Night, I am glad that you're all somewhere off the street."

Paislee gave everyone a plate, her insides warm and fluttery. He'd said *next year*, as if their being together was a fact to be counted on.

Everybody dished up their choice of pizza—veggie or pepperoni, or both—and then gathered around the kitchen table. Paislee consolidated the pizza into one box and moved it to the counter out of the way and to keep warm, throwing the other box away.

Mack and Paislee were drinking hot tea, Grandpa had whisky, and Brody lemon fizzy water. Wallace watched the proceedings, his bright eyes ready to catch anything that dropped.

After a bite of cheesy pepperoni with chili flakes, Mack said, "Now, tell me again what you heard, and who from?"

"Poppy Drummond, the manager of Oasis, the new hotel, used tae be a manager at the Dolphin, and she'd hired Ailis tae clean rooms. Guess Poppy didn't like Blake and when she found out about them using the vacant rooms tae party, or at least Blake, she told Ailis tae dump Blake or find another job. She had surveillance video of Blake coming in and out. Maybe he took Ailis's keys or something, and she didn't know, but chances are she was complicit in what happened." Paislee bit into her veggie pizza, sans chili flakes.

She always ordered extra pizza because she loved a cold slice of veggie for breakfast the next day. Mack also enjoyed cold pizza for leftovers. Grandpa and Brody would heat it up and thought cold pizza was disgusting—especially veggie.

"From the information we've gathered, Blake Harrington is a piece of work." Mack shook his head. "As for Ailis . . . it's hard tae know what she knew and what she didnae. Blake is still MIA. Poppy Drummond? I'll stop in and talk tae her aboot what she remembers. Mibbe where Blake used tae live or something. You never know what might lead tae the next clue."

"Pat Amblin, the chef at the Cawdor Café, is Poppy's boyfriend. He thinks that Poppy has ways of locating information," Grandpa said. "She said she'd put oot feelers, so . . ."

Mack started on his second slice of pepperoni.

"Simon told us tonight that jewelry was stolen from the DC's private rooms that night," Paislee said. "And we know that the gate was broken along the river." She kept the information about the ghost of Muriel to herself. Mack wouldn't appreciate it.

"Four miles for someone fit is not a big deal if they were going tae walk from Cawdor tae the Rait Ruins," Brody said. "And if ye can run? Even faster." He also didn't mention Muriel's ghost.

"Besides the emerald found in Ailis's collar," Grandpa said, "Simon mentioned that diamond necklaces were stolen, among other items. The DC doesnae care for Simon and blames him for the theft occurring at all."

"And the Fabergé egg!" Paislee said.

"A real egg?" Brody asked.

"No, son, this is covered in jewels and famous because there was a limited edition." Grandpa slurped his whisky. "Poppy asked if Blake had killed Ailis."

"That's right!" Paislee said. "I thought it odd tae have it framed so boldly. Well, Mack?"

Mack nudged his now empty plate aside and placed his elbow on the table. "I cannae have you three ganging up on me like this."

Paislee studied the DI next to her. Was he really upset? He let his serious gaze land on each of them, settling on her. Was that disappointment?

He didn't understand. Brody had been deeply affected by the tragedy. "We're helping!" Paislee insisted.

"Help like this I dinnae need." Mack sipped his now cooled tea. "What if you were tae get hurt?"

"How could we?" Brody asked. "We're careful."

Mack exhaled. "Nairn is a safe shire—so far. There have been rumors of radicals infiltrating crowds on the street tae encourage rioting. Folks get riled up during Bonfire Night. Add alcohol, and hot tempers? The fireworks last year became weapons—not just in Edinburgh, but closer to home in Dundee."

"We watched the drone video of what happened in Edinburgh in class," Brody said. "Simon said it might be even worse this year. The Thane of Cawdor wants tae have the fireworks re, ri—"

"Regulated," Grandpa said. "The law would be put intae effect tae protect the Scots—however, most dinnae want more rules."

"Poppy didnae like that idea either," Paislee said.

"You heard the radical rumor from Simon Sinclair?" Mack took out his phone and opened the notes app, typing the name in, right after Poppy Drummond. "Interesting."

"Yes," Paislee said. "He's great mates with the thane, and also Corbin and Lydia."

"I'm familiar with both men, who have been lobbying for control of the fireworks. I agree that something should be done. A friend of mine was injured in the riots in Dundee last year." Mack gripped his upper arm. "Lost his arm from the elbow doon."

"What if you were hurt?" Paislee's heart raced. "I'm glad Amelia is still in constable school." She drank her tea. "Constable Payne, Constable Monroe. Surely, our community here in Nairn wouldn't participate?"

"Nairn is growing, Paislee." Mack looked at her with a half smile. "That means that there are more people and not all of them are going tae be as goody-two-shoes as you."

"I am not!" Paislee looked around the table at Grandpa and Brody to have them come to her defense. She absolutely was not a goody anything. Brody was proof of that.

Brody snickered and pinched his thumb and forefinger together. "Could be a wee bit true, Mum."

Paislee ignored them all to get another slice of pizza, opting for pepperoni.

"I promised that I would find oot what happened tae Ailis, and I will. It just takes time, and when we have the possibility of mass rioting in our shire, it complicates things." Mack pushed back a bit from the table. "Is Ailis's death a separate issue from the theft at Cawdor? Or are they related?"

"Where do the vandals fit in?" Brody asked. He was on his fourth piece of pizza.

"Guid question," Mack said. "The last election didnae go well for the Scottish National Party, the only group that demanded total freedom from Great Britain." He pointed to the high table with Grandpa's puzzle on it. "These problems all have solutions. It's a matter of finding the next piece, which will lead tae the next one, until the answer is right before us."

"What are the chances of radicals on the beach tomorrow here in Nairn?" Paislee asked. "It makes Bonfire Night seem menacing." In her lifetime, it had been a party before her birthday party, and all combined for fun.

"It started off as menacing when a radical Catholic, Guy Fawkes, wanted tae overthrow the king in 1605, so, there is that." The edges of Mack's mouth tilted upward toward a smile.

"You have a guid point," Grandpa said. "We were talking

aboot that earlier. Scotland is full of history and some of it is verra bloody."

Paislee turned toward Mack. She couldn't imagine him in the line of fire. Well, she could actually, and her stomach knotted. "What should we do? Will you be in danger, Mack? Please, call in sick or something."

"I'll be fine," Mack said. "I've been doing this for a verra long time. I'll be a lot happier knowing you'll be safe too. The rooftop of the Oasis sounds idyllic."

"It was lovely," Paislee said. "Maybe when you visit Poppy later you can ask her tae take you up tae the dome?"

"Mibbe." Mack's phone dinged and he read it with a groan. "Poppy is the only person tae have a negative experience with Ailis, so far, so I'm eager tae interview her. Halloween is a crazy time, and things are even worse this year than normal."

He stood and pushed back his chair.

Paislee snapped her mouth closed as she'd been about to give him a lecture on taking care of himself. Of not taking stupid chances.

Mack Zeffer was an excellent DI. Thanks to his training, combined with his bravery, the shire, Nairn, was in the best hands. She would not turn into a harping shrew just because she loved him.

"Thanks for stopping by, Mack. I'm glad tae share a meal anytime. Just let me know when you can break away."

Mack nodded at her, his gaze warm.

"Glad you dropped in," Brody said. He swallowed the last bite of his pizza.

Grandpa raised his tumbler to Mack and swirled the peaty whisky. "I'll pour you a dram when this business is over."

"I'll take you up on that." Mack pocketed his mobile in the interior of his suit. "Walk me tae the door, Paislee?"

"Of course." Paislee took a swig of lukewarm tea to make sure there wasn't pizza in her teeth or on her breath.

Anticipation hummed in her veins.

They went down the hall to the foyer. Brody and Grandpa noisily packed away the pizza boxes and rinsed dishes.

"I cannae help but worry aboot you, and now Brody and Angus too," Mack said. He slid his hand in Paislee's hair to sweetly tilt her head.

"I'm concerned about you, too." Paislee held his gaze, signaling strength from her to him. "Will you wear protective gear tomorrow night?"

She put her hand over his racing heart.

"I take educated risks when necessary," Mack said. "I am not foolish or reckless."

"I didn't think you were," Paislee said. "I'm not sure how tae feel, or what tae be concerned about. This is so new for me."

"And me." Mack stared into her eyes. "I made a promise tae my sister that I wouldnae be the constable or detective inspector who embarrassed her and the weans with underage hookers, or a gambling habit. No dying because I've fallen off a cliff trying tae rescue a wayward cow. I was tae have integrity and common sense, and only then would she give me her blessing."

Paislee burst out laughing. "I can't wait tae meet Michele."

Mack rubbed his thumb along her chin. Her body heated in immediate response.

"She wants tae meet you too. When I told her aboot you, she had a million questions. I gave her your social media information. She's probably been gently stalking you since Halloween."

"Gently stalking?"

"It doesnae hurt, but it's still dangerous." Mack's light touch as he smoothed her hair over her ear brought alternating shivers of cold and hot.

This was torture, and yet she wanted more.

Mack leaned down to brush his mouth against Paislee's, the pressure there and gone, and back again. She stood up on her tiptoes, pressing into his body.

He placed his hand on her hip, balancing her. When his tongue brushed her lower lip, her knees buckled, and it was good that he had his hand on her waist, or she would have fallen.

He cradled her to him, and she covered his heart with her palm. She could feel his heart pound. Her senses melted. Her face flamed as she gave a little moan of pleasure. Embarrassed, she tried to step back and duck her head, but Mack didn't let her go.

"You, Paislee, never have tae hide your feelings from me. Never." The promise was followed by another kiss that was the perfect mix of hard and soft.

He tipped her chin up and his eyes were as dazed as hers had to be. She was on the verge of telling him she loved him. Not to go into the line of fire. To stay in her house forever.

The spell was broken when his phone rang. They jumped apart, breaths heaving.

Laughing with nerves, Paislee opened the door, staying in the foyer and still attached to Mack at the hip. Cool air soothed her heated skin.

She kissed him as she helped him put on his overcoat, a kiss for his cap, and a kiss for each glove. This was silly and yet she couldn't stop grinning. Their mouths fused and they went in for one more kiss, and then another.

"Will I see you tomorrow?" Her question was breathless.

"Aye." Mack's expression darkened. "Mibbe?"

"I hope so. I, I really care for you. I promise not tae nag at you about the investigation," Paislee said. "I just want tae know you're okay."

"I am determined, Paislee, tae find oot what happened tae Ailis. I dinnae take my promises lightly. Gathering information aboot Ailis isnae as easy as one might think. Aye, there is her social media presence, but was that her true self? I have a call in tae Rooney Crowe. Thanks for that tip. While Ailis was popular with her peers, Rooney wasnae. I've studied her last social media posts for clues. She seemed like a spirited lass on her way tae a costume party, not a thief on her way tae break intae a castle to steal an emerald she didnae like. How did it get there?"

Paislee smoothed Mack's coat over his shoulders, believing in him. "Her words on Brody's mobile are kind—she wants tae find his phone and return it tae the ice rink."

"Pah!" Mack shook his head but smiled at her. "We should have the medical examiner's report soon. Tonight, we're training and going over protocol with our newbies on staff at the station."

They kissed one last kiss, and yanked themselves apart, breathing heavily.

Mack, his jacket buttoned wrong, just laughed and hopped into his SUV. Paislee waved to Mack, watching as he drove away.

Sure enough, the curtain across the street swayed closed. Paislee truly didn't care what Mrs. Florence thought.

Chapter 12

Paislee woke up at the sound of the newspaper hitting the cement steps on the stoop, and shrugged her robe over her flannel pajamas, sticking her feet into fleecy slippers.

Yawning, she made her way downstairs and opened the front door to a gust of brisk fall air. She sucked in a breath, grabbed the plastic-wrapped roll and darted inside, quickly shutting the door.

Her phone, in her robe pocket, dinged.

Mack? She'd dreamed of him all night and was tempted to take a very cold shower before she went into Cashmere Crush today.

She shuffled down the hall, passed Grandpa's closed door and the bathroom, to the kitchen and clicked on the electric kettle on the countertop to the right of the kitchen sink and window.

The gray skies were dark, and she realized it wasn't quite six yet, and early. She didn't mind and took the opportunity for this rare moment of quiet to think over the events of the last few days.

This time of year, so close to her birthday, made her thoughtful as she considered all she'd learned during the prior year, and made personal goals for the next one.

Change had come at them with a vengeance, painful but necessary.

The electric kettle clicked off, the water hot, and she got out a tea mug, and some Brodies tea, bringing it to the table.

She removed the newspaper from the wrapper, in a Zen mood, but once again Darcey McClintock destroyed her easy, mellow vibe.

Blake Harrington was on the front page, arguing with Ailis, the picture from someone's mobile, grainy and out of focus.

The headline, in bold, read—"Did Blake Kill Ailis?"

The article went on to share that Blake had driven with Ailis from their flat in Inverness to be with her family for Halloween. Ailis and Blake got into an argument, and Blake took off in Ailis's car, leaving Ailis at Rait Ruins. She had agreed to play a prank on Brody Shaw, all in good fun, and now the family believed that Blake must have returned shortly after, and they possibly argued again. Something happened and Ailis was killed. Help Find a Killer was the next tagline.

"What on earth is Darcey thinking? There are more missing pieces tae this story than an expert knitting pattern," Paislee groused. Beginning patterns walked a knitter through each step of the process whereas sometimes, not always, the more complicated patterns had intuitive steps as the knitter assumed expertise before tackling a tough project, such as a lace shawl.

Her phone rumbled and she brought it from her pocket. She'd forgotten about the earlier notification. Her heart slowed as she read that it was from Simon, not Mack. He'd sent the Muriel Campbell footage, and apologized for not sending it last night, as he'd been hung up with the thane. He would see her tonight at the Oasis, with Pat Amblin and the Barron-Smythes.

The second text was from Lydia, about the article by Darcey, and Blake Harrington.

KILLER? Should I be worried about you?

Grandpa came out of his bedroom and scuffed his slippers, blinking like an owl, into the bathroom across the hall.

In that instant Paislee could easily imagine her son as an old man. Three generations under one roof—she was grateful for it.

No. We are fine.

Call me ASAP.

Paislee got up and reheated the water in the electric kettle for Grandpa and stepped out onto the back porch to call Lydia, who answered on the first ring.

"Morning!" Lydia's tone was far too chipper. Paislee had been expecting avoidance and exhaustion, or concern.

"And hello to you too." Paislee flipped on the electric heater and grabbed a blanket to wrap around herself. Wallace was still upstairs asleep with Brody. It was the first night that he hadn't been on the couch since the incident.

"Did you know Ailis was murdered?" Lydia asked in a sharp tone.

"It's not for sure that she was killed. Tae my knowledge the medical examiner hasn't concluded the cause of death. I knew it was under investigation," Paislee said.

"I read the article, and had Mum read it too. It seems verra emotional and not verra fact-based."

"That is very kind, Lydia. The piece had more holes than a spider web."

Her bestie snorted. "Well, now that you mention it," Lydia said.

They laughed.

"I'm already in a better mood now," Lydia said. "I miss you. Any chance we can do lunch today at Cawdor Café, like you agreed?"

"I said maybe, Lyd. I'm not sure it's a good idea." She thought of the orders to do. "I'll close Cashmere Crush early though, tae meet you at five at the Oasis rooftop."

"Fine," Lydia said. "Will Mack be able tae join us tonight?"

"No. He seconded what Simon had mentioned over whisky yesterday that there are rumors of coordinated efforts tae cause rioting in Nairn."

"I dinnae like it," Lydia said. "Corbin, his da, and his brothers went on and on all night while we were there for dinner. Like Sorcha and Shannon's places, there was no permanent harm done tae the property, though it felt like an invasion of privacy. Mum and I were completely ignored. Da was pulled intae the conversation a wee bit when he shared his terrifying experience in Edinburgh last year."

"Are they worried?"

"Aye, but the house and shop are locked up tight this year. Da's got the entire block under video surveillance. It's cheap at half the price tae put cameras all over and have it come tae your personal mobile." Lydia whistled. "Corbin wants tae set us up just like that so that when we're away from the vineyard, we'll have drone footage of the property."

"That's impressive," Paislee said. "I'm glad that your parents are here with you if things go sideways."

"Me too," Lydia said. "Think it came as a shock tae the laird, and everyone, that Garrison is a mere mortal man."

Garrison Smythe was more at home in a kilt than street clothes. "Not the easiest revelation, I'm sure."

"No." Lydia's exhale rattled the mobile.

"I'm sorry." The thing that Paislee was sorry about most was that Lydia had to deal with the Smythes at all.

"It's fine." A pause and then Lydia said, "I was hoping tae sleep in but woke up with the roosters this morning. Please reconsider joining Mum and I for lunch at Cawdor Café? I was thinking we'd go as an early birthday present for you. I also selfishly need some girl time."

Paislee considered her schedule. "Maybe? I didn't go back tae the shop yesterday and I should see what is happening. I'll call you."

Lydia snorted. "That means no. Hey, can you take tomorrow off?"

"No."

"But, it's your birthday!"

"And I still have orders tae do. Why don't we do lunch tomorrow at Cawdor Café instead?" It made sense to her to celebrate during the actual day.

"I am juggling things as well. I was gathering information, as you like tae say." Lydia chuckled. "I want you tae keep your evening after five p.m. tomorrow free—promise?"

"Sure." Paislee recalled the cryptic looks Brody, Grandpa, and Lydia had shared yesterday and knew she would need to be "surprised" for her birthday party.

It was a wonderful blessing to have such close friends and family. Would Mack be able to come?

Thinking of Mack reminded her of the danger he might be in tonight if things in the shire went nuts. She would stop at the church today and light a candle for his safety, as well as the rest of the Nairn police.

"Okay. I hope tae see you later today," Lydia said. "I'd be willing tae go tae the Lion's Mane since it's closer tae the shop, even though Pat Amblin is reported tae hang oot at the café. He's a cutie."

"That might be more doable, but Pat is charming and talented. The tasting menu he did yesterday was indescribable—go tae the café. You won't regret it. You and I will be able tae catch up later at the rooftop dome." Paislee could hear Lydia's need and would try. "What did you think of Poppy?"

"She was verra feisty," Lydia said. "I like that. Reminds me of you when you get your feathers ruffled, actually."

"Hey!"

"Think her and Pat will last?"

"I don't know. Funny that we both wondered about that, though," Paislee said. "Could be the clash of the egos."

"Pat's is justifiably huge, he's an incredible chef, but Poppy is on the up-and-up. And, I just dinnae ken what tae think aboot Ailis and Blake. Did they meet at university? What if he was a bad influence on her? What if she didnae even know he was using her keys tae party in the hotel rooms?"

"That's a lot of what-ifs, Lyd. The fact is that Ailis knew about the parties when Poppy confronted her, and she chose tae stay with Blake." Paislee wrapped the blanket around her shoulders. Two squirrels chased each other from the tree to the clothesline. "She seemed tae be a sweet person."

"Some women have tae be with a guy no matter what and dinnae understand that being single is better than being with a jerk. Single, you can take responsibility for your own choices and not be dragged doon by someone else."

"Lots of girls are like that." Paislee shrugged. "Not us. I think Sophie would have had our heads if we'd been like that. Your mum was a great influence when we were teens."

"That she was. I'm so glad she's here. I had no idea how close the riots came tae their place last year on Bonfire Night. Mum didnae tell me because she didnae want me tae be worrit."

"It isn't right that innocent people are hurt by bad apples. Most folks are good." Ailis came to mind.

"Simon has been pounding the pavement with that petition on behalf of the thane. He feels terrible that it was his idea for the fundraiser. The ten thousand pounds raised tae help the injured farmer was a drop in the bucket compared tae the jewelry stolen. Corbin's stepmum is a fount of gossip and Mary said that the DC froze the rest of the family oot, when they were already on shaky ground when it came tae keeping the peace. I've never met the Dowager Countess of Cawdor, but between Simon and Mary, I'm shaking in my Jimmy Choos at the idea."

"She is formidable. Imagine Lady Leery and DC Grant combined. A powerhouse, yes, but also protective of the castle . . . the fact that her jewels were stolen felt like a personal attack."

"It doesnae explain the Guy Fawkes character in the tower. The holly tree isnae worth money. Mibbe as a collector's item, but the diamonds and the jeweled egg are the pieces of financial value. What do you think?"

"Simon just sent the Muriel footage this morning, so I will look at it."

"Call me afterward?"

"All right."

Paislee stood and allowed the warm blanket to slide from her shoulders to the chair, and turned off the heater.

Brody opened the back door and let Wallace out, nodding a good morning to Paislee before closing the door again. Paislee stayed outside and watched Wallace run around.

"Being an activist for a cause is not in your nature, but we might need tae peacefully protest or something if we have thugs in Nairn tonight," Lydia said.

Because they were best friends, and discussed everything under the sun, Paislee knew Lydia had been like her—a Liberal Democrat, leaning toward the Labour Party. Her parents were Labour, like Grandpa. The Smythes were Conservatives. Labels lumped people together but in the end, it was up to the individual.

"I'm concerned," Paislee admitted. "I will do whatever it takes tae keep our shire safe for the next generation."

She went inside, where Grandpa and Brody sat at the breakfast table. Toast and cereal had been prepared, juice for Brody and tea for Grandpa, the paper dispersed to the parties' preferences, the article with Blake on the front page set to the side. It was obvious from how Brody kept glancing at it that her son had read it. Had Blake killed Ailis?

"Call me!" Lydia said.

"I will—bye." Paislee pressed the end button.

The snug kitchen provided warmth and shimmered with love. She thought of poor Julie Barclay, waking up on this Tuesday without her daughter. Her son, Darryl, her husband, Doug, all trying to find solace and getting smacked by the article from Darcey accusing Blake of murdering Ailis.

Another piece of news where the journalist had crossed the line.

Was she so powerless that she couldn't act? Angry, Paislee called the newspaper office. She reached a recording and left a brutal message on the answering machine. "Darcey McClintock is unprofessional and deserves tae be reprimanded."

Brody and Grandpa both looked at her with alarm when she slammed the phone down to the charging base.

"What's the matter, Paislee?" Grandpa asked. "Darcey is all aboot selling papers with seedy headlines. It's her MO."

Paislee tapped the picture of Blake and Ailis on the table. "It's not okay. Put yourself in Julie Barclay's shoes."

"Mum, calm doon."

Grandpa sucked in a breath and shook his head at Brody. "Never tell a woman, especially an angry redhead, tae calm doon."

Paislee's face burned with temper. Was steam coming out of her ears? She wouldn't be surprised. She counted to ten. Fifteen . . . twenty. Fifty. There was no phrase in the world guaranteed to tip the scales of anger like *calm down*.

When her eyes had uncrossed, she tried again, going to the tea kettle to prepare herself a fresh cup. She turned, her hip to the counter as she spoke over her shoulder to them.

"In my opinion, Darcey McClintock is going too far tae sell a paper. Setting up Blake and Ailis like that? We don't know the truth yet. I can easily imagine Julie's pain, because this just happened a few days ago. We stumbled across someone who had died. We don't know how. This is libelous."

"Sairy, Mum."

"It's fine." Paislee paced to the kitchen window and focused on the chestnut tree. She empathized wholeheartedly with the Barclay family. She made a mental note to drop by later with something from Tesco. Perhaps a large lasagna, or shepherd's pie.

"Come and eat your toast," Grandpa said.

Paislee found her calm, let Wallace back in, and joined them at the table. "I hope Darcey calls me back."

"She's probably quaking under her desk," Brody said. "I've never heard you that mad."

"Darcey McClintock is a very tough young woman." Paislee recalled their face-to-face meeting in her office. "She doesn't scare easily. I really thought after our last conversation that she would have been more considerate of grieving families."

"I guess not," Grandpa said. "This is pretty blatant, and has a picture of the family, including Darryl and Ailis."

"Darryl should be at school today, and this will put him in the spotlight. Not okay." The tips of Paislee's ears burned with emotion.

"Cannae I stay home?" Brody asked.

"No."

"You didnae even think aboot it," Brody said. He placed his hand over his belly. "I could have a cold or the flu."

"Do you?" Paislee's brow winged upward.

"No."

"All right then. You just have tae get through today and tonight we'll get tae see fireworks from the best seats in the shire."

Paislee would bring Poppy a knitted cashmere scarf as a thank-you. She'd promised to bring the pumpkin table decorations to Pat Amblin. *Later.*

"I cannae wait," Grandpa said. "Paislee, any word from the DI?"

"Nope. Mack has been suspiciously quiet. I think he doesn't want tae encourage us, but, well, we want answers."

Her phone dinged. Lydia, asking if she'd seen the Guy Fawkes figure on the Muriel Campbell video yet.

Her phone dinged again—Sorcha, Dowager Countess Grant, promising to have Darcey's job, in truth this time.

Paislee nibbled a corner of her toast. "We need tae see the Muriel footage. Simon just sent it."

"Oh, yeah," Brody said. "Before school for sure. I had dreams last night that Muriel in blue had combined with the Wraith of Rait Ruins and didnae have hands." He shivered. "If it's real enough we can show Mack. He'll know if it's a fake."

Paislee went to the downstairs computer, an updated laptop in the lounge, and brought it back to the round table. Grandpa moved her toast plate and the paper.

She fired it up and opened the email from Simon. "Here we go," she said.

Simon's email said, *Security footage from inside C Castle. Motion activated. Nobody was supposed tae be in the* locked *tower.*

Brody, munching toast, stood behind her on the right and Grandpa to the left. At last, the video loaded, and she hit the play button.

"The tower was locked," Grandpa said. "That alone is eerie. Who unlocked it? Muriel?"

"And the cameras are motion activated," Brody said. "What kind of energy would a ghost have in order tae set off the alarm?"

They each hunched over her to peer at the laptop screen. Paislee waited, holding her breath, for something to happen.

After just a few seconds the black screen flashed on—the camera was trained on the petrified holly tree. Nothing moved. Suddenly there was a splash of Cawdor Campbell blue and green, like a smudged watercolor, in front of the camera, which swiveled to locate what was moving. Paislee leaned closer, her mouth dry. The camera zeroed in on the staircase of the tower and . . . Guy Fawkes. "Huh?"

"It's a guy in a costume," Brody said.

"Right." Paislee put her hand to her galloping heart. She hadn't understood what Lydia had meant when her bestie had mentioned it.

The smudge of blue whirled around the figure, who screamed in terror. A man? A woman? It was impossible to tell.

"I did that too," Brody said. He was pale. "I feel ya, bro."

The action and sound set off the tower alarm and the costumed figure ran back out of sight.

"The blue tornado was Muriel," Paislee said decisively.

Brody plunked down in his chair, elbow smacking the table. "It had tae be Muriel." Her son held out his trembling hand. "For real. Not a prank."

Grandpa sat at the table and removed his glasses to pinch the bridge of his nose. "It could have been . . . activated by the joker coming doon the tower stairs, and that's what alerted the camera."

"Grandpa, that's not what happened." Brody nodded toward Paislee. "Right, Mum?"

Paislee's skin was covered in goose bumps and her stomach was clenched tight. "It could be coincidence, but it could also not be. There is more tae this world." Her voice shook. "Why not Muriel protecting the castle, specifically the holly tree? It's been there since forever. The castle was built around it."

"Why Guy Fawkes?" Grandpa asked. "It cannae have been a random costume choice."

"I see where you're going," Paislee said. "Guy Fawkes was a Catholic radical who wanted tae overthrow the Protestant monarchy. Not the same instance here."

"Has the vandals' propaganda ever been religious in tone?" Grandpa's question made sense. Religion didn't actually track.

"Not really. SAORSA. Down with Tories. Freedom. Freedom from what? That seems more political. Guy Fawkes was willing tae blow himself tae Kingdom Come for freedom. Today is Guy Fawkes Day. There will be fireworks and effigies of Guy Fawkes burned all over Great Britain and Scotland."

"People are encouraged tae be a little mental," Grandpa said. "In this particular climate, that's not guid."

Lydia texted and Paislee replied that they'd just finished watching the footage.

She called, and Paislee answered, putting the phone on speaker. "Hi!"

"Well—what do ye think?" Lydia demanded. "That had tae be Muriel the ghost, right?"

"I think so, too," Paislee said. "We all do."

Brody and Grandpa chorused agreement.

"What aboot the Guy Fawkes character in costume?" Lydia asked. "Simon cannae believe that somehow, he got past the guards. There is a padlock on the door that he must have unlocked. A key? A bobby pin?"

"Was it locked on the way oot?" Grandpa asked. "He ran when the alarms went off."

"I dinnae think so," Lydia said. "We can ask Simon. He wants tae help find the intruders, and the jewelry, tae get back in the family's guid graces."

Brody leaned back against the kitchen counter. He was dressed for school already in his blue uniform. Hair combed, but a spot of milk from his cereal glistened on his upper lip.

"Guy Fawkes wanted tae overthrow the government." Brody swiped the milk off with the back of his hand. Paislee gave him a napkin. "In the old days war was aboot religion, and now, it is supposedly politics . . ."

"Aye," Lydia said. "The vandals, the graffiti."

Pushing from the counter, Brody walked around the kitchen table, smacking his fingers to his opposite palm. Grandpa crossed his arms as he watched Brody pace from the sink to the table.

"What if it isnae politics or religion—no ideals. What if this is all a big fake oot?" Brody swiped his hands together. "Grandpa, we talked aboot this on Halloween. What else are people willing to fight for? Family, food, shelter and . . ."

Paislee put her hand to her mouth. Simon and the thane both thought that the holly tree was the real target that night. Were they wrong?

"Money?" Lydia said.

"Buckets of it," Brody said. "How much are diamond necklaces worth?"

"Brilliant," Grandpa chortled. "Secondary school is really paying off."

Chapter 13

"Protesting the power of the nobility might be a ruse," Lydia repeated. "Tae make people think that the vandalism is political in nature, hence the Guy Fawkes costume."

"And what they really want is money," Paislee said. "I don't know . . . that is a big risk to steal jewelry that will have to then again be sold."

"We should question the religious part of the equation as well," Grandpa said. "There hasnae been a single instance of it in the vandals' threats. The pamphlets of the unicorn stomping on the lion?"

"Supposedly a desire for freedom," Lydia said. "But, I think Brody is on to something regarding a sleight of hand."

"Let's examine this again from all angles. Why did the only theft happen at Cawdor?" Paislee mused. "Thank goodness for Muriel setting off the alarm. The man was not expecting a ghost."

"It doesnae feel great tae be tricked, even if it is supposed tae be in guid fun." Brody wadded up the napkin and tossed it in the trash. "Now, I'm not sure what I believe with me own eyes."

"You are too young tae be cynical," Lydia declared.

Paislee's heart ached for her son. She glanced at the time on her phone and swallowed a squeal. "We've got tae get moving. I'm going tae officially decline lunch. I have a feeling today will be a long day and I should keep my schedule open."

"I'm being turned doon for nothing?" Lydia asked in disbelief.

"Lyd, come tae the shop if you want tae—you are always welcome. I gotta go!"

"You, bestie, are something else. For sure a date tonight at the hotel at five?"

"Promise!" Paislee ended the call, flustered.

"You should go tae lunch," Brody said. "With Aunt Lydia and Sophie. It would be a break, and you always work so hard."

"She says she has plans for tomorrow and can't go tae lunch, but we have plans with her tomorrow night. What am I going tae do for my birthday lunch?" It felt odd that Lydia wouldn't be a little more forthcoming.

Brody and Grandpa both adopted innocent expressions.

"Fine. I will go with the flow, but that means I should be at work today tae get things crossed off the never-ending projects list." She hadn't checked the Cashmere Crush website, where folks could order bespoke items, for several days.

The coin purses in the Grant tartan were in constant demand, as well as scarves, hats, and gloves in matching colors. Sweater vests were also popular. Fall, while slower in the shop itself, usually allowed her to build her inventory for the Christmas season.

Paislee closed the laptop and brought it back to the small desk in the lounge. There was room for everything, and it didn't look messy so long as everything was put back in its place. What had Gran used to say? *A place for everything, and everything in its place.*

She would claim that slogan for the back room at the shop.

"I'll be there at noon," Grandpa said. "If it's slow like it has been, Rhona and I can handle it withoot a problem."

"I know you can." Paislee sighed. "I'll think about it." She went upstairs to shower and get dressed for the day, choosing tan khakis and a pretty burnt-orange shirt with yellow flowers that usually cheered her up.

The busy morning had dampened all romantic thoughts of Mack, and Mack's kisses that had sweetened her dreams.

At 8:45, Paislee and Brody were on their way to his school. His backpack was at his feet, and he wore a lightweight jacket. She went just a touch over the speed limit. "How are you doing?"

"It feels weird not tae have a phone," Brody said. "At first, I didnae mind it, but I keep checking for messages and then reminding myself that the DI has it, looking for clues."

Brody twirled his fingers near his temple.

Paislee laughed softly.

"I'm losing it."

"That's all right. Tomorrow, you can borrow Grandpa's if that will make you feel better. We can get you a new mobile this weekend at Tesco. I want tae pick up some food for the Barclay family." She glanced at Brody, who stared out the passenger window. "I don't think we should stick tae your plan of not getting a new phone until Ailis's death is resolved." Mack was always reminding them that investigations took time.

"It seems like Blake might have had something tae do with it," Brody said. "When will they know for sure?"

"Mack said that he hoped for the medical examiner's report soon."

"Darryl must be gutted aboot that article," Brody said. "I kinda hope he doesnae come tae school today."

Paislee nodded in understanding, still angry with the reporter. If Darcey didn't call her today, then she would take Sorcha up on her offer of drastic measures.

"I cannae believe we saw a ghost on the footage from Cawdor." Brody ruffled his hair around his nape. It was growing in and often tickled. "Edwyn wouldnae believe it—he's always looking for a gimmick. Mibbe he's right? Emma and Sam would think it was brilliant."

Paislee turned down the street the school was on. The brick building grew closer, and she continued onto the paved road. School started at nine and they had a whole five minutes to spare. "You can't really talk about it tae anyone, remember?"

"I dinnae have anyone tae talk tae, anyway," Brody said. The bell rang. "Dang it. There's Darryl, and he's with Jimmy. You cannae drop me off here, Mum. Go around the block or something."

Paislee wanted to protect Brody, and she wanted to confront the boys, but she couldn't do either. She held back a little in the queue. With the autumn mornings cooler, most of the kids and staff were already inside.

Darryl, his eyes red, Jimmy at his side, darted into the building. They didn't see the teacher behind them juggling a mug and a briefcase.

Paislee stopped at the drop-off spot. "Oh no!"

Brody hopped out to help, grabbing his backpack without a word to her. He rushed forward and arrived in the nick of time to grab the briefcase.

"Have a good day," Paislee said as the car door shut.

The two went in while the warning bell clanged.

Paislee couldn't get Darryl's ravaged expression from her mind. How dare Darcey add salt to the gaping wound the Barclays felt right now?

Despite her tight schedule, she decided to pay Darcey another visit at the paper before going to Cashmere Crush. The office was open at seven in the morning, so Darcey, by not returning Paislee's call, was ignoring her.

Paislee drove to the newspaper building and parked in the lot by ten after nine. She went inside and directly to the office that Darcey shared with another reporter.

Darcey saw her coming and held up her hand. Silver rings shone from several fingers and a blob of ink was on her palm.

"I'd like a word with you," Paislee said.

The other journalist rose from his desk with a snicker. "I recognize that voice from the recording on the machine. Paislee Shaw. Mitch Duprey. Nice tae meet you." Mitch stepped toward the door. He had wild green hair, and yellow trainers. His suit was gray.

"Dinnae leave me," Darcey said as Mitch left, closing the door behind him.

Paislee's face heated with anger, and she crossed her arms, stepping closer to Darcey. "You have some nerve, really tearing apart a family in their time of grief."

"Dinnae start with me, Paislee." Darcey sat back in her chair, which was on wheels and scooted several inches. Her ensemble was black on black, including her leather boots. "I'll have you know that I wrote that article on behalf of the Barclay family."

Paislee stopped in mid-stride. This woman was delusional. "How could you?"

"Did you hear me?" The chair creaked across the tiled floor as Darcey rolled it to the desk. "Mrs. Barclay begged me tae write that piece. Julie believes that Blake Harrington is guilty of more than just being a bad boyfriend, if ye ken what I mean."

Paislee inched back as Darcey stood up from behind her cluttered desk.

"I don't understand." Paislee scowled at Darcey.

"Darryl told us that he and Blake were in contact the night of Ailis's death. When she went tae Rait Ruins?"

Of course they would have been, since they were setting Brody up. Oh, Blake and Darryl . . . not just Ailis. There was more to the story. "And?"

"And, when Ailis didnae answer Darryl's phone calls, he called Blake tae have him check on his big sister." Darcey's gaze was steady as she made her points.

"Did Blake do so?"

"Darryl said that he asked Blake tae check on Ailis, around nine thirty. Blake agreed but is now in the wind. He's disappeared. We know from multiple sources that the couple had argued. The live video from the harbor, and the social media post of them arguing, where he'd kicked her oot of her own vehicle." Darcey shrugged. "This is a ploy tae close the net around Blake until he surfaces and confesses."

"Your awful headline is meant tae sell papers."

"Well, yes." Darcey looked at Paislee like Paislee was a moron. "It's also meant tae get people tae contact us with information if they've seen Blake—he isnae just a university student playing coy, he is wanted for questioning in the circumstances surrounding Ailis's last night."

Paislee slowly relaxed as she saw the merit of the scheme. "Nine thirty?" Brody would have been long gone, and she and her son hadn't come until an hour later. Blake had known where Ailis was.

"Aye. I did this at their request." Darcey lifted her chin in a self-righteous manner. "I believe an apology is in order."

"Sorr—" Paislee stopped, hoping she wasn't being had. "I'll check with the Barclays. If one is owed, you will get it, but not until. I can't imagine grieving parents going along with this headline."

But, the more she thought about it, the more she could see another side.

If this was a chance to drive Blake into the open? From the Barclays' point of view, she could imagine them using whatever tools necessary, even a reporter.

"I'll be in touch," Paislee said.

"I like chocolates," Darcey said snidely. "Skip the flowers."

Paislee left Darcey's office, worried she'd made a blunder.

"Paislee?" Mitch stopped her in the lobby. There was nobody at the reception desk today. Maybe Susie hadn't come in yet.

"Yes?" She turned to face the other journalist.

"Hey. Want you tae know that I really like your spunk." The journalist ruffled his green locks, going for charm that fell flat. "You dating anyone?"

Ugh. "Yes. The detective inspector on this case," Paislee said in a short tone. This guy didn't stand a chance to gain her interest, let alone her affection.

"My bad!" Mitch jerked his chin toward the offices. "Darcey can be extra. She knows what buttons tae push."

"Is it true that the Barclays wanted her help tae locate Blake?"

"Sort of." Mitch stepped closer to Paislee, glancing down the hall to be sure they were still alone. "She went tae them for an interview and skewed it so it seemed like she was doing them a favor.

In a way she is, if it gets the slimeball Blake intae custody. It's always the lover in these situations."

Paislee scowled toward Darcey's office. That was not worth an apology. She'd been played just now by a champ. "Not always. I can't believe her!"

"She's got brass balls, that one. Has tae have them, being as Darcey's a card-carrying member of the Scottish National Party. She wants total freedom."

The SNP? "No way!"

"Yep. Had a bumper sticker but took it off when her car was egged. Silly goose," Mitch said. "What can you do?"

"So, she is all about freedom—same as the vandals?"

Mitch's eyes widened. "That I dinnae ken. She's sly as a fox." The reporter left Paislee in the lobby with interest in his gaze. Would he be poking around to see if Darcey had some aerosol cans tucked away?

It was now quarter till ten and she had to get to work. Rhona would be there, as would Jerry McFadden to drop off her Tuesday morning yarn delivery.

She put tricky Darcey, who wanted FREEDOM, from her mind. She parked behind her shop as Rhona and Jerry chatted on the stoop, early birds.

"And here's our Paislee Shaw," Jerry said. He had brown hair, a thick mustache and beard. Gray canvas coveralls with heavy boots for work were his delivery uniform.

Rhona said, "I was getting worried aboot you. You are never late tae the shop."

Brody's school sometimes, but hardly ever anymore.

Paislee smiled at Rhona, who had her braids coiled on top of her head. Cashmere Crush didn't have uniforms, so she dressed in an ankle-length cocoa-colored skirt and trainers in pink and brown plaid, with a thick brown jumper.

"Yes, I decided tae give Darcey McClintock at the newspaper a piece of my mind. I don't trust that woman a bit, not as far as I can throw her." Paislee trembled with adrenaline.

"Are you talking aboot the brazen headline accusing Blake of killing Ailis?" Rhona patted a flyaway strand of brunette hair and tucked it into her braids. "My parents couldnae believe it."

"Well, Darcey claimed that the Barclay family wanted her tae post the article in order tae get Blake tae come forward." Paislee unlocked the back door and opened it. "And it was kind of true, but then the other reporter clarified that she'd gone tae their house for an interview and skewed it so that it would seem like their idea."

"What a dafty!" Rhona said.

"Can you talk tae the Barclays?" Jerry asked. "Find oot the truth from them personally. They've got tae be devastated."

"They weren't around this past week at church," Paislee said. "I plan on going tae Tesco this weekend tae pick up some dinners for them. I'll chat with them then. Do you know them, Jerry?"

"Naw. Seen them around the shire, but not tae say that we are friends. Same for Freya. We feel awful for them though. Let me know if we can help oot in any way?"

"I will."

Rhona and Paislee went to the register and put their handbags under the counter while Jerry brought in two boxes of yarn. The beige merino wool was her best and most consistent seller.

"Here you are," Jerry said, giving her an invoice.

Paislee, after counting the skeins in the boxes to be sure it was the correct order, wrote a check for the exact amount.

"Thank you," Paislee said. "How's Freya?"

"Grand. She's verra excited about the new puppies she's training for JoJo's Farm. Working at the Scottish games reignited her love for them, and of course getting Rolly for herself made it a natural extension." He pulled his mobile from his pocket. "See?"

The photo of Freya, Jerry, and a black-and-white border collie puppy named Rolly was captured in that perfect moment of sheer joy. Jerry, in his forties, had never been in love before Freya. Like Paislee, he'd been a late bloomer.

"That's wonderful news. Rolly is almost as cute as Wallace. Be sure tae give her my best," Paislee said.

"That I will." Jerry doffed his cap. "See you next week."

"Bye." Rhona walked Jerry to the back door and quickly joined Paislee at the counter. "He's so nice."

"He is a genuine person, which is rare these days." Paislee opened the safe and set up the money in the register.

"Like Artie, too," Rhona said.

"And Aibreann, and Lydia—we have good taste in our friends, Rhona," Paislee said with a laugh. "We are ready!"

Paislee and Rhona smacked hands, and at exactly ten in the morning, Rhona opened the door.

Paislee logged on to the store laptop, mentally running though her schedule. She had an order for a knitted blanket in a couple's combined clan colors that wasn't due until their anniversary in spring, but other than that she was caught up. Getting Sorcha's wedding order would be a boon, and she could get started once she had a conversation with Sorcha, and probably Robert as well. Exact instructions would be paramount.

As she waited for her website to connect, she heard Rhona say, "Guid morning, DI."

Paislee, heart skipping with happiness, looked up from the laptop as Mack Zeffer strode toward her. This blue suit was denim in color and covered by a Police Scotland raincoat that wasn't buttoned. His smile didn't quite reach his seafoam-green eyes.

"Hi," Paislee said, her voice shy. Now was not a convenient time for the memory of their kisses that had kept her up last night.

"Hey, yourself." Mack rested his forearm on the counter. Drops of rain were in his russet hair and on the shoulders of his jacket.

"How's it going?" She kept the question general, but hoped he'd tell her more about Ailis or Blake. She couldn't wait to get Mack's take on Darcey McClintock's article.

"Could be better, but things are looking up." Mack winked. "Can we talk in private?" He walked into the back storage area.

It needed an upgrade, especially if it was going to be seen by so many members of the public. "Sure. Rhona, will you mind the front?"

"Of course." The teenager took the feather duster and walked toward the front of Cashmere Crush, to give them even more privacy.

"Can I get you a cup of tea?" Paislee joined Mack by the armchair. "I could absolutely use one!"

"I'm tea'd out." Mack kept his jacket on. Did this mean he wouldn't be staying long? What did he have to say?

"Okay." Paislee put on the electric kettle and chose a large mug, and a Brodies tea bag, prepping the mug as she waited. "What is it?"

"There was an attempted break-in at the station last night in the wee hours of the morning." Mack held her gaze, his voice steady as a rock despite the news he'd delivered.

A break-in at the police station, with actual constables on duty. Paislee had to have heard that wrong. She jiggled her ear lobe. "What?"

"Nothing wrong with your hearing, sadly." Mack glanced toward the front, but Rhona wasn't paying them any attention as she sang along to the store music pop tunes she kept on low volume. "Specifically, someone wanted intae the evidence room."

"That seems very risky," Paislee said.

"A desperate move, aye."

"What's in there?"

Mack tucked his hands into the pockets of his raincoat and leaned toward her to murmur, "The emerald found at the scene on Ailis's Halloween costume."

Paislee's mind leapt ahead. "And Brody's mobile."

Mack gave a grim nod.

"Are the items still there?" Paislee studied Mack's dear face for a hint of whether or not she should be worried a little, or a lot.

"Yes. We are assuming those were the targets, as the burglars went straight for that room rather than an easier access point, like the bathroom. The window there has always been a concern. The only other things in evidence belong tae closed cases."

"The emerald is worth money," Paislee said.

"Possibly," Mack replied. "Constable Jays was on duty and heard a ruckus. He realized that the cameras outside the station had been blacked oot and the noise turned oot tae be a cement cutter used on the wall. Barely made a crack. Jays ran oot after the culprit, locking the door and following protocol. The criminal was in a ninja costume, all black. I am beginning tae hate Halloween. While I believe the emerald might have value, I really think they wanted Brody's mobile."

Paislee brought her hand to her chest, her heart thumping. "It must have something of import on it that someone believes is worth breaking into a police station for."

"The video techs already have the video on their program, which leads me tae believe that we are missing something on it." Mack's voice was low. "Something in plain sight."

Paislee's stomach clenched. "Not good," she said.

"Not even a little bit." Mack looked into her eyes. "You need tae stay home tonight. I realize this will be a disappointment. I can bring a case of sparklers."

"What? It's Bonfire Night. You agreed the Oasis Hotel would be a safe place. Did you see the rooftop when you talked tae Poppy?"

"I havenae spoken tae her yet. It's on the agenda for today."

"Poppy might be able tae help you find Blake. I'm assuming that he's still on the run?" Paislee scowled toward the electric kettle. What was taking so blasted long?

"Trust me—like the DC of Cawdor, we are spread verra thin with our staff. I wish Amelia was finished with constable school but that isnae done yet for another eighteen months. We have two newbies, as well as Inspector McCleod, and Constables Payne and

Monroe. Maybe twenty-five officers in total. Our informants have all come back with rumors of a riot planned on the beach."

"In Nairn?"

"Yes. In Nairn, and Inverness."

Paislee exhaled. This was home.

Mack touched her arm. "There is more."

"What could possibly be worse? We haven't even talked yet about Darcey McClintock's article." Paislee crossed her arms at her waist. The cheery print of her blouse was failing miserably to lift her mood.

"Aboot that—the phones are ringing off the hook with Blake sightings, thanks tae that headline accusing Blake of killing Ailis."

The emotional and possibly sue-worthy article. "Did he? Darryl was in touch with Blake on Samhain around nine thirty, according tae Darcey."

Mack shrugged. "We are collecting evidence. Information. Blake Harrington is a key part of the puzzle."

Blake Harrington, uni student who liked to party. Was he a bad example for Ailis, or was he the mastermind behind the theft at Cawdor?

What had they been arguing about so viciously? "Have you seen the clip of Ailis and Blake yet?"

"Aye."

Paislee tucked her hair behind her ear. She'd left it down today rather than in her customary clip. "Darcey manipulated that poor family into giving their permission tae print that article," she said. "She had a purpose in mind when she went for an interview tae get them tae open up about their tragedy. Tap into their angst."

"Mibbe so. I can send an officer tae talk tae her at the paper."

"You can't do it?" And there she'd gone and added more pressure to the DI. Mack. "Sorry!"

"It's all right. But, aye, I'm too busy tae track Darcey doon." Mack rocked back on his heels. "I want you tae come tae the station."

the door on the way oot as he took off on foot after the car. Well, it's actually a truck."

"Not a chance of catching the driver. Not even if he was as fast as Brody."

"No. However, Jays was able tae cut across the grass and get a description of the getaway vehicle before it disappeared. We wouldnae have that key information withoot his quick thinking. He then returned tae the station, reported the incident and sent oot an alert. He traversed the area in his police car but never located the truck." Mack rested his hand on Paislee's lower back when they passed Scoops on the corner. It didn't open until eleven, but wonderful smells escaped the kitchen area.

After crossing the street and heading right, they reached the station. Mack opened the door for her, and they entered.

Inside, Paislee took a second to let her eyes adjust. Constable Payne sat behind the front desk where Amelia used to answer phones when she was a receptionist, before she decided to break all the rules she'd grown up with in her family to follow her dream to be a constable.

The dark-skinned officer always had a smile for Paislee and granted her one now. He'd shared with her once that he made the effort to see the joy in the small things or else he risked being lost in the bad stuff.

He saw people at their worst and wanted to help those in need while protecting them from criminals. He'd taken Amelia under his wing, as had Constable Monroe.

Monroe, at Amelia's old desk, was teaching a newbie male officer Paislee hadn't met before how to keep up with the phones. All five were ringing.

"The receptionist called in sick," Payne said. "It's chaos. Nice tae see you, Paislee!"

"Hi, Constable Payne. How are you?"

The plump officer shrugged, his uniform tight across the shoulders but not from muscle.

Kitty-corner to Payne, a young woman in a navy-blue constable uniform was sorting phone messages that had been piled up—all pink notes. Her brown hair was slicked back in a bun. The station was making an effort to build rapport in their community and move away from the old-school tactics of fear-based rules and they'd relaxed the tattoo requirements. She had a heart peeking from the sleeve of her short-sleeved top. Her tag read, D. MCPHERSON.

"I'm all right," Constable Payne said. "We sure miss Amelia around here. Teaching Constable Jays tae answer more than three lines has been a challenge. I needed a break, so it is Monroe's turn."

The young man scowled at the phone system. "Trying me best here. I'm a little freaked oot that someone tried tae break intae the police department with a cement cutter. That's crazy, right? I wish I'd caught the bloke. Dressed like a ninja. Fast too."

Constable Monroe gave the young man a very stern look that he ignored.

"Only stuff in there is that kid's phone, and an itty-bitty jewel." The phone rang again, and Constable Jays ignored it. "Bunch of dead cases."

"It seems like a big risk," Constable Payne said in a calm tone.

Constable Monroe eyed the ceiling in frustration. "Jays, you have got tae answer the phone. *Nairn Police Station.* I am this close tae losing my temper." She stood, leaving him to sink or swim. "Payne, you have the printoots?"

Payne tapped a sheaf of papers. "Yep. Right here. Your office, Zeffer?"

"Aye." Mack explained to Paislee, "Our tech team has pulled the CCTV info from the corner of A96 as the cameras on the building here were disabled." He opened the door to his office. When they'd first met, he'd had the big one that Inspector McCleod currently occupied, and now used a smaller one to the left.

Monroe and Payne joined them, and the plump constable placed the stack on the corner of Mack's desk.

"Here's two photos from the CCTV footage." Monroe tapped

her finger on the top pages. She flipped through the images and then selected a section to put in a separate pile. "These are from the verra, verra grainy images off of Brody's mobile." She passed them to Paislee. "Do you know this bloke?"

The picture was of a man with a fake Viking beard and horns. The passenger wore a cap and dark clothes. Was it part of the ninja costume? It was too shadowed to make out.

"No, I don't think so." Paislee picked up the ones off of Brody's phone. She squinted, trying to bring the image into sharper focus but it didn't help because the photos were bad to begin with. A blob was just a blob. Her shoulders bowed.

"It was worth a shot. Well, we'll run them through the system just in case we get a match for his identity. The truck was dark, the plate blacked oot." Monroe returned the photos to the top of the stack with a dejected sigh.

"Police work is tedious," Mack said. "We will get a break. Paislee, what aboot these images that our tech slowed doon from the video?"

Paislee accepted a stack of twenty as she sat down in an office chair. "These aren't much better."

She put herself back at Rait Ruins and recalled what she'd seen. Rait Tower, crumbling into literal piles of dirt to the right, and the cemetery to the left. Trees, boulders, Ailis in a dramatic swirl of white, dressed as the Wraith of Rait Ruins. There hadn't been a car in the lot, but she'd passed a truck parked on the side of the road. "I realize there is no way tae tell for sure, but I remember a truck on the road, similar tae this make, when Brody and I had returned tae the tower."

"A truck?" Mack opened his notes. "Did you tell me that earlier?"

Paislee wasn't sure. "It was parked toward the cemetery. That's where I'd felt like I was being watched from the direction of the oak tree." What if the truck hadn't been empty?

She rubbed her arm. The tech had blown up a shadowy figure

wearing a cape. Was that a tricorn hat? It was eerie and reminded her of the Guy Fawkes costume worn by the person in the tower at Cawdor, who'd been focused on the holly branch before being scared off by Muriel the ghost.

Paislee examined the image. Perhaps a stretch but it felt right. "Have you seen the security footage from Cawdor Castle, and the man in costume, breaking into the tower that protects the holly tree?"

Mack nodded.

Monroe and Payne did too.

"We had tae really press tae get that footage," Mack said. "You've seen it?"

"I can't share my sources"—Paislee would check with Simon first—"but this could be the same costume."

"Unfortunately, the Guy Fawkes is a verra popular costume on Halloween," Monroe said. "We were checking that angle already." She held out her hand and compared the photo from the tech with the one on Brody's phone. "I agree that this might be the same costume. Is it the same man?"

Mack rhythmically tapped the table with a firm forefinger, jaw tight.

"What are you thinking?" Paislee asked.

"It's just an idea that needs proof one way or the other." Mack leaned back in his office chair. "It's possible that Ailis saw something she shouldnae have, and that's why she . . . died. There is not a single snapshot of Blake Harrington in a Guy Fawkes costume—not with Ailis tae dress up, or prior Halloweens."

"We've pored through all of his social media photos," Monroe said. She had taken up a seat on a plastic bin used for storage. Payne was in a chair opposite Paislee. "He liked tae drink, he liked the ladies, and he didnae seem tae care aboot costumes. Not even as a wean, according tae his mum in Inverness. She hasnae seen him for a week."

Paislee swallowed. "Could Ailis's death have been a tragic accident?"

"Dunno," Mack said. "I'm afraid if I bug the ME one more time, the file will never be closed."

Paislee, through the slightly open office door, heard the phone ring and Constable Jays answered it. "Nairn Police Station."

Monroe splayed her hands over her knees. "Finally."

They all waited, listening.

"I'll be sure tae let the constables know. Thank you."

Jays came into Mack's office with a pink message slip.

"And?" Monroe prodded.

Jays offered Mack the piece of paper. "Another Blake sighting. This one sounded legitimate. You can tell when someone wants their two seconds of fame. This woman had a muffled voice, like she didnae want tae be recognized."

"We could use a break," Mack said.

"Where?" Constable Monroe asked.

"The caravan park a mile away. I can run over," Constable Jays offered. "It will just be a few minutes."

"All right," Mack said. "Take McPherson with you. Ride your bikes tae be on the downlow and let us know right away. Blake is central tae this investigation."

"You got it," Jays said. The young constable eagerly left the office. "McPherson. Let's ride!"

"Love his enthusiasm," Payne said with a weary smile. "I remember being that young and green. You?"

"It's been a while," Mack admitted. "It's refreshing. Paislee, thanks for coming doon here this morning. I think you're right aboot the Guy Fawkes mask in the trees." He nudged the photo across the desk. "How does it connect tae Ailis?"

"We were talking this morning over breakfast, wondering if the vandalism might be a ruse. Perhaps tae point tae politics, but it's really about something else."

"Go back tae work," Mack directed her firmly. "At your yarn shop."

Paislee stayed seated and studied the pictures of the driver and passenger one more time. A Viking costume, and a ninja. "The

Viking doesn't come close tae resembling Blake. He had longer hair, a broader forehead, and a narrower nose." She glanced at Mack. "The article seems to have helped though, even if Darcey is on my bad list."

Monroe's mobile phone rang, and she checked the time as well as caller. "Jays. Seven minutes—that was fast." The redhaired constable answered, putting him on speaker. "Monroe."

"We've located Blake. He's at the caravan park, space ten. Hurry!"

Paislee wished she could go with them, but knew it wasn't her place. "Let me know what happens," she said.

"If we can," Mack said. "You know the drill."

Monroe and Mack left the office with Paislee, leaving Payne with Inspector McCleod. As she walked back to Cashmere Crush, she couldn't get the youthful faces of Jays and McPherson from her mind. They were so young, and there were rumors of riots from reliable sources.

"What happened?" Rhona asked as soon as Paislee returned to the shop.

"The article from Darcey worked very well, and they are inundated with Blake Harrington sightings."

"But no Blake?" Rhona asked.

"No Blake." Paislee checked the Cashmere Crush website. "Yet." Two online orders for matching holiday jumpers, both medium in size. It was her favorite kind of order as the design was up to her. To be delivered December 20th.

Which would coincide with the cashmere for the Grant clan wedding. She put them on her calendar.

Would there be violence later? Concerned for the constables and Mack, dear Mack, Paislee was close to jumping out of her skin waiting for someone to call her with more information.

Grandpa arrived at noon, and Paislee had her keys in hand. Her heart was racing, and one thing that she did when she felt out of control was to pray. "Where you off tae in such a hurry, lass?"

"Church. I've got tae light some candles for Nairn and Bonfire

Night—the new constables are so green behind the ears. I'm glad that Amelia is still at school." Paislee showed Grandpa her phone, which had no messages from Mack. "I think Blake must still be at large."

"Mack would tell you if Blake was in custody. Say hello tae the Big Guy for me." Grandpa removed his jacket and tam to hang in the back room.

"Will do," she said.

"Aibreann and I will go tae the Lion's Mane when you get back," Rhona said. "Should we bring you some curry chips since you are praying through your lunch hour?" The teenager's mouth lifted in a teasing grin. "You still need sustenance."

Guy Fawkes Day, Bonfire Night, had a festive feel to it, but Paislee was so worried that she couldn't relax and just enjoy it like she normally would.

"No, thank you. I'll get something." While at church, she'd corner Rooney about Ailis and Blake. He'd made derogatory comments that needed an explanation. If Blake turned out to be innocent, then who else had known that Ailis would be at Rait Ruins? Rooney, that was who. He'd been the town crier and followed Ailis on social media. They'd had a summer love, whatever that meant.

The whole drive to the church, Paislee thought over the men in the photo caught on CCTV. Neither were Blake. Could one of them have been Rooney? The ninja had been thin, and wore a cap. Why would he want the phone or the jewel? Who had taken the video of Blake and Ailis?

Parking in the church car lot, Paislee hurried in as it started to drizzle.

Rooney, dressed in a Henley and jeans rather than business attire, sat at the welcome desk in the lobby of the church office. Father Dixon's office was directly behind him, and the church itself was to the left. She had coins in her pocket to put into the donation box for candles and special prayers.

"Hi, Paislee." Rooney gave her a worried smile. "Did you see the article in the paper this morning?"

"I did." Darcey certainly had sold papers with that headline. "What do you think?"

Rooney frowned. "I've always thought Blake could have hurt Ailis. I warned her. Seems like I was right." He shrugged, the movement lifting the three-quarter sleeve of his shirt to reveal a unicorn tattoo.

"Where did you get that?" Paislee pointed to the unicorn that was very similar to Poppy's in design and placement.

"What?" Rooney tugged the sleeve down to cover it.

"The tattoo, Rooney." Paislee shook her head. What a clown.

"Not that it's any of your business, but I went tae university in Edinburgh for a while before returning tae Nairn."

"And you randomly decided tae get a unicorn tattoo on your inner forearm?" Paislee tucked her hand in her pocket, jingling the coins. This guy was something else.

"It might have been a club thing."

That made sense, as Poppy had said she'd been wild during her youth in Edinburgh. "Do you know Poppy Drummond?"

"No."

Had that been a hesitation? Knowing Poppy would give Rooney some cachet in the world, considering that they were on opposite ends of the popularity spectrum. "Did Ailis have that tattoo?"

"Not during our hot summer of love. I worshipped every inch of her body." Rooney sighed, eyes half-closed as if he was lost in the memory. "We were both young teens then. I didnae have any ink either."

Jealousy was a common motive for passion escalating out of control. Maybe there was something on the phone that proved it was Rooney. "Do you drive?"

"Aye. I've got a truck. It's a new Ford Ranger tae pull my boat. Why?"

The getaway vehicle had been an older truck. Probably not

Rooney but she couldn't, and the constables shouldn't, rule him out. "No reason." She glanced at Father Dixon's closed door, having heard voices.

"If you want tae talk tae Father Dixon, he's in with the Barclays."

"Oh?" Paislee would like to chat with the family and share her condolences in person. She'd gladly take up the baton on the Barclays' behalf and maybe get Darcey booted from the newspaper. "I'll go light some prayer candles while I wait. Rooney, do you know about Ailis and Blake partying together at the Dolphin Hotel?"

"Partying?" Rooney shook his head at Paislee's ignorance. "Blake was charging by the hour for a little extra money."

Paislee's knees buckled. "No. No way. Ailis could not have gone along with that—what woman would?"

"Listen, I warned you that Ailis was not as sweet as she appeared, didnae I?"

"Yes." It was true that he had. Paislee hated that she was shocked by people's choices in their behavior.

"Well, we talked at church when she visited her family last, and she told me she planned on dumping Blake as payback for his crappy treatment. You know what I think?"

"No, what?"

"I think Ailis told Blake she wanted tae call things off, and he didnae go for it. He left her there at the ruins alone on purpose tae die. What if the Wraith scared Ailis so bad, she had a heart attack?"

"Just . . ."

"Why not? Her heart might have exploded due tae being pure terrified." Rooney leaned toward her. "Do they have a cause of death yet?"

"No. I believe everyone is still waiting for the results."

"I'm telling you, that's my bet. Scared tae death."

"I am not placing a wager like that, Rooney." Paislee stepped toward the prayer room.

The door to Father Dixon's office opened. "We will prepare

the funeral mass for next Saturday." In the Catholic religion, Sunday was traditionally kept for worship unless there were special circumstances.

"Thank you, Father," Doug Barclay said in a somber tone.

The trio made it as far as Rooney's desk before looking up and realizing that Paislee was standing there.

"I'm so very sorry for your loss." Her heart ached for them.

"Thank you." Doug's reply sounded as if he was on autopilot.

Julie's gaze flamed with fury.

Paislee edged back, her hip hitting Rooney's desk hard enough to bruise.

"You, Paislee Shaw, found my daughter. You didnae save her. You havenae reached oot, nor sent a consoling word. Not the person that I thought you were. Agnes would be verra disappointed in you. Darryl was right tae blame you, and Brody."

Stunned, Paislee didn't know what to say. She and Brody had done nothing wrong.

"Darling," Doug said, putting his arm around his wife's bowed shoulders. "Let's go home." He looked at Paislee. "It's the grief talking, but it seems odd that you havenae reached oot tae us."

"You and your family have been in my prayers since the moment I discovered Ailis at the ruins, please believe that." Paislee raised her chin as she conveyed empathy with her gaze. "If there is anything that I can do, please, say the word." They were hurting and lashing out.

"Find Blake Harrington and bring that fool tae justice." Julie fell into her husband. "It took Darcey McClintock tae get things moving."

Father Dixon ushered them to a wooden bench in the waiting room, but the couple ignored it and sailed out the door. It seemed Mitch had been right about Darcey coercing the family during their tragedy to make headlines.

"That was awful," Paislee said. "How can she blame me, and Brody, when Darryl was the one tae set everything up?"

"Pointing fingers at the aggrieved is not helpful," Father Dixon said.

Rooney snickered.

Paislee was ready to pop the immature man.

She could imagine how that would go down in the press. Angry mother lashes out in church. Instead, she went inside and lit several candles, kneeled, bowed her head and prayed.

She prayed for peace—peace for the Barclays, for her son, for the church, and for the constables in their shire. She prayed for Mack.

Her phone, on silent, buzzed repeatedly.

Concern for Brody cut her prayers short, though her load was a wee bit lighter as she left the dark room for the lobby.

Rooney was on the reception phone, and Father Dixon's door was closed. She scanned the messages.

Lydia, lunch.

Shannon, lunch—at the Cawdor Café.

Sorcha, lunch—at the Cawdor Café.

With the Dowager Countess of Cawdor, in—she gulped—fifteen minutes.

She sped from the parking lot, getting to the massive Cawdor property in record time—she'd tried to call Lydia on the way, but it had gone to voice mail.

Dialing the shop, she was glad when Grandpa answered. "Cashmere Crush."

"Hi—it's Paislee. It seems that I have a command invitation tae Cawdor Café after all, thanks tae the ladies."

"Ach, lass, that's fine, that's fine. Things are calm as can be on this end. I'll have Rhona go tae lunch with Aibreann?"

"Perfect. Let me know if you need me tae come back early. I feel like I'm being ambushed."

"Didnae you just spend an hour praying?" Grandpa teased.

"Thirty minutes, that's all. My phone kept buzzing in my pocket and I was worried it concerned Brody, not *lunch*. Have you heard any news from the constables?"

"Not a word."

"Me either." It was like juggling cats. The facts were squirmy, and the information ever-changing.

"Dinnae fret, lass. Things have a way of working oot." Grandpa said goodbye and she was listening to static.

Paislee parked and raced into Cawdor Café, quickly finding Shannon, Sorcha, and the DC of Cawdor, along with Sophie, Lydia, and Pat Amblin at the corner table with the most seats and privacy.

"Hi! And don't be mad. I wasn't late—I was just invited twenty minutes ago and happened tae be at the church." Paislee exhaled, her nerves on high alert, and faced them all as if they were a firing squad.

Lydia's lips twitched. Was she fighting a smile? The rest of the crew, regal and haughty, remained quiet. Sophie glared at the others. Lydia tilted her chin. "And this is what it takes for you tae come tae lunch with me?"

"Are you mad? I can't take it if you are for real. The Barclays blame me for not saving Ailis." Tears clouded her vision.

"Nonsense." Sophie got up and drew Paislee into a comforting hug. "Nobody is mad, dear. Lydia and I had no idea that Shannon and Sorcha were meeting with the DC of Cawdor when we arrived for our meal. They kindly included us, and we got tae chatting, sharing information. We realized that you needed tae be part of the conversation, so we'd all be on the same page as tae what happened tae puir Ailis."

Paislee allowed herself to be guided to a chair between Sophie and Lydia. Lydia put her arm around Paislee and squeezed. "I could never be mad at you, Paislee. I was sure you would ignore my invite as well as the noble summons."

"I wish I could have, trust me." Paislee bit her tongue so she didn't share about the possible riots tonight and the reason for her prayers. It wasn't hers to share. "We need tae find answers for the Barclays."

"Saw the paper this morning," Shannon said. "Couldnae believe it, not after we'd all had a chat with that journalist, Darcey McClintock."

Paislee accepted a glass of water that Lydia poured for her from a pitcher. "Thanks. Darcey told me that the Barclays wanted her tae do the piece accusing Blake of harming Ailis, but Mitch Duprey said she coerced them during an interview, tae sell papers."

"That's her job," the DC of Cawdor said.

"Tae put minors in danger?" Paislee shook her head. "I don't think so. Darryl . . . well, he's hurting like his mother, and looking for someone tae blame."

"And what if Blake is guilty?" Shannon asked.

"The constables are doing all they can tae find him," Paislee said.

"Poppy had a bead on him earlier today," Pat said. "Sent the information tae the station, though she was reluctant tae be involved."

"Okay, then." Paislee blew out a breath. "Now what?"

"Lydia said you saw the Muriel footage?" the DC of Cawdor asked.

"Yes." Paislee sipped her water. "And the person who had broken into the tower. We think we might have seen that costume at the cemetery, in the trees. Unfortunately, it's a popular costume, and the image was blurred."

"I dinnae like politics, but I can hardly stick my head in the sand," Shannon decreed. She pulled out the pamphlet with the unicorn trampling the lion. "I received this the day that my property was graffitied."

Sorcha pulled a pamphlet from her purse and placed it next to Shannon's. "I received this—exactly the same. With the word SAORSA."

"Freedom," Sophie breathed.

"I have one of those as well," the DC of Cawdor said. "It was tacked tae my front door." She pursed her lips. "Randall discovered that one of the guards had been knocked oot. Didnae want tae admit it, but the keys were taken at that time."

"Do you trust Randall?" Shannon said.

"Aye. I have tae trust someone. He's been in love with me since our youth."

"Like my Gavin," Shannon said. "I trust him with my life."

"I had someone like that in my life once upon a time. Tae lose them hurts," Sorcha said slowly.

Was she thinking of her dear friend Finn?

"Strong women need a strong man," Sophie said.

"It's true." Lydia smiled at Paislee. "You have that in Mack."

"Slow down with that, would you?" Paislee raised her hand. Though it did make her feel warm and fuzzy inside to think that she had possibly found her person. Her other half.

Just then all of their phones went off, from texts to calls.

Paislee stood, walking toward the front of the café as she answered the call from the shop to hear Grandpa say, "Blake is in custody!"

Chapter 15

Blake in custody—that was a relief. Now, they could get answers at last. "That's grand!" Paislee said. "Has he admitted tae anything?"

"Not yet," Grandpa said.

"Where was he?" Paislee paced the lobby near the check-out register. Plants in pots decorated the space interspersed with narrow wooden chairs.

"Not sure," Grandpa said. "It was on social media when Aibreann picked up Rhona for lunch, and they shared the news. I promised tae call you with it."

"Thanks, Grandpa. I'll see you"—she looked at her watch—"in an hour or so, I hope. Lydia was here and she and Sophie had joined the noble ladies, and Pat, the chef. I don't want tae be stuck here all day."

"Paislee, lass, please just enjoy the break," Grandpa said. "You work too hard as it is. Eat lunch."

Paislee turned and realized that Shannon and Sorcha were motioning for her to come back to the table. Gorgeous green salads were being served. "All right. Bye!"

She returned to her seat between Lydia and Sophie, turning off her mobile and placing it in her handbag.

"Things all right at the shop?" Sorcha asked.

"Perfect." She smiled at everyone. "How was Blake captured? Grandpa didn't know the details."

Pat lifted his phone. “Poppy came through for us. She put the word oot among her staff, some in the party scene. The constables found him at the caravan park.”

“That’s terrific.” She wondered if it was the same tip they’d received while she was at the police station to identify the driver of the getaway truck. She hadn’t had a second to share with Lydia, her bestie, about the attempted break-in. How desperate did you have to be to get *inside* a police station filled with constables?

“What an idiot tae not leave the shire,” Shannon said. “Blake Harrington. Sounds handsome, and wealthy. No brains.”

“I’ve seen his picture, so yes, he was cute in a boyish way. Mibbe with the heat on him, he was pinned,” Sophie suggested.

“I suppose,” the DC of Cawdor said. “Shall we?”

The salads were delicious with a dressing that Paislee doubted she would ever get tired of. Garlic, rosemary . . . it was incredible and so deceptively simple. Pine nuts, butter lettuce.

“This is really good,” Paislee said.

“All the veg are grown on the Cawdor property,” Pat said.

“The dressing?” Lydia asked.

“My own,” Pat said.

The DC of Cawdor put down her fork, only halfway through with the greens. “I pray that Blake will tell us where he hid the stolen jewels. The diamonds have been in the Campbell family for centuries. The egg is an original Fabergé gifted tae me by my mother, created in 1902. Its value is around 25 million pounds but that is for insurance purposes. Tae me, it is priceless.”

“It’s a shame,” Shannon said. “Tae be so violated.”

Paislee couldn’t fathom anything she owned that valuable. She’d heard of the Fabergé eggs but had never seen so much as a picture of one. “What did it look like?”

“Gold and platinum for the base, decorated with emeralds, diamonds, sapphires, and rubies.” The DC pursed her lips. “We are entrusted with these treasures for the next generations. I feel as if

I've let my mother and my ancestors doon. I'm tempted tae haunt the place like Muriel when I die, just tae continue tae be part of it."

Paislee didn't think she was joking.

Sophie, about to pat the woman's shoulder with commiseration, opted to fold her fingers around her teacup instead. This dowager countess was not one to let her guard down easily.

"What a brilliant idea." Sorcha's gaze twinkled. "I've considered doing the same, havenae I said so, Shannon? I'll inform Robert immediately that if he doesnae behave, he'll have me tae contend with, even in the afterlife. He's getting married this Christmas."

"Please send an invite. I would love tae attend," the DC of Cawdor said. "I've never been tae Ramsey Castle."

"You are quite welcome—it will be an intimate affair. Less than a hundred," Sorcha said.

"Even better. The older I get the less I like crowds. I dinnae really know anyone in the Highland social circle anymore. I've spent my free time with Randall, designing our gardens."

This noble attendance would make Robert Grant's nuptials the wedding of the year.

No pressure on Paislee for the bespoke cashmere vests or sashes for the ladies. She wanted to get started right away, yet recalled Grandpa's advice, and enjoyed another bite of salad.

"Lady Barron-Smythe here is an adored member of our social set, as is Lady Leery, so now you know two people tae befriend," Sorcha said.

"Anytime you want tae duck away from the limelight, come find me," Shannon murmured. "Overlooking the ballroom provides the best view for a blether."

The DC laughed. "Splendid." She looked at her delicate gold watch. "I must go. The insurance agent will be here soon, aboot the stolen jewels. I was hoping they'd be returned by now, but Randall says this is no time for hoping. The sooner we can make a report the faster pictures of the pieces can be sent around so that they willnae be auctioned for sale."

"Guid idea," Sorcha said. "Now that Blake is in custody, perhaps we will get answers."

The DC stood, signaling the end of lunch. Paislee barely stopped herself from licking the plate. She rose, hoping to get a private word with Lydia.

Pat cut between Lydia and Paislee, taking Paislee aside. "Poppy asked me tae remind you that you should be at the rooftop tonight by five. Her chef is making tapas and had the nerve tae ask for my brown sauce recipe! Can you imagine? Cheeky. I've made the desserts. Toffee apples, for one. I heard they're Brody's favorite."

"And one of mine. Thank you, Pat."

Paislee grabbed her jacket and handbag. Lydia and Sophie urged Paislee forward as they were bottlenecked by the kitchen of the café. "I know you're busy so we can catch up tonight!" Lydia said. "Mum and I have a few errands." Yet, she and Sophie waited with Pat, talking animatedly.

Paislee had no choice but to let it go and joined Shannon and Sorcha in the cramped café lobby where Sorcha struggled with a twisted coat sleeve.

"The DC inviting herself tae your son's wedding will make it the event of the season, Sorcha," Shannon murmured.

"I was just thinking the same thing." Paislee straightened Sorcha's sleeve and helped her into the jacket. "Are you sure you want me tae do the sashes and vests?"

"You are the most talented young woman in Scotland when it comes tae knitting. Mibbe all of the UK. Of course I do. Dinnae back oot on me now, Paislee. My to-do list just jumped in anxiety."

Shannon, in a large shrug with armholes, was ready and opened the door to the parking lot.

"Thanks," Paislee said to Shannon, then told Sorcha, "I won't back out. My mind is spinning with possibilities."

"We can talk next week when you refill the cashmere stock at the castle for the giftshop," Sorcha said.

Paislee had only seen the woman shaken once—but this was a close second.

They reached the car park. Sorcha was driving a fancy SUV, and Shannon walked toward the passenger side.

"I hope Blake spills the beans aboot the vandals and the theft of the jewels," Sorcha said. She clicked her key fob, and the doors unlocked.

"From what I've discovered aboot Blake, he's all looks and not verra bright," Shannon said. "Let's keep our expectations low."

"What do you mean?" Paislee asked.

"Well, I dinnae think we can assume that the Blake and Ailis situation is the same as the vandals situation." Shannon paused at the rear of the SUV and peered at Paislee.

"Why is that?" Paislee had been lumping the problems together in her mind as well. It would be easier. Life was messy and rarely easy.

"There was more than one person with nefarious ideas in Cawdor Castle on Halloween night. The timing for the theft of the diamonds, and the other of the egg, in a different part of the castle, and the sighting of the Guy Fawkes character, suggest at least three if not more intruders," Shannon said. Her shrug wrapped around her in cozy comfort to her hips.

"I guess I missed that portion of the lunch," Paislee said. "Thanks for filling me in. Three or more certainly broadens the net beyond Blake and Ailis."

"It really does." Sorcha opened the driver's-side door. "Randall told my grounds manager that Pat Amblin was with Poppy at her hotel on Halloween night, so not a suspect."

"Why bring that up?" Paislee asked.

"The police wondered if it could be an inside job," Shannon shared.

"The DC said that a guard was knocked oot for over an hour and his keys were stolen; well, that slants toward a stranger," Sorcha said.

"It does." It gave Pat and Poppy both alibis for the theft of the jewelry, unless they were lying for each other. Paislee couldn't see either of them behaving in a manner to destroy property.

Would Blake have any reason to be at Cawdor?

Paislee lifted her hand goodbye. Lydia and her mother hadn't left the café yet.

"I'll see you next week," Sorcha said. "At the castle. I know I can rely on you."

"That you can. All right. Happy . . . well, it isn't a very happy Guy Fawkes, or a Bonfire Night, is it? Celebrating the radicals against traditionalists when you are both Conservatives, a party I am leaning toward after all we've learned."

Shannon laughed.

"We've converted her," Sorcha said.

"Naw. Grandpa would have my head. Be safe tonight, my ladies."

"You too!" Sorcha and Shannon said in unison before climbing into Sorcha's vehicle.

Driving away from the castle grounds, Paislee chuckled, bemused that she'd made such strong women friends. It was a blessing, and a curse.

Today they'd been thoughtful to include her in gathering information, because she and Brody had found Ailis the same night as the theft at Cawdor.

Two separate things? She still didn't know.

She texted Mack that she'd heard about Blake with a "congratulations" emoji.

Her phone rang and she answered via Bluetooth.

"Hello, Mack!"

"Paislee! Where are you?"

"In the Juke. Just left Cawdor Café after lunch with Lydia, her mum, and the nobles. Grandpa said you caught Blake. That's got tae feel great."

"We are getting answers, but Blake isnae confessing tae anything. Not the theft, or harming Ailis. Can you stop by the station? I'll meet you in the car park and we can talk in the Juke. It willnae take long."

"Sure. Be there in five mi—"

But, Mack had already hung up.

He was either very, very busy or what he had to say needed to be in person.

Paislee arrived at the station. Mack was outside, on the phone, his arms gesturing as he spoke. He saw her and his frown changed to a smile. He stepped toward the car as Paislee unlocked the door and he climbed in.

"Hey, Mack. I realize you've got a lot going on, so we don't have tae talk right now."

"We do. I promised tae keep you in the loop the best I could." Mack reached across the console for Paislee's hand. "Blake was partying all night on Halloween. He's on CCTV buying drinks at ten and then eleven. He was never in costume."

Paislee drew up the memory of the time when she and Brody had been at Rait Ruins. "Ailis was dead by ten thirty."

"Aye. He said that Darryl had called him, but because they'd already been in a fight earlier, he ignored the summons."

"Jerk."

"The medical examiner places time of death within an hour of when you found her at ten thirty," Mack said.

Tears stung her eyes. "If we'd come earlier, would Ailis still be alive?"

"You cannae think that way." Mack's gaze was earnest. "What's going on?"

Paislee withdrew her fingers. Even though she understood that the family was in pain, their accusations still had stung. "The Barclays lit into me at church today."

"You didnae do this, and Brody didnae do this. They are hurting, so it isnae personal."

"Did Blake kill Ailis?"

"It's not likely." Mack sighed. His gaze went to the windshield and the view of the park and barren field. The oak tree with missing leaves.

"Could she have tripped on the rocks and hit her head—an accident?"

Mack returned his compassionate gaze her way. "It's not looking like that either."

"What do you mean?" Her chest ached.

"Paislee, I cannae tell you details."

"That isn't fair." She rested her hand on the steering wheel. "If you wanted tae drag this out, why bother meeting me in person?"

"There is something else," Mack admitted.

"What?" Paislee glanced from the field to Mack, swallowing the bitter bite of disappointment.

"We actually got a hit on the identity of the truck driver."

"We knew that neither person in the car was Blake—who was it? Rooney Crowe?"

Mack didn't answer but instead shared, "We wondered if Blake could have been behind the scenes as part of the heist, tae account for his hanging oot in Nairn without Ailis. He's been here several times in the last month on his own."

Paislee's pulse sped. "I didn't realize that he had been. Maybe he had family?"

"No family in Nairn, but lots in Inverness. Blake's been seeing a young lady who lives at the caravan park. On the side—we think Ailis found oot aboot it, and that's why they were arguing."

"Dang it."

"Yes." Mack sighed. "Rooney had been suspicious and suggested that Blake had been messing around. He was right."

"You talked tae Rooney?"

"I called him intae the station this morning. Nice new truck," Mack said. "Not a match for the getaway vehicle. He was the one tae post the video of Blake and Ailis. He says he was worrit aboot her and that's why he followed her and Blake tae the ruins. That was at eight."

"Rooney took the video? He sounded jealous of Blake." Paislee tilted her head. "Do you believe him?"

"It checks oot on CCTV with his truck. He was at the church at eight thirty, helping with the haunted maze. Lots of witnesses."

"Who is the girl Blake is dating?"

"You might know her—she was a dancer at the Nairn Highland Games. Fern McElroy? She says that when she found oot aboot Ailis, she made Blake break it off or she refused tae see him."

"That sounds right. She's a sweetheart." Paislee wished she could ease the frown lines between Mack's brows. Grandpa texted, wanting to know where she was. "I should get going."

Mack nodded but didn't leave the car. "Why were you at church?"

"I prayed for you today. I'm a wee bit worried about how things might go tonight, with the threats of rioting. I'd hoped that Blake would be the key tae the vandals and give up the stolen jewels."

"He's just an awful boyfriend," Mack said. "Cannae toss him intae jail for that."

"The cells would be full." Paislee sent Mack a sad smile. This wasn't the answer she'd hoped for.

"Overflowing," Mack said. "How was lunch otherwise?"

"Informative. Pat Amblin and Poppy Drummond are each other's alibi for the night in question. The fundraiser for the injured farmer was from seven tae nine, and Darcey McClintock was there tae cover the event, and was gone by eight. There were at least three intruders inside the castle that night, but probably not an inside job considering the guard was knocked out and the key tae the tower stolen." Mack's eyes widened. "Did you know that *all* of the nobles received the pamphlet with the lion being trampled by the unicorn?"

"Even the DC of Cawdor?" Mack shook his head. "She didnae mention it when I was just there for the police report. I swear, they want me tae keep them safe but dinnae give me all the information."

"That doesn't seem fair."

But Mack helped them anyway. "It's not. Fair is not part of the job description. Lawful and just."

"Shannon, Lady Leery, didn't think that Blake had the smarts tae plan a heist or care more about anything but the next party."

"She pegged him right." Mack reached across and took her hand, "Any other news?"

"The DC of Cawdor told Sorcha that she would attend the earl's wedding at Christmas—that will make it the event of the season."

"And you," Mack said with pride, "will be knitting their bespoke vests and scarves."

"Aye." Paislee still couldn't quite believe it.

"Cashmere Crush and its owner will be on the map of local celebrities in Nairn." Mack squeezed her fingers.

"Wouldn't that be something? I'll save any extra income for Brody's choice of university, if he doesn't get a scholarship," she said. "But I bet he will. He's very determined."

"Like his mum," Mack said warmly.

Her phone rumbled. "I have tae go, Mack. Grandpa sent another text."

The warm moment cooled when he cleared his throat.

She braced herself.

"I hate tae ruin the mood."

"But?" Her body tensed.

Mack exhaled and held her hands. "We finally got the medical examiner's report back, with the cause of death."

She closed her eyes, hoping with all of her heart that it would be accidental.

She knew it wasn't, even before Mack said, "Blunt trauma tae the temple. There is no way that Ailis could have hit her head against the tombstone tae cause it."

"Poor Ailis."

Mack nodded and released her fingers. "It's been ruled as a homicide. The video and pictures on Brody's phone have her last minutes on it."

Chapter 16

"Homicide . . ." Unfortunately, that had the ring of sad, tragic truth. Paislee looked closely at Mack. "You'd mentioned that you discovered the identity of the men who'd broken in tae steal whatever was in the evidence room."

"Just the Viking." Mack rubbed his thumb over her knuckles. "The driver is Alan Martin. He's a known radical of the Scottish National Party. He's been charged twice but both times they were dropped."

"Darcey McClintock is also a member of the SNP. Makes sense that the slogan would be freedom." The Scottish National Party was the only government faction interested in complete separation from Great Britain. "Have you talked tae her?"

"Not yet. Why did Alan Martin and his accomplice want Brody's phone? What did either of you see, or capture? Is it why Ailis was killed? We cannae ignore the timing." Mack's voice lowered as he held her gaze. "What if you are in danger?"

"We are fine," Paislee assured him. "You are the one putting your neck on the line. You and the other constables. Our officers of Police Scotland." It was so very brave of them.

"I signed up tae do it. It is important tae me. I feel one hundred percent okay answering for everyone inside the department—they all believe the same way."

"Even Constable Jays? He's nervous."

"He is, but he's committed. Inspector McCleod wouldnae have hired him if he wasnae."

Grandpa sent another concerned text, so Paislee answered, letting him know she was on her way.

"I'm sorry the DC of Cawdor didn't tell you about the pamphlet with the unicorn trampling the lion. Sorcha didn't want tae... neither did Shannon, actually, but when I stressed how it wasn't giving you all of the information, they agreed. They trust you, Mack, though they've had bad experiences with the police before."

"Because of you," he said. "What can I do tae help?"

"Find the stolen jewels. The DC of Cawdor has closed the castle for the Christmas season, except for the café, which is outside of the grounds, and can be locked up tight. She will protect the holly tree and the power of the thanes."

"I appreciate that dedication," Mack said.

"She wants tae be a ghost like Muriel when she passes, tae make sure that the future generation doesn't mess it up." Paislee laughed. "Sorcha also thought it was a good idea tae come back and haunt her kids."

"You dinnae believe that blue blur was Muriel, do you?"

"Maybe?" Paislee sighed and patted Mack's clenched cheek. "I think it was something."

"I'll catch the actual Guy Fawkes character and then we will find the truth."

"She'd prefer the jewels tae the truth, if she had tae pick. I almost choked when the DC mentioned the insurance value of the Fabergé egg. It had emeralds, diamonds, and rubies. Twenty-five million pounds."

Mack sucked in a breath. "Was there a picture of that egg?"

"I don't know. I imagine so. She had a meeting with the insurance adjuster today, so she's at the castle if you want tae ask her."

"I am going tae pay her a visit right now." Mack had his hand on the interior passenger door but turned around to face her. "Please be careful."

"You too, Mack."

He leaned toward her, and they kissed over the console. "This is life with an officer of the law. It's not easy. I will try tae make it easier."

Paislee grabbed his shoulder. "I never asked for easy. You don't have tae change for me either, Mack."

His eyes warmed and he exited the car, going to his SUV rather than inside the station.

Paislee drove behind Cashmere Crush, parked, and went inside. Because it was Bonfire Night, the shop was closing early at five, like many of the other businesses did. She made the executive decision to close at four.

"Hi, Paislee," Rhona said. "Can you believe they finally caught Blake?"

"It's about time." Paislee quickly brought Grandpa and Rhona up to speed. "So, they don't think Blake is guilty of either the thefts, the vandalism, or Ailis's . . . death." She looked around to be sure they were alone. "It was murder. She was hit in the temple by a blunt object. I was hoping it would be deemed a tragic accident, which would have been more natural and not so violent. Still awful but not murder."

"How sad for the Barclays." Rhona sniffed back a tear.

"We need tae send a large bouquet tae the service on Saturday as well as several meals."

"I can make them chicken and dumplings," Grandpa said. "I'll do it tomorrow . . . oh, not tomorrow but the day after. We can bring it tae them on Thursday."

"I saw them at church earlier. Julie Barclay said that Gran would have been disappointed in me." Paislee placed her palm over her heart.

"Ach, she was just striking oot because she's hurting." Grandpa squeezed Paislee's shoulder.

"Still, that wasnae nice," Rhona said in Paislee's defense.

"It's all right. If anything happened tae Brody, I'd be a complete mess." Paislee looked at Grandpa and Rhona. "They were able tae match the driver from the CCTV footage in the getaway car for the break-in at the police station last night. Some guy named Alan Martin. He'd dressed as a Viking, and the passenger, we think, was a ninja. They don't know his identity yet."

Grandpa sat on a stool at the high-top table.

Paislee placed her mobile on the counter, thinking of Brody's phone, and the emerald. "The emerald! I wonder if it could be part of the DC's missing jewels? Like, part of the Fabergé egg? It was worth twenty-five million pounds tae insure."

"What a haul!" Grandpa said. "And, if sold, could tie intae the money motive."

"Mack was sure in a hurry tae get a picture of the egg." Paislee exhaled with relief. "The emerald must be what the men breaking into the police station were after. That makes me feel a lot better about going out tonight." She pinched her fingers together. "I was very close tae staying home with Brody."

"Bonfire Night is the best night of fall," Rhona said. "Should we be worrit?"

"Just be careful . . . I love it too." Could she tell Rhona about the rumor of riots without betraying Mack?

"I'm glad you're okay with things," Grandpa said. "It woulda been a shame tae miss the fireworks from the rooftop."

Rhona rubbed her arm against Grandpa's as if for luck. "Angus mentioned you've been invited to the dome. You'll have the best seats no matter the weather. The Oasis Hotel is *fancy.*"

Maybe Paislee should have prayed for rain. Would that stop rioters? "Have we been at all busy today?"

"Not really. Oh, that healthy lady popped in for a knitting pattern. She is verra pretty when she's in actual clothes. She was a knockout in jogging togs."

"Marion? I think she might be very wealthy. I saw her at the new hotel. Seems like everyone is getting short spiky blond hair. Are you planning tae do it?"

"Mum would kill me if I cut off my hair. Aibreann was talking about it though. There was an actress who recently lopped off her long tresses and dyed it white. Shana Fox. Aibreann would be cute with it."

Paislee texted Mack, eager for answers, but there was only silence.

Constable Payne came in. His raincoat and cap were dry. "Afternoon, Shaws. Rhona. Zeffer said I could bring you guys in the loop." He showed them the mug shot for Alan Martin, then a photo of another man. Brown hair, dreamy blue eyes. "And this is Rob McGinty, a known acquaintance. He's got a rap sheet so long I couldnae print it all oot. Alan is a saint compared tae this bloke. He might be the passenger but it's hard tae be sure because he's wearing a cap. The DI okayed me dropping this off at the newspaper too."

"Tae Darcey McClintock?" Paislee blew out a breath.

"No, some guy named Mitch Duprey. He said Darcey has been MIA all afternoon."

"Mitch told me that Darcey is a member of the local Scottish National Party." Paislee sat on the stool behind the register. "She printed the picture of the vandalism at Lady Leery's estate without questioning where it came from."

"Interesting. Could Darcey be involved?" Constable Payne asked. "Working at the paper puts her front and center for the news."

"No way," Paislee said.

"Dunno. If Darcey believes her cause is right, no matter what the consequences, that makes her dangerous," Grandpa said.

"She was at the fundraiser at Cawdor Castle tae cover it but stayed less than an hour. However, the DC said Randall Fowler, head of security, had chased off two people with spray cans at midnight on Halloween." Paislee stabbed her knitting needles into the skein of yarn. "I forgot tae tell Mack."

"I'll let Zeffer, McCleod, and the other constables know," Payne said. "Thanks, Paislee. Enjoy the fireworks tonight."

"Thanks. Please be safe." Paislee patted Payne's arm. "I will be worried all night."

"We've gotten training on what tae do if a riot erupts in Nairn like it did in Edinburgh, or Dundee. I cannae imagine anyone tossing a petrol bomb at us here. We know almost everyone," Payne said.

"That's true," Paislee agreed. It was why she didn't believe it would happen in their shire.

"See you later," Payne said.

As soon as the door closed, Rhona asked, "Did the constable just say that there might be a riot in Nairn?" Her eyes widened with apprehension.

"There have been rumors but so far, that's it. I'm glad he mentioned it because now we can talk about it and come up with a plan. Where are you going tae be tonight?"

"The bonfire on the beach," Rhona said. "My folks will be with Garrison and the family having the traditional bonfire on the Smythe property. Da was adamant not tae be cowed intae not celebrating."

"I'm glad that Garrison is on the mend." Paislee was still concerned that the Scotsman would push his body to the limit. "Listen, you're a smart lass. Have fun but just be aware in case things get heated—make a plan."

"I'll do that."

At three on the dot, Darcey McClintock, bleached blond hair wild, entered Cashmere Crush. She was in the same all-black ensemble from earlier in the day. A blue smudge of paint was on the toe of her black boot. "You, Paislee, are a troublemaker."

"Me?" Paislee, who'd completed a scarf and was putting it on the shelf for sale, stood her ground. Grandpa rose from his seat on the stool.

"Aye. I got put on leave, thanks tae you. I was expecting accolades for getting that article intae the paper, that led tae calls for Blake's arrest." Darcey patted her chest, her face in an angry snarl. "Practically sacked instead."

"Blake wasn't guilty," Paislee said.

"What?" Darcey stopped shouting insults long enough to hear Paislee.

"Haven't you been tae your office? Well, Constable Payne dropped off the scoop of the year regarding the driver of the getaway truck, a fellow SNP member that you might know?"

"Who?" Her voice grew quiet . . . the quiet before the next storm.

"Alan Martin." Paislee watched the journalist closely for an eruption.

"Unbelievable." Her eyes narrowed. "Who got the scoop?"

"Mitch Duprey."

"Damn it." Darcey flung her arm to the side and paced from the front door to where Paislee stood and back again. "I worked my arse off tae get that story. It's not fair!"

The woman was mental. Grandpa held the broom from the back room. Rhona had her mobile ready to dial for assistance.

Darcey faced Paislee. "Who killed Ailis if it wasnae Blake?"

"Her death is still under investigation," Paislee said. "What do you know about the vandalism on the nobles' estates?"

Darcey clamped her mouth tight.

Paislee asked, "You have the unicorn tattoo?"

Darcey faced Paislee in disbelief. She touched the spot on her arm that matched what Poppy had, and Rooney. In a rush, she left without a goodbye.

"What was that aboot?" Grandpa leaned the broom against the shelves of yarn.

"Rooney from the church also has that same tattoo, in that same place. So does Poppy Drummond. I'm not sure what it means. Rooney tried tae pass it off as a club thing."

"Poppy admitted to a wild youth in Edinburgh." Grandpa put

the broom in the back room. Rhona slipped her mobile into her pocket.

Paislee knew she wouldn't be able to concentrate on anything business related and tapped her hand to the high-top table.

"You know what? Let's call it a day. Me and Grandpa will go get Brody. You and Aibreann have fun with Artie and Foster, but please, be cautious. I'm hoping the rumors remain just that."

"Sounds good tae me." Rhona hugged each of them. "See you tomorrow. Cannae wait tae celebrate your birthday and have this night behind us."

It took Paislee a while longer to lock up but by three thirty they were in queue to pick up Brody. Her son was by himself, his backpack hanging by a single strap over his arm. He had a cap pulled low on his forehead, his gaze on the Juke.

As he reached for the car door handle, Emma called out, "Brody!"

Her son turned and Emma slipped a note into his hand and then darted off before he could talk to her. The teenager had red cheeks, and a canvas coat over her school uniform.

He got into the car in the seat behind Grandpa and buckled up.

"Love note?" Grandpa quipped.

"Probably not." Brody dropped his backpack to the floor. "More like a hate note."

"Are you going tae read it?" Paislee asked, curiosity on high.

"Not now." Brody's voice trembled. "In my room."

"Fine." Paislee gave him one last imploring look before she began to drive away from the school.

"And before you ask, we werenae assigned homework, Darryl went home early, and Jimmy stayed tae himself. Edwyn acts like we are strangers. Okay?"

Grandpa laughed.

"Are you saying my questions are predictable?" Paislee fought a smile, poking fun at herself.

Brody kept his focus out the passenger window. "Just a wee bit."

They arrived home and Brody went to his room with the note. They were leaving at half past four for the Oasis, to account for traffic, which gave them ample opportunity to change into fancy clothes and feed Wallace. Paislee was grateful that the dog wasn't bothered by fireworks. Snowball, Amelia's pup, was also unaffected.

By the time the Shaws piled into the car, Brody didn't seem as sad, but he didn't share what Emma had written. It was difficult not to pester him.

They were pulling out of the carport when Mack arrived, blocking them in with his SUV.

Paislee rolled down her window, watching in her side mirror as he exited and strode toward them to her driver's side.

"Hello, Shaw family," Mack said. "This is the last chance tae accept my offer of a crate of sparklers the size of the back garden shed. Stay home?"

"We are going, Mack," Paislee said.

Mack put his gloved hand on the open window ledge. "Even though Blake wasnae the one involved with Ailis's demise, I dinnae want you sleuthing tonight. I want you tae enjoy the fireworks and the bonfire and come straight home."

The DI made eye contact with each of them.

"All right?"

"I hadn't planned on sleuthing or staying out late," Paislee said, affronted. She'd already decided to come straight home but didn't share that with Mack.

"That seems a wee bit bossy," Brody said.

"I realize that, but I care aboot you three and I cannae focus on my job properly if I am wondering what you are doing. For whatever reason, you attract trouble."

"Hey!" Grandpa protested.

"You cannae deny it's true," Mack said.

Paislee's shoulders settled as she realized that Mack spoke out of love. "And what are you doing tae protect yourself tonight, among the possible riots?"

Mack opened his jacket to show protective gear rather than his blue suits that he favored. "I promise tae check in every few hours via text. Can you let me know when you get back? Last year the riots erupted at midnight. After that we should be home free."

"Mum's birthday." Brody nodded. "This is the first time I've missed having a mobile. I have no intention of leaving Mum's side."

"Guid lad."

Mack kissed Paislee firmly and returned to his blue SUV.

Her lips tingled. They hadn't stopped tingling. "Let's go have some fun."

When they arrived at the posh new hotel, the businesses next to it were hopping. The arcade had the door propped open as people were in a constant stream of in or out. Lights flashed and buzzers sounded.

"Can we go play some games?" Brody asked as if pulled by the frenetic energy.

"Not tonight, hon. Unless you get bored, then maybe Grandpa or I can go with you. I can't imagine that you will, though. Fireworks, food, and conversation."

"You're right. Is Uncle Corbin going tae be here? He's so funny."

"Yes."

Corbin and Lydia had so many nieces and nephews to spoil that they didn't plan on kids of their own, which meant Brody benefitted from the latest cool gadgets.

Mostly he was into football, but he wasn't immune to video games.

"We can go this weekend tae get a new mobile from Tesco," Paislee reminded him. *Mobile, food. Mobile. Food.*

"Thanks, Mum."

They entered the hotel. The lobby was opulent and covered in lights, outshining the beauty of yesterday. Poppy and her staff had outdone themselves to create a magical venue. The rope lights on the dolphins in the fountain made it look like they were leaping in the water.

People were dressed to the nines for a cocktail party at the lower level. Paislee recognized several A-listers from the telly.

"Did you see . . ." Brody started to say.

"Yes!" Paislee said. It was incredible. The beautiful people were even more beautiful in person.

"Can we get an autograph?" Brody headed toward the star but Paislee tugged him back.

"No, lad, that isnae how it's done." Grandpa smoothed his beard. "They're on a holiday, which means we have tae pretend that they arenae famous."

"It's not fair," Brody said, but switched tactics. "Grandpa, can I borrow your phone tae take pictures?"

"Discreetly." Grandpa gave his mobile to Brody. "Sly, now. I want one of his girlfriend too."

Paislee's phone dinged. Lydia, already upstairs, texting her to hurry.

The atmosphere in the lobby was festive, and Paislee was swept up in it. The fireworks wouldn't start until nine, with the bonfire afterward at ten. Kids still had school and work the next day, so the festivities had been curtailed.

Fine with Paislee.

Poppy was there with Pat by the elevator. The couple were arguing in muted voices. Pat's body language exuded annoyance. What was this about?

"We are through," Pat said. His voice rose. "You were using me! *Me*."

"I wanted your sauce recipes. So what?" Poppy shrugged, her eyes slitted like a cat's. "What is the crime in that?"

"I am not a piece of meat, Poppy."

Paislee, about to wave, lowered her hand.

"If I apologize, can we get through the night?" Poppy asked coldly. "We have guests upstairs."

Grandpa astutely ushered Brody into the elevator as it opened. Paislee kept her eye on the broken-up couple as the door closed.

"Awkward," Grandpa mouthed.

"Ten?" Brody asked, oblivious, thank goodness.

"Yes." Paislee felt sad but not surprised by the revelation that Pat and Poppy wouldn't go the distance.

Brody pushed the button, and they reached the top floor in seconds.

When the door opened, Lydia waved to them, gesturing to three seats around a table near them. It was cozy and inviting.

Sofas and stuffed chairs, lots of benches, and a view of the Moray Firth. The sunset would be spectacular; almost as phenomenal as the fireworks.

"Several bonfires along the beach are already started. You see the effigy of Guy Fawkes?" Alistair said to them. His eyes glittered with excitement.

"That's the biggest one ever," Brody said. He went to the glass and peered out.

"It's sure tae be on TV later. This is so amazing," Sophie said.

Simon showed up with Poppy on his arm. He was smooth, a real charmer, as he talked with everyone, not just the women.

The space had been set up so that people could play games while they talked and snacked on popcorn, pretzels, and toffee apples. A makeshift stage had been put against the wall.

"How are you doing?" Paislee asked. Her best friend had shadows under her eyes. "How's Corbin's dad?"

"Fine, fine. There's going tae be a comedian at eight," Lydia said. She pointed to a set of closed doors where the most amazing smells escaped from. "And food. I peeked into the micro kitchen because I'm starving and saw Chef Pat and the hotel chef going at it."

"Poppy wanted Pat's sauce recipes," Paislee whispered. "They broke up just now. How did he beat us up here?"

"No way!" Lydia briefly covered her mouth with her fingers. "There's a private elevator in there."

"Lyd, look at this!" Corbin called.

Lydia got up to peer out one of six telescopes along the perimeters inside as the dome circle enclosed the entire roof, but quickly returned to her seat when Pat set out a fresh tray of appetizers, including a selection of his signature sauces, all meant to be dipped into with skinny breadsticks.

So much for following Poppy's directive to stick with the desserts. Had the manager been worried that her chef wouldn't be able to compete with Pat Amblin, superstar?

Paislee shared a glance with Grandpa, who was sipping on some topnotch whisky. Pat filled baskets of artisan bread, but there was no sign of Poppy. Paislee drank champagne but would only have a glass or two as she was driving and wanted to be on her game if something happened, like rioting in the streets.

She could imagine it easily because of the video footage from last year. It was impossible to forget the sound of screaming innocents. She would sign the petition to regulate the fireworks.

Mack had texted at seven that he was okay. He'd text again at ten. Then at one. Midnight would be the difficult hour. She hoped to be home by eleven, with Brody and Grandpa.

Lydia, next to her, was doing her best to maintain her big smile, which was another clue that something was going on. No matter how many times Paislee suggested a quiet talk in the corner, her bestie rebuffed her.

By eight o'clock the party was in full swing, with a comedian about to start on the far side of the large chamber.

Paislee, Brody, Corbin, and Lydia sat on one side of a table overlooking the dark sky alight with smaller fireworks. Grandpa, Simon, Alistair, and Sophie sat on the other as they played poker for candied peanuts.

It was a magical night. She laughed so hard during the comedy show that her stomach ached. Brody was also swept up in the joy of the night. "No sparklers though. Mibbe we can do some when we get home?"

Paislee had bought a box last week, and they were in the shed. "In the back garden, for sure."

The fireworks went off at nine. The show was spectacular. It was ten times better than Hogmanay. Not being cold? Also a win.

Paislee prayed that Mack, Payne, Monroe, and the newbie constables were all okay. Between bursts of bright light, Corbin's phone rang. He turned off the sound.

Annoyed at first, his expression as he listened to the voice message became concerned. He whispered into Lydia's ear. Her best friend covered her mouth with her fingers.

"What is it?" Paislee asked.

"Corbin's brother left a message. The vandals have returned with a Guy Fawkes effigy on the property, and another with his dad's picture. Garrison isnae taking this lightly."

Corbin stood, his back to the glass where fireworks erupted in full glory. He texted his brother, radiating angst, anger, and sorrow.

"We should go," Lydia said. She started to rise but halted and sat down again. Corbin was texting, his thumbs moving quickly, and not looking at Lydia.

"You shouldn't leave right now," Paislee said. "What can you do? The roads will be a mess." Her intuition was saying they should all stay together.

"Paislee's right," Sophie said. She reached across to Lydia and put her hand on her daughter's knee. "It could be dangerous. Who can we contact?"

Paislee thought of Mack and the members of Police Scotland, the office in Nairn. Surely, they already were aware. She hated to distract Mack with a personal message.

Simon shot off a text. "Tae the thane, warning him tae be on guard tonight. Were the earlier attacks practice for the main event?"

"Lady Leery, DC Grant, and DC of Cawdor," Grandpa said. "They should all be notified tae make sure they are okay. What if they are victims too?"

"I will call the DC of Cawdor," Lydia said. "I have her number from earlier."

Simon nodded. "Brilliant."

"I'll call Shannon and Sorcha," Paislee said, quickly dialing their numbers. The phone wasn't picked up at either place. She left voice messages.

She decided to text Mack and let him know what was happening but that she was fine. He didn't answer. Her nerves tightened, on edge, her body braced for an invisible enemy.

Poppy and Pat must have been alerted that all was not right at Oasis as Pat left the small kitchen and joined them in the room with his brow arched in question as Poppy, in a hoodie and jeans, arrived from the main elevator bank. A familiar-looking man followed her.

Alan Martin? The Viking. The getaway driver. Before Paislee could call a warning a huge explosion went off outside—bigger than the fireworks—and the hotel went dark.

Chapter 17

"Brody!" Paislee called, her hand unerringly going for his arm in the dark—only her son wasn't there.

"Brody!" Her stomach clenched with fear so tight that nausea rose up her throat, burning her esophagus.

A crash sounded to her left.

Pat Amblin cursed.

Simon put on his flashlight app to illuminate a part of the room, but it wasn't enough to reveal all. It was distorting rather than illuminating. The fireworks went off outside the dome, adding to the sensory confusion.

A door slammed in the kitchen to her right, and Paislee raced for the sound, bumping into chairs and tables. "Brody!" She opened the door and shoved it wide.

The generator kicked to life, allowing Paislee to make out the back of Poppy's bleached blond hair as she disappeared behind the doors of a private elevator that hummed closed.

She heard her son's muffled voice.

Paislee, engulfed by rage, found a center of calm she never dreamed she would possess in a situation as terrifying as this one.

Lydia, Corbin, Pat, and Grandpa crowded into the kitchen. Pat found a regular torch and turned it on, setting it on the counter like a lantern for camping. The lights were dim, as if at only half power.

"Poppy has Brody," Paislee said coolly. "Where would she take him? Why?"

"She wouldnae," Pat said.

"She did," Paislee said with certainty. She pointed to the elevator. "Where does this go?"

The generator roared and brightened the overhead lights before dimming.

"It's a service elevator tae the lobby, the kitchen, and then the basement," Pat explained with confusion on his handsome face. "It doesnae stop at any of the floors with rooms or suites, for speed."

"What's wrong with the lights?" Lydia asked.

"It's a new hotel," Pat said. "Has all the bells and whistles but is in energy-saving mode and will only use half-light in the designated areas."

"Are there stairs?" Paislee pushed on several doors—all cabinets.

"Here," Pat said. He showed her a narrow staircase. Dark.

Paislee started down it. "Lyd, maybe try the other elevator tae the lobby? I'll take the stairs. I don't understand what's happening." Moving toward her son was all that mattered.

"Stop!" Alan Martin entered the kitchen, pointing a gun at them all.

Paislee froze, partially in the kitchen, and half in the stairwell.

Alan grinned—eerie and wicked on his boyish face. This man had driven the getaway truck from the attempted break-in at the police department. She had a vague recollection of seeing him somewhere. Where was his partner, Rob?

"Stop, Paislee. I will shoot."

Paislee couldn't listen and jumped into the staircase, slamming the door behind her. She hoped that Corbin or Pat would stop Alan from shooting at her, but she had to focus on saving Brody. She descended the stairs three at a time, going so fast she tore the skin from her palm on the handrail.

She didn't waste time thinking of why but simply sent prayers skyward to keep Brody safe. She prayed to God, to Gran, to Brody's angels, to her da, Bruce, to Brody's da, Calan, to God again.

Poppy had a curvier figure than the blonde with Alan coming off the main elevator before the power went out, but Paislee had been confused by the short white hair. White hair. Darcey McClintock also had short white hair. Darcey didn't like Paislee. Would she kidnap Brody over it?

Paislee reached level three and paused to listen for her son. There was no noise. Taking a huge breath, she raced until she reached the lobby and shoved open the door. Nothing.

She went down to the next floor, the kitchen, and slammed the door open. It hit the interior with a loud smack.

The kitchen workers all looked at her, nonplussed. They had meals to prepare even if the power was operating at half light. No Brody. No Darcey or Poppy.

The basement, then.

Paislee's heart hammered in her chest as she reached the final option. She pushed open the door to see Brody shoved forward. He had tape over his mouth and his hair in his eyes.

Only, it wasn't Darcey either. The tall slender figure that she'd seen with Alan before, at this very hotel, was Marion. Rob McGinty, on one side . . . of Marion *McGinty*. They shared vibrant blue eyes. The supersweet traveler from Glasgow, who'd bought a knitting pattern to while away the time.

Was there a lot of downtime between murders?

"Brody!" Paislee shouted.

Her son struggled against Marion. He was taller than his abductor, but she didn't give him time to get balanced. She was lean and strong. A scrapper.

Red rage filled her.

Paislee looked around for anything to use as a weapon. If Brody and Marion made it outside, then they could disappear into the crowd of Bonfire Night revelers. Was that what her plan had been all along?

"Marion!"

From behind a stack of crates, open boxes filled with weapons as well as fireworks, came a man in a Guy Fawkes costume. The height and breadth of his shoulders matched the figure on the security footage from Cawdor Castle.

It all clicked together. Alan, Robin Hood; Marion, as Maid Marian; and Rob as Guy Fawkes, in costume when they'd entered her shop the day after she and Brody had discovered Ailis. They'd known where to find her, thanks to the articles from Darcey or Mitch about a yarn shop owner in Nairn.

Marion had chatted with Rhona, probably to discover what they had witnessed, and that's when they'd learned about the video Brody had recorded.

Dirt caked the wooden boxes. Moss, like from the trees at the cemetery, snagged on the corners. Rob pointed a gun at her feet. "Hold up, sis," the man told Marion. "Lady, turn around and save yourself."

Paislee gasped in outrage. "I am not leaving my son."

"Then you die."

Life without Brody? Not a chance she'd give up on her only child.

"Stop talking, Robbie." Marion had Brody captured with his wrists behind him in zip ties, a knife at his waist. She maneuvered Brody toward the crates.

Rob removed his mask. She knew from watching movies that this meant they didn't expect for Paislee or Brody to make it out of this situation alive.

"Why are you doing this?" Paislee asked on an exhale. *Think, think, think.*

"What did you see on Halloween?" Rob countered.

"Nothing. We didn't see anything," Paislee said.

She inched closer to Brody.

"Dinnae move another muscle," Marion instructed, poking Brody harder.

Her son moaned.

She froze in place.

"I dinnae believe it," Marion said. "You were all up in our business. You and that stupid Ailis twit."

Brody struggled and Marion popped him on the head with the heel of her knife. Her son went down in a faint.

Tears of fury slipped from Paislee's eyes. She waited, watching for his breaths to continue, and then focused on Marion and Rob.

They would pay dearly for this.

Brody was alive. Ailis was not. She would find a way to bring closure to the Barclay family while getting out of this with her son.

Paislee didn't have her phone, which was on the table next to her drink and her handbag. Stupid.

Did Brody still have Grandpa's phone? She couldn't remember if it was sitting on the table next to hers or not.

They'd put the Find My Location feature on all the mobiles after Grandpa had slipped in the River Nairn a few months back. Had it been powered on, or off? Phones were so important and not just as a means to communicate but for safety.

Why hadn't she put hers in her pocket?

She would get Brody one tomorrow. They would make it.

"The police are coming," Paislee said. She'd sent a reassuring text to Mack so he wouldn't have cause for concern. The hotel had gone dark. Who all was in on this? Could Poppy be involved? She had the unicorn tattoo. Had grown up in Edinburgh.

"So?" Rob shrugged.

"The power in this hotel is mostly oot along with the entire block." Marion paced from Rob to Paislee and Brody. She wore a gold chain that had a large diamond ring on it. "We're waiting for our convoy tae arrive and pick up the fireworks and guns, and then it doesnae matter. This country thrives on chaos. We will deliver."

"When will they be here?" Paislee's voice sounded scratchy and scared. She hated to share her true feelings.

"How long do you have tae live, you mean?" Marion pointed

her knife from Brody to Paislee. "We'll use you—one at a time, or both, or neither—as a hostage tae make sure we make our escape."

"A hostage?" Paislee repeated like a demented parrot.

Rob looped the Guy Fawkes mask over his wrist and checked the large screen on his phone, which showed the exterior of the new hotel. "Ten tonight." He watched the surveillance cameras.

In the movies Paislee had seen that hostages had a fifty-fifty chance of living through the exchange. Their chances were even less because they could identify their kidnappers. She had to keep them talking and find a chance to negotiate for Brody's safety.

"Rob McGinty. The police have footage of you trying tae steal the holly branch from Cawdor. Why take that chance? The tower was locked. Protected by cameras." And the ghost of Muriel.

"Ain't you nosy?" Marion asked with disapproval. "Dinnae answer her, Rob."

Brody stirred. The tape on his mouth loosened and slipped. Paislee shifted her stance to hide his movement. Unfortunately, that meant she was no longer able to see what Rob was doing.

"It seemed tae me that you were scared off by the ghost of Muriel Campbell." Paislee put extra emphasis on the word *scared*.

"Nobody else was there," Marion said. "Was there, Rob? You didnae say that."

"Nah." Rob glared toward Paislee. "Shut it."

"Not a person," Paislee said. "The ghost that protects the castle was there and stopped you by tripping the motion alarm. It was a big risk. Why did you want the dead branch? It seemed like a stupid move in an otherwise commendable plan." She shrugged.

"Tae show the thane that the power between the Tories and the monarchy is over," Rob said. "I planned tae use it as a symbol of their defeat as we ride intae Inverness in victory. We want anarchy." He shivered and scowled at Paislee. "There was no ghost, dafty lass. That's fine. I will still lead our convoy without it."

"Park it." Marion eyed Brody and then motioned for Paislee to sit down next to him. "Dinnae like you hovering." Paislee did, cushioning his head on her thigh. Blood stained his shirt at the waist. "Rob's always been a poet. Me and Alan want enough money tae set ourselves up in the Bahamas."

Sick, Paislee scanned the wooden trusses in the ceiling, looking for anything that might help. "He needs a doctor."

"Ridiculous. He needs tough love, like we got growing up," Marion said derisively.

"A poor upbringing is no reason tae kill someone." She looked at Rob from her seated position. "Why did you kill Ailis?"

"I didnae." Rob kept his focus on the screen of his phone, turning his shoulder to his sister. What was he watching so intently?

Marion puffed her chest. "I did it. Stupid chit got too close tae us as we were hiding the weapons we'd bought by Rait Ruins. Nobody's been there for ages and then all of a sudden it was busy as Kensington Palace. You had tae have seen us or heard us."

"No, we didn't." Paislee hoped they'd realize they weren't a threat after all.

"Well, little Ailis did. She called oot when she heard us. On reflex, I reacted and threw the fancy egg at her," Marion said. "I was always a guid shot with the rocks. Had tae be tae protect us from the bigger kids when we were little."

"An ace," Rob said proudly.

"It all happened so fast." Marion spoke in a giddy tone. "We were coming back from the castle tae add what we'd stolen tae our stash when you showed up. I learned from chatty Rhona that your son had video of that night. We had tae stop him, and you, from identifying us before our plan tonight. After this, it doesnae matter."

"The photos were too blurry tae make out." She thought of the mounds of fresh dirt by the tower. "You didn't have tae do this. You can still change your mind."

"What planet are you from?" Marion asked with a twitch of her lips.

"You don't have tae be rude," Paislee said.

A knock pounded on the other side of the door. "Open up!" It was too muffled to make out the voice.

Rob checked the cameras and his video from his mobile. "Cops."

"Be quiet!" Marion said, her eyes filled with menace.

Paislee wanted to scream but knew if she acted now, she would be signing their death warrants. They needed to be a commodity, not a hindrance.

Marion selected a gun from the open crate, one that fit into her hand like it was made for it. She pointed the weapon at the door.

Rob raised his palm and shook his head.

Whoever it was, went away.

"Stupid coppers," Rob said. He read the time on his phone. Perspiration dotted his forehead. "Twenty minutes until our team gets here. Then, all hell will break loose."

"What do you hope to achieve with all of these weapons?" Paislee asked.

"We've been collecting since last year. The riots in Dundee were disappointing. We decided tae make this coast as effective as Edinburgh," Marion said.

"Effective?"

"The people want freedom." Rob left his position by the door to stare at Paislee. "Freedom from rules and government."

"Chaos," Marion said, her gaze bright.

"Organized chaos will bring change," Rob said. He placed his hand over his heart, the mask of Guy Fawkes dangling against his waist. "'Tis worth all of the pain."

Organization meant planning. How big was this rebellion? "Are you members of the Scottish National Party?"

Marion shook her head. "Dinnae be an eejit. We have moved *beyond* the party. We want tae have fun. No rules. Lots of money."

"The police willnae be prepared for the firepower we have. We will destroy the current mess and take over the government in Inverness just as Dundee, and Glasgow, and Edinburgh will fall." Rob showed a gun in a holster at his side, hidden in the cape of his Halloween costume. "Midnight."

Marion pumped her fist and jumped from one crate to the next, to the floor by her brother. "It's our time. We are going tae shine."

"Aye." Rob put on his mask. "We will succeed. Sometimes you must sacrifice in order tae win, blood must be shed. The lives lost will be worth it."

Paislee didn't agree with that. This was a dangerous plan.

Marion peered into a crate and used her gun carelessly to move the fireworks and other weapons. Paislee winced, anticipating something firing.

"Where is the petrol?" Marion asked with suspicion, as if she didn't quite trust her brother.

"Outside, already in barrels."

Marion looked at her watch and her phone, then touched the diamond on her necklace. "Where is Alan?"

"Alan was caught," Paislee said, hoping her words were true and that he hadn't shot anyone.

"You are a liar." Marion whirled her weapon toward Paislee. She slipped the ring hanging from the chain onto her finger, but it was way too big so she put it back. "Alan stole this lovely bauble. We're gettin' married when this is all over. We're gonna have a big house and new cars. A pool. Mibbe our own island."

Marion sounded like a dreamer. She wanted money, yet her brother was on a different page. Sometimes there might be multiple wants that collided, creating even more chaos.

Rob tossed a rock at his sister. "Be quiet. People are outside."

Brody's eyes opened, and he winked at Paislee. Had he been awake and listening this whole time?

Paislee kept her expression blank.

He nodded toward his feet and moved the tape from his mouth. He mouthed, "Mobile."

She widened her eyes.

He had Grandpa's phone!

"Location." His mouth moved but no sound emerged. "On."

She wanted to cry with relief.

He was so smart, and they had so much to live for. She cautiously put the tape loosely back in case Marion looked over their way.

She gave him a quick smile.

They would get out of here.

She just didn't know how—yet.

Chapter 18

Paislee's watch showed the passing of minutes simultaneously slowing as well as speeding by.

The radicals had put together a plan to be even bigger than last year in Dundee, which hadn't been as big as Edinburgh or Glasgow.

There had been over 50,000 injuries from the event.

And that wasn't enough?

The voters proved in the last election that they didn't want to leave the EU. They didn't want to leave Great Britain. While the Scottish National Party had spun a golden tale, it had fallen apart with embezzlement and money laundering.

The good ideas they'd had were taken on by some of the other parties, such as the Labour and the Lib Dems, as well as the Conservatives.

"Here come the cops again," Rob said, sounding annoyed. "I'm going tae shoot them through the door if they dinnae go away."

"Not smart," Marion cautioned. "We gotta wait for the others."

"We cannae let them trap us inside here." Rob sounded worried. "How far away is the lead truck?"

Marion sent a text. The reply was almost immediate. "Ten minutes. I let them know aboot the police being so close tae us. Tae be careful."

"Why?" Rob's tone grew angry. "We can handle this."

"I dinnae want them scared off, that's all. They need these weapons. You gotta know your worth, Robbie," Marion said.

"I dinnae need your sass right now, baby sis." Rob gestured to the crates of fireworks and guns. "Your impulsive behavior is the reason we are in this predicament."

"What are you going tae do aboot it?" Marion strode ahead, gun pointed toward her brother.

Paislee tensed, worried that they might hurt one another, and her and Brody while they were at it. They didn't care about their lives.

If there was an explosion caused by a shoot-out in this basement, then where could she and Brody hide? It was made of cement block with several cement pilings.

The staircase was also cement. Would it be safer to hide behind a pillar, or under the stairs?

She looked around to be sure there were no better options.

As she stared at the cement, she realized that what she had assumed was a crack in the wall was opening slightly. A crack in a brand-new basement? It had to be a cellar door.

Constable Jays slipped out, in his Police Scotland gear, followed by Mack. They were in the basement, low to the ground by the wall. The pillar partially hid them from the front.

Mack!

They were going to be okay.

"Make a decision," Marion taunted Rob. "Shoot the police or shut your gob and wait for the convoy tae back us up?"

"You are the one tae blame here, sister. You never should have stolen the fancy egg or killed that university girl. You got all eyes on Nairn and Cawdor Castle too early."

"And you, with the epic fail of stealing the holly branch?" Marion scoffed. "Paislee here was right and it was a big risk that almost got us busted that night."

"You and Alan are the reason we were almost caught," Rob

said. "You both messed up by stealing from the castle. It wasnae the plan. You killed Ailis."

"Shut up!" Marion said. She paced between the crates, the diamond bouncing from the chain. "We did what we had tae do in order tae have a plan for when this is over."

"Where is Alan? He should have been down here by now." Rob looked at his phone in angst. "If he's not here, I will leave him behind."

Paislee did her best to keep her gaze from the wall opening but it was very, very hard. What if she gave away their position?

"I told you that Alan was caught upstairs," Paislee said. She hoped to keep the siblings arguing.

"You're not leaving Alan," Marion said. "I willnae go with you."

"You want tae die?" Rob shook his head. He sounded nervous. "You're not following the plan, again!"

The pounding on the outer door continued. "Police! Open up!"

Brody shifted and Marion whirled to him with her weapon pointed. "Get up, kid. Rob, shove him oot as a human shield."

"Hang on!" Rob said. He pressed buttons on his mobile. "Damn it. They've blocked the cameras ootside, and I cannae see who is oot there or where."

Marion reached down for Brody, but Paislee stood. "Use me."

"You both are going tae die," Marion scoffed. "Fine with me if you go first."

Constable Jays, slight in stature, hid behind the thick cement pillar. He'd been given a gun, and it was trained on Rob. Officers were not usually issued weapons unless it was by special dispensation.

Like, riots.

Where was Mack?

Where was Alan? What if he joined them at any moment?

Constable Jays lowered his hand in a motion for Paislee to duck.

Paislee dropped her body over Brody's as shots rang out.

Marion spun on her heel, a hole in the palm of her hand.

Rob staggered into the wall, blood blossoming on his shoulder, as the door was rammed open from the other side.

Constable Jays had Marion in cuffs just as Mack had Rob also subdued, with zip ties.

Paislee sat back off of Brody. "Are you all right, son?"

"Yes, Mum. Thanks tae you."

Constable Monroe hurried toward them, using her knife to slice the plastic manacles from Brody's wrists.

"Thank you!" Brody said.

"How did you know where we were?" Paislee asked. She'd been very scared that it would be up to her to figure out a solution on her own.

"We were able tae track the location on Angus's mobile," Monroe said.

"The phone is in my pocket," Brody said. "Marion nabbed me so fast that she didnae bother patting me doon." He gingerly touched his head and winced.

"Rookie mistake," Rob shouted at Marion. "Impulsive, sis!"

"Shut up! Shoulda used the sleeper on you," Marion yelled back. "Moron."

"How did she get you out of the main room?" Paislee had Brody bend so she could see his head, which had a lump, but no blood. She kept turning and patting him to make sure that he was okay. "I thought it was Poppy at first. I was concerned for her safety when I saw Alan behind her when they exited the elevator. But it was Marion, all along."

"It just happened so fast. Marion was really strong and had my mouth taped and the zip ties on before I understood what was going on." Brody rubbed the red marks on his wrists.

"And," Mack shared, "Alan sang like the proverbial canary when we caught him. We knew the plan, down tae the convoy that the police have already stopped en route."

The constable and the DI looked at all of the firepower in amazed shock.

"This was meant tae harm thousands of lives." Mack scowled at Marion and Rob. "You deserve tae be behind bars. You wanted freedom? You should have stayed oot of trouble."

The medics came in to check out Brody and Paislee.

"Any injuries?" asked a tall man with a very calm expression. He skimmed his gaze over Paislee and then Brody.

"I'm fine." Paislee's heart had calmed down to a fast beat rather than manic. "My son needs tae be checked out."

The medic nodded at a spot of blood on Brody's shirt. "You're right."

"His head too," Paislee said.

"Heya," the female medic said. "We should be able tae patch him up here. The roads are blocked because of the rebellion." She gave a cool look to Marion.

"We need tae be free," Marion said. A third medic was wrapping gauze around her hand.

"You were free and behaved immorally," Paislee said. "How is that fair tae anyone besides yourself?"

The tall male medic nodded at Paislee. "Point. It's ridiculous tae think that human lives are *not* all equal."

"It's all aboot equality until it's not," Monroe said. She studied Brody and Paislee with concern. "Then someone wants something that doesnae belong tae them and equality goes oot the window." She flicked the diamond on the chain on Marion's neck.

"How come you have a gun?" Brody asked Constable Jays. "That's so cool."

"A crack shot, too," Mack said. "Right through Marion's palm." Her handsome DI was patting Marion down and sat back with a nod as he pulled the stolen Fabergé egg from her pocket. She had so little care for the historic twenty-five-million-pound piece that she'd wrapped it in a sock.

"That's mine!" Marion said.

Mack examined the egg that was missing an emerald sure to match the one in the evidence room at the police station. "Guid tae know. I bet the curve of the egg here will match the divot on Ailis Barclay's temple. Heard you say you were a crack shot."

"Never seen that before in me life," Marion said.

Mack patted her down further. He removed the chain around her neck and placed it in a bag. "Where are the other diamonds?"

Marion pressed her lips together.

Constable Monroe, searching Rob, said, "I have two necklaces here. Will I find the third?"

"No," Rob said. "Dinnae know nothing aboot them."

"So what are they doing in your pocket?" Monroe asked.

"Alan Martin told us that you sold one for supplies," Mack said. "Will the one on Marion's neck be part of the Cawdor heist?"

"She wasnae using it," Marion said.

"Inspector McCleod gave us special permission, considering the riots and threats for tonight," Constable Monroe said. "Tae carry guns."

"I'm so glad that you are all safe," Paislee said.

Fireworks erupted outside the hotel, the sound coming through the open door of the basement.

"I'm glad too," Brody said. He hugged Paislee with his good side once the medic had bandaged him up.

"No stitches, but check in with his physician tomorrow tae be sure. He might need a tetanus jab." The medic took off her gloves and tucked them in her pocket. "You're fine?"

"Yes," Paislee said, "I am." She was floating on adrenaline.

The door from the interior staircase flew open with a bang. Paislee stifled a squeal. Brody jumped.

Lydia, Grandpa, Corbin, Alistair, and Sophie crowded at the threshold before descending the steps with cries of joy.

They hugged one another in relief with lots of exclamations

and retellings of what had happened and how Mack and Constables Jays and Monroe had saved them.

Mack stayed within Paislee's orbit. Every time she looked up, he was watching her with love in his seafoam-green eyes.

"We Shaws are in the pink, aren't we?" Paislee said—not seeing the rubble or blood, but her family. "Our luck has finally turned around."

Chapter 19

"I want tae go home," Brody said, a half hour later. Tidying up after a big arrest and kidnapping, sorting illegal guns from the industrial fireworks, not to mention the entire box of homemade petrol bombs, took time.

Paislee and Brody sat together on the steps, with Lydia and Corbin behind her, and Alistair, Sophie, and Grandpa behind them. Brody had started to shiver from cold and shock. Constable Monroe had given them each a thin emergency blanket.

Hating to bother Mack when he needed to sort what was happening, Paislee walked to him with reluctance and tapped his shoulder. "Hey. Can we get out of here? I promise we'll all go straight home. Lydia and Corbin too."

Laird Garrison Smythe had tapped into his Highland warrior roots and fought the vandals off of his property. He'd earned accolades from Corbin's brothers and a smile of pride from Corbin as he heard the story that Paislee knew would become family legend.

Mack turned, understanding at once as he looked over her shoulder to the cement stairs and her exhausted family.

"I can provide a police escort from the hotel. Monroe, you okay transporting the criminals tae the station in Inverness?" It was big enough to hold plenty of bad guys.

"Aye," Constable Monroe said. She'd holstered the gun and used the taser to get Marion to cooperate. SAORSA had fallen apart thanks to the information from the informants who had valued this shire and community.

Constable Jays had a slightly gobsmacked expression as he too holstered his gun. "What a first week on the job," the newbie said.

"It's true," Constable Monroe agreed. "If we had more weeks like this then I'd want tae retire."

"Fair." Mack nodded. "But, please dinnae. I need your cool head and expertise."

"I'm not really going anywhere," Monroe said. "It feels good tae capture criminals and place them in the legal system, tae pay their dues."

"I liked following through on clues tae not only find Brody and Paislee but also capture a caravan of criminals," Jays admitted. "*Before* they used the weapons."

"Thank goodness!" Monroe clapped her hand on the young recruit's shoulder. "You really did terrific tonight. I'm sairy I wasnae verra patient aboot the telephone system earlier."

"I'll figure it oot," Jays promised.

Constable Payne entered the basement from the outside with Constable D. McPherson. She eyed Constable Jays with respect. "I heard you helped free the hostages."

Constable Jays puffed his chest. "It was nothing. Just following orders."

Paislee stifled a tired smile. Romance possibly in the air? Or better, a mutual respect between equals. Payne and Monroe were friends.

Paislee peered around the basement. Constable Payne had Rob McGinty ready to transport, and Constable Monroe had Marion. Constables Jays and McPherson were to stay and catalogue the weaponry. This was sure to get them each a commendation of some kind. She worried that regular policework would become dull after such a thrilling start.

Poppy arrived as Monroe and Payne were leaving with their charges. "Wait! Is that Marion McGinty? And Rob? I saw Alan Martin being put intae the back of a police car and knew they had tae be around too."

"You know these two?" Mack demanded

"Part of my wild youth," Poppy admitted.

"Are you a member of SAORSA?" Mack asked.

"No, no—that was too wild for me. I like my luxuries and things I can afford because I work hard for them. I didnae steal or have visions of grandeur. We met at uni in our government class. Had some drinks and got the unicorn tattoo, determined tae right the wrongs of Scotland. I just thought Rob was cute." Her mouth turned down. "I fell for his ideals."

"You and Marion have the same hairstyle," Paislee said.

"Us and a thousand other ladies copying Shanda Fox. She had long glorious locks and chopped them off for a role. I'll switch mine tomorrow," Poppy said.

"I have an excellent hairdresser," Lydia said. She and her mother, Sophie, both enjoyed changing up their hairstyles.

"Thanks. I have one already." Poppy stared at Marion and Rob with distaste and distrust. "Why are they here?" The constables had stopped moving them toward the exit at Poppy's entrance. "At *my* hotel?"

Constable Payne looked at Mack with the silent question of how he wanted to handle this new information.

"Poppy, were you complicit in any of the raids or destruction of property in Nairn in this past week, or ever?" Mack asked.

"No." Poppy replied firmly.

Paislee thought it was smart not to ask about Edinburgh. It might muddy the waters for what happened recently here.

"When was the last time you saw Rob, or Marion, McGinty?" Mack asked. He had his phone app out and tapped in notes.

Poppy tilted her head. "Ten years ago, at least. Mibbe longer."

"If we need tae question you further, will you be here in Nairn?"

"I have a suite in this hotel," Poppy said. "I've made a life here and I'm not going anywhere. I better not get sacked because of these numpties. Why are there crates of fireworks and weapons in the basement? This wasnae here yesterday."

"We moved it this morning," Marion said with a smirk. "You didnae notice a thing."

"Why would I have?" Poppy ruffled her hair in anger.

"Where from?" Mack asked Marion. The radical had stopped talking at her brother's urging, but Poppy's appearance merited response from the old rivals.

"Rait Tower. The ruins were the best hiding spot—until Ailis, Brody, and Paislee showed up and stumbled on us as we were burying . . . things."

"How long have you been using the ruins as a hiding ground?" Mack asked.

"This last year," Rob said. The fight had left him as he realized that he was well and truly caught.

"I want this stuff oot of here," Poppy told Mack. "Puir Ailis was innocent after all," she said. "I never want tae see you McGintys again."

Poppy turned on her heel and went back inside the narrow staircase going up to the lobby of the hotel.

"Me either," Brody said.

"You might have tae testify but it will feel guid tae put them behind bars," Monroe said to Brody.

Paislee stood next to her son. If he didn't want to, or didn't feel comfortable, they would find another way.

"Too bad," Marion snarked.

Monroe adjusted the zip ties to jostle Marion's wounded hand. The criminal yelped.

"Sairy," Monroe said in a cheerful tone. "There are days when I really enjoy my job."

"If it means doing the right thing, I will," Brody said.

Paislee patted his shoulder. He was a good person from the inside out.

Men in protective gear arrived to move the weapons and industrial grade fireworks that had been used against the police in prior years. One talked to Constable Jays, who faced Mack, Paislee, and her family.

"We have tae clear this space of all civilians," the young constable said, sounding more confident by the second. "You should all go. We've got this from here."

"I'll be in touch—let me know if you need anything. Well done, Jays." Mack ushered them all into the staircase and they exited at the lobby level from a side entrance.

Poppy had turned off the festive lights, probably to save the drain of power from the generator, leaving the fountain silent and dark.

"What happened with Alan?" Paislee asked Lydia. "I just remember him aiming a gun at us, but I had tae get tae Brody."

"Pat Amblin hit him over the head with a solid oak charcuterie board," Lydia said. "Knocked him right oot. Corbin and Simon tied him tae a kitchen chair with dish towels until the police arrived."

"I thought Marion was Poppy or Darcey. Came as a big surprise tae discover the sweet, healthy tourist from Glasgow was who'd kidnapped Brody from the room." Paislee hated feeling like she'd been taken advantage of.

"I have never seen anybody move as fast as you did after him," Lydia said. Her eyes welled. "Best mum, Paislee."

"You didnae stop tae give Alan's threat with the gun the time of day but darted doon the stairs after Brody," Grandpa said. "I thought I was going tae have a heart attack on the spot."

"You didnae though," Corbin said. "You called DI Zeffer while we tied up Alan, after Pat clonked him on the head."

Mack shook his head, his skin paling as he understood for the first time the real danger Paislee and Brody had been in.

"Angus remembered aboot the location app on the mobile phone," Alistair said, clapping Grandpa on the back.

"And showed it tae the DI when he arrived," Grandpa said.

"I was ten minutes away," Mack said. "I ran from the station rather than try tae drive with the traffic so congested. I wished I could fly but couldnae be here any faster."

"Thank you, everyone, for all that you've done," Paislee said. She took Mack's hand, and Brody's.

Poppy arrived with a small trolly with all of their personal items from the rooftop room. "Here you are. Handbags, phones, keys. Jackets. This was all that was left. Everyone else is gone. I am so sairy that this happened."

Pat arrived behind her, shrugging into his jacket. Simon wasn't around.

"It wasnae your fault, Poppy, darling," Sophie said. "Thanks for bringing this doon."

"Corbin—how is your dad?" Paislee scanned her phone. The noble ladies had all texted that they were okay. Sorcha and Shannon both had to put out literal fires, but they were fine. The radicals were arrested.

Unfortunately, this would put a bigger divide between the top and the bottom of society. Paislee would think about that tomorrow.

"Da is the man of the hour. My stepmum is making sure he's resting with the dogs and a large whisky," Corbin said. "My brothers are handling things. It's not an emergency for us tae brave the roads tonight. We'll set up a video call when we get home."

"It's midnight," Lydia said, nudging Paislee's arm.

"Midnight?" Paislee blinked. Midnight would have been when the radicals had set off the explosives to take over the government.

But, thanks to this wonderful group, the radicals were arrested.

"Instead of the Gunpowder Plot failing like it had for Guy Fawkes, this was the SAORSA Plot failing," Brody said. He pumped his fist.

"Happy birthday, Paislee," Mack said. He looked into her eyes and her skin warmed.

As she scanned their tired and dirty faces, she felt like she could float from pure joy. "Best gift ever, is having my family here and everyone safe."

Chapter 20

The morning of Paislee's thirty-first birthday started off with Wallace, Brody, and Grandpa bringing her pancakes in bed.

They sang to her, and she may have cried a little. She blamed the tears on the adrenaline coursing through her from the ups and downs of the previous few days.

The three went downstairs as the house phone was ringing off the hook.

"Hello!" Paislee answered in a cheery tone, expecting it to be her mother, or Emma for Brody, or someone to wish her a happy birthday.

"It's Darcey." The woman's voice was gruff.

The only Darcey Paislee knew was Darcey McClintock from the Nairn paper.

Where was the paper? "Did we get the newspaper?" Paislee asked, covering the receiver so that Darcey didn't hear the question.

Grandpa went to get it, and brought it in, slipping it from the wrapper before placing it on the table.

Mack texted her to call him immediately. Lydia called on her mobile, sure to leave birthday wishes galore.

Chuckling, Paislee said, "Morning, Darcey."

"Paislee Shaw. I'm calling for a quote. How do you feel aboot the shops on Market Street being burned in the riot?"

"What?" She blinked and fell against the kitchen counter. Did she say *burned*? She thought of the inventory of yarn and bespoke items in Cashmere Crush. The time and money spent to build up the shop. Her neighbors on the block—were they all right?

"Och, you didnae ken?" Darcey said snidely.

"Is everyone okay?" Paislee pinched the inside of her wrist. People mattered most. Ritchie, across the street. "What happened, Darcey?"

"The brick didnae burn like it might have. Folks from the Lion's Mane alerted authorities. Still standing."

"I thought the riots were over? And, weren't you laid off for your tricky interview of the Barclay family?"

"They will want me back. Your reaction tae the story is definitely going tae sell papers." Her laugh was ugly.

"Mum!" Brody said.

"What is it, son?" Her life flashed before her eyes. Her way of earning money, to take care of Brody and Grandpa and Wallace.

Hadn't she thought that her luck had finally turned around? She was an eejit.

But, it had.

It had. Paislee had to trust in that.

She hung up on Darcey.

Paislee answered Lydia, who was on her third call.

"Yes?" Paislee exhaled, the expectation for birthday felicitations crumbled. Of course, Lydia would know when Paislee's world was sinking.

"I'm headed tae the shop now," Lydia said. "Meet me there?"

"All right." Paislee nodded, numb.

Paislee hung up. Mack called. She answered in a low croak of hello.

"Morning, Paislee. Listen tae me, all right? The brick on the shop has only been scorched and the window boxes are gone. Nobody was injured. Can you meet me here?"

"Yes." Her eyes felt three times their size and she forced a blink to focus on the round table where Brody and Grandpa had spread out the paper for her to read the article.

The front page was a montage of photos of the fires from last night—both bonfires and organized attacks on noble properties all over Scotland. The story of the brand-new hotel, Oasis, being used to transfer weapons bought with stolen goods from Cawdor Castle and stored at Rait Tower in the base of the ruins. Ailis had been an innocent caught in the crosshairs of a radical section of the SNP called SAORSA. The SNP was denying any credit or knowledge of the actions.

"I can't believe what I'm reading," Paislee said, her body shaking.

"Drive safe. There is *no* danger."

"Easy for you tae say," Paislee replied in shock.

"It will be okay," Mack said.

No matter what happened? He was right.

Grandpa handed her a cup of strong tea in a to-go mug. Brody hugged her over and over. "Should we go with you tae the shop?" Brody asked.

"I don't think so. Someone tried tae burn the businesses on Market Street."

"We heard," Grandpa said. He removed his glasses and tossed them to the paper in disbelief.

Paislee looked at the time. Half past eight. Her family was in no way ready for the day. "Brody, can you call Edwyn tae get a ride tae school?"

"I'd rather call Sam or Emma."

He didn't argue, which was good. Paislee nodded.

Paislee blinked and then started to laugh. "Mack said that Cashmere Crush is still standing. And you know what? That is a bonus. I have you both, and after last night? Everything else is just stuff. I can make more of it. I can't replace either one of you."

She felt Gran's love in the kitchen surrounding them as they gave each other hugs. Wallace wanted to be held, so Brody included him in the hugs too.

After getting dressed, Paislee drove to the shop, arriving at the same time as Lydia, who exited the Mercedes as Mack walked toward them from the police station. Most of the shops opened at ten, except for Scoops, which opened at eleven, and Margot's walk-in clinic, which opened at eight.

"How did you know?" Paislee asked her best friend. "Before I did."

"I wasnae able tae sleep so I went tae the beach tae sit at the bandstand and watch the sunrise. It's almost the same view as from the condo. Smelled the smoke and noticed the fire truck but there werenae any more flames when I got here."

"You called right after Darcey McClintock. She wanted my reaction, hoping to get back in with the paper with this article. The pictures were all from last night, so this would be for tomorrow's news."

"I passed Darcey McClintock around six. She was jogging and seemed verra off this morning," Lydia said.

Mack arrived and stood next to them. Paislee was doing her best to not stare at the missing window boxes on each of the storefronts. Ritchie opened at eight as well. He came out and waved at her, blowing her a kiss and miming a phone call to talk to him later. All those businesses across the street were fine. The Lion's Mane at the far corner was also still standing. They didn't open until eleven but the cooks or waitstaff had alerted the fire trucks.

"Like how off?" Mack asked Lydia.

"Like, distracted." Lydia palmed her keys. "I said hello, but she barely acknowledged me. Guess she was focused on getting tae the office."

"Interesting," Mack said. The wheels were churning in his handsome head. He leaned over to kiss her cheek. "You okay?"

"Surprisingly enough, I am fine. Darcey has it in for me," Paislee said.

"Why?" Mack asked.

"That's not right," Lydia said. "Her actions got her sacked. She's not an ethical journalist."

"The headline accusing Blake of killing Ailis?" Mack tucked his hand into his jacket pocket. "Crude but effective."

"Poppy had another lead so maybe Darcey's false accusations weren't necessary." Paislee exhaled and turned to look at the outside of Cashmere Crush. Scorched marks on the brick where the wooden flowerboxes used to be. She would need to check inside for smoke damage. "I'm so glad that it wasn't worse."

"I think it's strange that the fire from the riots came this far," Mack said. "It was mostly on the other side of the village with the new builds and the big traditional estates. Lady Leery, and the Dowager Countess Grant, and Dowager Countess of Cawdor. The Smythe Estate. Three others between here and Inverness. The plan was tae burn everything doon and start over."

"Did you catch all of the vandals?" Lydia asked.

Mack lifted his shoulders. "It would be impossible tae know for sure."

"I think we should go pay a visit tae Darcey. Mitch, her co-worker, said she was a member of the SNP. I thought I saw paint on the toe of her boot yesterday when she accused me of meddling in her career."

"Being a member of the Scottish National Party is not a crime," Mack warned. "They are denying involvement. However, if she knows anything about the damages done here locally, I need tae know. Graffiti and vandalism are chargeable offenses."

Paislee was walking toward the newspaper office, just two blocks away, as they talked. She was very angry about Darcey's cavalier attitude regarding the fire when she'd called this morning.

I guess you didnae ken?

Mack and Lydia easily kept pace with her as they both had longer strides than she did. Lydia was a yoga nut, and Mack was very fit through his job.

They turned the corner as Mitch Duprey, green hair wild, was escorting Darcey out toward her car.

"Fired means fired," Mitch said. He washed his hands together.

"Dinnae come back. You're lucky the editor decided not tae press charges."

Darcey saw Paislee, Lydia, and most importantly, Detective Inspector Mack Zeffer coming toward her.

She hopped into her car and turned it on, revving the engine before she peeled out, smoke from the burning rubber wafting upward.

Mack had his team of constables on speed dial, quickly giving them the coordinates and make and model of Darcey's car.

"She willnae get far," Mack promised.

Sure enough, a crash sounded as Darcey drove into a street sign. Smoke and dust plumed, the scent mixing with the burning rubber.

Mitch joined them, out of breath from running half a block to the crash site.

"She smelled like petrol. I accused her of starting the fire for a story and she lost her mind. She blames you, Paislee. I told her tae take a guid look in the mirror for some self-reflection." Mitch used his mobile to take pictures of Darcey, Darcey's car, and Darcey being arrested by Constable McPherson.

"She'll get time for that in jail," Mack said.

He went to investigate the contents of the boot and pulled out a plastic bag of aerosol cans in a variety of colors. It was the motherlode of evidence as she was also passing out the SAORSA pamphlets with the unicorn trampling the lion.

"Why was she lucky not tae be turned in?" Paislee asked Mitch.

"She was using the newspaper tae print these pamphlets oot." Mitch shook his head. "The owner is friends with the thane and didnae take it well."

"Awful."

Mitch looked at Paislee. "Why are you here?"

"We were wondering what Darcey could tell us about the fire on Market Street," Paislee said. "You mentioned she smelled like petrol?"

"She did. Damn, I'm really sairy, Paislee. Is your shop okay?"

"I haven't checked inside yet, but all along the row I think the main loss will be the flowerboxes out front."

"You have the cutest street." Mitch sighed. "I love Scoops. Never been intae Cashmere Crush."

Paislee smiled. "Do you knit?"

"Nah."

"Paislee is a yarn *artiste,* Mitch," Lydia said. "She has cashmere at the Ramsey Castle gift shop. She sells the finest quality, from hats"—she touched her head—"tae scarves, vests, jumpers, and socks. Any woman in your life would love a gift from there."

"Oh?" Mitch looked at her differently.

"You cannae tell anyone, but she will be doing some of the Grant wedding accoutrement in December."

Mack joined them toward the end of Lydia's endorsement.

"I hope tae put in an order for a cashmere scarf myself before you get too busy for us regular folk." Mack's half smile made her heart soar.

"I'll be sure tae stop in. Detective . . ."

"Detective Inspector Mack Zeffer. I would love tae talk tae your boss aboot this incident."

"He's in the office right now," Mitch said.

"Do you mind going back tae the shop on your own?" Mack said. "I'd like tae get notes while the accident is still fresh. You were right aboot Darcey wanting revenge."

Dismissed, Paislee thought with a chuckle. "Not at all."

"Dinnae forget dinner tonight for Paislee's birthday," Lydia said with an arched brow at Mack.

"As if I could!"

Mack and Mitch walked toward the Nairn newspaper office, Mitch talking a mile a minute about Darcey and all of her various faults.

Lydia put her arm through Paislee's. "Can we walk back along the water?"

"Yes, of course."

Paislee hoped she would finally get to the bottom of what her bestie was upset about. If it was Corbin's stepmother again, then Paislee would have her hide.

Lydia's sleep was vital to her, and she required eight hours every night. For her to not be getting it meant that she was very worried about something.

Like for Paislee, the ocean brought solace to Lydia.

"Want tae grab a coffee and sit at the bandstand?"

"No coffee. I've been verra thirsty for plain water. I think we need tae fix the filter at the property in Germany."

"Will that be expensive?" Paislee asked.

"I dinnae ken. Corbin is in a different space aboot those things, and he will just do it despite the cost," Lydia said with a laugh.

"I forget, Lady Lydia Barron-Smythe, that you are part of the local nobility."

They reached the bandstand and sat, facing the water. Lydia pulled two cans of water from her massive handbag.

"Here," she said, cracking the top.

Paislee did too.

They tapped cans with a laugh. "Slainte."

"Happy birthday, Paislee." Lydia glanced at her and wiped a tear from her eye.

Lydia cried beautifully as she did everything else. As her best friend, Paislee had learned to let it go.

Paislee had left her handbag in the Juke at Cashmere Crush so didn't have anything but her mobile and keys. No tissue on hand to offer.

She patted Lydia's shoulder. "What is it? You haven't been yourself since you returned from Germany."

"I know it. I was blaming the water filtration system." Lydia pointed to a spot of acne on her chin. "See this?"

"No. I didn't. Not until you pointed it out."

"I was nauseous over breakfast yesterday and Mum said that she was that way when she was pregnant with me. I was horrified."

Paislee's jaw dropped. She studied her friend closely—the shadows beneath her eyes, the acne, the lack of sleep.

Water, and ice cream rather than whisky, which hadn't tasted good.

She'd barely touched her champagne.

"Well?" Paislee said, crying with happiness.

"I've got an appointment tomorrow at Doc Whyte's." Lydia showed Paislee a picture of a pregnancy test on her phone. It was pink for positive.

Paislee threw her arms around her best friend in the world.

"What does Corbin think? He must be ecstatic."

"He doesnae know."

Paislee's happy tears dried. "Oh."

"Mum went with me tae buy the kit. She doesnae know the results yet. It was why I was up so early, so that Corbin didnae see me. I was hoping tae have the flu." Lydia glanced at Paislee in misery. "We didnae want children."

"Birth control?"

"IUD." Lydia continued crying. "What will happen now? Somehow, the rules have changed. I dinnae want tae be in Germany raising a baby withoot you, and Mum."

"Lydia, sweetheart, you need tae tell Corbin. He will surprise you, I think, with his response. You will be amazing parents."

"I dinnae ken the first thing aboot it," Lydia fretted. "You are an awesome mother. I need you by my side."

"I am here, always. Your mother will also be wonderful and on hand. She was such a great role model for us." Paislee cried and wrapped her best friend in a hug. "You can do this. I will be a phone call away. We will figure out the Germany thing."

"You're sure?"

"I know it." Paislee couldn't stop grinning. "I get tae be an aunt."

"Yeah, now that is a role I knew how tae play, hands down."

"You've set the bar high," Paislee said. "Brody gets a cousin. More family tae love."

A splash sounded in the water.

"Look!" Lydia said.

"Dolphins. Now, that is good luck, Lydia. Will you please call your husband? I know you'll be pleased by his reaction. He loves you, and he will love the wee bean growing inside you."

"I will. Love you. Dinnae be late for dinner tonight. Six sharp." She wagged her finger as she called Corbin, asking him to meet her at the bandstand.

Paislee walked the few blocks to Cashmere Crush. Grandpa had texted that Sam's mum had driven Brody to school.

It was ten on the dot when she arrived at the back entrance to Cashmere Crush. Rhona was in tears, holding a balloon bouquet for Paislee's birthday. "Paislee! There you are. You left your handbag in your car. I was worrit you'd been kidnapped or something awful."

Grandpa, having walked to work early, stood next to Rhona on the back stoop.

"I was concerned," Grandpa said. "And told Rhona what happened last night."

"Why you both aren't taking the day off is beyond me." Rhona wrapped an arm around Paislee's shoulders.

"Let's go inside." Paislee couldn't stop grinning.

"What is the matter with you?" Grandpa demanded. "You've been hittin' the whisky this morning?"

"Nope." She unlocked the door and gestured for them to come in.

The landline in the shop was ringing.

She raced to get it. "Cashmere Crush."

"It's Mary Beth. Are you all right? Should I come over?"

"I'm fine—we are fine. I . . ."

"I'm coming. I'll be there in ten minutes."

Paislee was listening to a dial tone.

Rhona beelined for the front door and unlocked it even though they weren't ready with the register. She opened it and peered out along the street. "All the window boxes are gone?"

"Yes." Paislee held up her hand. "Come on in. Darcey McClintock is the one who tried tae burn the Market Street businesses down, and make it look like it was part of the riots. She blamed me for losing her job at the paper."

"Rats!" Rhona said. She closed the door, but it opened again as Margot, Elspeth, Susan and her service dog, Rosie, came in.

"Are you all right?" Elspeth asked, looking from Paislee to Grandpa with watering eyes.

"I couldnae get in earlier," Margot said. "They had the street blocked. I called Susan tae not come in right away. I have never missed a scheduled day of work. It all happened so fast. You're okay?"

"Yes, I am." She sniffed the air, which had a slightly burned scent.

"Let's prop the back door open," Grandpa said.

"Good idea." She would need to hope that the yarn at the front of the shop didn't smell like smoke.

"Who is responsible? We will find them," Elspeth said.

"Actually, it was Darcey McClintock. Mack already has her in jail," Paislee said.

The other business owners stopped in to check on Paislee throughout the day. The worst thing for them all was the loss of the flowerboxes and a slightly burned smell that faded when they propped their doors open. None of her yarn or bespoke items had been ruined.

Gemma, Artie's mum, and her boyfriend, Lachlan, arrived with the shelving for the back storage room. "Our gift tae you, Paislee. Rhona showed us the design you'd created online, and we wanted tae help."

She was truly speechless by everyone's kindness and concern.

At noon, Paislee was sure that everybody in their beloved shire had dropped in to make sure that she was okay.

This was community. Since they were going to have a fancy

dinner with Lydia later, she decided to order sandwiches from the Lion's Mane and eat in. It was a party atmosphere.

Julie Barclay came in with her husband, Doug.

"I want tae apologize, Paislee," Julie said. "I was oot of my mind." Her husband held her elbow, as if she was a fragile piece of glass.

"No need. All I kept thinking the whole time was how I would feel if our situations were reversed. It could have been Brody."

"We are going tae therapy as a family," Julie said. "Darryl is weighted doon by guilt. He cannae look at Brody withoot feeling worse for his actions. He considers Brody a friend. He was crazy aboot his sister."

"That's a relief tae hear. You and your family are in our prayers."

Grandpa walked to join them. "I'm verra sairy for your loss. We'd like tae send over some chicken and dumplings tomorrow, if that would be all right?"

"Too thoughtful, and thank you," Doug said.

"I'll be going tae Tesco this weekend and I was going tae pick up some other meals tae tuck in your freezer. Is there anything at all I can do? We will be at the service on Saturday."

"That's enough," Julie said. "I was awful."

Paislee hugged the woman to her. "There is nothing tae forgive, all right? We are mums, doing our best for our families."

Julie inhaled and took her husband's hand. "Later, then?"

"Tomorrow," Grandpa said, "and Saturday."

"We heard aboot Darcey being responsible for the fire on this street. She was rather mental in the end," Doug said. "But even if she was wrong aboot her methods for finding oot what happened tae Ailis, we learned that it wasnae Blake."

"Our darling was not a thief, just a high-spirited young woman in the wrong place at the wrong time." Julie exhaled, her eyes clearing. "Thinking the worst while trying tae find her killer was an added grief that we can let go of now."

The Barclays left. Paislee and Grandpa shared a sad smile. Letting go was the key.

"Should I close up?" Rhona asked Paislee at half past three. "You deserve tae take the rest of the day off."

"We have Lydia's at six. I can work until five." She hadn't even thought about what to wear later, when Grandpa handed her a box from a high-end clothing store.

"I think that's a guid idea, Rhona," Grandpa said.

"What?" Paislee didn't understand. She had scarves to work on, matching jumpers, the blanket with the clans united, and a back storage room to organize.

"This is tae be opened after your massage at four."

"What massage?" Paislee didn't have time for such things.

"Part of me and Brody's birthday gift tae you is a massage and a facial and nails at the spa before we go."

Rhona clapped in delight. "Spa day!"

Paislee plopped down on the stool, not releasing the fancy box. "But . . ."

"And dinnae nag at me for more answers," Grandpa said with a twinkle in his eye. "You willnae be getting any."

Chapter 21

Paislee, brushed, coiffed, waxed, and lotioned, was as limp as a string of yarn when the spa experience was over.

Nobody answered her texts.

Her family and her friends were ghosting her, plain and simple.

"Just relax," the handsome masseur said. "Or you will undo all of the magic of these hands." He splayed them. On his left was a thin gold wedding ring.

"We can't have that. Gerard, are you sure that I'm not supposed tae tip you?" Paislee sat up, the satin sheet around her body.

"It has all been taken care of, I promise."

It had to be very expensive, but no matter how hard she'd tried, Gerard hadn't given up the name of her benefactor.

"Now, hang on. Marni will be in tae help you dress. You didnae peek, did you?" Gerard asked.

"No."

It had been tempting but she'd promised Grandpa that she wouldn't.

"Guid. I can tell you that this dress is from a verra sought-after designer."

"I don't really like fancy dresses. Cinderella? Poofy skirts?"

"Trust us, Paislee. We just need tae style your hair and then you can get intae the dress."

She was glad that he hadn't said *gown*. Gowns were for other people, not knitting shop owners with a ten-year-old SUV and a hundred-year-old house.

Maybe Lydia was surprising her with dinner at the Nairn Golf Club, with Blaise and Shep. Or, it could be another posh place—possibly in Inverness.

Her stomach fluttered with nerves.

Gerard put his hand against the pulse at her neck. "Relax. I want a picture before you go." He handed her a glass of champagne. "Sip."

Paislee did. It was delicious and crisp.

Marni, an adorable redhaired pixie with green eyes, who had been in charge of shaping and waxing Paislee's brows as well as painting toes and fingers, had assisted with the hair and makeup. The perfume they'd chosen was so light as to be a whisper of scent.

"One doesnae want tae overpower the senses," Marni had said earlier.

Now, it was time to see the dress. Marni entered the private salon as Gerard exited.

Paislee lifted the top of the shiny opalescent box and moved aside gossamer tissue to see fabric of ice blue.

"Like your eyes," Marni said.

"Oh!" She thought of her dad, Bruce, who used to comment on the color as being a unique and lovely feature.

Her pale skin without freckles, and copper hair as fine as cornsilk, hadn't been put together in a way that she'd ever felt especially pretty. As Marni helped her into the dress and showed her in the full-length mirror, she sucked in a happy smile. "This is really lovely."

"As are you," Marni said.

The style had little cap sleeves and an empire waist, like something from the eighteen hundreds, but it was modern in that it fell to just above her knees. The open-toe heels were only two inches, in nude to show off her pedicure.

"What if I ruin it?"

"The fabric is more durable than it looks. You can take it tae the dry cleaner and any stain will come right oot. Isnae it comfortable too?"

"Aye." It was made to flatter without being restrictive. She could walk, talk, and twirl.

"This is genius," Marni said, showing Paislee a hidden pocket in the dress just large enough for her phone.

"Awesome!"

Her hair had been styled so that it was straight to her shoulders, with an angel clip at the side.

"I heard the last few years have been rough ones," Marni said. "But your luck has certainly turned around."

Marni unknowingly echoed Paislee's belief. "It has."

Marni handed her the flute of champagne. "Gerard! Let's get this girl oot the door tae the limo."

"A limo?"

"Yes, princesses dinnae drive themselves around. They are driven. It will be a nice change of pace for you not tae have tae be the one in charge, eh?" Marni asked. Her tone was bordering on teasing but it was a serious question.

"I don't mind," Paislee said.

"You are unbelievable," Gerard stated. "So genuine that you dinnae even know how much you take on."

"It's my job."

"And you can go back tae it tomorrow, but for tonight, just enjoy the magic," Gerard said.

He stood next to Paislee on one side, Marni on the other, and she snapped a picture with her phone of them all.

"It's time," Gerard said.

"Do I turn into a pumpkin at midnight?" Paislee asked, not really kidding.

"This is your life always," Marni said. "Come back and see us."

Gerard opened the door as a silver stretch limo pulled up to the salon by the sea. The driver got out to open the rear passenger door.

"I want tae go pick up my son and grandfather," she told the man.

"Mum!" Brody poked his head out and grinned, waving at her. "We are already here."

Paislee climbed in and sat next to Grandpa and across from Brody.

"You look beautiful, Paislee," Grandpa said.

"You really do, Mum."

He studied her fingernails—a silver polish that matched her toes.

She didn't really wear fingernail polish that often as she didn't have time and preferred her nails plain and short.

"Do you know where we are going?" Paislee asked.

"Mibbe," Brody said. He was dressed in a stylish suit that she was sure Lydia had picked out. Grandpa looked snazzy too.

"You guys are so handsome."

"It's comfy," Brody said, stretching his leg to show her a dress shoe of stylish leather. "I bet I can run a mile in these."

"Grandpa?"

"I'm not running in these togs, but I do look pretty dapper." He smoothed his beard and then his hair.

Brody had gotten a trim as well.

"Who do I thank for this largesse?"

"We pitched in," Brody said.

"Thank you."

Grandpa squeezed her hand. "Happy birthday."

"I just don't know what I've done tae deserve all of this," Paislee said.

"You deserve tae be spoiled."

"You do, Mum." Brody sipped a can of fizzy water.

Grandpa offered her champagne, but she didn't want to spill anything on her dress. They arrived at Lydia's at six. That was one way to ensure that your guest of honor wasn't late.

Mack walked toward the limo with a single red rose wrapped in an ice-blue ribbon and opened the door.

"Ladies first," Grandpa said.

Mack effortlessly lifted her from the back. His suit, a blue to match her dress, had to be brand-new and fit him perfectly.

Lydia and Corbin came next. "Happy birthday, Paislee."

"I feel so spoiled." Paislee squeezed Lydia's hand.

Corbin couldn't stop grinning at Lydia or touching her hip.

He knew, and was happy. How could he not be?

"Let's go in, Shaw family."

"I feel like this is something you do for a fiftieth birthday," Paislee said. "Not thirty-one."

"You're old, Mum. But still bonnie," Brody teased. He didn't leave her side. Grandpa was on the other side of Mack, who held her hand.

"Tae the ballroom," Mack murmured low. "You look beautiful, Paislee."

She patted his arm and accepted the rose. "Thank you. You are always handsome tae me. Now we have matching clothes. It's a little cutesy, but I don't mind."

Mack's mouth twitched. "Cutesy?"

"Like when you're dating as a teenager and have matching everything. Never thought I would see the appeal." She smiled up at Mack.

Brody practically hummed with excitement.

"Sweetheart, calm down."

"Mum, I think you should close your eyes."

"Oh, guid idea," Lydia said. "Close 'em tight, Paislee."

She did and couldn't see. Mack held her by the elbow. "I've got you."

That he did. She'd never dreamed of being so supported, literally.

They entered the room for a hundred people that Lydia had designed with dances and dinners in mind. Soft music played overhead and around them from wall speakers that were out of sight. Corbin liked his gadgets.

They stopped. Paislee's senses were on high alert with her eyes shut.

"When can she open them?" Brody asked in a loud whisper.

"I'm right here, hon." Paislee put her hand on Brody's shoulder, eyes closed. His voice had sounded farther away.

"On three," Lydia said. "Everyone—one, two, and three!"

When Paislee opened her eyes, she couldn't believe it and blinked hard. Across from her, just three feet away stood Rosanna. Her mum, beautiful and blonde, and Natalie and Josh before her. She had the kids with her. Her brother and sister. Here.

"Oh!" Paislee didn't think there was anything else that could surprise her, but this, this was it. She sucked in a dragging breath. Mack had his hand on her back.

"That was Josh," Brody said, observing Paislee very closely as if to see if she was okay.

"You sound alike." She looked at Lydia, crying, beautifully crying, and reached for her. "Thank you." Next, she clasped Brody's hand. Was she dreaming?

"Are you glad tae see us?" Natalie asked, her eyes wide.

That broke the spell.

Paislee kicked aside her heels and raced with Brody across the room, hand in hand. They dropped to their knees, as did Rosanna, to engulf Natalie and Josh.

"Is it okay?" her mother whispered, her throat thick. Her arms were around them. "If you want me tae go, I will."

"No, no, no. Don't leave." All of the years of bitterness faded. Aye, Paislee had a right to hold onto a grudge as her mum had deserted her for a new life in America, yet her mother had braved Paislee's rejection to surprise her on her birthday.

She had to let go of the anger and disappointment, to be in this moment of forgiveness.

"I'm sorry, Paislee. I know my actions hurt you," Rosanna said. She, thank God, cried like a regular person, and her cheeks were as splotchy as Paislee's.

"It's okay. I was a bratty teenager."

"I wanna know all aboot it," Brody said. Her mum snuggled him close.

Paislee's arms were around Natalie and Josh, then her mum. Grandpa joined the circle. Then Lydia, Mack, and Corbin.

Grandpa helped Rosanna to her feet. "It's guid tae see you," he said. "You havenae changed a bit."

"As much of a charmer as always," Rosanna said. "Angus, this is Natalie and Josh." The kids shook his hand, not leaving Paislee.

Mack had helped her up, and brought her heels. "Never knew you could run so fast," he said to Paislee. "Hi, Rosanna. I am Mack Zeffer. Josh, Natalie. Hello."

"Did we surprise you?" Natalie wanted to know.

"Yes. That was the best surprise ever."

"Mum, you looked totally gobsmacked," Brody said. "We got her, Grandpa."

"Gobsmacked?" Rosanna said. "I haven't heard that word in a very long time." Her mother looked at Lydia. "Thank you for arranging this. It has meant the world."

"Lydia is our fairy godmother," Paislee said.

She didn't mention the baby, and wouldn't until she'd gotten the all-clear from Lydia. What a lucky baby that would be.

"Dinner will be served in thirty minutes," Lydia announced over the din. Paislee figured there had to be seventy-five people or more here tonight. The space was full but not crowded. "Get appetizers, drinks, and mingle. The birthday girl will be over here if you want tae say hello."

Before she knew it, Paislee was seated in an armchair before the fireplace with a glass of champagne in hand.

Mack was always nearby, but also allowing her space to converse. She saw him talking with her mother. Her. Mother. And then Lydia. He hung out with Brody, Corbin, and Grandpa. Natalie and Josh. Her little brother and sister were so stinking cute.

Josh followed Brody around and Brody ate it up.

Sorcha arrived with Shannon. They beelined to Paislee. "Did we miss the maternal reunion?" Shannon asked.

Paislee nodded.

"Darn it. My fault. I had tae stop and fill the tank, and that guzzler takes more than my weight in petrol."

Paislee laughed. "Can I say how much I love that you get your own petrol, Sorcha? Most people in your position have it done for them."

"It's crass," Shannon said, lifting her nose. "But she willnae listen." Lady Leery noticed Paislee's dress and heels. "Gorgeous. Simply stunning. I had no idea you could dress up so prettily."

"Eh, thanks?" Paislee said.

Mack arrived with a fresh glass of champagne. "Paislee, I'm here tae walk you intae dinner. Ladies. How are you?"

"Just fine, thank you," Sorcha said. "Grateful we didnae miss the meal. Lydia told us Pat Amblin is cooking. They'd arranged the menu yesterday and we had tae walk you oot so you wouldnae catch on. As if I cannae fix me own sleeve!"

"I'm glad you are here," Paislee said, meaning every word.

"What are we having tonight?" Shannon asked.

"I have no idea. But the way he cooks?" Paislee shrugged. "It will be delicious."

Mack tugged her back to walk her in last.

"I've always known how beautiful you are."

Paislee rolled her eyes. Her face turned red. The only reason she didn't look like a raccoon from all the tears was because Lydia had warned the spa to use waterproof makeup. "You don't have tae flatter me."

Mack dipped his hand into the interior suit jacket pocket. "I want tae give you this, as a token of my love. I would like tae flatter you and make you blush for the rest of our days."

He opened the box. He knew her so well. It wasn't a blingy five carat but a lovely smooth platinum band that wouldn't snag on cashmere. The large circular diamond was set in a bezel design for the same reason.

"Mack!"

He dropped to one knee. Paislee was vaguely aware of cameras flashing but she only had eyes for Mack. His seafoam-green eyes had flecks of gold. Why was he rushing her? She had to raise Brody. That came first.

"I can see you lining up your arguments and would like tae plead my case." He wasn't joking around. "You have raised an incredible young man who has integrity. Honor. Guid values. You have done that, Paislee. I would like tae point oot that I also strive for those qualities. I feel like I can add tae your life—tae all of your lives."

Paislee tugged him upward, but Mack wouldn't budge.

"I am steady as a rock. Your life, Paislee, is full the way it is. I would like tae add just a little bit tae make it sweeter." He freed the ring from the box.

"I . . ." Paislee looked behind Mack to see Brody nodding and giving two thumbs-up. Grandpa, next to him, pumped his fist.

She peered down into Mack's eyes, then dropped to her knees so they were face-to-face. He kissed her thoroughly.

Lips tingling, she accepted the ring on her left hand.

"Aye, I accept your proposal." She kissed him and pulled back. "I want tae raise a fine young man, and you are the best example I can think of tae add tae our family."

Applause sounded as paper birthday horns were blasted.

Mack stood and helped her up. "I asked your son, and your grandfather, and your mother, tae be in your life, but the one I wasnae sure of was you."

"Mack! I love you."

"I know you do, so I had that in my corner."

"Then what?"

"Well, I wasnae sure how serious you were aboot waiting until Brody turned eighteen." His warm breath skimmed her knuckles, and she shivered. "Tae have a relationship in all ways."

"Mack Zeffer!" Mack swept her into his arms. "I look forward tae our wedding day, and night."

"I'm happy tae hear you say that." He touched her cheek and gave her a wicked wink. "You're blushing."

Acknowledgments

I am thankful to my amazing editor, John Scognamiglio, for his understanding when I was juggling time away from my desk in Florida to be in Washington with my mom, and my grandmother, who passed away at ninety-six, January 2025.

I am thankful to my agent, Evan Marshall, who helped me navigate career stuff while I dealt with messy life things. I am thankful to everyone on the Kensington team, from the editors to the cover artists, to the marketing team. Larissa Ackerman is an incredible publicist and has led the charge for spotlighting the cozy mystery genre.

I am grateful every second for my family: Judi Potter, Mom, who kept me in coffee and peanut butter toast while I wrote in the back room; my son, Brighton, who literally sent me a laptop when mine broke and I had the hinges taped with packing tape; my daughter, Destini, who promises she doesn't mind driving to the cozy conferences and doing my hair; and Kennedi, my granddaughter, who I hope will someday love reading as much as we all do. My daughter-in-law, Ceci, has been such a blessing!

I want to send a big thank-you to Mom's Tuesday morning coffee ladies. I really appreciate you letting me occasionally crash the party. Sheryl McGavin, for your assists at the beta reader stage and knitting knowledge.

This page could not be complete without a thank-you to my husband, Christopher, for sharing his family with me. I love you guys!